Welcome to Deer Creek!

This is the third book from Karin Richardson featuring the intriguing cast of characters who make their home in the sleepy little town of Deer Creek, Colorado.

Sleepy?
Yeah, Right! NOT!

Deer Creek seems to be plagued by a series of mishaps, all centered around a mystical aquamarine necklace inherited by one of the town's residents. Follow Ruth Ann and her friends from Deer Creek to the frigid fjords of Sweden, and now to the gorgeous tropical island of Jamaica. But what started out as a romantic getaway turned into yet another mystery surrounding the mystical gem known as Blue Ice. But this time there's an ancient voodoo curse!!!

What readers are saying about Richardson's books:

☆☆☆☆☆
5-STARS

Jaw Dropping – kept me on the edge of my seat! (TT)

This book was so suspenseful from start to finish. The voice of the characters was so strong I felt like I was right there with them all searching for the necklace! Awesome, quick read!

Couldn't put it down (AJ)

I loved this book. Every time I thought I had it figured out there was another twist and turn. A great read and now I anxiously wait for the next one!

Love the dialogue between characters. East to pick up if set it down. Keeps you guessing.

A charming mystery!!

A great read. Perfect for a book club. Looking forward to the next one in the series!

Great read!! Love Ruth Ann! Can't wait for the next book!

A Deer Creek Mystery

BLUE ICE

Karin Richardson

It began with the letter & took them on a desperate race from Colorado to Sweden, searching for an heirloom necklace. Was this fabulous gemstone really cursed?

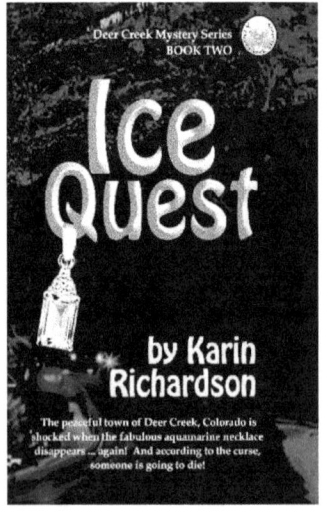

Deer Creek Mystery Series
BOOK TWO

Ice Quest

by Karin Richardson

The peaceful town of Deer Creek, Colorado is shocked when the fabulous aquamarine necklace disappears ... again! And according to the curse, someone is going to die!

BLUE ICE & ICE QUEST are available from Amazon.com as either a paper book or for Kindle

CURSED ICE

Karin Richardson

CURSED ICE is also available as a Kindle edition from
Amazon.com

10 9 8 7 6 5 4 3 2 1

ISBN 978-1-57550-103-1

Printed in the United States of America
Cover Art by Johanna M. Bolton

*CURSED ICE is a work of fiction. All the characters and
events portrayed in this book are fictional, and any
resemblance to real people and incidents is purely
coincidental.*

I dedicate this third book in
The Deer Creek Mystery Series
To
Wilma Longman
for all her help editing
CURSED ICE,
And to Johanna M. Bolton
for making the books possible.

I'd also like to mention the Caribbean, the inspiration for this third story. My husband, Kerry, and I made many wonderful memories as we traveled the Caribbean and visited the islands there.

Recipes

WARNING! Once again, as with the scrumptious recipes in Karin's second book, Ice Quest, neither the author nor publisher will be responsible for any weight gain due to the abuse of the recipes included in the book! They are truly delicious and the temptation to over-indulge is considerable. They should be consumed only under the careful supervision of a responsible adult!

Chapter 1

"John!" I screamed in horror from the shoreline. I was frantically running up and down soft pearly white sand of the Caribbean beach.

I was too terrified to go in the water since I had a horrible fear of sharks. A friend of mine once told me that sharks hunt their prey close to shore. That thought paralyzed me as I watched my longtime boyfriend, John Wilkinson, wipe out on his paddleboard when a large wave crashed into him. John didn't see the wave approaching so he wasn't prepared as the rush of water took him under. I saw the whole event just as I was cooling my toes in an inch or two of water. The temperature outside was a grueling ninety-five degrees with ridiculously high humidity.

"John!" I shouted, when finally, a young man came running toward me and asked me what happened. "Didn't you see that huge wave knock my friend off the board?" I asked, panicked.

The college age man nodded, but didn't appear concerned. "Just give him a minute, ma'am. I'm sure he'll pop up somewhere near where he wiped out." I turned around slowly to face him. First, what's with the *ma'am* comment? I despised when strangers called me that! In my opinion I wasn't that old, just hitting my prime. Second, what was his problem? Why didn't he rush out there and try to save John? His golden brown tan, muscular build, and nearby surfboard told me he was an experienced surfer. It took me only a second to get my wits back when I yelled at the poor boy, "go out and help him!" I quickly added, "please."

He looked around hoping one of his friends would come to his rescue. When that didn't happen he shook his head and ran out into the water within seconds of John's submersion. The beach was fairly empty since it was right before Thanksgiving. Most tourists were back in the United States with their families about to sit down to a holiday dinner.

John and I needed a break. I had been through a horrific month or two and John, who also happened to be the Chief of Police back in our hometown of Deer Creek, Colorado, whirled me away on a long overdue tropical getaway.

My life had been fairly normal, except for the fact that I became a widow at a very young age. My first husband died in a plane crash while we lived in California. I was left alone with very young twin daughters. The pain was so unbearable for me that I left with my daughters, Lynne and Nancy, and moved to the small town of Deer Creek, Colorado.

Fast forward twenty years, my pain had healed and I led an active, fulfilling lifestyle until the infamous Blue Ice necklace appeared in town and the crime rate skyrocketed.

I opened up my dream business, Ruth Ann's Antiques (named after me, of course), and my twin daughters were living in town after returning from college. Lynne owned a bakery, Sinful Sweets, and Nancy was a high school history teacher. Both were unmarried, much to my chagrin, but I couldn't beat that dead horse into the ground any more without them ganging up on me for not moving on myself.

However, I did move on in my own way. I was dating the Chief of Police, John Wilkinson, and we were extremely happy with our current arrangement. John agreed to date only me and I agreed to date only him. There had been a slight snafu recently when John hired a young, ambitious detective named Judy Lynch. Judy was brought here mostly because of me. The crime rate had escalated so quickly that there was need for additional help.

John had been a friend of Judy's parent's years ago. When he found out Judy was now a big city detective nearby, he contacted her and she dropped her job and rushed to Deer Creek. I never trusted Judy's motives because I felt she was excessively flirtatious with him. John didn't knowingly return her sentiments, but he was clearly too nice to her. He had professed to me over and over that Judy was too young for him, and she wasn't interested in him that way. "You're blind," I said to him, but he chose to ignore the truth. I truly believed he secretly got a kick out of it.

Getting back to why the extra police were needed in Deer Creek. A mysterious package addressed to me was sent to the town's bank president, Doug Albertson. A letter attached to the package clearly stated the item inside was cursed and to proceed with caution. Doug ignored the message, but chose to hold on to the package for a little while before informing me of its presence. He took it upon himself to open it and discovered a beautiful, radiant blue emerald shaped gem.

It was the most amazing piece he'd ever laid eyes on. Doug didn't realize the significance of the gem. It was securely fastened to a white gold chain, but when he was alone with the necklace one Friday afternoon he was violently attacked, robbed of my necklace, and severely injured. I just happened to be strolling by the bank at the same time of the robbery and ended up being the one who found Doug unconscious. Unfortunately, the robber also spotted me just as he was trying to make his getaway.

The necklace was stolen, and the town went into an uproar. John, Doug, and our local doctor, Doc Albert, decided to keep the reason for the attack under wraps to the public and reported it as a common robbery. We gave the necklace the name "Blue Ice" shortly after we got it back after a long, grueling chase that led from Deer Creek to Stockholm, Sweden!

Prunella, yes, that's a long story in itself, but I'll be brief. Prunella sent the gem to the bank with help from her lawyer, Michael Swenson. Prunella was married to a ruthless man, Axel Eklund. Both Axel and Prunella's families had a long, violent history with the piece. Prunella fell in love with Axel and once they were married he quickly turned on her and she felt her life was being threatened. She stole the necklace from Axel and sent it to the only other living relative her lawyer found, me, Ruth Ann Conroy (Liljestrom).

After much snooping, I discovered it was Axel Eklund who purchased a large estate just outside Deer Creek and that he had masterminded the theft from the bank. I was kidnapped and hauled overseas to Axel's Stockholm estate. Axel gave me the freedom to roam his household, but not to go outside of the mansion. Being an overly curious person, I discovered a young woman living in the estate's attic. After pushing my way into this woman's life, I discovered it was Axel's second wife, Prunella. She was faking a terminal illness so Axel would feel sorry for her and not kill her for stealing the necklace. Axel was actually not a horrible man; we had many long, fulfilling talks, and I liked him. He was so obsessed with his family's heirloom that it made him act out in desperation.

On a hunch, John and Judy flew to Stockholm and rescued me, Prunella, Inga (Prunella's housekeeper and loyal friend), and Sherman (Prunella's devoted long-time butler). Axel was supposedly hauled off to jail to spend the rest of his life behind bars. However, as the story goes, it didn't end there. Axel was reported dead after being transported from the jail to a hospital.

I convinced Prunella, Inga, and Sherman to come back to Deer Creek. Prunella took over Axel's estate since she was still legally his wife and sole heir. There was one glitch with her plan, Bert. Bert was Axel's butler in Deer Creek and he was angry about Axel's imprisonment and death. He was bitter, old, and held a deep grudge. Prunella was as sweet as he was nasty. She wouldn't fire anyone just because they were in her husband's employ.

Now, back to a couple weeks ago. It was Halloween in Deer Creek. The big resort in town was holding their annual Halloween party. I just happened to be close friends of the owners, Richard and Carol Dickson. I thought it would be nice to invite Prunella and her staff to attend the party so they could get to know some of our local residents. They were all thrilled, except Bert. He flatly refused to go. Prunella insisted, actually ordered, him to attend. I supplied the costumes for the party from my daughter's high school theatre department. Bert just about blew a gasket because I picked out his costume. He was to be a pirate, along with Sherman.

Long story short, the evening ended with a burned body dangling from the ceiling and the townspeople shocked and horrified. Bert had been murdered, but by whom? Prunella felt immense guilt for forcing the poor old guy to attend the party, and John, with the aid of Judy, started up another investigation.

It was quickly discovered that Axel wasn't dead or even locked up in jail anymore. He was in town, with Prunella's Swedish lawyer's cousin, Steven Svenson. He was the black sheep in the family, and about as shady as they come. Axel needed someone cutthroat to get him out of jail and back into the states to retrieve his assets and the cursed Blue Ice. However, Steven got greedy and became obsessed with the gem. We discovered that Steven and Jimmy killed Bert and a few innocent others. Once Axel learned the truth, he turned on Steven and his hit man, Jimmy.

Once those two were taken down, Prunella and I were finally able to move forward and grew closer as cousins until another newcomer, Alex, appeared. Alex showed up just as Steven and Jimmy were about to be captured at Axel's estate in Deer Creek. Stunned by his announcement that he was related to us, Prunella and I listened as Alex told us about another branch of our family and their knowledge of the infamous Blue Ice. The story continues from here.

Chapter 2

John decided that I needed a trip; far away from Deer Creek and all the troubles it had brought me recently. John knew that I really wanted a vacation alone with him, but he never had the time. But after the fiasco with Axel Eklund and Steven Svenson, he decided it was vital to get me out of town for a few days.

John knew that I loved swaying palm trees and shimmery ocean waters. He decided to contact the one and only travel agency in town to speak with Julie, the owner. "Julie?" John asked, as a woman's voice picked up on the other line.

"Nope, sorry, this is her daughter, Tiana. Can I help you?"

"Oh, yes, hi Tiana. This is Chief John over at the police station."

Tiana's voice stumbled over her next few words, "Is there something wrong, sir?"

"No, no, I'm sorry, let me start over. I'm actually calling to book a trip."

"Oh," Tiana replied, cheerily. "I was scared something happened to my mother!"

"No, no, everything's quiet," John hesitated, and realized he might have jinxed it by saying everything was quiet. "Is your mother working today?" John asked, wanting to get a move on. He still had so much paperwork to do with Eklund's case. Axel was pardoned of all his crimes since he helped the police capture the real murderers of Bert, Helena, and others.

"No, she's off on a cruise with my father, but I can help you."

"You're a travel agent too?"

"Of course I am," Tiana answered, indignantly. "I'm twenty-three and I took the training at the local college in Grand Junction."

"That's great, Tiana," John said. "So, here's my dilemma. I want to take Ruth Ann, oh, I mean Mrs. Conroy, on a well-deserved trip."

"It's okay, Chief. I call her Ruth Ann, too. I'm not a child anymore remember."

"Sorry, Tiana, I wasn't sure the etiquette on that one. Can we just get back to my trip? I've gotta get back to work." John waited for Tiana to reply, but the line stayed silent so he continued. "I'd like to take a quick, but nice trip somewhere warm."

"How long do you want to be gone?"

"I figure I can be away about five days. Can we go far enough away, but not spend a whole day traveling?"

"Sure, there's lots of places you two can go," Tiana said, giggling. Suddenly, John became embarrassed that he was making plans for himself and Ruth Ann. They weren't married and that could look inappropriate to Tiana.

He regained his composure and said, "Okay, here are my requirements and I need you to tell me if it'll work. First, I need a place that's warm and sunny overlooking the ocean. Second, there have to be palm trees. Ruth Ann has this obsession with them and I want her to relax and stare out into the water and watch the palm trees sway. Can you do that?"

John could overhear the keyboard keys snapping away in the background as Tiana said, "Of course. I've already pulled up several options, but," she stopped, and paused a moment. "But, I need to know your budget?"

"Ah, yes, money," John stated. "Let's just say I don't want some run down motel, but yet I don't want to break the bank on this. How about we say somewhere in the middle."

"Okay, so here's what I think," Tiana started to say. "I have two perfect options for you. One's an all-inclusive resort in Jamaica. It's not that far away, but still has everything you need. The other option is a nice cozy place in the Bahamas. There's also," she said, blasting away at her keyboard, "the Florida Keys."

"No, I want an island. So either the Jamaica or the Bahamas resort will do. You pick the best one and I'll trust your advice."

Tiana perked up at his compliment and said, "I would definitely go to Jamaica because you get more for your money. I can book five nights at a four-star all-inclusive resort. That way all you have to do is go there and plop yourselves down and let the staff pamper the both of you. All your food and drinks will be included so you really don't need money down there except for gifts and stuff like that. How does that sound?"

"Sounds perfect!" John answered, thrilled with her news. "Now, what are the dates and how much will it set me back?"

"I can get you a really good deal if you go next Saturday and return on Thursday."

"Wait, come back on Thanksgiving?" John asked, worried about the dates.

"Yep," Tiana answered. "You'll be back before the Thanksgiving meal."

"I don't know if I can get her to go away those dates, but…" John stopped talking to contemplate the plan.

"Well, maybe this will make it sound better to you. I can get you 50% off for those dates."

"Really?" John asked, perking up. "Maybe it wouldn't be so bad after all. I'll get Ruth Ann back in time for dinner with her family. Okay, let's do this."

"I'll run over the flights with you and you can tell me if it works. One thing, Chief," Tiana started to say. "This is non-refundable once I book it. Do you want to check with Ruth Ann first?"

John immediately replied, "No! Sorry, I mean no I don't want to check with her. It's a total surprise so…yes, let's book it."

John and Tiana spent the next few minutes finishing up the details and he hung up wondering if he just made a huge mistake. Would Ruth Ann be willing to drop everything and go off with him four days from now? She'd finally gotten her life back again and was thrilled to be working at her antique store. However, it was a short trip and we had never discussed our plans for the upcoming holiday. But, it was a crazy time with the holidays coming up and

Ruth Ann's Antique Shop did quite a lot of business this time of year. It was the busiest and most lucrative time for her business. John's mind was reeling when there was a knock on his office door.

"Come in," John yelled loudly. The door had been closed to give him the privacy he needed to make the call to Deer Creek Travel.

When the door opened, John looked up to see Judy, his partner in crime at the police department. Ruth Ann's nemesis was standing just inside the door with a huge grin on her face. "What're you doing locked away in here, John?"

John looked strangely at her and replied, "Paper work." He lied a little, but didn't want to discuss booking a romantic trip with Ruth Ann. "I can't believe all the papers we have to fill out regarding Eklund."

"Well, the guy got off without a slap on his wrist! I don't know how that happened with the list of crimes he committed, but somebody likes him enough to release him of all responsibilities."

John's face said it all. He couldn't believe it himself. Axel Eklund committed a kidnapping or two, accessory to murder, and a host of other crimes, but when he turned himself in, he was immediately pardoned of his crimes not only here in Colorado, but also in Stockholm. "I don't even believe it myself, Judy, and I thought I've seen it all."

"Why would the Governor pardon him? He was ready to admit his guilt, but they stopped him."

"He must have friends in high places, Judy. There's no other explanation."

"Not really fair for the average Joe, is it? I mean if you have enough money you can buy yourself out of a long prison sentence. Not very just!"

"Nothing we can do, Judy. I have to finish this paperwork before I," John stopped before he stuck his foot all the way into his mouth. He hoped she wouldn't question him on his comment, but we knew that wouldn't float.

"What do you mean before you…?"

"Umm," he couldn't figure out what to reply fast enough.

"C'mon, what's up?" she demanded. "You got a secret?" Judy's eager look of curiosity forced John's hand.

"Okay, I'm going to tell you something, but you have to swear not to say a word to anyone until it's confirmed." He watched her expression change to worried and not so sure she wanted to hear what he was about to tell her. "Well, can you promise me?"

Quickly, Judy shook it off and replied, "Of course, whatever you want, John."

"I'm going to take a few days off starting this Saturday. I'll be back on Thanksgiving."

Judy looked deflated. "Oh, that's all? What's the big deal about you taking a few days off? You've been through a lot with the slew of criminal activity this past month, and then going off to Sweden to rescue innocent little Ruth Ann."

John wasn't happy with Judy's evaluation of Ruth Ann. "Innocent and little?" he questioned her.

"It's a joke, John. Geez, lighten up." She smiled and made her way to his desk and sat on the side of it. "So, where you going?"

John thought about it for a moment wondering if he should leak the surprise before he sprung it on Ruth Ann. "I'm going to take Ruth Ann to Jamaica for five days. She's been wanting to get away and after everything she's been through, I thought it was the perfect time." He held his breath waiting for a snarky comment, but she just stared at him, dumbfounded.

"You all right, Judy?" John asked, trying to break the awkward silence. "You can't tell me you're surprised that we'd be going away together, are you?"

Judy, sitting on the edge of his desk, hopped off and snapped her mouth shut after it had been hanging wide open in confusion. "I, I didn't know you two were that close."

"Really?" John asked. "We've been dating for a long time so it shouldn't surprise anybody that I would do this for her."

"Oh, well, yeah, but I guess I just didn't expect to hear that from *you*."

"Why not?"

"Because you're all about the job, John. I just don't envision you as the gushy type that goes harrowing off on some romantic getaway."

"Gushy type?" John asked, offended. "I don't think I act that way or ever will. However, going off on a short trip with my girl-friend shouldn't have to be labeled as gushy or romantic."

"So it's not a romantic getaway? Or are you embarrassed to admit that to *me*?"

John was becoming flustered and yes, embarrassed, with the direction the conversation was going. He didn't feel he needed to justify himself. Ruth Ann couldn't stand Judy, and trying to explain to Judy why he was going away was ridiculous and none of her business. "Enough talk about this, Judy. Just keep it under wraps until I ask Ruth Ann if she can get away."

"Has Ruth Ann said she wanted the two of you to go away together?"

"Not exactly," John admitted. "She's hinted as much though."

"Oh, okay. Good luck with that, John," Judy replied, hurrying out of his office.

Well, that was awkward, John thought. Was Judy showing signs of jealousy or just surprised that Ruth Ann and he were close enough to go away together? He shrugged it off and went back to the never-ending pile of paperwork.

A short time later, John drove over to Ruth Ann's Antiques and made a surprise visit. He found me in my office working on paperwork behind my desk, I looked up and shouted, happily, "John!"

Instead of easing into his news, he blurted out, "I booked a five-day trip to Jamaica!"

"For whom?" I asked, shocked.

John's facial expression faded when he realized I might not want to go away with him. "Uh, I thought it would be just the two of us." Before I had a chance to respond, he added quickly, "If that's alright with you?"

I jumped out of my vintage leather desk chair and ran to the other side of the desk. I threw my arms around his neck and stood on tippy toes to plant a huge wet kiss on his cheek. I was aiming for his mouth, but lost my balance as I tried to reach up to his face. I was only a little over five foot three, while John was a couple inches over six feet. He realized I missed and then grabbed me around my waist and held me up in the air with my feet dangling several inches from the ground. "I take that as a yes?" he asked, as I hung in the air.

I kissed him smack dab on his full lips and let the kiss linger for several seconds. "Wow," John said, setting me back down on the ground. "If I knew I'd get that kind of reaction I would've done this ages ago!"

"I've told you I wanted to go away with you many times, John."

"Yes, but I wondered what you would tell your daughters," he replied.

"Lynne and Nancy are thirty years old. I think they can handle it. Plus, it's been a long time coming for the two of us. It's our turn to have alone time, just you and me." I smiled at him and he melted. It was amazing at even his age, in his middle fifties, that he could still feel such excitement and desire for a woman. He never really expressed how much he cared for me, actually, that he loved me. I was such a fiery person at times that he often wanted to throw me in a jail cell, to be honest. On the other hand, I was kind, loving, and some may even say kind of pretty for a woman in my fifties, too. He said I was beautiful for a woman of any age, and he wanted me to know that this trip would be taking our relationship to a whole other level, but did I want that, too? Of course I did!

"John?" I questioned him, because he was suddenly silent. "You're awfully quiet. Anything wrong?"

John woke from his trance and replied, "Oh, no, I was just thinking about how nice it'll be lying on a sandy beach with a cocktail and you by my side. However," John stopped, and I eyed him strangely.

"However, what?" I inquired.

"I haven't mentioned one tiny minor detail with the trip."

"Oh, no," I said. "What's the catch?"

"No catch, Ruth Ann. It's just that I booked it already and I didn't get your approval for the date."

"Oh, no biggie. I'm sure whatever the date it'll be great."

"Okay, we're leaving in four days!"

"What?" I hollered, stunned at his announcement. "I ... I can't leave that soon. Thanksgiving's next week and my store's swamped. Christmas is right around the corner!"

"If you think about it, it's really the perfect time. We leave Saturday and return on Thanksgiving Day in time for dinner up at Prunella and Axel's place." He waited for me to speak, but my mouth hung open in confusion. "I'm assuming that's where Thanksgiving dinner will be since they have the huge mansion and staff?"

"Well, yes, Prunella did say she was excited to have the family for the holidays this year. And since Prunella and Axel had reconciled, Axel was there too. They were all pretty excited about having a huge family get together. Inga would be cooking her first ever Thanksgiving meal and she's been asking me tons of questions. How will I help her if I'm out of the country?" I went into my own thoughts, but popped out quickly. "I don't want you to think I'm not eternally grateful to you for planning such a wonderful trip. I just need to figure out how to make it work."

John was worried that he just lost a large sum of money when I decided that it could work. "So, you think we can do this?" he asked, hoping the answer was positive.

"Of course we can!" I announced. "I'm not passing up a trip like this, never!"

"Phew," John said, wiping his perspiring brow. "I really wanted to surprise you, and Tiana over at the agency gave me such a good deal."

"Tiana?" I questioned. "Where was Julie, her mother?"

"I don't know. All I cared about was she booked a nice place for us to stay."

"Is it all-inclusive?"

"Yes," he replied, wondering what I knew about all-inclusive resorts. "Have you been to one before?"

"Oh, yes, I've been to them, but it was years ago. They're fantastic! You get all your meals, drinks, and activities included in one price."

"Yes, I know. Tiana explained it to me."

"So, I have so much to accomplish in the next four days. I'll talk with Prunella and Inga. Inga will need Lynne to help her since she's the baker in the family. Nancy doesn't do too well in the kitchen. She's more of the book smart kind of gal, but that's okay, too. I'll have to see what I need to pack, and..." John threw his hands up and laughed. "What?" I asked him.

"I give up! I wanted to plan a nice, romantic getaway for us and all you can think about is what you need to do for a Thanksgiving meal that you're not even preparing. I think the staff up at Eklund's' place can handle that."

My smile diminished. "Wait, did you say *romantic getaway*?"

John's face flushed and he replied, "Yes. I was hoping we were on the same page."

I wrapped my arms around his waist and gave him a squeeze. "We are on the same page. I've waited so long to spend time with you and not your job."

"I know my job's interfered, but lately, it's been your family that's done all the interfering."

I could've become angry with him, but I had to admit, he was right! The crime rate soared in Deer Creek ever since I discovered my cousin, Prunella, her husband, Axel, Inga the housekeeper, and Sherman, the butler. But, it was mostly because of the precious Blue Ice gem, not the people. The necklace made people crazy like it was cursed or something. Actually, I hadn't seen it in the last couple weeks. Prunella had it locked safe and sound up at their estate on the mountain.

Now that Prunella and Axel reunited, they were madly in love again. I wasn't sure this was the right thing, but since they appeared to be so happy, who was I to muck it up? Inga, the loyal housekeeper, wasn't as positive about the couple as I tried to be. She was faithful to Prunella and didn't want her hurt again by Axel. On the other hand, Sherman, the butler, was thrilled they were together. We recently discovered that he was Prunella's great uncle, and he loved working for their household. Sherman loved the rules and formalities of a large estate.

"Are you okay, Ruth Ann?" John asked, watching my expression change from a tad bit angry, to not so bad, to smiling.

"I'm just great!" I replied, cheerily. "It's true what you just said. Deer Creek was a safe, quiet town until my long lost family appeared from Sweden."

"I didn't mean to imply that *your* family has caused *all* the crime in town, just escalated it."

"I can't disagree with you." I shook it off and then realized what was really happening. "Wait a minute!" I exclaimed. "We have to get packing and shopping since we're leaving in four days.

I have to go and tell Prunella and my girls that I'll be away until Thanksgiving!"

"I'm sure they'll survive without you for five days," John said, smiling.

"Very funny, John. I know my girls are grown up and so is Prunella."

"Plus, she has Eklund by her side again."

"I can't believe Axel isn't in jail. I still don't understand how, but it's not my place to judge. There's a higher court he'll have to face one day."

"That's pretty deep, Ruth Ann," John said. "But, you've got a point."

"As soon as I talk to Meme, I'll pop over to Lynne's bakery and tell her what's going on. Then I'll drive up the mountain to Prunella and Axel's place and tell them. I know they'll be excited for me."

"I hope so," John mumbled.

"Why would you say that? Are you worried they won't approve?"

"Seriously?" John asked, letting out a little howl of laughter. "No, no, I just don't want your daughters or the others giving you a hard time for not being here right before the holiday."

"Wait, you're the one who told me not to worry, and it's not a big deal."

"It isn't, at least in my opinion. Hopefully they'll be okay with it, too." John watched as I turned around and walked over to a tall, bronze coat rack and pulled off my winter white coat. "Hey, do you want me to go with you?"

"No, I'm better off going by myself. I'll give you a call after I'm done speaking with everyone. Nancy's still at school so I'll have to wait till later to talk to her and by then I'm sure Lynne will have already filled her in."

"Great!" John answered. "I have to go back to my office and get that damn paperwork finished. It's been a thorn in my side for the last week or so. If some politician's going to pardon Eklund then he should have to fill out the piles and piles of paperwork."

"Someday you'll have to explain that one to me. Don't get me wrong, I'm happy for Prunella, but he did a lot of illegal things, and now he's a totally free man."

"He had to have quite the deal worked out or..." John stopped talking after he realized he shouldn't have said 'or'.

"What do you mean, John?" I inquired.

John knew I wouldn't let him get away without explaining himself. I can be such a busybody! "Umm, maybe Eklund has something on the governor or someone over in Stockholm."

"THAT'S IT!" I hollered. "I bet he blackmailed somebody to get himself free."

"It's a possibility, Ruth Ann. I know it happens, so why not for Eklund?"

"I wonder if Prunella knows anything? I may have to ask her a few questions when I see her."

"Let it be, Ruth Ann," John suggested. "Don't open Pandora's Box!"

My lack of response made John uneasy. Life had just started to get back to normal so he really wanted me to stay out of trouble. However, he knew when something got in my head I wouldn't stop until I felt it was solved. Little did he know what 'box' we were about to open.

Chapter 3

John said his good-byes and headed back to the police station to finish his paperwork. I walked out of my office and through the storage room into the showroom. It was a beautiful store. The antique store was built specifically with my instructions to look like a two story Victorian home. At the moment, the store was loaded with wonderful pieces for the upcoming holidays. I have many contacts around the world who communicate with me when they have a piece I might want to put in the store. Of course shipping from afar costs me a pretty penny, but I am passionate about my merchandise and fortunate enough to afford it.

Meme was my very young assistant manager. She was a single mother of a two-year-old, Elijah. I did whatever I could to make sure I paid Meme enough money so she and her son could live a comfortable life. I was fortunate that money wasn't an object. When my husband was killed in that tragic plane crash over twenty years ago, he left me a sizable amount of money. My fortune had grown over the years with the help of a thriving business. It wasn't a fortune like Prunella and Axel had, but a very comfortable life where my daughters will never want for anything. The only thing that could make life better would be if my two daughters would marry!

"Hi, Meme," I called as she was standing on the second to top rung of a tall ladder cleaning one of the crystal chandeliers on the first floor showroom. "Be careful up there!"

Meme turned around and carefully stepped down. "Hi, Ruth Ann. Are you leaving?"

"Why are you asking me that?" I asked curiously.

"Because you have your coat on!"

"Oh, I do, don't I?" I asked laughing, remembering my coat was still on. "I've got to run out and I probably won't be back to-day."

"What's up? Did I hear John here just a few moments ago?"

My face reddened a bit when she mentioned John's name. "Uh, yes, he stopped by to give me some news."

"What news? You look like you're about to burst."

"He asked me to go away on a trip," I blurted out. Meme giggled a little. "Really? Just the two of you?"

"Yes," I replied, wondering what her giggle meant. "We haven't really done that before."

"How exciting for you! Where are you going and when?" Meme asked, truly excited for me.

"He surprised me with an all-inclusive trip to Jamaica!"

"Jamaica! I'm so jealous," Meme cried out. "I would love to go to a tropical island." She added, "And with a man would be even better!"

"Meme, you're embarrassing me." I laughed, and said, "No, not really. I'm just kidding you. I have one teensy weeny problem though."

"What on earth could be a problem with a romantic trip with John?"

"We leave in four days!" I waited for her reaction. I was worried Meme wouldn't be comfortable running the store at this time of the year without me.

"In four days? Wow! That's fantastic!" She bellowed, surprising me once again.

"You're okay with this?"

"Of course," Meme immediately responded. "Were you worried I wouldn't be okay?"

"I didn't want to upset you and leave you in a lurch the week before Thanksgiving."

"Of course not!" Meme replied, emphatically. "I'm sure while you're gone we'll actually be kind of quiet here. Most people aren't shopping that week except for food."

"You think so?"

"Definitely. John picked a perfect time for you to get away. Plus, you need it. You've had rough couple months, and to sit on a fluffy white beach is something you love."

"You're right about that, Meme," I said, dreamily. "I just have to pop over to Sinful Sweets and tell Lynne. I hope she's okay with it."

"Why wouldn't she be?"

"I have to admit it's kind of awkward telling your daughter that you're going away with your boyfriend."

"I can see that, but knowing Lynne and Nancy, they'll be happy for you. I wouldn't worry about it at all," Meme said, unequivocally.

"Thanks, Meme. I'm going to head over there now. Just lock up the store when you're ready to go. Don't stay too late."

"I have to pick up Elijah at Kiddie Care at five so I'll lock up at about four forty-five if that's okay with you?"

"Perfect, thanks. I'll see you in the morning," I said, and then turned on my heels and headed back through the double swinging doors into the storage room. I made sure I closed my office door, and then headed out the back door into the alley behind the store.

It was just after three in the afternoon and extremely cold outside. I looked over at my yellow SUV, but passed right by it. My daughter's store, Sinful Sweets, was only two businesses down. I buttoned my coat and slipped on my white leather gloves. "Brrr," I said out loud as I walked down the alley.

About a minute later I reached the back door of the bakery. I reached out and grabbed the handle and pushed it open. I didn't like that Lynne left the back door unlocked during business hours. I didn't dare say anything to her because I knew Lynne would snap back that it was "her store, her rules".

Once inside the bright kitchen of the bakery, I immediately felt the warmth coming from several ovens. "Wow, it's really cold out there," I said, shivering a little.

"Hi Mom," Lynne called out to her from a stainless steel workstation in the middle of the kitchen. "What're you doing here? Isn't your store still open?"

"Oh, yeah, Meme's still there. I wanted to come and see you."

Lynne looked at me suspiciously. "Either you want some chocolate or you have something to tell me. Which is it?"

I laughed and slipped off my coat and threw it on a metal stool. "You know me so well." I spotted the delicacy Lynne was working on. "What are you making, Lynne?"

"Oh, I'm making spiced pumpkin balls for Henry and Lulu Hamilton."

"Why?" I asked, curiously. Henry and I went way back and he was our current Mayor in Deer Creek. His wife, Lulu, was quite a few years younger than him. She was what most people would call a diva.

"Mayor Henry said he loved the variety of dipped balls I make and he's having his family, including that wife of his, over for Thanksgiving dinner. I'm practicing making these to see if they taste any good."

"Do they?" I asked, extremely interested in being the guinea pig taster. "I'll try them!"

Lynne laughed and said, "I kind of figured you would. You like everything I make, don't you?"

"Well," I said, wondering how to diplomatically answer that question. I didn't exactly like *everything* she made.

"What?" Lynne asked, surprised at my initial response. "You *don't* like everything I make here?"

"Well," I said again. "I do love *most* of what you make."

"Really? What don't you like?" Lynne asked.

"I don't like baked goods with nuts in them. There, I said it. I'm very sorry, dear, but I don't like nuts in my brownies or in coffee cakes or in the frosting."

Lynne let out a laugh that was so loud it startled me. "That's just fine, mother," she replied. "I'm not a fan of them either, except for my almond biscotti. I do like the nuts in those."

"Oh, so do I! I love almond biscotti, but that's the only exception I can think of."

Spiced Pumpkin Balls

1 - package spiced sandwich cookies
   (These typically come out in the fall so grab
   a few packages of them)
1- 8 oz. package Neufchatel Cheese, softened
1 -12 oz. package of white baking chips or
   any brand of almond or white baking chocolate

Crush the cookies either by hand or in a food
processor. Take the softened cheese and whip it up in a
mixer (table or hand). Add cookies and mix
thoroughly. Shape into small balls (your preference on
how big or small) and place on a waxed paper lined
cookie sheet. Then chill in freezer for fifteen to thirty
minutes.

Melt white chocolate in microwave according to directions, and then quickly (white chocolate
hardens fast), dip balls into chocolate and place back on
to the waxed paper lined cookie sheet. Put back into
freezer for about five minutes. Store in refrigerator and
enjoy!

"Okay, Mom, what are you really doing here before your store's closing time?" Lynne demanded.

I picked up a spiced ball and quickly popped it in my mouth. I was nervous for some reason in telling my grown daughter that I was about to go away on a trip with my boyfriend, John.

"C'mon, Mom, spill it!" Lynne insisted, waiting patiently for me to finish my treat.

"This is really tasty, dear," I said, avoiding her demand. "You should put these on your menu during the fall or actually, you could sell these all year long." I waited for my daughter's reply, but Lynne stood frozen in her spot staring me down.

"Fine," I said. "It's not really a big deal. I just came by to tell you that John and I are going away for a few days. We're leaving Saturday."

Lynne sat down on the nearest stool and didn't say a word. She looked down at the cookie sheets filled with her newest creation. Finally, after a long, nerve racking few seconds, she lifted her head and said, "Where you going?"

I didn't care for her initial reaction; she wasn't showing any excitement for her mother. "Well, John made a reservation for us to stay at an all-Inclusive resort in Jamaica."

"Jamaica!" Lynne blurted out loudly.

"Are you upset about this? Because you don't seem too happy for me."

Lynne pulled herself together and walked toward me. She put her arms around me and said, "Of course I'm not upset. It just wasn't what I expected you to say. I figured it had something to do with Thanksgiving next week." Lynne stopped talking for a brief moment, and then cried out, "Hey, wait. Are you going to be here for Thanksgiving?"

"Of course! We'll be back by then. This is just a short five-day trip. John promised that we'd be back in time for Thanksgiving dinner up at Prunella and Axel's place."

"That's cutting it kind of close, but it's not like *you* are doing any cooking. Inga is preparing the main meal and Prunella asked me to make pumpkin and apple pies."

"Lynne, you must be mad at me or you wouldn't be so sarcastic about my not doing any cooking. I was the one Inga went to for the menu since they've never made Thanksgiving dinner before. Living in Sweden, Inga didn't understand the necessary food items. So, I've been helping her with recipes and serving suggestions. Yes, I'm aware I won't be *making* any of it, but she might still need my help."

Lynne smiled and then apologized. "I know you're a huge. I wasn't trying to be sarcastic. I was just pointing out it's fine that you and John go away for a few days. Just as long as you're back for Thanksgiving dinner."

"Are you sure this doesn't make you uncomfortable?"

"What?" Lynne asked innocently, even though I knew she understood my question.

"Lynne, you're my daughter and no matter how old you are, it's gotta be kind of weird having your middle aged mother trot off to an island with her boyfriend."

"The way you just described it does sound a tad inappropriate, but I know you have been close for quite some time. I'm okay with it, really. I was just taken by surprise, that's all. Let it go, mom. I'll be fine with the idea once I've gotten used to it. You really do need a break from all the chaos around here, so go, have a great time!"

I didn't want to push it any further so I dropped it. I asked if she thought I should tell Nancy or if she wanted to do the honors. "Let me break it to her so you don't get upset with her reaction like you just did with me."

"Wait a minute!" I bellowed. "I was fine with it, you had a slight issue at first."

"I admit it felt a little weird, but after the initial blow, I'm fine."

"Okay, why don't you fill your sister in and then I'll speak with her this evening, too."

"Sounds like a plan. I'll pop over to Nancy's apartment when I get home."

"If you both want to see me afterward, just call me. Otherwise, I'll call Nancy later."

"Okay, see you soon, mom," Lynne called as I put on my coat on and headed out the back door. That was not how I thought the conversation would go. I'm aware the girls knew about my relationship with John. However, I've never talked about the *intimate* part of our relationship. In fact, John and I barely talk about it! Outside of professing his love for me after our escapade in Stockholm, he really was very conservative with me. I was secretly hoping that would change when we were alone on our trip. It was time John and I committed to our relationship, and maybe even discussed the possibility of a wedding. Of course that would include a serious discussion about his current status with his detested detective, Judy Lynch!

I decided it was time to head up to Axel and Prunella's massive estate about twenty minutes up the mountain on the one and only road out of town. Deer Creek is nestled at the bottom of Deer

Creek Mountain, giving both the town and it's one and only resort, Deer Creek Resort, their names.

In November high season was in full blast. Our town thrived during the ski season and then in the summer with the fishing and hiking season. The locals loved wintertime. If they owned any type of business, it was the most profitable time of year. I happen to be fortunate because my business was profitable year round, but during the holidays, I really made a bundle.

The quaintness of our town's Main Street and its friendly business owners prompted many tourists to come back year after year. We rarely had a slow winter season unless we didn't get much snow.

Deer Creek Resort, run by Richard and Carol Dickson, is a massive structure smack dab in the middle of Main Street. They inherited it from family, but they've added on and spruced it up so it is a luxurious place to stay and ski. They've sponsored many wonderful events there. Unfortunately, their Halloween party last month ended with the horrific murder of Bert, Axel's butler. I was so thankful it hadn't ruined their bottom line or caused a loss of guests. The murder was my fault, I believe. I was the one who convinced Prunella, Inga, Sherman, and even Axel to move here from Sweden.

I made my way back to my bright yellow SUV behind my antique store. My thoughts were running rampant, but I had no choice but to drive up the mountain and explain my plans to Prunella. I was a bit nervous as I drove up the mountain. The weather was fine, that wasn't what was causing my anxiety. I always felt a strange sensation of fear when I drove up there. I've done it more times than I can count, but each time my mind wandered to bad times I experienced there. I should just put those out of my head and concentrate on the fact that I had doubled my family size and we were all very happy.

Before I knew it I pulled onto Lookout Mountain View Road. It wasn't really a road, just a gravel path that led to the large estate. The roads were clear, thankfully, but the weather was changing. I felt a storm was brewing with the ominous, gray clouds that lingered so near I felt I could put my hands through them.

I pulled up to the circular drive with a massive covered fountain in the middle. I parked my car right outside the front entrance.

Axel bought a fantastic piece of property, a hidden gem. There was the main house with its two white columns and red brick exterior. Behind the house a path led to the massive garage. Behind the garage was the secret part of the estate. There a grass path led to another building, the guesthouse. It was a large and beautiful home whose massive two-story great room was filled with warm and woodsy decorations.

I hurried up the steps that led to the ornate double front doors of the main estate. I was about to see if the door was unlocked when the door flew open. "Sherman," I cried out, startled. "You scared me!"

"Sorry, Ruth Ann," he said, smirking. He caught me off guard and it must've amused him for some unknown reason. "I was walking through the foyer from Mr. Eklund's library and I saw you pull up."

"Oh, that's alright. I was just caught off guard for a moment. Is Prunella with Axel in the library?"

"Nope, just Mr. Eklund."

"What's he up to?" I asked him, curiously.

"He's been on the phone all day with people back in Stockholm," he replied.

"Stockholm?" I repeated, surprised a little. "Is he reviving his shipping industry back there?"

"I don't know much, but I overheard him with contractors."

"Contractors for what?" I inquired.

"He's rebuilding the pier so his ships can be docked there again, I guess. Remember Ruth Ann, you blew up the pier not too long ago."

"I didn't blow up any pier!" I stammered. "Bertha and her brothers, and that Finn character took care of that. I was just in the wrong place at the wrong time."

"Funny, it seems so long ago that it happened, but it really wasn't."

"So much has happened since then. I can't believe we're all here in this house and Axel's free."

"Amazing, isn't it?" Sherman asked.

"Hey," I said, quietly. "You're here all the time. How are they *really* doing?"

"Who?"

"You know…Prunella and Axel?"

"Oh," Sherman loudly responded.

"Shhh," I whispered. "These walls have ears!"

Sherman lowered his voice and said, "Now that you're asking, they seem almost too happy."

"Too happy?"

"I get the feeling that when someone's around, like Inga or me, they turn on the charm and appear as a loving, newlywed couple."

"Hmm," I said out loud, but didn't mean to.

"What?" Sherman asked quickly. "Do you think something's going on again?"

"No, I mean, I don't know, Sherman. I was just wondering how they could go from such a hateful place to being a lovey-dovey couple."

"I agree, but we have no reason to doubt them, do we?"

"I don't know," I repeated. "I will tell you this, I'm going to pay close attention to the two of them and how they interact."

"I'll do the same!" Sherman exclaimed. "And I'll tell Inga to do the same."

"No, no, Sherman," I stammered. "You don't do anything, let me handle this."

"But Prunella's *my* niece, remember?"

"Yes, of course I remember. You hid that information from us and caused a lot of time and heartache, Sherman."

He turned a bright shade of red and slowly said, "I had no choice then. Now it's all out in the open and I have no other secrets."

"I sure hope not, Sherman," I stated. "We don't need any more wild goose chases around this town or back in Sweden."

"Why would we? There's nobody after us anymore. Is there?" he asked, studying the blank reaction on my face because I was hoping the same.

"Nope, nobody chasing us or threatening us anymore," I replied.

"Wait a minute, Ruth Ann," Sherman snapped. "Are you worried about that new kid, Alex? Do we really know what he's told us is true?"

"Alex? He seems genuine to me. He's young, and was originally after our necklace, but once he heard our side of the story, I think he's resolved to leave it alone."

"How long is he going to stay here?" Sherman asked.

"How would I know. It's not my home he's staying in." I added, "Is there a problem with him living here?"

"No, he's been polite and stays out of Mr. Eklund's way. In fact, he's too quiet if you ask me."

"Am I asking you?" I replied, apprehensively. "You seem to want to get something off your chest regarding Alex. Why don't you just tell me what it is."

Sherman gazed around the large grand foyer to see if the coast was clear. "Let's go into the kitchen, Ruth Ann. I don't feel safe talking out here in the open."

"There's nobody around. You told me yourself that Axel's in the library. Inga's probably in the kitchen, but you didn't mention where Prunella was."

"She went upstairs to rest."

"To rest?" I questioned him, strangely. "What's she resting from?"

"I have no idea. I just overheard her tell Mr. Eklund that she was going upstairs to lie down for a little while. She saw me as she exited the library and asked me to rouse her by five."

"It's getting close to that time now. Maybe I'll go up there and knock on her door. I need to talk with her anyway." I chose to wake Prunella rather than gossiping with Sherman in the kitchen.

Sherman eyed me suspiciously. "What about?"

I laughed and said, "You'll hear in due time, Sherman." I turned and headed toward the grand staircase before he could reply. Just as I put my foot on the first stair I spun around and asked him, "Where's Alex now?"

"He's somewhere around here. I told you he's so quiet you don't hear or see him until he sneaks upon you."

"I'll look around for him after I go and get Prunella. Don't worry about him, I'm sure he's perfectly normal." I suddenly felt uneasy after talking with Sherman. First, why would Prunella feel the need to lie down? She's only in her mid-thirties and shouldn't be tired in the middle of the afternoon. Second, were Sherman's suspicions of Alex correct? Was he up to no good? I hurried up the wide, red velvet lined runner as fast as I could so I could speak with Prunella.

I walked down the long hallway on the second floor. I was told that Prunella and Axel were sharing a room again. I'd find out in a moment if that was actually true. I made my way to their room and found the door shut. I was about to knock when a thought crossed my mind. Before I knock on their door, I would check inside my room that was next to theirs. I was curious if Prunella borrowed my room to take her nap. I reached to open the door handle when a voice startled me. "Ruth Ann!" a man's voice called out abruptly.

I spun around and found Alex standing behind me. Sherman was right; he does sneak up on you without any warning. "Alex," I cried out, in surprise. "I didn't hear you." I looked around the empty hall and asked, "Where did you come from?"

Alex shuffled his feet from side to side nervously and replied, "I, I was in my room when I heard footsteps in the hall. So, I opened my door and spotted you right outside of Prunella and Axel's door. But then you came over to this room, why?"

"Why?" I asked, wondering how and why he was flipping the questions back to me. Very suspicious!

"I'm sorry," Alex said. "I didn't mean to intrude. You have every right to be anywhere in this place."

"Actually, Alex, the room I was about to enter is *my* room."

Alex looked confused, and asked, "but I thought you didn't live here?"

"No, but I've stayed here many nights so they let me decorate a room with stuff from my store."

"Oh, that makes sense. Sorry to bother you." Alex was about to turn and go back down the hall, when I stopped him.

"What are you up to, Alex?"

"Me?" he looked around to make sure I was conversing with him. "I don't really have any plans yet. I was just reading a book in my room so I stayed out of everyone's way. I probably should just pack up and head back to Chicago."

"No!" I blurted out, loudly enough to cause another door to pop open.

"Who's out here?" Prunella called out from her doorway. She looked down in front of my room and said, "Oh, it's just you two. What's up?"

Well, Prunella answered one of my questions. She did exit the bedroom she claimed she shared with Axel. I was happy they appeared to be back together, but time will tell the whole truth. "Hi, Prunella," I said. "I was coming to look for you when I ran into Alex."

"Alex, were you hiding up here in your room, again?" Prunella asked him, with a strange look on her face. What was that look? I felt a slight uneasiness forming between the three of us, almost as if *I* was the one intruding.

"Ah, yes, Prunella," he stumbled on his words. "I was looking over that book you loaned me from the library."

I watched Prunella's reaction carefully, but she didn't respond to him, so I did. "What book?"

"The works of Stanley Liljestrom," Prunella answered, rapidly. "He was curious about our relative who was the famous painter."

"Oh, that makes sense," I said, feeling a little better. "He was very talented. Did you learn anything?"

Alex appeared caught off guard by my question. "I didn't have enough time to study his work. I…I just flipped through some pages. He does seem to be very talented."

"Of course he was!" I retorted, becoming frustrated with the two of them. "What's going on here?" I asked, cutting straight to the point.

"Ruth Ann, what on earth are you talking about?" Prunella answered, coming to Alex's defense. "Give the guy a break, he's only been here a couple weeks."

"I'm sorry, Alex," I said, honestly. "I guess I'm so used to being in attack mode that I get suspicious with everyone these days."

Alex looked uncomfortable and said it was all right. He was going back into his room, located directly across the hall from Axel and Prunella's room, to clean up for dinner. Just before he closed his door he stuck his head out and asked me, "Will you still be here when I get downstairs, Ruth Ann?"

"I didn't plan on being here long, but I can stay a while. I have a few things to discuss with Prunella."

"Me?" Prunella pointed at herself. "Is something wrong?"

"Can we go talk somewhere private?" I asked her quietly. "How about my room?"

Prunella nodded and we waited for Alex to close his bedroom door before we opened my door and went inside. "So, what's up, Ruth Ann?" Prunella asked, before we had both feet in the room.

I wanted to talk with her about my trip, but first, we needed to get the elephant out of the room. "I want the truth from you, Prunella."

"About what?" she asked, innocently.

"I saw those funny looks you shared with Alex. What's up between the two of you and don't tell me it's nothing!" I stood my ground and wasn't going to budge until I got a sufficient answer.

"Are you implying Alex and I are acting inappropriately?" Prunella asked, her stern eyes glaring in my direction.

"If you're not then you should have no problem telling me what's going on between you two."

"Fine," she snapped at me. "I'll tell you what's going on, but it's not what you're thinking."

I walked over to my couch and sat down, exasperated. Instead of relaxing, I sat upright and rigid. I folded my arms across my body and waited for Prunella to explain what was going on. Prunella noticed my attitude, and finally relaxed her own fury so she could calm me down. She lost the intense glare in her eyes and replaced it with her usual soft sparkle and sweet smile. She sat down next to me and put her hand on my forearm. "Ruth Ann, I hope by now you wouldn't think that I would cheat on or plan anything evil against Axel or any of you."

"You have to stop with the secrets, Prunella," I said, frustrated. "We've been through so much recently and I thought we'd grown close. However, you still feel the need to hold things from me, and it really needs to stop. I can't take much more. I'm just calming down from when you and Lynne were kidnapped."

"I know, I'm sorry. You need to remember that I came from a childhood with lots of secrets and hatred toward people who wronged my family. I don't trust easily, but I really am trying."

Well, those words made me feel awful. Prunella's right, I should put myself in her place. It wasn't her fault that she had problems trusting people. I just thought I was different and it hurt a little that she didn't completely trust me, yet.

I unfolded my arms and grabbed Prunella's hand. "You're right. I am sorry. I need to give you more space and hopefully you'll see, in due time, that I can be the person you trust unconditionally. Just remind me once in a while when you feel I'm attacking you." I laughed at my last statement which lightened the moment. Prunella joined in and we sat in contentment for a couple minutes. Unfortunately, it wouldn't last for long.

Chapter 4

"So, Ruth Ann, do you want me to explain what's going on with Alex?" Prunella asked, trying to get back to the topic at hand.

"One of these days I'm going to confuse Alex with Axel! Their names are too similar."

"Maybe they're more related than any of us know," Prunella commented, out of nowhere.

"That's not possible, Prunella," I exclaimed. "How could Axel have anything to do with a young man from Chicago?"

"You and I didn't know we were related and you're from Colorado and I'm from Stockholm. Look at us now, we're not only cousins, we're *close* cousins, and in a short amount of time!"

"Well, I don't think there's any relationship between the two of them, but what does that have to do with the looks you and Alex were throwing back and forth a few minutes ago?"

"Actually, nothing," Prunella answered. "It just popped in my head."

"Why don't you fill me in on what's going on? I have something to tell you, too, and it's almost time for dinner."

"You're right. I've been sworn to secrecy by Alex, but I will tell you since you'll probably find out anyway."

"I'm not sure if that was a compliment or not, but you're starting to worry me."

"No, Ruth Ann, Alex and I are doing something good, not something sneaky or bad."

"C'mon, tell me. I'm getting anxious waiting for you to spill it!"

"It's not that big of a deal. Alex came to me a couple days ago all sullen and depressed. I asked him what was wrong, but he denied having a problem. Well, I must be hanging around you a lot, Ruth Ann, because I wouldn't let it go. I pushed him all day until he finally got me alone after dinner."

"Once again, I'm not sure if that was a compliment or not," I said, irritated. "I don't push and push people, do I?"

Prunella laughed and nodded her head gently. "Well, you do have a way of getting people to do what you want. So take that as a huge compliment!"

I wasn't so sure, but I wasn't going to push it just to prove a point! "Go on," I said instead.

"Everyone left the dining room except Alex and me. Inga was going in and out clearing the dishes, but I didn't think she caught on to anything out of the ordinary." She paused and waited for me to interrupt, but time was ticking and I needed her to spit it out. "So, I was about to get up when Alex asked if he could talk privately with me. Of course I said yes, but I had an uneasy feeling for some reason. I waited until Inga left for the kitchen, then I told him to tell me."

"Was he acting depressed, too?" I asked her curiously.

"Kind of. To be honest, he's been so quiet since he arrived that I didn't notice a difference until I really paid attention to him. He's been here a couple weeks, but he doesn't really do anything. I didn't want to bring it up to him, I figured he would either leave here or find a job. I know he just graduated from college with a good degree."

"Engineering, right?" I asked Prunella, trying to remember.

"Yes, but there's not a lot of work here in town. I don't know what he could do here."

"We'll come up with something," I responded. "I'd hate for him to leave right after he came into our lives. It's fun expanding our family!"

"I agree, so that's why when he asked me to help him I couldn't say no. I knew you'd understand, Ruth Ann. Axel's suspicious about him, but I'm not."

"Wait, what?" I asked, confused how Axel got in on this.

"Let me explain. Axel doesn't know I'm helping him right now. He's just mentioned he thinks it's strange that this young man is still hanging around here. I agreed with him until Alex poured his heart out."

"He poured his heart out to you? I wish I was here," I said, regretfully. Prunella was able to form a close bond with Alex and I wasn't a part of it.

"Don't worry, you'll have plenty of time to get close to him, he doesn't want to leave here. He told me he really loved the thought of having family. Remember, he doesn't have any parents or siblings back in Chicago. He's been on his own since his mother died."

"That is sad, Prunella," I replied. "So, tell me what you're doing for him?"

"That's just it. I haven't lived here long enough to really help him. That's what I told him, but he said he didn't feel comfortable speaking with Axel."

"Axel? Why him?" I inquired, curiously.

"Axel used to run a humongous shipping company and he's trying to rebuild that company as we speak."

"Sherman filled me in a little of that," I admitted, without thinking if I should have.

"Sherman?" Prunella quickly questioned. "How does he…wait a minute," Prunella said, thinking out loud. "He's overheard Axel, hasn't he?"

"I don't think I should've said anything. I ran into Sherman when I arrived here and he told me Axel was in his library. It was my fault because I started bombarding Sherman with questions. That must be that personality trait of mine pushing people until they cave!"

"Funny, Ruth Ann," Prunella said, giggling. "But yes, I was going to fill you in on everything once I knew for sure what Axel's plans were. He's still trying to figure it out himself."

"I'm okay, just tell me what Alex has to do with it?" I inquired.

"He figured he can work on some of the ship's designs from here, you know the mechanical part of it. I asked him what I could do to help, and he asked if I could smooth things over between him and Axel. Alex is extremely intimidated by him."

"Axel can come across that way, Prunella. He's always been a powerful businessman, so I see why Alex would be afraid of him."

"Well, he thinks if I fill him in on Axel's past, he would be able to understand why he did the things he did."

"Oh, I get it," I said, interrupting her. "Alex wants to work for him, but isn't sure if Axel's doing legitimate business or not, right?"

"Exactly!" Prunella cried out. "Poor Alex thinks everything Axel's done has been illegal."

"Well," I mumbled quietly, but Prunella heard me.

"He's not a crook, Ruth Ann! My husband's been cleared of all charges, and he's working very hard to get his life back, including his businesses."

"Easy, Prunella, I get it. I've always liked Axel, except for the brief time back in his office in Stockholm. He really went off the deep end trying to recover our necklace."

"He's admitted as much, but he's really trying to get back in everybody's good graces."

"I see that," I said, smiling over at her noticing how revved up she was getting defending her husband. "He's been working very hard at reclaiming his life. I think some people believe he got off a little too easy, but I'm not here to judge."

That comment didn't calm her down. Her facial features hardened and I didn't want her to be upset with me so I tried to diffuse the situation. "I didn't mean anything cruel, Prunella. You have to admit Axel had friends in high places who got him pardoned of his crimes. Most people would've gone to jail for those offenses." I wasn't helping matters so I immediately added, "Please, we're digressing. I like Axel, I always have, so let's get off this topic and get back to Alex, please."

Prunella accepted my attempt at an apology and calmed down. "I know. I was there for most of his crimes, Ruth Ann. I feel like all I do is defend the man and to be honest, I'm tired of doing it."

"You can't blame people, even Alex, for being afraid of him. Give it time; Axel's doing the right thing now. He's making amends and becoming a legitimate businessman. So, what does Alex need to know and why, again?"

"I've given him some background on Axel's life and my own. He knows all about my parents and how Axel's father ruined my father's business. I even told him about my stay at our estate back in Stockholm with Axel's first wife. He knows all about the chase for the necklace, which is something he was very interested in. He still claims he came here just for that, but I think there was more to it. I think we're missing some detail. I just don't know what, yet."

"Prunella, why does he have to know all the bad stuff? Can't we just focus on where we are now and the fact that we're all together as a family?"

"Yes, he is, but he needs a job, and that's where I came in to help him smooth things over with Axel. I told him once he's ready, I'll confront Axel, alone, and see if he's willing to take Alex on. Maybe one day Alex can run the whole business!"

"Wow, that's a big step from trying to get a job designing parts for a ship," I mentioned. "You really think there's more of a connection with Axel than he's leading on?"

"I don't have any proof, just a peculiar feeling," Prunella responded. "You're famous for your premonitions and hunches."

"Me?" I asked, surprised at her statement. "Why would you say that?"

"Because since I've known you, you been able to go after some pretty nasty people. You have a purpose and nothing will stop you from achieving your goal. I think it's highly admirable, Ruth Ann. I hope I can get more of your moxie. I'm too wishy-washy."

"Okay, let's put this hunch you have on hold for a minute and get back to you telling Alex all about Axel's past," I said.

"My past too, Ruth Ann," Prunella interrupted me. "I haven't been a saint, either."

"You've done what you had to do to survive, Prunella," I reminded her.

"But I could've chosen not to seek revenge against the Eklund family."

I reminded Prunella of one important point. "It actually was your parents that put the idea in your head."

"I knew better!"

"If there's one thing I've learned over the years it's you can't change the past. Forget about it, Prunella. Why don't you tell me Alex's reaction to everything you told him?"

"He was calm and quiet, just like he's been since he arrived here."

"He's a shy fellow, isn't he?" I questioned, wondering if "shy" was the correct word.

"You know on one hand I would agree, but there's a part of me that wonders if he's manipulating us all."

"For what greater good, Prunella?" I asked, extremely curiously.

"Well, think about it. When he first arrived at the estate, he was armed and ready to force us to hand over our necklace. Now, he's shy and willing to learn all about Axel's past and his business."

"Don't forget you filled him in on your past, too. Did you willingly offer up your past or did he ask?"

Prunella rubbed her forehead, puzzled. "I, I really don't know. At the time I didn't think so much about it. Now, I'm wondering if I'm getting played!"

"Maybe we are thinking too much about it. We've been so involved with chasing down murderers, kidnappers, and thieves that I believe we've become paranoid!"

"You think so?" Prunella asked, hopefully.

"Why don't we give Alex the benefit of the doubt unless he gives us a reason not to."

"That sounds like a plan, Ruth Ann," Prunella agreed.

"So, let's leave it alone. You've done your job explaining to Alex about Axel's and your turbulent past, and you've given him suggestions of how to confront Axel so he might fit him into the family business, right?"

"Yes. I'm tired of this topic, Ruth Ann. Let's get back to why you came up here in the first place. Not that I don't love your visits!"

"Oh, yes," I said, excited about filling Prunella in on John's invitation. However, that wasn't to be. A sudden loud knock on my bedroom door startled the two of us.

"Who did that?" Prunella asked.

"I don't know, let's find out," I replied, and then called out, "Come in."

The door flew open and in stomped Inga. Prunella relaxed after seeing it was Inga and said, "Oh, it's just you. You knocked so loud it terrified me for a moment. What's up?"

"Sorry, but I was worried when you weren't in your room. I panicked a little, I guess. I ran back down stairs and almost knocked Sherman over. He was standing at the bottom of the staircase wondering what the loud knocks were about. How did you two not hear them? You're just one room over."

I looked over at Prunella, and she shrugged her shoulders. "I guess we were too involved in our conversation and didn't hear you, right Ruth Ann?"

"Yep, I didn't hear any knocking either."

"Hmm," Inga said, unsure of our response. However, she continued, "Sherman told me Ruth Ann was here so I came back up and checked. What are you two up to?" Inga eyed us suspiciously.

"We weren't up to anything, Inga," I replied. "Prunella and I were just chatting about Alex, and then I was about to tell her some news on my end."

"News?" Inga inquired, curiously.

Prunella stood up and said, "It'll have to wait until after dinner. I'm assuming you were looking for me to tell us it was time to eat?"

Inga looked irritated because she wasn't getting the news I wanted to discuss with Prunella. "Oh, yes, it's time for dinner so why don't you both come down to the dining room, unless…" Inga looked eagerly in my direction and added, "Unless Ruth Ann wants to tell us her news?"

I stood up now and answered, "later!"

"Fine," Inga snapped, and turned her heels and stomped down the hallway.

"Ooh, I don't think she was too happy with me," I said to Prunella.

"She's just being a busybody," Prunella replied, taking a hold of my arm and leading us down the hallway toward the stairs. "I'm hungry, let's go eat."

"I guess I could eat a little," I said laughing. I always had room for Inga's cooking. She was a fabulous cook, and I was looking forward to seeing what she prepared this evening. However, a thought just popped in my head. I had to put on a bathing suit in a few days, uh-oh. Maybe I'll just nibble at dinner.

Chapter 5

Inga quickly took the back staircase down that led into the butler's pantry. Prunella and I chose to descend down the main stairs that led into the grand foyer. Waiting for us at the bottom was Sherman. "So, Inga found you?"

"Yes, Sherman," Prunella answered. "What's her problem? She had quite the attitude with us. Did you two talk about anything I should know about?"

Sherman nervously swayed back and forth before responding. "No. She came barreling down the stairs a few minutes ago demanding your whereabouts, Prunella. I just told her you and Ruth Ann were upstairs talking."

"Did she wonder what we were talking about?" I asked him quickly, before Prunella probed him with another question.

"Of course!" he announced. "She hates to be left out of your conversations. You know her, she's a busybody!"

"Really, Sherman?" I asked, laughing. "And you're not?"

"Me!" he bellowed. "I could care less what you two were talking about. I was doing my duties as the butler, that's all."

Prunella walked closer to Sherman and he held out his arm for her to grab. "That's a good one, Uncle Sherman! You know you're dying to know what Ruth Ann came all the way up here to tell me."

"Maybe," he said, lowering his head in embarrassment. "Well?"

"Well?" I repeated. "I never got the chance to speak with Prunella about it yet. I will after dinner."

"Why so secretive?" he asked. "Just tell us what it is. I'm sure it's no big deal, right?"

"Of course it isn't. I just have some news I'd like to share with Prunella first, that's all," I said, walking to the hall to the dining room. "Let's go, I'm hungry."

Prunella gave Sherman's arm a little squeeze and dragged him into the dining room. "What's for dinner?" she asked, sitting down at the seat next to the head of the table. The head seat was reserved for Axel, who was still missing from the room. "Hey, where's my husband?" she asked Sherman.

"Last I knew he was still in the library on the telephone," Sherman replied. "He's been trapped in that room since earlier today."

"I know; he's really trying to get his pier rebuilt at Eklund Industries. Ever since the explosion there's been no work for his employees. Axel wants to get the company up and running quickly. The town's shipping industry counts on Axel."

"I'm sure they're still employed there, aren't they?" I inquired. "I mean the actual building didn't blow up, just the pier."

"You're right, Ruth Ann, but it cost the company millions, and until Axel got pardoned, he couldn't conduct any business. Now that he's in the clear, he's free to start up the company."

"I'm glad to hear that," I said. I sat down opposite Prunella. I softly asked her, "Axel doesn't blame me for the explosion, does he?"

"Of course not!"

Suddenly, a strong male voice announced, "I don't hold any of the blame against you, Ruth Ann."

"Axel," I said, looking up to see the tall, lean mid-sixties man standing in the doorway from the kitchen to the dining room. Axel was a handsome man, still active and energetic and I can see why Prunella was so attracted to him. "I didn't hear you come in."

Axel sauntered over to Prunella and bent over to give her a kiss on her cheek. Prunella's face lit up with joy as he made his way to the head of the table. "You've been busy today," she said, smiling at him.

His cheery demeanor changed to a gloomier expression. "I have to admit this is more work than I thought trying to save my family's business."

Prunella truly looked concerned and devoted to him. "I can help. Just tell me what you want me to do."

Axel grabbed her hand and took it gently in his. "You're so sweet, Prunella. After everything I put you through, I can't believe how you're still standing by me."

"I love you, Axel," she said quietly, blushing over at me. "Remember, I am a business woman, too. I can get down and dirty with the rest of them!"

"I know you can," Axel replied, amused. "I'll let you know what you can do after I eat something. I don't think I've had any-thing to eat since breakfast!"

Sherman cleared his throat. We turned our attention to him at the large serving buffet. "Uh, sir, I tried to bring you lunch, and then tea, but you were so engrossed in your phone calls that you waved me away."

"I'm sorry, Sherman. I didn't mean anything by it. I had a long day, and hopefully some good will come out of it. I won't ignore you again. Plus, your family now, old man!"

Sherman scowled at Axel's "old man". "I am part of the family. I'm Prunella's great uncle and I can help with your busi-ness, too."

Before I jumped in and agreed to help Axel, he said, "I know you all are being very kind to me. I think I'm going to have this settled soon. So, if I need any help from any of you, I will let you know." Axel looked over at Inga, who had just walked into the dining room with a platter of steaming spaghetti and meatballs. "That looks good, Inga. I want a huge plate full of spaghetti."

Prunella and I noticed one person missing from our cozy group. I decided to ask where Alex was. Inga answered. "I just came from his room and he said he would be right down. He said you all should begin eating and not wait for him."

"Oh, well, then," Axel said. "Let's dig in!"

Inga took that as her cue to load our plates with piles of spaghetti and one of her massive meatballs. "These are gigantic!" I exclaimed, sticking my fork into the nearly baseball sized meatball. "I've never seen one this big."

"I watched a food show on television and these were all the rage. I wanted to experiment with them, and when I tasted one, I thought they were quite good."

"They look fantastic, Inga," Prunella said. "Can you hand me the bowl of parmesan, please?"

"Me, too," I said eyeing the large, china bowl full of freshly shredded parmesan. "You can never have enough parmesan!" I waited for Prunella to barely sprinkle a bit of cheese over her meatball. Normally, Prunella would eat a bite or two then proclaim she was full. I couldn't wait to watch her dig into this meal. There was no way she'd be able to finish even an eighth of her meatball!

I patiently waited for Prunella to hand the cheese to Axel, who declined the cheese, and then hand it to me. All eyes were on me as I dumped layers and layers of the cheese over my meatball and the tomato sauce covered noodles. "Really, what's the big deal?" I asked everyone. "It's just that I like a taste of the parmesan in each bite. Haven't you ever seen anyone do this before?"

Axel and Prunella laughed as I set the bowl directly in front of me. Inga grabbed the bowl and disappeared into the kitchen. Knowing Inga, I'm sure she went back to fill the bowl with more cheese. "So," I said, swirling a couple long noodles up in my spoon and taking a bite. "I do have some news. I was going to speak with Prunella, but the rest of you might as well hear it. Especially, Inga."

"Me?" Inga inquired, entering the dining room with a heaping bowl of cheese and setting it in front of me. I grabbed the bowl and reloaded my plate with more. "Why would I be interested in your news?"

"Because you've been working on our Thanksgiving meal."

"Oh, yeah. Do you have some more changes for me with the food?"

I was about to tell everyone my news, again, but once again, I was interrupted. Alex entered the dining room without anyone noticing. He quietly sat down next to me and Inga placed a heaping plate of food in front of him. I held out the bowl of parmesan for him and he smiled and took it. We all watched as Alex dumped more cheese on his plate than I did. I let out a howl, but Prunella was the one who spoke up. "Wow, Alex, I thought Ruth Ann put a lot of cheese on her pasta, but you actually beat her!"

Alex blushed and set the bowl back down between the two of us. "I'm sorry, did I use too much?"

"Of course not!" Prunella exclaimed. "Just before you came in here, we watched Ruth Ann dump a ton on her plate. We thought it was hilarious!"

"Oh, okay. I have to admit I really love covering my pasta with loads of cheese. My mom used to go through bags and bags of parmesan cheese with me." Alex wound a large forkful of pasta and a chunk of meatball and realized it was bigger than his mouth. He delicately bit off about half of it then chewed it carefully.

"You don't have to be so formal," Axel joined in. "It's a messy meal so dig in and enjoy!"

Alex smiled and did just that. He ate more pasta than I've ever seen anyone eat before. "Glad to see you have an appetite," I said, cheerily.

"Okay, Ruth Ann," Prunella said, sternly. "You keep saying you have news, but you still haven't told us what it was. Now you say Inga's involved. So what is it and no more distractions!"

"Fine," I stammered. "It's no big deal, just thought I'd come up here and tell you all that I'm taking off for a few days."

"That's it?" Inga bellowed. "What's that got to do with me?"

"Yeah," Prunella agreed. "When and where are you going?" she asked, suddenly becoming curious.

"Well, that's why it involves Inga. I'm leaving on Saturday and won't be back until Thanksgiving Day." I paused, waiting for their reaction about my timing with the trip.

"What!" Prunella cried out, loudly. "You're going to miss our big dinner? But it's because of you we're doing it!"

"No, no, I'm going to be back by lunchtime on Thanksgiving. John promised me that we'd be back by then."

All eyes were upon me now. Prunella's mouth slammed shut, Axel grinned broadly, and poor meek Alex shoved more pasta in his mouth. Inga was the only one who spoke. "Um, Ruth Ann, so what you're saying is that you're leaving for four or five days, *with John*, but you'll be back here in time to celebrate Thanksgiving?"

"Yep," I answered.

Inga shrugged her shoulders and said, "So what. We can handle the preparation for the day. It's not like you were going to do any of the cooking anyway. That was between Lynne and me."

I was a tad insulted by Inga's reaction. I guess being here isn't that important to them. Thank you Prunella for not being as blasé as Inga. "Ruth Ann," she exclaimed. "Did I hear you correctly? You're going away *with John*?"

"Yes, John just came over to my shop and sprung it on me." I waited for Prunella's response, but she just stared at me without any expression on her face. I wasn't sure if she was upset, surprised, happy or what! "So, are you okay with my news?"

Axel stopped grinning and answered for the now speechless Prunella. "Of course we're okay with it! In fact, it's great news!"

Prunella woke up from her silence and said, "Yes, yes, Ruth Ann. I think it's great that John's taking you away for a few days. I know how much you've wanted to spend alone time with him. I was just caught off guard, that's all."

"Great," I said. "I haven't exactly had positive reactions from anyone I've told so far. Once they got used to the idea, it was all right, but not initially."

"Who else have you told, Ruth Ann?" Inga asked. "I thought you just found out."

"Yes, I told Meme since she'll be alone for a few days in the store during my busy season."

"That makes sense," Inga said.

"I'm sure Meme was thrilled," Axel said. "She can handle the business herself, can't she? If she needs help, I'm sure one of us can pitch in, too."

"Thanks, Axel," I said, a little surprised with his offer. I couldn't picture him ringing up customers! He wasn't exactly the 'customer service' type of individual.

Prunella chimed in now and asked me, "So, besides Meme, who else knows?"

"Just Lynne. I walked over there right before I drove up here. She also was shocked with my news, but once she had a minute to digest the information, she was fine."

"Of course she is," Prunella answered. "It's not that any of us are upset or overly shocked, it's just the holidays and all."

I laughed quietly and said, "That's probably why John booked it!"

"What do you mean, Ruth Ann," Axel asked.

"Because I'm sure he got a good deal on the trip!"

"Oh, being so last minute or during a time most people don't go away?" Axel inquired.

"Both!" I replied. "I have to admit, I was rather stunned at the timing, but I wasn't going to turn it down! It has taken so long to get him to take me away, I'd never say no!"

"No way," Alex looked up from his pasta and declared. "I barely know you and could've figured that one out."

We all laughed heartily at Alex's comment. "You got that right!" Axel bellowed.

"Really, Ruth Ann," Prunella said seriously. "I truly am very happy for you two. I think you'll have a fabulous time. In fact, I'm jealous!"

"Jealous?" I questioned her. "Why would you be jealous of me? You and Axel could go anywhere at any time!"

Axel looked up from his plate and quickly added, "Definitely! If you want to go on a trip, we'll go. In fact, we could join John and Ruth Ann and make it a double date trip."

Prunella and I looked at each other in horror. I was happy that Prunella said these next words instead of me, "Axel! We could never interfere with their trip!"

"Why not?" he asked, confused. "We'd have a good time, wouldn't we?"

"Yes, but it's not our place, Axel," Prunella commented, nodding her head in my direction trying to be discreet.

Axel finally caught on and said, "Oh, I get it. You two want an *alone* trip!"

I turned three shades of red in embarrassment. Prunella sensed the awkwardness and said, "Axel, you're embarrassing Ruth Ann. I think we should plan another trip later on, not this one. Leave Ruth Ann and John to get away and relax alone.

"Thank you, Prunella. It's not that I wouldn't thoroughly enjoy the company, but you have to understand that I've been trying for so long to get John away from here, and now he's finally done it and booked a trip all by himself!"

"You were just in Sweden with John not long ago, Ruth Ann," Sherman interjected. "That's away."

"Really, Sherman. You count that as a relaxing trip with my boyfriend?" I glared at Sherman with evil eyes.

"He's just kidding you, Ruth Ann," Prunella quickly said, diffusing the situation.

"Ah, yes, I was just kidding," Sherman replied, unaware he had said anything wrong. "I'm just going to help Inga clear the table," he said, hurrying to grab our plates and head into the kitchen. Inga stood by the buffet laughing to herself and shaking her head.

"What's so funny, Inga?" I asked, angrily. "Are you laughing at Sherman or me?"

Inga quickly sobered and noticed the looks on Prunella and Axel's faces. "Oh, I was amused by Sherman's lack of common sense. That's all."

"Oh, sorry, Inga. I guess I'm a little self-conscious about the whole situation. I'm not used to telling my family I'm going away with someone who's not my husband. It feels strange, but don't get me wrong. I can't wait!"

"You're not a teenager, Ruth Ann," Axel stated. "You can go and do anything you'd like. Plus, it's not like John and you are newly dating. You two have been together for a long time now, right?"

"Well, yes, I guess," I answered, a bit perplexed. "We've known each other for years, but a solid commitment between the two of us is fairly recent."

"So, in the past you two could date other people?" Alex asked me, curiously.

"I guess so," I answered. "We assumed we'd be exclusive, but until the wild exploits in Stockholm and the scares we've had lately, we never said it out loud. Now we have."

"It's all good, Ruth Ann," Prunella said. "You and John belong together. That's all that matters."

"I don't get why you all are beating this to death," Inga exclaimed. "So what, you're going away. If someone doesn't like it, too bad!"

"That's right!" Axel agreed. "You two go and have a blast. We'll be here waiting with Thanksgiving dinner on the table."

"Thank you, Axel," I said, finally relaxing. "I'm going to head out soon because I need to still call Nancy. Lynne said she'd break the news first, but then I said I'd call her tonight."

"It's so silly how you feel you have to break the news," Prunella said. "You act like you're the daughter instead of Lynne and Nancy."

"Ah, Prunella, you didn't take the news that well initially either!"

"Touché!" Prunella laughed vigorously.

Inga, with Sherman's help, cleared the buffet and table quickly. She walked back into the dining room with a large silver platter filled with chocolate éclairs. "Wow, I said staring at the pile. Those look delicious!"

"They ought to. I got them from Lynne's bakery," Inga announced.

"She makes éclairs, too?" I asked, surprised.

"Sherman took me over there earlier today to pick up something sweet for tonight since I didn't have time to bake anything. She told us that her customers loved éclairs and she added them to her menu a couple days a week. Today was our lucky day. Sherman and I taste tested them at the bakery and they were scrumptious!"

"Hey, Ruth Ann, what ever happened to the shop Lynne was supposed to open at the resort?" Prunella asked, curiously.

"That's opening December 1st," I announced.

"Is it still going to be called, 'She's Got Balls'?" Axel inquired. "That's a catchy name."

I laughed and said, "Yes, that's the name. I came up with it a month or two ago and when I talked to Carol over at the resort about it, she was thrilled. They already serve many of Lynne's baked goods at their restaurant. Now they'll have a small store next to the gift shop. Lynne's been very busy with the holidays and opening up the new store."

"Perfect timing for it, don't you think?" Axel asked. "I mean with the holidays; she'll take it a large sum of money."

"I do believe she'll be making a profit immediately," I replied. "Carol and Dick already had the space for her so all she had to do was decorate it and fill it with her goods. It's been a lot of work for her, but it could've been worse it there wasn't an existing space set up for her."

"That's great!" Prunella said. "I'll be her first customer!"

"You'll have to beat me to it," I said, smiling.

"We'll go together!" Prunella announced. "In fact, we'll all go. How's that? We could show family support."

"Sounds like a plan," Axel said, and then stood up. "Well, ladies, and Alex, I've got more work to do before I call it a day. If you'll excuse me," Axel bent over and gave Prunella a kiss on the cheek and walked out of the room.

"He sure works a lot," I said after he disappeared. "I hope it ends well with his company in Stockholm."

"It will," Prunella responded. "I think by the time you get back it will all be settled. The problem is..." Prunella stopped, abruptly.

"What?" I asked. "What could be a problem?"

"After everything that's happened over there I sure hope the people will accept him and still want to work for him."

"If he pays his employees enough money, I'm sure they will. And in time, they'll forget what happened."

"Don't forget the other issue. If this works out, and his pier gets rebuilt, and Eklund Industries reopens, he'll be gone a lot."

"Oh, that's right," I said, understanding her reason for distress. "He'll have to go to Sweden regularly."

"Or..."

"Or what?" I asked immediately, knowing what she could say.

"Or he'll want to move back there!"

"No, you can't, Prunella! You have to stay here, with me!" I bawled. "We just found each other. I can't let you go."

"I will fight it every step of the way, Ruth Ann. I don't want to move back there either. Too many bad memories."

"Yes, that's a good thing to point out to Axel if he asks you to move back with him."

"I will," Prunella said, glumly.

"Cheer up! It hasn't happened yet, and hopefully won't even be mentioned," I reminded her.

Inga plopped another of Lynne's éclairs down on my plate. I knew I should tell her to take it away, but they were so good. The smooth, cool cream custard filling, the perfectly puffed pastry, and the rich chocolate glaze topping were calling my name. "Eat me, Ruth Ann, I'm so good!"

Prunella watched me argue with myself. "I knew you couldn't resist it, Ruth Ann."

"I'm not happy with myself. I have to put on a dreaded bathing suit in about four days. I should be starving myself! Instead I'm eating spaghetti and meatballs *and* two chocolate éclairs!"

"Don't forget about all that parmesan cheese, too," Inga reminded me, sarcastically.

"Gee, thanks, Inga."

After I finished my two desserts, I looked over at Prunella's plate. She had taken only one éclair and barely ate a quarter of it. "Didn't you like it?" I asked her.

"It's delicious, I was just too full from the pasta," she replied.

I laughed to myself. Prunella barely ate any of her pasta. On the other hand, Alex had polished off two platefuls of pasta and meatballs, and he was working on his third éclair. "Now, Alex, you look like you really enjoyed the éclairs."

"They're really good," he said, through a stuffed mouth. "Your daughter's bakery must do really well. Her stuff is amazing!"

"Thank you, Alex. She does pretty well for such a small town," I answered.

"I also have a major sweet tooth. I love dessert!" he stated, enthusiastically.

"Maybe you should learn how to bake," I said. "Lynne could teach you."

"Naw, I just like to eat it. I don't really like baking or cooking," he replied.

"What do you like to do?" I asked him, curiously. "Sports or computer games…"

"Um, what I'd really like is a job so I don't just sit around here feeling like I'm useless."

"You're not useless!" Prunella bellowed. "You just got here, give yourself some time to adjust."

"Yeah, Alex, give yourself a break. I bet Axel could give you a job with something." Oops, I did it again! I put my foot in my mouth. I wasn't supposed to know about Prunella helping Alex get a job with Axel. Maybe he would believe I just came up with the idea myself.

Prunella glared at me, and Alex looked imploringly at Prunella. "Please tell me you didn't talk to Ruth Ann about me," he asked her.

"Um, I only told her that you were interested in getting an engineering job and that maybe I could talk to Axel and see if he had any ideas."

"Alex, don't blame Prunella. I knew something was up between you two. I'm not stupid; I knew you two were conspiring about something. It's not a big deal anyway. I'm sure Axel will be thrilled to give you a job once his business is up and running again."

"You think so?" he asked, perking up.

"Of course. I think it'll help you if you not only have Prunella on your side, but me."

Alex suddenly appeared more energetic than I've seen him since he's been here. "You're probably right!"

"Let's give Axel until Thanksgiving to see what happens with his company. Then Ruth Ann and I will double team him and convince him you'd be a perfect addition to his company. What do you say?"

"I'd be eternally grateful," Alex answered, sweetly. "I can wait another week."

"Good, that's settled," I said. "Now, I have to get out of here and get home. I need to look through my closet and see what I have for this trip!"

"I'm so excited for you, Ruth Ann," Prunella declared, standing up and walking with me toward the front door. "I'll go shopping with you if you need more clothes, too."

"That would be fun, Prunella." I said my good-byes to all and headed out to my car. I was even happier when I sat down and realized Sherman had started my car and it was toasty warm!

Chapter 6

I made it back into town in no time. I went straight to my house after passing by Sinful Sweets and Ruth Ann's Antiques. Except for the security lights, the lights were out in both places so I knew Lynne had left for the day. Her days began early so I was happy to see she wasn't still there baking for the next day.

I contemplated stopping by the resort to see how Lynne's store was coming along, but decided against it. I really needed to get packing. The next day was Wednesday, which meant Saturday would sneak up on me fast. I had so much to accomplish before John whisked me away to Jamaica for our romantic getaway.

Once inside my garage I noticed the light didn't turn on. For a split second, my heart skipped a beat. I knew immediately why I needed this vacation. I was a nervous wreck wondering who was waiting for me inside my very own garage. My imagination went wild, but then I told myself to knock it off. Not everything that went wrong was because someone was after me. It was over, nobody was waiting to kidnap or hurt me. After a few seconds, my heart rate slowed, but I quickly got myself inside and bolted the door.

Ever since my kidnapping, I found it comforting to walk into a well-lit house. Even if I left in the morning and knew I'd be gone all day, I still left several lights on. So, when I entered my small kitchen, I took in a sigh of relief that I could see most of my living space. It was a cheery home, with bright colors and cozy furniture.

I wanted to call Nancy as soon as possible. Lynne had probably calmed her down, but I needed to hear her voice. I dropped my purse onto the tall kitchen island and grabbed my cellphone. I hit the speed dial and while I waited for it to connect I walked over to my stove and grabbed the bright red teapot. I filled it with some water and put it on. One ring, two rings, three rings... "Hello, this is Nancy, I'm not here at the moment, leave a message and I'll get back to you as soon as I can."

I hated hearing that message. My daughters were so naïve. I kept telling them to use the generic voice mail message! I didn't want someone getting a hold of my daughters and causing any harm. I know that may sound old fashioned, but after what I've been through the past month or so, I was allowed.

I left Nancy a message and then hurried over to the screaming teapot. I grabbed one of my favorite mugs and filled it to the brim. I picked out a small piece of dark chocolate candy from the bowl I always kept full on my island. For a split second, I contemplated those two éclairs I ate, but dismissed the thought. I always had chocolate with my tea!

Twenty minutes later I was showered and standing inside my walk-in closet. "Now, time to pull out some clothes," I said to myself.

After much frustration, I stood in front of the couch and stared at the pile of clothes. "Five days in Jamaica. I'll need at least three bathing suits, five pairs of shorts and tops, five sleeveless dresses with a light sweater or two." I sorted the pile into categories and got to work.

About a half hour later, I had several neatly organized piles of clothes. I didn't feel like I've gained any weight since I've worn the shorts, but still planned on waiting until the morning to try them on. The dresses were fine since they were stretchy. Now, the bathing suits...nobody looks good without a tan in a bathing suit! I'm not even going to put one on until I'm walking out to the pool or beach. The suits I picked were cute for a woman of my age. I doubt John would expect me to wear a two-piece suit!

Once I finished with the clothing, I worked on the shoes. Shoes! That's where I failed miserably. I needed an entire suitcase just for shoes! I'm sure many women tear their hair out trying to pick and choose their shoes for a trip. I'm one of them. I've never claimed to be a good packer; in fact, I'm horrible at it. I hurried back inside my closet and pulled out all the shoes I wanted to bring.

"Ten pairs of sandals! No way," I exclaimed. I had to eliminate some. Of course I needed some gym shoes in case we did some exercise, and then a pair of hiking shoes for the outdoor walking. Oh, then I might need some shoes for the water, and my pool flip-flops...UGH, what am I doing? I can't seem to get a grip on the shoe thing!

I stomped away from the mess on the couch and hopped into bed. "Tomorrow," I said, admitting defeat for the moment. I looked at the clock on my nightstand and realized Nancy never returned my call. Should I call her back? Was she so furious that she wasn't capable of speaking with me? Ridiculous, I thought to myself. I will try her first thing in the morning.

I woke before seven the next morning with bright sunshine streaming through my bedroom windows. The warmth of the sun brought my mind back to the upcoming trip. I couldn't wait to lie in the sun, and float in the warm Caribbean waters, but for now, I had to get myself organized. I hopped out of bed and decided to call Nancy before I tackled the dreaded elliptical screaming for me in the corner of my bedroom.

Once I was dressed to exercise and had my first cup of tea, I punched in Nancy's phone number. It should be a perfect time to reach her before she headed out to the high school. One ring, two rings, three rings... "Hello, this is Nancy..."

"No way, again she's not answering my call!"

I quickly called Lynne's bakery because I knew she would be there and couldn't avoid my call. "Hi, Mom," Lynne called out cheerily. "Why are you calling so early?"

"I've tried your sister two times, and she's not picking up. Is there something wrong?"

Lynne didn't answer me right away, causing alarm bells to ring in my head. Or was it paranoia? "Did you talk to Nancy yesterday about my trip coming up on Saturday?"

"Yes, I talked to her briefly. I've been so busy with the baking that I didn't get to go see her so I just called her last night."

"And?" I inquired anxiously.

"What?" Lynne asked, innocently. "Oh, wait, you're wondering if she had a problem with you going away with a man!"

"Not just a random man, Lynne, it's with John!"

"I'm just giving you a hard time, mom," Lynne giggled. "Nancy's busy with school so she didn't really say much about it. She had the same concern as I did."

"Which was?" I asked, pulling information from her, which wasn't going smoothly.

"Oh, sorry, I'm baking a new ball right now for my new shop. My mind's on the ingredients and...what were we talking about again?"

"Lynne!" I yelled through the phone. "Just tell me what Nancy and your concerns are."

"Oh, just that you'd be back by Thanksgiving."

"That's it?" I asked, calming down. "She didn't have *any* other problems with the trip?"

"Nope," she replied. "Why? You think there should be some other reason for Nancy to be angry with you?"

"No, no, I'm just trying to make sure everyone's happy and okay with the trip."

"Mom, seriously, why would you care if someone had a problem with John and you taking a short trip? It's your life, and you're an adult. Let it go, mom."

"You are completely right, dear. I'll wait and hear from your sister when she has time." I hesitated a moment, and then asked, "Do you happen to know where your sister is right now?" I suddenly realized that Nancy may not have a problem with me, but maybe she was busy somewhere else and didn't want me to know where!

"I'm no snitch, mom," Lynne snapped. "I really have to go or I'll ruin this batch. Just leave Nancy a message and I'm sure she'll get back to you as soon as she can." Lynne hung up the phone before I could order her to tell me what she meant with the snitch comment.

Being full of pent up frustration, I decided to take it out on my elliptical. Maybe I could burn a few extra calories as anger raged through my body. Where could Nancy be? Or maybe I should be asking myself *who* was Nancy with at this time of the morning. My imagination went wild with inappropriate thoughts. I dismissed them and had the best fifty minutes on the elliptical I've had in a very long time.

Chapter 7

Once showered, I ate a quick bowl of cereal and then headed to my store. Not a peep from Nancy, and now she would be at the high school teaching her first class. I came up with a solution that helped me get through the morning. I would work hard at the paperwork at my antique store, and then at lunchtime I would pop over to the school and confront Nancy face to face.

"Hi, Meme," I said, smiling at my young, assistant manager.

"Good morning, Ruth Ann," she called back to me from the back storeroom. "Are you getting excited for your trip?" she asked, smiling broadly.

"To be honest, I can't get away soon enough!"

Meme stared strangely at me after my brash statement. "Are you alright?"

"I'm fine, just irritated with my daughter!" I snapped.

"Lynne?" Meme asked, surprised. "What did she do?"

"No, not Lynne," I responded. "Nancy."

"Nancy!" Meme bellowed. "Nancy never does anything do make you mad. It's always Lynne who speaks her mind with you."

Meme was so right! Lynne and I always clashed, but Nancy and I never did. She was the quiet, stay far away from confrontation type of individual. Maybe the last few years teaching high school students had caused her to become rebellious. No, that's not my Nancy. She was sweet, liked by everyone. Oh, no, what if some man was taking advantage of her innocence? "Ruth Ann!" Meme yelled. "What's going on with you?"

I shook off the internal conversation I was having and said, "I'm sorry, my mind took me to places I didn't want to go. Nancy hasn't returned any of my phone calls."

Meme shrugged her shoulders and said, "That's all."

"Well, yes," I replied. "Maybe I am worrying for no reason. I decided I would go over to see her at lunchtime. Maybe I'll be able to speak to her then."

"I'm sure it's no big deal. What's going on this time of year over at the school? She could be busy and just didn't have time to call you back."

"That could be it, but Lynne mentioned something strange when I asked her about where her sister's been."

"What?" Meme asked, curiously.

"She told me flat out that she wouldn't 'snitch' on her sister! What's that supposed to mean?"

"Oh," Meme said slowly, changing her tone.

"See, you think that's strange, too."

"Lynne could just be playing around. Go over and see Nancy in a couple hours."

"I plan on it," I said, walking into my office. I called out to Meme, "I can't go on any trip if I don't clear this mess off my desk!"

"Don't worry, you will, Ruth Ann," Meme said loudly, laughing.

She was correct. I wouldn't let my work pile keep me away from a trip to Jamaica or my daughter! I focused my energy on work and put my concerns about Nancy in the back of my brain. It worked for a couple hours until I glanced at the time and saw it was just before noon. I hopped out of my desk chair and hurried into the empty back storeroom. Meme was out in the showroom waiting on customers and moving items around. She was a genius with staging the showroom. Whenever merchandise sat too long, Meme would stage it perfectly so that a customer would feel she had to have it. Genius. That's why I made her my assistant manager at such a young age. Plus, I wanted her to be able to support her two-year-old son, Elijah.

"I'm heading out for a little while, Meme," I called out to her, sticking my head through one of the swinging double doors.

"No problem, Ruth Ann," she answered. "It's been slow in here this morning so don't feel you have to hurry back on my account."

"I guess you were right about the business the week before Thanksgiving. I sure hope it picks up after though."

"Oh, I'm sure it will. People will be doing their holiday shopping." Meme stopped dusting one of the several curio cabinets, and added, "Speaking of holiday, are we open the day after Thanksgiving?"

"I know we should because it's supposedly the busiest shopping day, but I don't want to work the day after Thanksgiving."

"Oh, okay," Meme said, glumly.

I picked up on her tone, and quickly added, "but I will definitely pay you for the day, Meme."

She perked right up and said, "Oh, that's so nice of you! Thank you!"

I turned and headed to the alley and hopped in my bright yellow truck. It was beginning to snow lightly outside. I wondered if we were in for a storm. Oh, no, what if we got snow on Saturday when we're trying to leave for Jamaica! I made myself a mental note to check what the weather was going to be like at the Denver airport.

I pulled the collar of my coat over my chin and hurried inside my truck. Once inside, I cranked up the heat and headed to the high school. Five minutes later, I was parking in the nearest visitor spot I could find. The wind had clearly picked up since this morning and now that it was snowing it made me more anxious to get out of town. Winters were pretty long here so any break was welcome.

I hurried to the main entrance of the school and walked inside. I made a left and went to the administrative offices. Nobody was allowed in the school without checking in. I spotted Tom Johnson, the Principal standing by the main desk. "Hi, Tom," I called out. "What are you doing working the desk?" Tom turned and smiled in my direction. "Lunchtime."

"Oh, and the Principal fills in during that time," I said.

"Not normally, Ruth Ann. The staff went over to the café for Emily's birthday. I said I'd man the desk for the hour or so."

"You're so kind," I said. "Did any teachers go, too?"

"Nope, I don't think so, why?" he asked, curiously.

"I'm here to see Nancy and didn't know if she took off somewhere for lunch."

"Oh, she did, Ruth Ann," he broadcasted, proudly. "I just happened to see her leave here about five minutes ago. Sorry you missed her."

I couldn't catch a break! Where'd she go to now? "You wouldn't by chance know where she went?"

"Sorry, Ruth Ann. I just got lucky when I told you she left. I happened to be looking out toward the hall and saw her with her coat on. She did look like she was in a hurry, though."

"Really?" I asked. "Hmm, I wonder where she went."

"Try your other daughter's place," he suggested. "Maybe she went to have a cookie or something.

"Oh, that's a great suggestion. I bet that's where she went." I thanked him and took off into the frigid afternoon weather.

I rushed down the slightly slick Main Street and pulled behind Lynne's store. I contemplated parking behind my store, but with the snow and dropping temperatures, I didn't even want to walk two doors down from the antique store to the bakery. I entered the bakery through the back door.

"Mom," Lynne cried out, surprised by my sudden visit. "What are you doing here? Need a chocolate break?"

"No, but actually, I could use some chocolate!" I sat down on a stool where Lynne was working. "Hey, those look good, what are they?" I asked, staring at the numerous red and green balls on a cookie sheet.

"Those are my new holiday balls. I haven't decorated them yet, but they'll be very festive for Christmas."

"What flavor are they?" I asked, trying to smell their aroma.

Lynne grabbed the cherry red ball and held her hand out for me to take it. "It is melted white chocolate with red coloring. The filling is crushed ginger snaps."

I popped the inch sized chocolate ball into my mouth and the strong, ginger flavor immediately melted on my tongue. "Mmm, these are delicious, and you're right, very Christmassy!"

"I think so. If I can decorate them with sprinkles or drizzle other colors over them, I think they'll be a big hit."

"What's inside the green ones?" I asked, holding my hand out to receive one.

"Those are chocolate chip cookie dough balls."

I popped the entire ball into my mouth and chewed slowly. The raw cookie dough tasted like real cookie dough. "Wow! Can I have one more? I ate that one too fast."

Lynne handed me a napkin with one of each. I ate each one slowly so I could savor every ounce. "These will be a huge hit in your new store, Lynne."

"I hope so," she answered. "Hey, is that why you came over here?"

"Oh, no, I hoped to see your sister here," I said, swallowing my last bite. "Is she in the front of the store?" Lynne looked at me oddly and stated, "Nancy's not here. Why would you think she was?"

"Because I stopped over at the school and Principal Tom told me she left. I figured where else would she go at lunchtime."

Lynne's expression changed and she lost eye contact with me. "Maybe she ran home," she hinted, weakly.

"C'mon, Lynne. I see the look in your eyes. You can't even look at me, so I know you're lying."

"Look, Mom," she said. "It's not my place to tell you where she is."

"Aha! So you *do* know?" I asked, angrily. "How's this, I'm your mother and I'm *ordering* you to tell me where your sister is!"

"Nope, not this time, mother," Lynne answered, sternly. "I will call her myself and tell her that you know something's up. I promise you she'll contact you this afternoon. How's that?"

"This isn't fair, Lynne! Is she sick or hurt?" I asked, worried sick.

"No, no, it's nothing like that. She's just..." Lynne shut her mouth and refused to say anymore. I stormed out of the bakery and headed back to my store. I slammed my office door and sat down behind my desk. "How dare they," I cried out. "And after every-thing I've done for them over the years!"

**HOLIDAY WHITE CHOCOLATE
GINGERSNAP BALLS**

1 - package white melting chips
    (or colored melting chips in red)
1 - box ginger snaps
1 - 8 oz. Neufchatel cheese
    Red food coloring/gel

Allow cream cheese to soften at room temperature.

Crush ginger snaps in food processor or in a large baggie until finely chopped.

Mix cookies with cheese until thoroughly mixed. Chill in freezer for thirty minutes to an hour. Roll into one-inch balls and place on waxed paper lined cookie sheet. Chill in freezer for fifteen minutes up to an hour.

Melt chocolate in microwave until smooth. Add in food coloring/gel and immediately dip balls into candy (add sprinkles) and place back on cookie sheet. Chill for ten to fifteen minutes. Keep in covered container or large plastic bag for up to two weeks.

About an hour later there was a slight knock on my door. "Come in," I snapped. I still was fuming mad at both daughters. I tried to calm myself down by purchasing merchandise, but it failed miserably. My mind couldn't stop wandering back to Nancy and what she could've gotten herself into.

My office door slowly crept open and Meme stuck her head in. "I didn't want to bother you, Ruth Ann, but I really thought I should check on you to see if you're all right."

"I'm sorry, Meme. It's not you," I said, calmly. "I'm just so mad at Nancy and Lynne."

"So, you didn't find Nancy at the high school?" she asked.

"Nope."

"Why are you mad at Lynne now?" she asked carefully, not wanting to upset me further.

"After I found out she wasn't at school, I figured she'd be over at the bakery."

"So you drove over there and confronted Lynne, didn't you?"

"Yes."

"Lynne wouldn't rat out her sister, would she?"

"No," I said, not liking the direction of this conversation now. "Wait, are you implying I shouldn't be mad at Lynne for not telling me where her sister is?"

"Look, Ruth Ann," Meme said sweetly, trying not to upset me. "I don't want to overstep, but maybe it's really nothing and you're getting upset over something you shouldn't."

"Really. You think so?" I questioned, wondering if I blew up over nothing.

"I can't say for sure, but why don't you put it in the back of your mind for the rest of the afternoon. Hopefully after you leave here, Nancy will tell you where and what's she's been up to."

"Hmm," I said, contemplating Meme's words. "You have a point, Meme. Maybe you're right!"

"I sure hope so! Because I wouldn't want you on my bad side!" Meme said, smiling at me to make me aware she was joking, but was she?

I glanced up at the clock and noticed it was almost three in the afternoon. I would give it to five and then I would find Nancy and force her to spill it!

Thankfully, I kept myself occupied with orders and phone calls and the time passed quickly. At five o'clock, I locked my office door and Meme locked the front door. "I'm taking off," I called out to her. "I'll see you in the morning, Meme."

"Okay, good luck with your daughters, Ruth Ann. Try not to be too hard on them. They really are good women!"

"Yes, they usually are," I said back to her.

I hurried out the back and stepped inside my freezing truck. I turned over the engine and cranked the heat to high. I hit the switch for my heated seats and within a minute or two I felt the warmth streaming through the vents and underneath my seat. "Ah," I muttered. "Now, off to the school. My daughter better still be there!"

I rushed down the freshly salted Main Street and pulled into the nearly empty school parking lot. I decided to drive around and locate Nancy's car before getting out and going inside. I couldn't find her car after going around the back. "She must've left," I said, frustrated.

I pulled out of the school lot and headed back down Main Street toward my house. I was really beginning to worry about Nancy. I almost turned and went to the police station to speak with John, but decided against worrying him. I didn't want John to have any distractions and tell me he didn't have the time to take off for our trip.

I opened my garage and pulled inside. I hurried into the kitchen and pulled out my cell phone. One last time, I dialed Nancy's number and hoped I wouldn't have to hear her voicemail message again. "Hello, Mom," a voice answered from the other end.

"Finally!" I muttered. "I've been trying to reach you since last night! Where have you been?"

"I've been busy," Nancy answered. "What's wrong?"

"What's wrong?" I repeated. "That's my question for you!"

"Nothing's wrong with me, Mother," she said. "You do realize that I'm an adult and I do have a life."

"I understand that," I snapped. "But when your sister tells me she couldn't tell me where you've been, and I couldn't reach you, well…a mother worries. Just wait until…" Nancy stopped me and said, "Don't go there, Mother!"

"Fine," I agreed. "But tell me what's so secretive that Lynne couldn't tell me where you've been lately?"

Silence. "Well?" I said. "Just tell me! If it's bad, I can handle it."

"Nothing is wrong! I already told you that. I'm just helping someone and I've been asked to keep it private. That's all!"

"That's the big secret! You're helping a student and putting in extra time, phew."

"Well, not exactly," Nancy said.

"Not exactly, what?" I questioned her.

"It's not a student, Mother."

"Then who is it and why are you helping them?"

"I told you, it's private!" Nancy retorted.

"Nancy, don't be snippy with me! I won't press you any more if you don't want me to know. I just was worried you were seeing a…"

"Seeing a?" she interrupted, and asked me what I meant by it.

"Okay, I was worried you were seeing a man that you didn't want me or anyone else to know about. Like a married man!"

A loud noise filtered through the phone. I believe it was laughter! "Are you laughing, Nancy?"

"Yes, that's hilarious!" Nancy howled, and couldn't stop laughing.

"Well, that answered my question of a married man. However, are you seeing someone you're not ready to tell me about yet?

"No. I'm not seeing anyone. I'm only helping someone." Nancy waited a moment, and then added, "I figure I should just come out and tell you. You're going to find out anyway."

"Mother's usually do!" I commented.

"How about I meet you over at Lynne's bakery. We can talk there."

"One last question. Does your sister know all about this?"

"Yes," she replied. "I'll meet you there in thirty minutes, okay?"

"I'll be there." I finished my call with her and felt an intense urge to throw my phone across the room. I chose to take a few deep breaths and count to ten. Finally, my heart rate returned to normal, I grabbed a bottle of water and went into my bedroom to put on some comfortable clothes. As I grabbed a pair of black leggings and a long, gray sweater, I passed my pile of clothing and remembered I had a trip in three days. I didn't want to leave town with anything unresolved, so I ignored the clothes and headed back over to the bakery.

A Few minutes later, I was opening the back door to Sinful Sweets. Julie, Lynne's assistant was making tomorrow's dough for the donuts. "Hi, Ruth Ann!" she said. "Lynne's in the front of the bakery. She's waiting for you."

I thanked Julie and walked through the double swinging doors that led into her cute bakery shop. I spotted Lynne standing behind her long counter wiping it down. "Hi, Lynne," I said, walking over to her and sitting down on one of the stools.

"Nancy told me we were meeting here." Lynne eyed me suspiciously, and asked, "Are you doing okay?"

"I'm fine, dear," I answered. "Isn't Nancy here yet?"

"Nope, she texted me she'd be right over." Lynne walked over to a large urn filled with chocolate chip cookies and grabbed a couple. She placed them onto a napkin and slid them over to me. "Maybe you should have a couple of these."

"What do you mean by *I should* have them?" I asked, inquisitively.

"You're always a little calmer after having some chocolate."

"Not that I agree, but I am hungry so I'll eat them," I said, grabbing one of the chewy cookies and taking a bite. "These are so gooey. How do you get them like that?"

"Lots of practice," Lynne answered. "I bake them every day you know!"

"Good point," I said. Just then the front door of the bakery flew open and in came Nancy. However, she wasn't alone. My mouth dropped open and suddenly I found myself speechless.

Chapter 8

Lynne saw the shocked look on my face and decided to intervene. "Hi, Sis, why don't you and Alex come over here and sit down."

Why was my just over thirty-year-old daughter coming here with our newly discovered family member. It seemed quite a coincidence that he would be involved in *another* secret with a family member of mine! "Hi, Mom," Nancy said, as she sat on one of the stools next to me.

I nodded to her, but kept my stare on Alex. Finally, after several awkward seconds, I got my voice back. "What on earth are you doing here with my daughter, Alex?"

He nervously stood behind Nancy pleading for her to answer. "Mom, leave him alone. We have something we want to tell you."

"Oh, no way!" I bellowed. "You and Alex?"

"No, no, that's not what's happening at all, Mom," Lynne replied for her sister. "That would be totally inappropriate. Alex is a member of our family, gross!"

"Well, he's a distant relative, like third or fourth cousin I would guess," Nancy added.

"So, if you two aren't involved, why would you be with him?" I inquired, greatly relieved that they weren't in a relationship.

"I'll tell her," Alex said, jumping into the conversation. "It's my fault anyway."

"Fault, what fault?" I asked, confused. "Is there trouble?"

"No, Mom," Nancy replied. "I'm helping him."

"With what?" I asked.

"Ruth Ann, you caught me with Prunella secretly trying to figure out this new family of mine and its troubles with the law. I'm not sure Axel will want to hire me, and I need employment. So, Prunella suggested I contact Nancy since she's a teacher here in town. I thought I could get a job teaching at the high school."

"Oh, but aren't you an engineer?" I asked.

"Yes, but I also have a Physics Degree. I can teach Physics if it doesn't work out with Axel. In fact, I like the thought of working with high school students, and maybe I can start coaching their football team."

"Football team," I questioned him. "You want to coach football?"

"Oh, yes, I played throughout my childhood and until my second year in college. I hurt my knees so I had to quit. That's why I originally majored in Physics, but I was worried I wouldn't make enough money so I added the Engineering Degree."

"You're way over qualified to be a Physics teacher!" I announced. "I'll speak with Axel. I know I can convince him to give you a well-paying job."

"Gee, thanks, Mom," Nancy moaned. "I'm sorry I don't have a well-paying job."

I realized I made a huge blunder so I quickly tried to make amends. "Nancy, you always wanted to be a teacher. Even when you were a little girl you would set up pretend classrooms with a chalkboard and do math equations. I'm just saying Alex wasn't planning on being a teacher when he graduated from college. He got his Engineering Degree so he should use it!"

"That's okay, Mom," Nancy said. "That's what I told him, too." Nancy turned around in her stool and told him, "I think I've finally convinced him, too."

Alex blushed, but said, "I know. I have to admit, I'm kind of terrified of him."

"Axel?" I questioned him.

"Yes, he has a strong personality. Also, his past kind of scares me, too."

I stepped in and said, "But he's not as bad as he looks on paper. I know he's done a lot of illegal things, but give him a chance. I'll go up there and talk with him. Don't worry, I'll get you a job!"

"But even Prunella told me she wasn't sure he would hire me. How could you do it if his own wife can't?"

"Because he owes me more than you know!" I said, smiling confidently. I knew I could make this work. Alex didn't have the personality needed to be a teacher. He was too quiet, and his confidence needed a drastic boost.

"Here's what I'm going to do. I'm going to pack tonight and tomorrow I'll pop up to the estate and have a nice chat with Axel. That way when I'm gone on my trip you can hash out the details, and when I return I expect to hear the progress you've made with your new job."

"If I get the job, Ruth Ann," Alex reminded me.

"Not if, but when," I reassured him. "Hey," I turned to my attention back to my daughters and said, "What was so secretive about this? You two made such a big deal of keeping this from me, why?"

Lynne eyed Nancy, and nudged her to speak up. "Fine, Mom," Nancy snapped. "I made Lynne promise not to tell you because I knew you would take matters into your own hand. I wanted to get Alex to admit he didn't really want to be a teacher without your interference."

"Wow, I'm that bad!" I exclaimed.

"No, it's not that," Lynne chimed in. "You just have this way of always trying to solve the problem, even when you shouldn't. Sometimes," she smiled at me to reassure me, "Just sometimes, we need to solve things on our own. Can you try to relate?"

"Well, I guess I have a dominant personality and I always want people to be happy and safe."

"I'll say!" Nancy stated. "Oops, sorry. I meant that as a compliment."

"Sure you did," I said, trying to smile. "But isn't that what happened anyway? I usually find out anyway, so why not omit all the secrets?"

"You're right, Mom," Nancy admitted. "We never got away with anything!"

"And look how well you both turned out," I said, adding a little guilt to my tone.

"Thanks, I guess," Lynne said. "So, I'm tired and have to come back here early in the morning. Why don't we let Mom take care of Axel, and change the subject for a moment?"

"To what?" I asked.

"To your trip!" Nancy said. "I hear you're taking a five-day trip to Jamaica with John!"

I watched her expression and couldn't tell if she was okay or upset. "And…"

"And what?" Nancy asked. "It's fine with me. You're an adult and can go away with whomever you please!"

"Really?" I questioned her, grinning broadly. "You're not upset about it?"

"Nope. Go and have a great time. Just make sure you both are back for Thanksgiving dinner."

"Great! Now I can pack with a clear conscience. Thanks, girls."

We said our good-byes and left Lynne's bakery. It was after dinnertime and I was a bit hungry, but after eating sweets at Lynne's shop, I decided I would go home and eat an apple. Bathing suit time was getting closer and closer!

After slicing an apple into about a hundred slices to make it look like I had a large plate of food, I dug in heartily. I headed into my bedroom and attacked the clothes and shoes spread over the couch and floor. "Now, I need to eliminate some shoes." After much deliberation, I was able to fit everything I needed into one very large suitcase. Unfortunately, there would be no room for souvenirs, but I could bet John would have plenty of room in his luggage. I decided that in the morning before work I would pop over to the station and see how things were coming on his end. I hoped there would be no calamities that would prevent us from leaving in just three days!

I woke up the next morning bright and early after having had a wonderful night's sleep. I hopped on my elliptical and strode away for almost an hour. Once showered, eaten, and dressed, I headed to the police station to see John. It was still early, but I was fairly confident he'd be there. I didn't have a lot of time since I had to get to my shop and open today. Meme was going to be delayed with Elijah over at Kiddie Corner Day Care.

"Hi, Judy," I said, trying to muster a big smile. "What are you doing at the front desk?"

"Ah, Ruth Ann, nice to see you," she said, not trying to muster any smile toward me. "We are short staffed so I'm helping out where I can. You know me, I'll help anyone at any time!"

That's a load of crap! She was kissing up to make herself look good. There wasn't a kind, generous bone in her body! So, I guess you wonder why all the angst? It was her, Judy Lynch, the newly hired, detective friend of *my* boyfriend, John! He brought her into the station as a temporary extra hand, but with the rise in crime in our little town, he offered her a permanent position. A position she took, of course.

"Yeah, okay, Judy. Whatever you say!"

Once she knew nobody else was around, she replied with her usual sarcasm, "What's that supposed to mean, Ruth Ann? I've rescued you from a lot of hot messes! Remember that?"

"I also recall you making some major mistakes along the way, Judy!"

"Ruth Ann!" a male voice called out, walking up to the front desk area.

Judy quickly changed her facial expression to that of a nice, happy, caring person, which we all know is a load of bull! "Hi, John. Look who came to visit you without an appointment?"

John gave Judy a funny glance, but ignored her comment. "Hey, I was going to stop by your store this morning if I hadn't heard from you. You've been awfully quiet the last twenty-four hours. All okay?"

I glimpsed in Judy's direction hoping John would get the hint to take me away from her. Thankfully, he grabbed my arm and we walked toward his office. "That was weird," he said. "Was she acting funny with you, too?"

"Who, Judy?" I asked him, not wanting to show him she still gets on my nerves.

"Yes. She's been acting goofy ever since she found out we're going away."

"Really?" I asked, grinning from ear to ear. Ha! She was jealous of me, now!

"Aw, forget about her. Fill me in on how everyone's taken the news about our trip. You know, it's just three days away!"

"I know," I said, sitting in one of the chairs in front of his desk. John plopped on the backside of his desk smiling that gorgeous smile of his. "I can't believe it's all coming together."

"I knew it would. You always make things work," John said.

"I do if I want it badly enough!" I replied.

"Ooh, that sounds almost inappropriate from you, Ruth Ann!" John said, laughing. "What is it that you want so badly?"

It took me a moment to figure out what he was talking about when it hit me. "John! You know what I mean. Get your mind out of the gutter!"

John laughed, but then got serious after a second. "You know I can't wait to get you alone. It's been a long-time coming."

"I couldn't agree more," I answered. "Oh, let me answer your original questions. My daughters are fine, and Prunella and the gang up at the estate are all on board for us going and returning in time for Thanksgiving dinner."

"That's great. What else is there to do?" he asked.

"Just finish packing, and, oh, that's a question I have for you," I said, stumbling over my words. John nodded for me to continue. "Will you have any extra room in your suitcase in case we buy souvenirs?"

"Ha! You've stuffed your suitcase, haven't you?"

"Yes. I've told you I'm a terrible packer. I need options."

"That's no surprise, and no problem. I'll have plenty of room in mine. I'll take a bigger piece just for you."

"Thanks, John."

"I could've used a duffel and had plenty of space. All I need are a couple swim trunks, shorts, and shirts. We're just hanging out at the beach and in the water."

"True, but there's meals, and if we go off on a hike or shopping…"

He looked at me peculiarly, and asked, "Do I need more clothes?"

"You'll be fine," I answered. "Well," I hopped out of the chair and said, "I gotta run. I need to open the store on time today."

"I'll talk with you later," John said, grabbing my hand and walking me out to the front of the station. He noticed Judy was staring at us as we walked hand in hand. I wanted her to see my next move so I waited until I was next to the front desk.

"I can't wait until Saturday, John!" I said, with as much enthusiasm as I could gather. Then I went on my tippy toes and kissed him right on the lips. It wasn't something I usually did so I caught not only Judy off guard, but John. His face turned red, but he went with it and returned my short, sweet kiss.

"Bye, Ruth Ann," he called out, as I sauntered out the front door feeling quite pleased with myself.

I hurried to my SUV and cranked up the heat. Once again, it was extremely frigid outside. I drove down Main Street past the resort and whizzed down the alley until I reached my spot. It was 9:30 in the morning and the store opened in thirty minutes. "Plenty of time," I said, out loud.

Once inside, I turned up the heat. I unlocked my office, turned on the lights, but didn't go inside. I went through the back storeroom and pushed open one of the doors that led into the front showroom. I flicked on several chandeliers even though the sun was shining brightly through the large front windows. I loved the sunlight, but it sure showed the dust. However, today I didn't see any dust! Meme must've polished them before she left last night. I always noticed the dust because it drove me nuts! I didn't know what I would do without her.

Thirty minutes flew by. I unlocked the front door and hoped we would have some sales today. Meme was correct about it being a slower time. I knew once Thanksgiving was over we would pick up immediately, but this was too slow. I looked over yesterday's receipts before I left last night and noticed we only had a few sales. However, one of the sales was a big one. A solid mahogany dining room table and eight chairs! That equals up for a whole month of sales in the summertime.

I was about to walk in the back room when the bell rang on the front door. I turned, and saw Lulu Hamilton, the Mayor's wife, stroll in. Lulu was young, beautiful, and a snob. I have no idea why she married a small town mayor like Henry. He was about my age, but round and bald. Not the most handsome man around, but he did come from money and I'm sure Lulu knew that when she married him.

"Hi, Lulu," I said, with as much excitement as I could. "What can I do for you this morning?"

"Ah, Ruth Ann, you're actually here," she said, sarcastically.

"Huh? I own the store. Why wouldn't I be here?"

"Because every time I come in here I'm being helped by Meme, your employee."

"Meme is my Assistant Manager, and quite capable of running the store when I'm not here." I didn't want to lose her sale so I changed my tone and shook her snootiness off. "What do you need or are you just browsing?"

"I would never browse in this tiny town. If there were more choices, I would probably rarely come in here. However, Henry wants to keep this place small and boring."

"I would call it quaint," I said, forgetting my manners. She was testing my nerves!

"Well, anyway, I need some help with my Thanksgiving table. I have Henry's mother's china, but it's so old-fashioned. I need something old, but with some zip to it. It's just got too much brown in it and I need something to brighten the table up. Any suggestions?"

"Of course," I said. "I bet we can make your table the talk of the town!" I said, knowing that line always worked on her. I did it recently with some old brass candlesticks she bought.

"Perfect. Tell me what I can use, please. I'm in a hurry," she ordered.

I walked over to a table and grabbed one of a set of glass serving bowls that would definitely brighten her table. "I also have an entire set of linens for your table if you need those, too."

"I'll take it all, Ruth Ann," she said, waving her arm in a circle. "Can you have it sent to my house?"

"Oh, sure," I said, wondering why she couldn't wait the five minutes for me to wrap it up. "I'll have Meme drop it off at your house this afternoon. Will that work?"

"Yes, and oh, bill me okay?" she demanded.

"We don't normally do that, Lulu, but I can have Meme pick up the payment when she brings it over. How does that work?"

"Fine," she snapped, and then turned and marched out of the store.

"Wow," a female voice bellowed from the back of the store. It was Meme, and she was laughing at my exchange with Lulu Hamilton. "She's a piece of work!"

"I'll say. Hey, did you hear the part about you bringing her merchandise to her later today and collecting payment?"

"Yes, that's no biggie. I'll do it at lunchtime. Then I can pop over to Kiddie-Care and take a peek at Elijah."

"What's going on with him? He's not sick, is he?"

"No, he's just having a hard time separating from me lately. I've been trying to get out more and I don't think he likes it very much."

"But it's great to hear, Meme! I've been telling you to socialize more, and you're finally listening to me!"

"Well, I've been going to the high school and taking an evening business class. I want to learn how to run a business so I can help you more."

"That's terrific, Meme! I think it's a great idea. What about your friends? Do you get to see them or maybe go on a date or two?"

"I'm getting there. Let's get Elijah used to me being gone a little more, and then I'll expand my horizons."

"Okay, I won't hound you anymore. If you need any help getting a date, just let me know. I can…" I stopped talking, and I realized my daughters were correct. I did try and solve everybody's problems and run their lives. Meme was waiting for me to finish my sentence, so I said, "I won't butt in on your social life. I think you can handle it just fine."

"I'm not your daughter, Ruth Ann. You can help me all you want. I won't ever hold it against you!"

"Thanks for saying that, Meme. I feel like I do get myself in trouble with them. I always thought a mother was supposed to guide her daughters through their lives."

"You can guide me any day, any time! I don't have a mother that cares as much as you do. They're lucky to have you."

"Thank you." I held back the emotion I felt overwhelming me and said, "I have to run up to Prunella's at lunchtime, can you hold the fort down later?"

"Sure. Do you want me to go and run my errands before you head out?"

"I think that would be best. It seems like every time I go up there I get held up, and I don't want you delayed in checking on Elijah."

"Sounds good. I'll leave here earlier then. How about I head out at eleven?"

"Perfect. I have more paperwork to finish up so I'll leave you alone out here unless you get swamped."

"I think I'll be fine, Ruth Ann. If it gets busy, I'll holler," Meme said, walking over to the front window and rubbing a fingerprint off with her shirt. "I love kids, but hate cleaning their little fingerprints!"

I laughed, and then agreed with her as I turned and went back into my office. I hit the books and tried with all my might to remain focused on finishing up the bills, orders, and anything that could possibly come up while I was gone. Once I felt fairly organized, it was time for Meme to head out. I took over for her in the showroom and walked around and around. I figured it was exercise at least!

I guess I could've rearranged some chairs and other smaller pieces, but Meme had done such a good job at arranging the showroom, it was futile. The place was spotless, organized, and ready for shoppers to come in and buy, buy, buy! I found myself bored, and becoming anxious, but what about? Everything was falling into place for my trip with John so what was starting to bother me? It had to be waiting for the trip to begin. I was ready, almost packed, and anxious for the next three days to pass.

"I'm back, Ruth Ann," Meme called out from the back of the store. "You can take off now, and don't worry if you can't get back here this afternoon. I'm sure you have a million things to do."

Do I? Outside of talking with Axel, I couldn't really think of anything else for me to do. "I plan on coming back here, Meme. Unless I get trapped up there talking to them."

"Well, don't hurry. I'm okay here. I was planning on changing a few pieces of furniture around, and then I was going to steam some of the drapes we're trying to sell. They get so wrinkled!"

"I could've done that while you were gone! I stammered. "I'm sorry, I thought the store looked great."

"It does, but I like to keep it fresh for customers. If they're repeat customers, I like them to think some of the old pieces were sold. If they come in here and see the same old stuff in the same old place, then they'll think we're not selling anything."

"Great thinking, Meme!" I said, wondering who worked for whom!

I headed out into the freezing afternoon air and drove up to Prunella and Axel's estate. I wondered if Alex would be hanging around so he could hear what I said to Axel. I wanted a few minutes alone with Axel before Alex gets involved. I just hoped I didn't confuse their names. Really! Alex and Axel, there has to be some connection between the two that we missed.

Within twenty minutes, I was stepping out of my SUV and walking up the freshly salted steps. The door flew open before I had a chance to step on the landing. "Hi, Ruth Ann," Inga called out.

"What are you doing answering the front door? Where's Sherman?"

"Oh, I just brought Mr. Eklund a cup of tea in his library. I noticed you pull up, and so I waited and opened the door for you. What are you doing up here? Did Prunella know you were coming?"

"No, she didn't. I'm not actually here to see her. I want to speak with Axel. Is he alone in there?" I turned my gaze toward the right side of the grand foyer and noticed the library doors were closed.

"He's alone, but on the phone. He's always on his phone."

"Did he seem like he was in a good mood or bad?" I asked, wondering how he might react when I try to involve Alex in his business.

"I really don't know. His head was lowered when I entered and he spoke very quietly. Almost like he didn't want me to hear what he was talking about!"

"That much I can figure out, Inga. But what's so secretive? Isn't he just trying to get his shipping business running again? That wouldn't cause him to be so mysterious!"

"Oh, no, Ruth Ann," Inga exclaimed. "Don't start imagining things."

"I'm not!" I snapped. "Anyway, I don't care. I'm leaving in three days and I don't want to get involved with anything that could deter my trip!"

"Then maybe you shouldn't speak with Mr. Eklund until you come back from your romantic getaway with John!"

I ignored her remark and pushed passed her to the library doors. I knocked gently, but didn't receive a response so I knocked a little louder. Perhaps he was still on his phone so I grabbed the handle and pushed it in a few inches. I stuck my face up to the opening and peeked in. Yep, he was on the phone.

The one-ended conversation I overheard wasn't pleasant. Axel didn't hear me knock because he was yelling into his phone. Inga was right, his head was lowered, but I could still hear him speak. "I'll get you the money as soon as my assets are unfrozen. Don't call me again!" Axel slammed his cell phone onto his desk and looked up to see me standing part way inside his library.

"Come in, Ruth Ann," he called out, from across the room. He was smiling and waving me in.

"Hi, Axel," I said, trying to act like I didn't hear any of the phone conversation. "You look busy, is this a good time?"

"It's fine. Um, did you happen to hear my last words, Ruth Ann?" he asked, inquisitively.

"Not much, Axel. I just got here," I said, trying to sound like I wasn't interested in his words about giving whomever the money once his assets were unfrozen.

"Oh, okay. What can I do for you? Are you looking for Prunella?" he asked, curiously.

"No, no, I'm here to speak with you."

"About?"

"Alex."

"What about him?" Axel asked, wondering where I was going with this.

I explained to Axel about Nancy and Axel trying out the whole teaching idea, when Axel interrupted me. "I know where you're leading, Ruth Ann."

"You do?" I asked, surprised.

"You want me to hire him, don't you?"

"Well, do you see why? He's such a smart young man with a heck of a degree. He's got not only his Physics Degree, but also a

Degree in Mechanical Engineering. I'm sure you could use him somewhere in your company. What do you say?"

"My company's in Sweden, Ruth Ann. Does Alex want to move over there?"

"Nope. He wants to stay here in town, near his family. I was hoping he could help you from here."

"I guess he could do the designing from a computer locally, but I'm not convinced about him yet."

"What are you worried about?" I asked.

"Not long ago, he came in here brandishing a gun demanding possession of your and Prunella's necklace." I was happy to hear Axel not claim any ownership to our necklace. That's how I knew he was moving on and not up to any funny business.

"He didn't know us. Plus, he was confused after his mother died. She told him all about the necklace and how he had to get it back. He did it for his mother. I think he's paid the price for that. He's lost his parents, and all he does around here is mope. I think he'll help you if you let him."

"Has he spoken with you, too?" Axel asked.

"Well," I stopped.

"Oh, wait. You forced him into telling you, didn't you?" he asked, smiling.

"I'm a little tired of everyone telling me I butt in too much! I'm just trying to help him, and you and I have an open relationship where we can talk about anything, don't we?"

Axel coughed slightly, "Ah, yes, of course we do. I didn't mean anything cruel by it. I have grown very fond of you, Ruth Ann, and I know you only have the best intentions. However, sometimes it's out of your hands."

"So, you're saying you *won't* hire him?"

"No, I didn't say that. I just wished the young man would've spoken to me directly."

"Oh, that's my fault!" I cried out. "I told him I would break the ice with you and see if you would consider it."

"But he still could've come to me first," Axel said.

"Yes, but," I hesitated, and tried to find the right words to tell him the poor kid was terrified of him.

"What is it, Ruth Ann?" Axel questioned me, wondering what my 'but' was all about.

"Okay, here's the truth. You have a rather colorful past, and he was somewhat worried about getting involved in something illegal."

"Oh, now I get it. You think I'm still a crook!" he exclaimed, looking quite upset at me.

"No! I never said that. It's just your past is a bit tainted, and you can't deny that."

Axel resigned to this and said, "You're right. I was pretty nasty not too long ago. But, what makes him want to work for me now?"

"He wants to be near his family, and he sees you differently. I think he just wanted to be filled in on everything so he knew what he would be getting himself into."

"Well, I guess that's good," Axel replied. "I guess I should give the kid a chance."

"My suggestion is that you don't actually call him *kid* when he speaks with you."

"I would never do that, Ruth Ann. So, when am I supposed to talk with him? I'm close to getting my stuff back," he stopped and cleared his throat. "Um, that's what I was doing when you came in here."

"Oh, you mean when you told whoever that your assets should be unfrozen soon and you'll get them the money then."

"Excuse me?" he asked, inquiringly. "I thought you didn't hear my conversation!"

My big mouth, again! "I'm sorry, I didn't want you to think I purposely listened at the door. I really did hear that only by accident."

"So, you're probably curious about who I was talking to?" Axel asked, with one eyebrow raised. I nodded because it did make me wonder if he was still on the up and up. "If you must know, I was speaking with the company's lawyer. He knows the last step before re-opening the doors of Eklund Industries rests solely on how fast the government unfreezes the hold on my money."

"But how have you been living here? You and Prunella spend money all the time!"

"Yes, but it's different with the company. There were crimes that occurred there and until Sweden's government releases me from all wrongdoing, they won't release the money I have over there."

"Oh, so you're fine in the states?" I asked, confused at how the law works from country to country.

"When I was pardoned in the states for my crimes, the money I had invested here was released to me. I have plenty of money, Ruth Ann, but not the kind of money needed to reopen Eklund Industries. That's what I'm waiting for. Once that's cleared up, we're up and running. It's just testing my patience, that's all."

"When do you think you'll have your money?"

"I'm hoping any day. That's why I got so crabby with the lawyer on the phone. All these delays are not only costing me money because my ships aren't being built, but it's costing my employees money by not working. That's very frustrating. I'm trying to make amends to them. I've always paid well, but let's just say I wasn't always the nicest boss to work for. It's time that changed."

"I think Prunella's been good for you," I said, knowing this softer, kinder side of Axel was because of my cousin.

"I agree." He stood up and walked around his desk and motioned for me to sit down on one of the two armchairs. I sat down and Axel sat in the other. "What's going on Axel?"

"I want you to know I'm very happy you're getting away for a few days. I know John is anxious to spend some vacation time alone with you. I'd like to do the same with Prunella. Once this mess is cleared up of course."

"I'm sure she'd love it. Make it a second honeymoon!" I suggested.

"It'll be more like a first honeymoon. I wasn't too compassionate back in those days, so I have lots to make up. The problem is I don't want to take her to Sweden for our trip just because I have to go there for business."

"Then don't," I said, confused why he would even think of Stockholm for their honeymoon.

"I'll be busy for quite some time, but if I come up with a great trip down the road, it'll give her something to look forward to."

"Oh, I get it. You want to plan it now, right?" Axel nodded and I continued, "I'll hook you up with Deer Creek Travel and you can speak with either Julie or her daughter, Tiana. They'll get you set up."

"Great. Now, why don't we go and find that young man and I'll convince him to come and work for me."

"Perfect!" I said, checking another box from my to-do list. "Where is Prunella, anyway? I didn't see her when I came in."

"She's been spending a lot of time alone up in our room. I don't know why. I ask her what's wrong, but she says nothing."

"That's odd," I said. "Maybe I'll have a talk with her."

"Of course you will!" Axel laughed. "I didn't mean it rudely, Ruth Ann. No matter what people say, you do get things done! That's why I like you so much."

"Thank you, Axel. Let's go find Alex *and* Prunella for that matter."

We walked out of the library together and found Sherman hanging around the foyer. "What's up, Sherman?"

He looked guilty as sin. My bet he was eavesdropping on our conversation and almost got caught. His hearing was not so good anymore, but he was still a busy body! "I was just about to knock on the library door and see if either of you needed anything."

"Nope," Axel responded. "Do you know where my wife is?"

"She just came down the stairs with Alex and they went to-ward the kitchen. Something about being hungry."

"Obviously it was Alex who was hungry. Prunella barely eats," Axel mumbled. I on the other hand, was more curious about the two of them always been caught together. It couldn't be any-thing inappropriate, they were related, but distantly, so…my mind was running a mile a minute. I dismissed those thoughts and sug-gested we go and get a snack ourselves. "I am a bit famished," Axel said.

Sherman followed us into the kitchen where we found Pru-nella and Alex sitting at the island laughing away. Inga was fixing a plate of sandwiches so we joined in. "Ruth Ann," Prunella cried out. "When did you get here?"

"Not long ago," I said, suspiciously. "What have *you* been up to?"

"Me?" she answered, innocently. "I was in my, excuse me, *our* room reading a book. I ran into Alex in the hall and he said he was hungry. I figured I could use something too, so we came down here and Inga was so kind to make us some sandwiches. Hungry?" she asked Axel and me.

"No, no," I said, quickly. "I've got to watch myself the next couple of days."

"Ah, the big trip is coming up," Prunella said, smiling devilishly. "I bet you can't wait to go and walk on the beach, and float in the water, and…"

"Prunella!" I exclaimed, embarrassed.

"I'm joking with you, Ruth Ann. Lighten up!" she said, grabbing a peanut butter sandwich and taking an enormous bite.

"You must be hungry, Prunella." Axel said. "I've never seen you eat a sandwich that fast!"

"I've never seen you *finish* a sandwich," I added, curious about Prunella's actions. I thought everything was out in the open with her, but somehow there was more I needed to get out of her.

Prunella didn't care for our comments about her eating habits. "What's the big deal? So I finish a sandwich. I love peanut butter, and it's lunchtime!"

"Why aren't we eating in the dining room?" Axel inquired, suddenly realizing lunchtime had passed and nobody came and got him to eat.

"Sorry, dear, that was my fault," Prunella interrupted. "I told them we'd be on our own for lunch today so you could concentrate on your company. I was about to come and bring you a sandwich, but you and Ruth Ann came in here first."

"Oh, okay," he replied, appearing confused. I didn't like the sudden tension I was feeling in the room so I knew I had to change the direction of this conversation. I surely didn't want to get involved in a marital dispute with Axel and Prunella. I only hoped it had nothing to do with Alex or he might as well kiss that job offer goodbye!

"Hey, Alex," I said, loudly trying to get all their attention. "After you finish eating, how about we have a chat?"

Alex nearly choked on his ham sandwich. "Excuse me," he said, trying to swallow quickly. "Is something wrong?"

"No, of course not. I just think it's time we get a few things settled."

"Ruth Ann," Prunella chimed in. "What are you up to now?"

"Nothing!" I snapped abruptly back at her. "I'm just saying that there are a few loose ends I thought could be tied before I leave on Saturday."

"Why can't we just talk in here?" Prunella inquired, looking over at her husband's blank face and then back to mine. "You two are up to something!"

"We're not the only ones," Axel muttered, referring to the constant togetherness of Prunella and Alex. I didn't like what was happening so I elbowed Axel in the side, but everyone saw me do it.

"Hey," Sherman tersely said. "Why'd you hit him?"

"She didn't hit me, Sherman. Ruth Ann was subtly trying to tell me I was being rude. I apologize, Prunella, and Alex. Let's drop this and get down to some business, shall we?"

Prunella didn't appear comfortable anymore. The laughter subsided, and she twirled around on her stool to face Axel and me. "*Business?*"

"Yes, it's time we get Alex some work. I just had a nice talk with Axel and he agreed completely, didn't you?" Axel nodded slowly, wondering who was offering whom a job.

"Oh," Prunella said, pepping up a bit. "I think that's a great idea. So, what's the job opportunity?"

I remained quiet, handing the reins to Axel. He took my cue and asked Alex to join him at the long kitchen table. Alex didn't dare say no, so he hopped off the stool and sat across the table from Axel. I, on the other hand, walked over to where Prunella was sitting and sat on the warmed stool Alex just left. I couldn't help but notice that Prunella didn't pay one lick of attention to me, but watched every move Axel and Alex were making as if something could drastically go wrong. I was so confused, what on earth was going on up here at the estate? I thought everyone was getting along splendidly, but obviously I was mistaken.

Chapter 9

Twenty minutes later, Alex and Axel had come to an agreement. Axel was willing to take Alex on as a Mechanical Engineer. He would be able to do his work remotely, to start with. After a ninety-day trial period, they would meet again to discuss how both sides felt the arrangement was working. I believed it was a fair deal, however, Prunella expressed concern.

"Why a trial period?" she asked. "I'm sure Alex will do the job perfectly! From what he told us he was quite the student."

"You just said it, Prunella." Axel looked at Alex and stated, "We just have *your word* on everything so far. I hope you don't mind that I add one stipulation." Alex's eyes met Prunella's for a quick second before he answered, "Of course I don't mind."

What was that look? I did the absolute wrong thing and blurted out, "I saw that! Why did you two look at each other before Alex agreed to Axel's conditions?" Neither one of them answered my questions so I added, "Is there a problem with your degrees, Alex?"

"Oh, no, I swear I have a double degree in Physics and Mechanical Engineering!" he protested, vehemently. "There wasn't anything with my looking at Prunella. It just happened at the same time Mr. Eklund, I mean, Axel, said he wanted to check my background."

"All right," I replied, pretty sure something else was happening, but it was obvious I wouldn't get anywhere at this moment so I'd table it until later.

Axel stood up, reached across the table and held out his hand. "Gentlemen shake on a deal. Are you okay with this until I check you out a little further?"

Alex stood, shook his hand strongly, and walked back to the island to finish his sandwich. I noticed his hand was shaking a little as he put the sandwich to his mouth. Prunella was watching me intently as I observed Alex's motions. She deflected the moment by reaching to the platter of sandwiches and grabbing a salami and cheese on rye for her husband. "Here you go, Axel. I know you're busy so we won't keep you any longer."

Axel didn't mind the hint since he was extremely busy settling his affairs. Now I added to his work, checking the background of an almost stranger that claimed to be part of our somewhat dysfunctional family. Actually, I doubted he would personally check Alex. I'm sure he would pass that responsibility down to one of his many lawyers.

Once Axel cleared the kitchen, Prunella turned her attention to me. "Well, you handled that one, didn't you?"

"Are you upset with me, Prunella?" I asked, wondering about her condescending tone.

"No, no. I just wished you had come to me first. I thought you and I were close, but you went directly to Axel."

"Hold on!" I bellowed. "You left *me* out on the whole Nancy/Alex thing in the first place. I was the only one who didn't know about Alex thinking about being a teacher. Nancy and Lynne confessed, which I knew they would, and you knew, too!"

"Well," Prunella stumbled. "It wasn't my secret to tell!"

"What is wrong with you lately?" I snapped, yes I admitted it. However, I kept going. "You've been acting strangely lately. Always hiding out in your bedroom, and every time I run into you, you're with Alex." I turned my head toward him and quickly stated, "No offense, I'm just concerned and annoyed that nobody wants to confide in me anymore. Am I that untrustworthy?"

Alex stayed completely out of the conversation. He sat quietly on his stool stuffing his face with another ham sandwich. Inga and Sherman on the other hand, were listening and watching every move. Inga immediately went to 'Ms.' Prunella's defense. "Hey, Ruth Ann, why are you being so hard on Ms. Prunella?" Sherman nodded vigorously, agreeing with Inga.

"Me being hard on her!" I cried out. "I think someone owes me an explanation."

Prunella realized things were getting out of hand. It was apparent that whatever the two of them had going on, she wasn't ready to tell me. She gently swung around on the stool and stood up. "Ruth Ann, you mean the world to me. I'm not doing anything to hurt or upset you. I know you're occupied with your upcoming trip so I don't think you should be getting so upset over nothing." I stood up and waited for her to continue speaking since I knew she wasn't done yet. "Hey, I've got another more important topic for you right now." She motioned for me to follow her out of the kitchen.

I wasn't the only one who followed Prunella into the foyer, but Inga and Sherman were right on my heels. I watched as Prunella sauntered over to the closed library doors. She turned her head around and said, "Can you give me one moment, please?" I was amazed at her change in attitude from being defensive back in the kitchen, to her normal, sweet self. My head was beginning to ache, but I knew I had to go on and see what she had planned for me next. "Fine."

Prunella disappeared inside the library and shut the doors behind her. I stood in the middle of the elaborate foyer with Inga on one side and Sherman on my other side. "What on earth is going on around here?" I demanded of both of them. "Don't tell me nothing! The air around here is so thick I could cut it with a knife!"

Inga truly looked baffled, but Sherman didn't. We turned on him and Inga let him have it. "Sherman, the great uncle of Ms. Prunella! What are you not telling us?" Inga stood frozen with her hands on her hips waiting for his response.

Sherman turned his eyes away from us and veered toward the library. "Oh, no you don't!" Inga shouted, grabbing his collar and yanking him back next to us. "You stay here and spill it! You've blown it in the past, remember? Don't try and keep whatever it is to yourself again. It'll just get you in bigger trouble!"

"I don't know anything!" he exclaimed. "I see everything around here just like you two. I know something's up, but I don't know what it is. I'm worried that Prunella and Alex are…"

"No!" Inga bellowed. "He's her cousin!"

"I put my hand to my mouth and gave a slight cough. "What, Ruth Ann?" Inga asked, angrier than I've seen her in a while.

"Inga, Prunella and Alex are *distant* cousins so if they want to, you know, they can."

"She wouldn't do that. She's married to Axel," Inga stated. "There's no way!"

"What else can it be?" I asked. "Why are those two always together?"

"Well, we need to figure it out before Mr. Eklund does," Sherman suggested, surprising Inga and me. He was such a big chicken that it amazed us that he would suggest interfering in their lives.

"And how do you suppose we do that?" Inga spat out. "You see and hear everything that goes on around here. I'm usually in the kitchen or cleaning. I hear things, but not nearly as much as you do."

"I promise to get to the bottom of this, but why don't we wait and see what Prunella wants to show you in the library."

"How do you know she wants to *show* me something?" I asked, curiously.

"Oh, I just assumed…"

"Sherman, if you don't know what's going on between Ms. Prunella and Alex, then you *do* know what's going inside that library!" Inga exclaimed.

"I agree with Inga," I said. "Do tell, and quickly."

Sherman didn't have time to leak what he knew, because the library doors flew open and Prunella waved us in. I was a bit surprised that Inga and Sherman were also allowed inside. They followed me into the spacious library. Prunella didn't direct us toward Axel who was engrossed in papers, but to the couches near the massive stone fireplace. "Please, sit down," she said, motioning for all of us to sit. Even Sherman and Inga were told to sit down. Prunella walked over toward the bookshelves behind Axel's desk and pulled out a familiar book. She glanced at Axel who nodded at her and walked back to the three of us sitting on the couches.

"What are you doing with that?" I questioned her, suspiciously.

"I want you to hear me out, Ruth Ann," Prunella said.

Sherman was about to speak, but Prunella stopped him. "I
want *all* of you to hear me out I should have said." Prunella waited
for our nods to continue.

"Okay, Ruth Ann, I know you're going to totally shoot me
down on this one, but I'm going to insist on it. I want you to take
our Blue Ice necklace and wear it while you're on vacation with
John."

In unison, Inga, Sherman, and I, bellowed out, "No way!"

"I told you, I insist," she said so quietly, but with such com-
mand, I slammed my mouth shut.

Axel couldn't help but hear our protests so he joined us for
the discussion. "Look, Ruth Ann," he started to say. "Prunella has
her mind set on this so you might as well agree. I think it's a great
idea, too."

"You do?" I asked him, completely amazed that he would
want the priceless piece to be taken out of his home. "But, it makes
no sense. What if I lost it or it broke off the chain? I would never
forgive myself!"

"It's fully insured, Ruth Ann," Prunella reminded me. "If we
have this beautiful piece, but keep it locked away in this book, why
have it? I think it should be worn and enjoyed. What better way to
show it off then on a trip?"

"I, I don't get it," I stammered. "I won't hear of it. You wear
it if you want to enjoy it. Don't put that pressure on me!" I
watched as Prunella took the necklace out of the built in safe and
held it high for us to admire. The necklace was just as stunning as
it was when I first laid eyes on it. The crystal clear, emerald
shaped, blue aquamarine surrounded by a couple diamonds was
glistening in the light. That's why Prunella and I gave it a name,
Blue Ice, because of its mind-blowing beauty!

"I'm just hanging around this big house, but you're going to
Jamaica and it'll be perfect for your trip. Let others see the beauty
in our piece."

"But it could be stolen, then what?" I said, struggling with
words to express how strongly I was against this.

"I insist," Prunella said, again. "I don't want to argue about it. It's a done deal as far as I'm concerned."

I pleadingly turned my attention to Axel. "Why are you letting her do this? I don't want the responsibility."

"Then don't think of it as a responsibility, Ruth Ann," Axel said, coolly. "I agree the necklace should be worn and admired by everyone. Just take it, it'll be fine. Look who you're traveling with, the Chief of Police!"

For one brief second, I thought it could work. I was traveling with John. He would never let anything happen to the necklace or me. Maybe it would be fun wearing it and showing it off, but at what risk? "Hmm," I said, not meaning to utter any words that showed I was actually contemplating their idea.

"See," Prunella cried out, happily. "You do want to wear it!"

"Of course I do!" I said, unexpectedly. "But, if anything happened to it I would never, ever, forgive myself."

"Nothing will happen, Ruth Ann," Axel said, returning to his desk and digging back into the pile of papers. "Now, if you all will excuse me…I have a few calls to make." Prunella took his cue, and suggested we leave her husband alone.

I don't know how I was convinced in taking the necklace. It wasn't until much later that I figured out the real reason why.

Chapter 10

I said my goodbyes and headed back into town. Prunella didn't even try to get me to stay later. I thought that, in itself, was very suspicious. As I drove back into Deer Creek I kept telling myself to forget it, let it go, you're going on a vacation, move on! Something was eating away at me, but I couldn't put my finger on it. I considered popping in and telling John, but I changed my mind. The last thing I wanted was to delay John or get him suspicious of anything. He would think I was thinking too much about nothing.

I stopped at our town's grocery store to pick up a pre-made salad. I walked inside to find the store empty, except for the owner, Chris Jenkins. Chris was stocking one of the shelves with cans of baked beans. "Hi, Chris," I called out as I entered the store. "Where is everyone?"

"Hi, Ruth Ann," she answered back, stepping down from the step stool. "It's been slow today so I sent my cashier home and said I'd close up today. What can I do for you?"

"Oh, just grabbing a salad. Got any left?" I asked, walking to the refrigerated section of the produce area.

"Wilma, over at the café, made some fresh salads and I think there are a few left. I'll help you."

I waited for her to make her way to the salad section and grab the last two containers. "This is all I've got. Ever since Wilma started creating these salads for me they sell out fast! People love the freshness, plus she makes all kinds of varieties."

"What are those two?" I asked, wondering if Chris was going to talk the whole time or show me the salads. I was on edge and just wanted to go home.

Chris held one up and slipped on her readers. "Let's see…this one has a variety of lettuces, tomatoes, black olives, artichoke hearts, and some feta cheese," she paused and wrinkled her nose. "I really don't like feta, but it's very popular right now!"

"Go on," I said, impatiently.

"Oh, there's cilantro," I cut her off and said, "no thanks! I can't stand cilantro. What about the other one, does that have cilantro in it, too?"

Chris sensed my tone and read the ingredients to herself. "Nope, this one is just a basic chef 's salad. Do you want it?"

"I'll take it, thanks," I said, walking with her to the register. "How much?"

"It'll be $8.00."

"Wilma's salads aren't cheap," I said, knowing it would be more than that if I went to her café and ordered a salad.

"Is everything okay with you, Ruth Ann?" Chris asked me, sensing my rotten mood. "I thought you'd be in such a good mood since you're going away in a couple days."

"Ah, you heard," I said, not surprised at news like this spreading.

"Of course. Wilma told me!"

"Ah, Wilma would know. She knows everything that goes on in town!" I said laughing, forgetting about my bad mood.

"That's the hotspot for gossip, Ruth Ann. If you want to know anything about everything, just eat at the café!"

I paid Chris, and then headed home with my chef's salad. I put what happened up at the estate in the back of my mind and turned my attention to eating my salad and giving my daughters a call. By the time I completed those tasks, it was time to go to bed. I wanted to go in to my store early and finish up the remaining paperwork. I only had two days left to work before John and I were flying to Jamaica.

I fell asleep immediately. I find when I eat somewhat healthy that I usually fall asleep without too much effort.

Tonight was a good night. I felt my eyes closing and turned off the comedy reruns I was watching on television.

I suddenly woke up and found myself lying on a deserted beach. John wasn't with me. Was I in Jamaica already? What was going on? I stood up and started calling for John, but he wasn't anywhere in sight. I walked up and down the deserted beach and realized it wasn't getting me anywhere.

I hurried over to a grass-covered shack that was near the entrance to the jungle. The doorway was blocked with several strings of beads that blew in the wind. I called inside, but nobody responded. I pushed a few strands aside and entered anyway. What was I doing? I knew it wasn't right to enter into somebody's home without permission. This had to be a dream...but it felt so real!

It was so dark inside the tiny shack. I tried to adjust my eyes since I just came in from intense sunlight. I opened and closed my eyes several times when I finally spotted a dim light coming from the back of the shack. I slowly walked toward the light when I noticed an older woman leaning over a small, flaming candle.

"Who are you?" the older woman asked me. "Why are you in here? You don't belong here; leave immediately before it's too late!" I asked her why, and that I needed her help finding my boyfriend. She told me with her browned, chipped teeth, "It's too late! Now go, and never come back!"

I suddenly woke up, shaking and sweating. "Wow, that was a horrible nightmare!" I immediately turned the television back on and frantically searched for a comedy. I needed a distraction from that frightening dream to get myself back to sleep. I glanced over at my cell phone that was charging on my nightstand. "3:30 am." I needed at least a few more hours of sleep to feel human.

Fortunately, watching television did the trick. I was able to get a couple hours of sleep, and then I did a quick hour on my elliptical, showered, ate and opened the back door of the antique store on time. With forced focus, I managed to clear my desk, and even helped Meme move some of the larger pieces of furniture. I told Meme to take off right after lunch and not to come in the next day except to pick up her check and go over some instructions with me. She refused at first, but when I told her I was ordering her to take the time off, and would pay her for her time, she happily left and had some well-deserved time off.

There were only a few stragglers that came inside the store to browse, but because we sold several profitable pieces of furniture earlier that week, I was okay. I closed the shop at five sharp and headed home. Only one more full day and then it was time to take off to the Caribbean. Finally, it was becoming more and more likely that this trip was going to take place. I had my doubts, with John and his work or with the strange stuff happening up at the estate, but the last twenty-four hours had been quiet, except for that crazy dream. I hoped I didn't just jinx myself.

I rushed home and checked my safe to make sure the necklace was still secure. I didn't like having the necklace in my home. It was terrifying. I hadn't told John or my daughters about it since they would just worry. I knew John would fear some stranger would wander into town and start a new crime wave over the piece, so it was best to leave it to myself until we arrived at the resort. That might not have been the best idea when I looked back on it!

I checked my many lists on the counter to see what I needed to accomplish on Friday. I knew I had to make a quick trip to the bank, and to the drugstore to pick up a few last minute items. Outside of that, all I had to do was make sure I stayed at the store during business hours, pay Meme, leave some instructions for her while I was gone, and then see my daughters and Prunella. Suddenly, I realized there was still quite a lot to handle.

I had a peaceful night's sleep with no wild nightmares. I woke up, exercised, and then hurried through the bank drive through and onto my store. I arrived a little later than I should have because when I unlocked the front door there were a couple people waiting outside. "I'm so sorry," I said to a couple I've never seen before. "Please, come in!"

"Thank you," the woman replied. She was well dressed in a pair of camel colored slacks and a beautiful winter white wool coat. I noticed she was wearing a large diamond ring on her wedding finger so I made the assumption that the man she was with was her husband. He also had a gold wedding band on and followed closely on her heels.

"So, are you staying over at the resort here in town?" I asked curiously, watching the woman pick up a very expensive crystal bowl from a table.

"Yes," she answered. "How much is this bowl? It's lovely!"

"It's a bit pricey since it's a well-known brand."

"How much?" the husband asked curtly. I glanced at him, shocked with his demeanor and noticed the age difference in the couple. The man was double the woman's age! He looked irritated that she brought him in my store, and from his antsy behavior I guessed he wanted out, quickly.

"It's a little over $600.00," I said, waiting for a shocked look in their faces, but I didn't get one.

"I'll take it," the woman snapped. "Pay her, would you please?" she directed her husband.

He pulled out a wad of cash and handed over $600.00 even. "It's actually $650.00," I said, not knowing how to deal with these people, but then I added quickly, before I lost the sale, "I'll take the $600.00 since you're paying cash."

He stuffed the remaining cash into his pants pocket, and looked away from his wife and me. "Would you like me to bubble wrap it or ship it to your home?" I asked.

"I'll just take it as is," the woman answered.

"But it'll only take me a minute to get the…" she held her hand up to stop my talking. She took the bowl off the table, turned and walked out of the store. Just as they were halfway out the front door, the man turned and said, "Thank you, ma'am."

"Well, that was rude! And I hate being called ma'am, especially from a man who was at least twenty years older than me!"

The time passed slowly afterward. Finally, Meme walked in the front door smiling broadly. "Hi, Ruth Ann! How's today been?"

I told her about the couple and handing over the cash. "Wow, must be nice to walk into a store and pay that kind of money for a glass bowl!"

"I know, but they were the most ostentatious couple I've ever had come in here, well, except for Lulu Hamilton. She can be a real pain in the…"

"Ruth Ann!" Meme bellowed, laughing loudly. "I agree though."

I left Meme in the front showroom for a couple minutes while I went in the back to get her paycheck and a pad of paper with my instructions. Meme was pleasantly surprised at the amount on the check. "Ruth Ann, this is way more than I usually make!"

"Consider it a bonus," I said. "We sold a couple big ticket items this week so I wanted to share."

"You don't know how much this helps me with Elijah. Two year olds cost a lot of money!"

"And so does all that daycare you have to pay."

"It's good for him and me!" she replied, happy. "I read over your notes and everything looks good. Now you can go and relax on your trip. Take lots of pictures, too!"

"I will," I said. "Go and enjoy the rest of your time off. We won't open until Monday morning."

"Not Saturday?" Meme asked, confused that I chose to close the store on a Saturday right before Thanksgiving.

"I figure we're going to have enough busy Saturdays after Thanksgiving so why not enjoy a long weekend. You're on your own Monday through Wednesday next week."

"Okay, you're the boss!" Meme declared. "I'll see you next Saturday! Have a wonderful trip." She gave me a huge hug and then headed back out the front door.

Now, only another hour until I closed up the store. I walked around both floors and inspected every last piece. I hoped more items would sell before I returned, but if not, I'm okay. Once I finished my rounds, I locked the front door and headed to my office. Everything was neat and tidy in there so I grabbed my coat and headed out into the freezing evening air. Should I stop by and see John and make sure he's caught up? No, I'll talk with him later.

I cranked up the heat on my car and quickly called Lynne. "Are you still at the bakery?"

"Yes, I'm making tomorrow's dough. Are you on your way home?" she asked.

"I'll pop in to see you. Is your sister there by any chance?"

"You must have ESP, Mom. Nancy just walked in the front door!"

"Great, I'll be right over," I said, driving down the alley and parking behind the bakery. I didn't want to walk the two stores over in these temperatures. My car was warm, and hopefully wouldn't take long to warm up again after I left the bakery.

"Hi, girls," I called out.

"Hey, Mom," Nancy said, sitting on one of the stools in the front of the bakery.

"Ooh, that looks good, Lynne. What is it?"

"Oh, it's another of my inventions," she said placing a napkin in front of me. I sat on the stool next to Nancy and picked up the round delicacy. I took a quick bite and said, "Wow, these are fantastic. Just what I needed!"

"Thanks, Mom," Lynne said from the other side of the counter. "I'm adding these to the menu over at my shop in the resort. "They're called Chocolate Chip Cookie Balls."

"Can I have another?" I asked. "I know I shouldn't, but one isn't enough." Nancy and Lynne cracked up as I shoved another ball in my mouth.

"I can't wait for your shop to open over there. What's left to do to get it up and running?" I asked.

"Nothing, we could open tomorrow if we wanted, but Carol already ran an ad specifying an opening date of December 1st."

"That's right around the corner, how exciting!" I said.

"So, did you stop by here to say goodbye to us?" Nancy asked, with a devilish smile upon her face.

"Yes!"

"Have a great time, and don't worry about us," Lynne said. "It's not like you're being kidnapped and held over in Stockholm. At least this time we know where you're going!"

"Very funny, Lynne," I said. "I gave you the name of the resort, right?"

"Yes, you've told us a thousand times! Don't worry; we'll be just fine. And when you come back, we'll be up at Prunella's waiting for you and John."

"Don't start Thanksgiving dinner without us!" I requested.

"Just as long as your flight's on time, and no big storms occur," Nancy said.

"I'm not going to even think that could happen," I said. I changed the topic and asked Lynne, "Do you and Inga have everything you need for the big dinner?"

"Yep, we're all good, Mom."

"Okay, then I guess I'm going to head up and say goodbye to Prunella and the gang." I stood up, hugged both my daughters tightly, and headed out the back into my frigid truck. Luckily, it heated up in about a minute.

CHOCOLATE CHIP COOKIE DOUGH BALLS

1-cup butter
1-½ cups brown sugar
2 t vanilla
2 cups flour
2 cups mini chocolate chips
1 bag semisweet or milk chocolate chips

Mix butter and brown sugar until mixed. Add vanilla. Stir in flour until well mixed. Add mini chips by hand.

Form into one inch balls and place on waxed paper lined cookie sheet. Chill in freezer 30 minutes or until firm.

Melt the semisweet chocolate chips in a microwave safe bowl. Use a spoon and dip the balls until well covered. Place back on the waxed paper lined cookie sheet and freeze until chocolate has set, about 15 minutes.

Store in a covered container or large plastic bag in the refrigerator.

Chapter 11

As I drove to Prunella and Axel's estate, I promised myself that I wouldn't stay too long. I wanted to say my goodbyes, check in with Inga and her plans for Thanksgiving dinner, and then head home to finish packing and check in with John. It seemed that every time I planned to get out quickly, something or someone prevents me from doing just that.

I wasn't received as quickly as usual. I knocked on the front door with one of the huge brass knockers, but nobody answered. I tried to open the door, but it was locked. "Hmm," I said. "This door is never locked during the day."

I banged louder and louder until finally, Sherman opened the door. "Gee, Ruth Ann, why didn't you just walk in?" he snapped, out of breath.

"It was locked!"

"Oh, I wonder who locked the door?" Sherman inquired, curiously.

"I did," a male voice called out from inside the foyer.

I slipped passed Sherman and went inside. Sherman and I spotted Alex standing smack dab in the middle of the foyer. "Oh, I didn't know you were in here," Sherman said, finally catching his breath. "I had to run all the way from the kitchen to open the door. Why didn't you answer it?"

"I wasn't down here. I was up on the second floor when I heard the banging. I came down, but you had already opened the door."

"Oh, okay," Sherman replied, appearing baffled still.

"Who cares, Sherman," I said. "I don't have a lot of time, but I wanted to come up here and make sure everything was set for Thanksgiving and say goodbye."

"Inga's in the kitchen, why don't you go and ask her?" he replied, turning and heading up the stairs.

"He's quite grouchy," Alex said.

"He's always that way!" I said, grabbing a hold of Alex's arm and leading him into the kitchen with me. "What are you up to? Have you and Axel started working together yet?"

"Oh, yes, he's given me tons of paperwork to read."

"Good, make sure you give it your all, Alex. I see Axel as a picky boss," I said, laughing. "But you seem the same way to me. I tell you, if I didn't know either of you I would say you two were related!"

Alex choked. That was rather odd, I thought. Why would he react as if I said something so absurd? I felt an odd chill run up my spine, which I haven't felt since all the murders that recently happened. I shook it off, even though deep down I should've known better. "You okay?" I asked him just as he recovered from his coughing spell.

"Fine, I, I just swallowed wrong. I'll get a glass of water while we're in the kitchen."

Inga was sitting at the kitchen table with cookbooks sprawled all over the table. Her hands were holding her head up in frustration. She perked up the minute she noticed us enter the kitchen. "Ruth Ann, you're back!"

"What's going on with you, Inga? You looked quite annoyed with the cookbooks. This doesn't have anything to do with Thanksgiving dinner, does it?"

"No, absolutely not!" she exclaimed. "I was looking for something else."

"Did everybody tell you to leave me out of it because I'm leaving in the morning?"

"No," she snapped.

"I don't believe you. I bet Lynne told you to leave me out of it now."

"Ruth Ann, can't you ever just let things be? I'm fine really."

Inga stood up and walked over to where Alex was trying to find a glass. "Let me," she said, irritated.

"I just want some water," he said, meekly. "I can find a glass. You don't have to wait on me."

"It's easier if I just do it," she said, trying to calm down. "Sorry both of you, I just have a lot on my plate."

"Aha! I knew it! Let me help you," I begged. "I've been cooking this dinner for twenty, maybe thirty years!"

"Fine," Inga spat out. "I can't find anywhere that explains how to make that rice pudding!"

I walked over to one of the cookbooks sprawled on the table and handed her a recipe my family used for generations. "Here, look toward the back of the book. You'll find Great Grandma Ruth's recipe there." I handed the book over to Inga. She grabbed it, turned to the correct page and whacked herself in the head.

"How did I miss that?" she muttered. "Thanks."

"No problem. You know; if you have any other questions, just ask Lynne or Nancy. They have the same cookbook."

"I'm good, now," she said, smiling calmly now.

MOTHER K'S RICE PUDDING

Cook 1-cup rice with 2 cups water 14 minutes.
Set aside.
Scald 1-quart milk with 1/8-pound butter.
Beat 4 eggs well, add 2/3-cup sugar & a dash of salt.
Combine all ingredients, adding 1-teaspoon vanilla.
Pour into a casserole dish.
Bake 30 minutes in 300-degree oven.
Then stir, sprinkle with cinnamon and nutmeg, & bake 50 minutes longer.
Adding raisins is optional.

I headed out into the foyer and walked toward the closed library doors. I was about to reach out to knock, when Sherman stopped me. "He's busy, Ruth Ann."

"I'm just saying good-bye, Sherman."

"He may not want to be disturbed," Sherman replied.

"He can tell me that himself. Why's everyone so crabby around here?" I asked, wondering why the last couple visits had been so tense.

"I'm not crabby! I'm just telling you Mr. Eklund gave explicit instructions not be bothered."

"Geez, Sherman. I'm just popping in to say good-bye. I can handle him." I ignored Sherman's instructions and knocked on the door. A loud, "What!" yelled back.

I opened the door and quickly stated, "It's just Ruth Ann. I've come to say a goodbye. Is it okay to come in?"

Axel stood up from behind his desk and said, "Of course, you're always welcome. I was just keeping that busy body, Sherman, out of here. If I didn't tell him I didn't want to be interrupted, he'd be in here every ten minutes!"

I laughed and walked over to the chairs in front of Axel's desk. He motioned for me to sit. We spent a relaxing fifteen or so minutes chatting away about nothing important. "Well, I'm going to find Prunella, and then head back home. I'll see you on Thanksgiving!"

"Have a great time, and relax, Ruth Ann. We'll all survive the five days you're gone!" He walked over and gave me a hug, and then he turned toward my face and our eyes met. We were within inches of each other's face when a wave of heat rushed through my body. For a moment, just a moment, I would've guessed he was about to kiss me, but that ridiculous thought was erased from my head. He quickly turned his head and kissed me on my cheek. "I'll see you soon," he said kindly, and then turned and went back to his desk.

My feet froze for a second, until I realized I was standing alone staring into thin air. "Okay," I said, awkwardly. "Good luck with Alex! Be patient with him, too."

"I will do just that, Ruth Ann!" Axel chuckled.

I hurried out of the library and headed straight for the main staircase. I rushed up the stairs and made my way down the wide hallway to Prunella and Axel's bedroom. I had the feeling Prunella was inside there like she's been lately.

"Come in," she called out from inside the bedroom.

"It's just me," I said, sticking my head inside the room. "I wanted to see you before I leave."

"Yes, of course!" she exclaimed, standing up from the couch she was lying on.

I noticed the blankets and pillows on the couch. "Were you sleeping, Prunella?"

"Oh, I was taking a little nap before dinner."

"It sure looks like you've camped yourself out on that couch. Is there anything you'd like to tell me, Prunella?"

Prunella glared at me and said, "There's nothing to tell. I've been a little tired lately, that's all."

"Why not nap in your and Axel's bed?"

"I'm more comfortable on the couch during the day."

"Oh, okay. If that's how you want to play it, I'll go along. However, when I come back, you'd better think of a better excuse than that!"

Prunella, quickly changed the topic, rose off the couch and grabbed my arm. "Let's go down into the living room. We can have a nice chat there before you have to leave. I'll have Inga bring us a cup of tea and one of the biscotti's you love so much."

"Perfect," I replied. We headed back downstairs and Prunella told me to go ahead into the living room while she asked Inga to make our tea. I nodded and walked into the formal living room. I grabbed one of the two-wingback chairs facing the front windows. There was a grand piano near the chairs, but I can't remember anyone ever playing. I sat down and stared straight ahead waiting for Prunella. For a moment I closed my eyes. I finally had a second to relax.

I found myself back on the beach in Jamaica. I was dressed strangely for a person in a warm climate. I was so hot. I looked down and noticed I still had on my winter coat. I ripped it off and threw it onto the sand. This can't be real! I turned around and looked back at the grass shack I just left. Why did that old woman tell me I had to leave before it's too late? I just got here, with John. Why would we leave when our vacation hadn't even begun?

I walked back toward the water's edge to look for John. He had to be here somewhere. I looked down and noticed I didn't have any shoes on. My feet were touching the warm, fluffy, sand. There wasn't a rock or shell in sight as I made my way into the water. Where were my shoes and why did I still have on long pants and a sweater? It was so hot in here...

"Ruth Ann," a female voice was calling me. "Isn't that tea cup hot in your hands?"

I opened my eyes, startled at my whereabouts, and looked at the hot cup of tea in my hands. "Oh, Prunella. I must've shut my eyes for a moment."

"You took the tea and pumpkin biscotti from me. How could you fall asleep?" Prunella asked, worried.

"I guess I totally relaxed and my eyes closed for a second. I'm okay, now."

PUMPKIN BISCOTTI

2 ½ cups flour
1-cup sugar
1 t baking powder
2 t cinnamon (I always add more!)
Dash of ginger
½ t salt
2 eggs
1 to 1 ½ t vanilla (I like more for flavor)
½ a can of pure pumpkin (not pumpkin
     pie filling)

Whisk eggs with vanilla and pumpkin. Set aside. Mix flour, sugar, baking powder, cinnamon, ginger, and salt.

Add the wet mixture to the dry mixture. Use your hands to lightly knead the mix, and form into two logs about 10 inches long by 5 inches wide (about ½ to 1 inch thick). Place loaves onto parchment lined cookie sheet and BAKE at 350 degrees for about 20-23 minutes. Should be firm to touch.

Let biscotti cool for 10-15 minutes (I usually don't have the patience and cut them pretty quickly!).
Using a serrated knife, slice diagonally into 1-inch-wide pieces.

Place one side flat side down and BAKE at 300 degrees for 6-7 minutes. Take out and flip to other side and bake another 6-7 minutes until hardened. Let cool completely. Enjoy!

We finished our tea in silence. I devoured the two biscotti she placed on my saucer. I was happy she didn't give me more of them because I probably would've eaten those, too. I noticed Prunella didn't have any biscotti, but she did have a couple crackers on her saucer. Something was beginning to add up with me. First, Prunella's always up in their room napping. She claims she's just tired. Second, she was eating less than usual, and now I see crackers with her tea. Thirdly, no! There is no third. She had to be pregnant!

I stood up abruptly, startling Prunella. She dropped her cup of tea on the chair, but thankfully missing her lap. "I'm so sorry, Prunella," I cried out. I didn't mean to scare you. Let's get Inga in here to clean that tea stain right away before it sets.

"It's okay, Ruth Ann," Prunella said calming down. "Why on earth did you jump out of your chair so quickly?"

I reconsidered my position. She had been acting so defensively with me that she may not confide in me just yet. I shrugged it off saying I had to get going because I realized I was running out of time. "That made you jump up?" she asked, not believing my explanation. "Come on, Ruth Ann. I know you better than that. You had a huge light bulb go off in your head, and now you have to tell me what it is."

"Me?" I questioned her, surprised. "You've been so sneaky lately. It's *you* who has to spill it! I'm tired of being the last person to know what's going on around here. Why don't you trust me anymore?"

Prunella was stunned. I thought I might have completely blown the chance for her to confide in me when she lowered her head and said, "You're right. I've been a horrible cousin. I'm so sorry, Ruth Ann. Can you forgive me and let me make it up to you?"

"Start by telling me the truth, right now!" I demanded, hands on my hips in a defensive stance.

"What are you talking about?" she asked, truly appearing confused at my request.

"I know you're pregnant! Why would you keep that from me?"

"*Pregnant*?" she repeated my word slowly like she couldn't believe the word spewed from my mouth.

"Yes! You've been tired, not eating, and now the tea with *crackers*. Who eats tea with soda crackers?" I waited and added, "I'll tell you who eats like that...a pregnant woman!"

Prunella plopped back down in the wet chair and stared up at me in shock. "You think I am pregnant?"

"Wait, you're not?" I asked, confused.

"No."

"But you have all the symptoms. Could you be pregnant and you don't know it yet?"

"That's impossible," she replied deep in thought.

I was curious what she meant by that. Were Axel and Prunella not sharing a married bed or maybe they were and she didn't think it would be possible to get pregnant with a man his age. Or...was there someone else?

"Prunella, you don't have to answer me, but is it even a possibility that Axel got you pregnant? Or is there something else you want to tell me?"

If looks could kill, I just got one. Prunella's glare up at me was chilling. "What are you implying, Ruth Ann?" she snapped.

"I'm not implying anything. I just was wondering if you and Axel ever..."

"Ruth Ann!" she exclaimed. "I don't think I need to answer that. I'm not pregnant so leave it alone." Prunella stood up, straightened her top and walked toward the foyer. "I know you have a lot to do before tomorrow morning so I won't keep you any longer."

It was my dismissal. I hated leaving on a bad note so I smiled as broadly as I could and told her I was sorry. "You know me; I have a curious soul."

"I'll say," Prunella answered, her mouth barely forming a slight smile. "Just forget about everything back here and go and have a wonderful time."

I gave her a tight hug, and said, "Thank you. I will."

Just as I was about to head out the front door, Prunella called, "Don't forget to wear our necklace!"

"I won't," I answered, still not feeling confident about bringing the necklace. My stomach did a minor churn, but I smiled and left the estate.

It was a very dark drive back into town. I didn't like how I left things with Prunella or Inga. Inga seemed overwhelmed with the menu for Thanksgiving dinner. I think I'll give Lynne a quick call when I get home asking her to give Inga a little extra help with the dinner. I was tired, and that dream was hovering around in my head. What was it all about? Maybe I was worried about leaving town and heading off to a faraway place.

Once home, I checked off all the items on my 'to do' list, and headed for the shower. Afterwards, I made myself another cup of tea and pulled out a small piece of chocolate. I walked back into my bedroom and plopped on the bed. I grabbed my cell phone and called Lynne.

"No worries, Mom," Lynne responded. "I'll help her out so it'll be just perfect."

"Thanks, dear." I hung up after saying another goodbye and pulled up the numerous texts I had ignored.

"Seven." I missed seven texts from John. I suddenly felt a slight panic when I called him cell. He better not tell me he can't get away.

"Hi, John," I said in a bright, cheery voice.

"Where have you been?" he asked, tersely. "I've left you several texts and you haven't answered one of them!"

"I'm sorry. I've been really busy getting ready for tomorrow. Please tell me there isn't a problem with our trip!"

"No, no, we're going no matter what!" he replied, loudly.

"What's that supposed to mean? Is there a problem you want to share with me?"

"No, it's all good, Ruth Ann. Just be ready at 4:30 am. I'm picking you up and we'll head out to the airport. Our flight was changed and it's taking off at 8:00 am instead of 10:00."

"That's great!" I blurted out, thrilled that we had *more* time together.

"Really? I thought you'd be upset at the early hour."

"I'm a morning person, John. You should know that!"

"Oh, yes, good. Try and get some sleep, and don't forget your passport!"

I hung up with John and ran to the safe I had built in my closet. "I don't believe it! I would've left without my passport. How could I be so stupid?" I opened the safe and pulled out the, oh so needed, passport. "Phew, that was a close one!"

It was after ten at night when I finally settled down and fell asleep. Right before I dozed off, I wondered if my dream was going to happen again. Thankfully, it didn't. I woke up to one of my favorite seventies songs blaring out of my cell phone. "The alarm!" I cried, pushing the button to turn it off. It was 3:30 in the morning, and even though I was exhausted, I jumped eagerly out of bed and threw myself into the shower.

Thirty minutes later, I was dressed and waiting at the front door with my luggage. John was early, he usually was. However, this time I shocked him and was ready. "Look at you!" he exclaimed, smiling. "I thought you'd be knee deep trying to get that suitcase of yours shut."

"I thought I'd surprise you and be ready," I replied. "Are you shocked?"

"I'll say."

"Let's go," I said, grabbing the handle of my suitcase and rolling it out the front door. John grabbed it from me, and I locked the door. We walked into the freezing November air and headed straight to the airport with no worries of a snowstorm.

As we sat side by side in our airplane seats, John looked over at me and said, "Well, we made it!"

"Yes, we did," I said, mentally crossing every 'T' that could be crossed. I didn't want anything to disrupt my trip with John.

Everything seemed to be going smoothly. We got out of town and to the airport in plenty of time. The plane even took off on time. Now it was time to enjoy our vacation! However, if anyone thinks that's going to happen, they don't know me very well!

Chapter 12

After a stop in Dallas and Miami, we finally landed in Kingston, Jamaica eight hours later. I guess I didn't realize how long it would take to get here. An entire day was blown on travel, which was disappointing, but I had to make the best of it. John looked okay, so I should be too.

"We're here!" I said, exiting the plane onto the tarmac. The air was warm, and the wind was blowing the palm trees surrounding the runway. "Ah, feel that warmth."

John grabbed my hand and gave it a little squeeze. "We are officially on vacation. Once we get checked into our room, let's grab dinner, I'm starving."

"Me, too. We haven't eaten much except for some airport food. I'm looking forward to a nice filet mignon."

John looked strangely at me. "Did you just say *filet mignon*? We're in the Caribbean. Most people say they're looking forward to shrimp or salmon or lobster!"

"I hate seafood! Well, I'll eat shrimp cocktail, but that's as far as it goes."

"I hope you won't be disappointed down here."

"I won't. There's always a ton of food at these all-inclusives. You'll see."

We walked through the tiny airport and grabbed our luggage. Thankfully, it was all here. John had arranged for transportation to the resort earlier that week. We hopped inside the air-conditioned van and the driver whisked us away to our final destination. "We can use our cell phones down here, right?" I asked John.

"Yes, but why would you ask that question? You're not planning on spending your time on the phone, are you?"

"No, no, I was just making sure there weren't any emergencies."

"Oh, okay," he said, wiping a drip of sweat running down the side of his cheek. It wasn't from my question, but from the intense humidity our bodies needed to get used to. The air was warm and steamy, unlike the dry climate back in Deer Creek.

The driver whipped around the winding one lane road, scaring me to death. The jungle enclosed the road on both sides, and I didn't want to end up wrapped around my favorite type of tree, the palm tree. John didn't seem bothered by it, so I decided to close my eyes and hope for the best.

"You okay?" John asked.

"Yep."

"Why are your eyes closed? You're not tired already, are you?"

I leaned over and whispered in his ear, "My eyes are closed so I don't see how this man is driving. He's driving like a maniac!"

John laughed and put his arm around me for protection. "We're almost there, so lean back and try and relax."

Once John's arms were around me I calmed down. I even opened my eyes and was ecstatic that I did. We were out of the jungle and nearing the many resorts on the Caribbean Sea. "Look at the size of these places!"

"They're huge," John replied. "I've been told that it's safe as long as you stay near your resort. No wandering off on your own, Ruth Ann."

"Why would I go anywhere without you?" I asked, wondering if he was going to make plans that didn't include me.

"You're not, I'm just saying if you took a walk down the beach, don't go far…and don't go without me."

"I promise, I'll behave."

Our driver made a sudden stop that caused us both to fly forward. He made a quick turn and we pulled into the most luxurious entrance I've ever seen. Besides the lush jungle trees and foliage, there was pond after pond with flowing fountains, and the most beautiful tropical flowers I've ever laid eyes on. "Wow, it's so green here!" I exclaimed.

"They get a lot of rain," John answered.

"It's a jungle, I get that, but it better not rain the whole time we're here!"

I still hadn't brought up the topic of the Blue Ice necklace. Don't think I've forgotten that small piece of information! I reached my hand up to my throat and felt, for the thousandth time, the chain and then the blue gem. Still there, phew!

John hadn't noticed it because I was wearing a short-sleeved button down shirt under my winter coat. I had it buttoned pretty high, but with the heat, I undid a few of the buttons. Being a male, he still didn't notice the necklace I daringly wore.

After a long drive up to the main resort, the driver pulled under a large covered entrance. He stopped, and jumped out of the van. John opened his side of the door and got out. I climbed out his side, too and stepped into air that made me gasp temporarily. "Whew, it's sultry here! We're so used to a dry climate. It'll take a little while to get used to it."

"If you want to go back home…" John said, jokingly.

"Very funny, John."

"Let's get inside and check-in," John said, grabbing our suitcases and rolling them into the open-air lobby. I looked around the massive room searching for the front desk. "I see it, Ruth Ann," John said, hurrying over to one side of the room.

I took my time reaching the desk because I was taking in the scenery. The main lobby was its own building. Trying to explain the lobby would be difficult because there were no words to describe the beauty. The large, high-ceiling lobby was filled with palms, bright flowers, and water features that sounded as if you were being soothed to sleep. I found John arguing with one of the poor desk clerks when I arrived next to him. "What's the problem?" I asked, curiously.

"They mixed up our room," John snapped, but quickly adjusted his tone with me. "They claim our reservations are for next Saturday and they're all booked!"

"What?" I bellowed. "Don't you have the paperwork with you from the travel agency?"

"Yes, I've showed it to this young man, but he said it's out of his hands."

I turned my attention to the young man behind the Guest Services desk. "If we have paperwork that explicitly states we have a reservation for today, then why is there a problem?" Before he answered, I raised my hand authoritatively and added, "Don't tell me you have no rooms. That, young man is not our problem!"

"But…" the man spat out.

"No buts, get me your supervisor so we can straighten this out," I ordered. He scampered away and John looked at me in amazement.

"Wow, you go girl!" he laughed. "But what happens when they tell us they don't have any rooms?"

"Easy. They find a room somewhere else," I stated.

"Oh, you mean at another resort?" he asked.

"Yep. We can handle it. I know you're hungry, but we'll have this sorted out quickly. Just don't let them see you acting indecisive. Look tough, but willing to work it out."

We waited for a few minutes, when the young Guest Services man came back. Sweat was rolling down his darkened face, but he had a huge grin upon it. "We have it figured out."

"Well?" I asked.

"It was our error. The paperwork is correct that you're carrying, but when we input it in our system, we put the wrong dates. So, we carry all responsibility, but we're still completely full."

"YOU'VE GOT TO BE KIDDING?" I screamed, scaring the young man half to death. "What are we supposed to do? We traveled a long way to visit *your* resort and now you tell us we're to sleep on the street!"

"No, no, we will find you other accommodations. My manager is working on that right now. We don't want any upset guests. Please, give us a few minutes. You can wait on those chairs right over there," the man pointed to the middle of the expansive lobby. There were several seating arrangements with small tables. Most of them were unoccupied since it was dinnertime. John didn't say a word. He rolled our luggage over to the chair and waited for me to sit down first.

"I'm sorry, Ruth Ann. This was supposed to be our first trip together and it's not going very well."

"It's not your fault, John," I replied. "It'll get handled. Give it a few minutes. If not, you'll see the real Ruth Ann come out to handle them!"

"Whoa, you're scaring me!"

"I'm just kidding, kind of. Don't worry, we will have a room within an hour," I declared, secretly hoping I was right, but not quite convinced.

Well, an hour later we did have a room. We were shipped to another resort, if you can call it a resort. We were promised we could use all the amenities back at the original place, but there wasn't anything they could do since there really were no rooms.

"This isn't what I planned for us, Ruth Ann. I don't know how I'm ever going to make it up to you!"

"John, we're still away from the cold weather and everyone we know. Let's make the best of it," I said, staring around the hut. Yes, I said hut.

John and I were escorted about five minutes down the beach with our original driver. He dumped us off at a small, but clean resort. The lobby was much smaller than the previous one. There weren't beautiful ponds with fountains, only a green pond without any water features bubbling out crystal clear water. There was a guest services desk, but this one wasn't of beautiful wood and neatly dressed attendants. The man behind this podium was dressed in a white (sort of white) tank top and ripped denim shorts. He had a cigar hanging from the side of his mouth as he spoke to us. "So, I'm told you need a room." John and I nodded, unsure of what we're about to get. "All I have left is one of our bungalows down by the water." He didn't have a computer to check this information out, but a yellow lined pad of paper where he kept flipping pages. "Ah, it's our best one!" he said, smiling his browned teeth from all the tobacco.

"Great!" I said, hoping with all I've got that it was as nice as he was claiming.

"Here is the information on the resort and where you should stay away from," the man said, handing a folded envelope to John.

"Wait, what did you just say?" John asked, coming out of his daze.

"I think he told us that we should stay away from other places, correct?" I directed toward the disgusting clerk.

"Yep. As long as you stay on our beach property and the properties to the north, you'll be safe. Just don't go south on the beach. There are unsavory people down that way. They frighten even me!" his gurgled laughter nearly made me lose what was left of the airport food I ingested earlier.

John shook his head in irritation, but took hold of my arm and pulled me far away from this man. "Let's check it out before we make any other plans."

"I agree," I said, watching John open the envelope and pull out the scrap of yellow paper the man scratched our room information on. "Looks like it's right on the water. That could be really nice, and private."

"Hmm," he said, placing the paper in his front pants pocket and leading the way down the winding sand path. We passed the one and only restaurant on the property. I spotted the stray dogs hanging around the other guests while they were eating inside the small, open air restaurant. We made our way past the pool. I guess it wasn't the crystal clear water I was expecting, but it might be a freshwater pool. At least I hoped that's why it was so green.

John was becoming angrier and angrier as we wound around the path that was surrounded by the jungle until we came upon the biggest surprise yet.

"It's gorgeous!" I yelled. "Look at this bungalow!"

John was speechless.

"We must've wandered into the other resort! There's no way this is the same resort we just left. This bungalow looks beautiful, and so new."

John remained silent until he stopped in front of the bungalow. "According to his map, this one is ours."

"No way!" I replied. "These don't look anything like the ones by the pool or the restaurant.

"Maybe they built some new ones and they haven't been trashed yet."

"Let's go inside. I'll reserve judgment until after I've seen the entire place," I said, reaching up my hand to open the door.

"Wait," John stopped me. "There's no key in the envelope." He searched the envelope and his pants pocket, but no key.

"You don't think they leave these unlocked all the time, do you?" I asked, becoming very worried and reaching up to feel my neck.

"No, that wouldn't be secure, especially since he mentioned it wasn't safe far from here."

"John, there's something I haven't mentioned to you yet," I started to say, but he stopped me.

"Don't tell me any worse news. Let's look inside first, and then if it's good enough for us, I'll walk back to the lobby and request a lock. How does that sound?"

"Sounds like a plan!" I said, feeling a little better about the situation.

Chapter 13

It took all of a minute to decide it was the perfect bungalow! John grabbed the door and opened it up wide enough for both of us to see inside. What we saw amazed us beyond our wildest dreams. The front of the bungalow was solidly built with a brick and wood framed exterior, but inside exuded a completely different vibe.

"Wow," I said, pushing past John and walking inside the wide-open room. "This place is huge, too!"

"It's beautiful, but not very private," John said, looking at the obvious flaw of the bungalow. "Anyone walking by on the beach can see in here!"

"We can just close the curtains when it's dark out," I suggested, noticing the massive sliding glass doors that spanned the whole backside of the bungalow. "But during the day we can keep it wide-open to enjoy that unbelievable view of the water."

"It is amazing, isn't it?" John asked. "I'm still confused about this place after walking through the lobby and other parts of the resort."

"I wonder if the bungalows down by the water are newer because it makes the resort look good from the beach," I said.

"How?" John asked.

"Well, if I was walking down the beach and saw this beautiful bungalow, I would be interested in looking into staying here, wouldn't you?"

"Oh, I get it," he said. "Yes, I agree, totally."

"Hey, where's the bedroom, John?" I asked, looking around the open room. "And the bathroom for that matter."

John walked to the left side and passed a kitchenette with a small refrigerator, sink, and rattan table with four chairs. The rattan themed furniture carried throughout the room. There was a large couch with floral cushions, and a coffee table in front of it. The couch was against the opposite wall of the kitchen area, near the massive sliders that opened up to the small patio with a couple of lounge chairs just waiting for us to use. Opposite the couch was a large, rattan entertainment center with a tiny television, a bunch of seashells, and other beach type decorations.

"Where's the bedroom?" he asked, confused. "There's only one other door, and that goes into the bathroom."

"You don't think the couch pulls out, do you?" I asked, quickly walking over to the couch and lifting a puffy cushion off. "Yep!" I replied to my own question. "It's a pull-out, John."

"Oh, well, maybe it won't be too bad. I mean, this place is terrific outside of that. Come over here and check out the bathroom, Ruth Ann. I think you'll be pleasantly surprised."

I hurried over to John who was standing in the doorway of the bathroom. "The door is see-through, John," I said, not too happy about that detail.

"It's right next to the kitchen area, too," he replied. He laughed and said, "Picture this, I'm cooking you some eggs in the morning and you're in there taking a shower. Now that makes for entertaining cooking!"

"There is no way that'll ever happen!" I exclaimed. "I'll throw a towel over the glass door, and then I'll have some privacy."

"I thought this trip was to bring us closer together, Ruth Ann," John said, jokingly. I didn't laugh back, and he quickly realized he shouldn't take this one too far. "I'm just playing with you, Ruth Ann. Of course we'll figure out a way to keep our bathroom duties private."

"Okay," I said. "Outside of those little issues, I think this place is perfect!"

"Let's unpack later. I'm hungry," John said.

"I agree. I guess we should try the restaurant we passed by, but I didn't like the stray dogs begging for food."

"You love dogs, Ruth Ann," John reminded me.

"I do, but I don't think it's very sanitary to have them jumping up on me when we're in a restaurant."

"We'll give it a try. This place is supposedly all-inclusive, too, but I'm not so sure we'll want to eat here for every meal. There's only one restaurant on the property as far as I know."

"Maybe we should ask where else we could eat while we're here."

John added, "And we need to see if they have a shop here or we'll have to go over to another resort. I know you like to shop in the hotels along the beach, right?"

"Definitely! I have lots of people to buy for now. Let's see, I have Lynne, Nancy, Prunella and Axel, Inga and Sherman, oh and Alex!"

"Why not buy gifts for the mayor, his wife, the pastor..." John laughed.

"Oh, you just reminded me of another person, Meme!"

"As long as I'm not spending these five days shopping, I'm good," John said. "I'd like to do some paddle boarding, and maybe we can use a kayak to take us around the area."

"Sounds great, John," I said, hoping I could just plop myself down by the beach and drink a few cocktails, and relax.

We stored our luggage in a large closet located off the bathroom. "First, before we eat, I need to get a lock for this place."

"I agree!" I said, remembering the necklace around my neck. I knew I didn't want to wear it down by the beach, but leaving it here made me terrified.

"What about asking about a safe?" John suggested. "I have my gun, money, and credit cards. What do you have?"

"Umm, I have a few items I'd like to put securely away. Let's stop back at the lobby and see if there's someone there who can help us better than the last guy."

We closed the door behind us. John wasn't thrilled about leaving our luggage, but we sure didn't want to haul it all the way back up to the lobby and restaurant. We didn't notice anybody else wandering around with their luggage, so he came to the conclusion it was safe, temporarily.

"There's a little gift shop, Ruth Ann," John pointed out. He spotted the small shop attached to the restaurant. The sign on the door said they'll be back in an hour. It was an old-fashioned, cardboard sign with a clock face and black plastic hands that could be manually changed. I walked over and put my face up to the window and tried to peek inside.

"It looks like they have refrigerated items in the back, John," I said, spotting a large glass cooler full of wine, beer, pop and water.

"That's good. If we need snacks or refreshments, we can come here."

"I'm hoping drinks will be brought down to the beach directly to me," I said. "Plus, an all-inclusive should give us all the food we need, John.

"I hope so," John said, walking over to the hostess at the restaurant.

The large, hut shaped facility was open on the sides except for the posts that held up the grass covered roof. It had a high ceiling and fans circulating to keep the air moving. It was still quite steamy inside the room, but the fans helped, a little. I completely forgot to see if our bungalow was air conditioned. I don't recall feeling overly hot, so maybe it was and we just didn't notice.

"Two, please," John said to the pretty young woman who was obviously the hostess. She smiled brightly at John, and I even think she giggled, and waved her hand for us to follow. She took us past a few occupied tables and sat us directly underneath one of the fans. She pulled out my chair, and waited until I sat down to explain our meal.

"The waitresses will come over and take your drink order. If you would like water, you need to ask them for it. They won't automatically bring it to you like in the states."

"Okay, thanks," I said, wondering how she knew we were from the states. "Do we just go and grab our plates and get food?" I asked her, looking at the buffet stations in the back of the restaurant.

"Yes, you may eat as much as you like," she replied, and turned and left.

"That's interesting," I said.

"What?" John asked, confused.

"How'd she know we were from the states?"

"We probably look American, Ruth Ann. We're pale, and don't exactly look Jamaican."

"Ha, ha," I said. "Should we wait for the waitress to order our drinks or go and grab food first?"

"I'm grabbing food," John stated, and stood up. "How about you?"

"I'm coming, too," I said, standing up and following John to the back of the restaurant to see what food we'd be eating for the next few days.

As we walked toward the back I noticed there weren't any dogs hanging around. Oh, well, on to my next curiosity, the buffet. I felt the heat coming from some of the stations as we approached them. The sweat started forming on my forehead. "Whew, it's really hot over here!" I stated.

"I know, I'm sweating all over the place," John agreed. "Let's hurry and get food so we can move away from the chafing dishes."

Chafing dishes? He was right. The buffet tables were set up like a U. There were two tables at the very end and two tables forming each of the sides of the U. At the very back of the room on the two side by side tables were the heated dishes. I noticed the food was inside silver chafing dishes with little flames burning underneath them to keep the food warm. "Interesting," I said, out loud. "It seems so formal for a beach resort."

John ignored my comments and walked over to the first container and took off the lid. "Pizza!" he cried out.

"Pizza?" I questioned him, taking back my comment about being too formal.

"Yes, how strange." He took a couple of pieces and placed them on a large plate he was holding and moved on to the next dish. "Fish and chips," he called out to me. How odd, I suddenly felt like we were in a fast food place. "Mac and cheese! What's going on around here," John exclaimed.

I wandered off to the side tables and spotted different salads, fruits, and there it was…the dessert table! I quickly filled my plate with a hot dog from the heated section and some French fries. Then I grabbed a bowl and filled up with some of the salads and fruits. I walked back to the table and set my plate and bowl down and turned and hurried back to the dessert table. "I'm not waiting," I said to John, who was watching my moves very carefully. "I'm grabbing one of everything for us to sample."

"Sure you are, Ruth Ann," he said, laughing. "You sharing a dessert! That's a good one."

"I want to sample a bunch of things tonight so we'll know what we like," I said, grabbing a large dinner plate instead of one of the smaller dessert plates they had piled next to the station.

However, when I looked at each of the desserts, I had to admit I was a tad disappointed. They all jiggled! Who wants a piece of chocolate cake that jiggles? I took one, though, just to try it. I piled some coconut cake, cheesecake, and a few cookies on my plate. I passed by the chocolate covered strawberries and bananas to get to the huge pile of cookies. "Lemon, chocolate chip, oatmeal raisin…I think this one has cranberry chunks and white chocolate chip…" I grabbed one of each and sauntered back to my seat where John was waiting for me to begin eating.

"Does something look funny to you, Ruth Ann?" John asked.

"What?" I questioned back.

"I have one plate and you have *three*!"

I looked at the amount of food set in front of me and bawled out laughing. John reached over and snatched one of my chocolate chip cookies and took a large bite. "Not bad," he said, with a full mouth.

"As good as my daughter's?" I asked, curiously.

"Of course not, but for where we are, not bad."

We sat and gorged ourselves for a few minutes when finally, a waitress appeared out of nowhere, startling the two of us. John choked on a piece of chicken, and I swallowed a bite of my hot dog the wrong way. "Would either of you care for a cocktail?" she asked.

John asked for a local beer, while I asked for a Pina colada. At first, I didn't take too much notice of our waitress, but when she brought our drinks back I couldn't help but observe she wouldn't leave our table. John eyed me peculiarly, but didn't say a word. I, on the other hand, said, "Can I help you with something?"

The pretty young woman, who I would guess was in her twenties, stood motionless, staring at me. "Excuse me?" I asked her. "Is something wrong?"

She woke from her trance, looking terrified, and ran away as fast as she could. "What on earth was that all about?" John asked.

"I have no idea, but I'm going to find out." I looked around the room for the hostess, and when I caught eyes with her I waved her over.

"Is there a problem?" she asked.

"Yes, who is our waitress?" I inquired, giving no other information yet.

"Isabella," she answered. "Did she do something wrong?"

"Not exactly," I began. "But when she dropped off our drinks, she stood frozen, staring at me in horror."

"Really?" the hostess questioned. "I'll go speak with her at once." Without letting me say I didn't want the poor girl in trouble, she abruptly turned and left.

"That didn't go very well," John said, stuffing a fork of the oddly colored mac and cheese in his mouth.

"No, it didn't. You'd better be careful eating all this strange food. It's like they're trying to serve American food instead of local food."

"I have a tough stomach. I'll be fine," he said, jamming a handful of French fries into what I think was catsup and eating them.

We were almost finished with our food and drinks when the hostess returned to our table. She looked nervous, almost afraid of us when she arrived. "I'm sorry it took me so long."

"That's okay, but what's going on?" I asked.

"Isabella explained to me why she acted the way she did," the woman started to say.

"And…" John said, trying to get her moving quicker.

"She saw something that gave her a scare."

"With me?" I asked, stunned at her statement. "What could I have done to scare her?"

"It's not something you've done, it's…it's what you are wearing." the young woman said.

I looked down at my clothes and all I saw was a shirt and shorts. Maybe I was dressed somewhat casually, but it wasn't that bad. John stared me down and shrugged his shoulders until... "Ruth Ann!" he bellowed. "I can't believe you're wearing that!"

"What?" I cried out, and then it hit me, my necklace. "Oh, are you referring to my necklace?" I asked the hostess, ignoring John's outburst for the moment.

"Why yes," she said, backing off a little and standing closer to John's side of the table. "Where did you get that?"

"It's a family heirloom. Why would it bother any of you?" I asked, baffled and insulted at the same time.

"You don't understand our culture down here, Miss."

"Ruth Ann, you can call me Ruth Ann," I snapped.

"Oh, okay. Ruth Ann, we have superstitions that are unlike anywhere else in the world. When one has a, how shall I describe it to you...a feeling that something is wrong, we don't hide our feelings very well."

John interrupted and declared, "I don't understand, Ruth Ann. You should never have brought that piece down here! It's a precious family heirloom all the way from Sweden! How could you?"

"I can't say if that's actually correct, sir. Maybe the gem came to be in Ruth Ann's possession from Sweden, but there are very strong vibes illuminating from the stone that may scare away some locals."

"Really?" I said, stunned and annoyed at the same time. "That's impossible. This necklace and the gem have been in my family for generations. Nobody knows how far back it goes."

"But maybe, ma'am, it originated from down here and somehow ended up in Sweden."

"Nope," I announced. "You must be incorrect."

"Okay," she conceded. "But if you have any further strange reactions from others around here, just beware." The woman didn't wait for John or me to question her further. Beware, beware of what?

"That was weird," John said, finally finishing his food.

"I know," I said, losing my appetite.

"You barely ate anything, Ruth Ann," John said, eyeing my three plates that were still full.

"I'm not that hungry anymore," I said. "What do you make of the waitress, Isabella, and the hostess? Do you think it's true what she said?"

"No, it's just island superstition. Jamaica's into voodoo and witchcraft."

"It is?" I asked, suddenly feeling uncomfortable about where we were vacationing. "I knew I should've never agreed to wear this thing!"

"Why did you? It's not very smart, Ruth Ann. I mean anyone could rip it off your neck and then the famous Blue Ice would be gone forever!"

"You make it sound so dramatic, John." I felt my neck and looked down at the piece. It was truly a beautiful stone; it couldn't be part of some evil past. "Aha!" I bellowed, scaring John half out of his seat. "I wonder if this is why anyone who took possession of it was either cursed, injured, robbed, or killed!"

"Now who's being dramatic," John said, reaching over and stealing my plate of desserts. He stabbed a piece of jiggly chocolate cake with his fork and stuck a hunk in his mouth. The drips falling from my plate to his mouth turned my stomach. "This is really bad," he said, scrunching his face. "I don't think baking is their thing down here. Maybe if we go somewhere else it'll be better."

I ignored John's rant about the quality of desserts. My mind was racing with thoughts of what has gone wrong with this necklace. However, there was some good, too. I met Prunella, Inga, Sherman, and even Axel. I'm being silly, I thought to myself. I expressed my concern again to John and he mentioned, "Don't forget about the newly discovered young man, Alex, Ruth Ann."

"Ah, I forgot about him already," I said. "He seems like a nice enough person; don't you think?"

"I don't really know him, Ruth Ann."

"Well, it appears he'll be sticking around for now. Axel's given him a job. He's going to teach him the family business."

"That's interesting, and quick," he said. "How do you know he's on the up and up?"

"I'm sure Axel has thoroughly checked out his background by now. I think it's great! Our family is growing, and that makes me really happy."

"I have a question, Ruth Ann," John said, swallowing the last bite of the cake. "How did they convince you to wear the necklace? I thought that thing was tucked safely away in the safe."

"So did I," I replied. "I was two-teamed by Prunella and Axel. They pushed and pushed until I agreed. I didn't want to bring it, but somehow they convinced me to do it. Plus, they said it was heavily insured."

"Hey, I'm curious, did Axel get all of his financial investments back? Like the shipping company, and his overseas money?"

"Why would you ask me that," I said, confused at his abrupt change of topic, but then it dawned on me. "Oh, I know where you're going with this. You think they pushed me to wear it because they *want* it stolen so they could collect the insurance money!"

"It's possible, don't you think?" he asked.

"No way!" I answered, confidently. "It's more likely they knew the stone was from here and they knew the locals would think it was actually cursed. Then I would get rid of it or someone would convince me to hand it over."

"That's ridiculous, Ruth Ann! How could anyone just plainly ask you to give it to them. You would never fall for this voodoo stuff, would you?"

"No," I replied slowly, suddenly not as confident as I was feeling earlier.

"Enough of this," John stammered, and hopped out of his chair and pulled mine out with me still in it. "I forgot. We need to get a lock for our bungalow. All this talk about stealing and voodoo makes me nervous our stuff is sitting in there without any protection."

"You're right, let's get going," I said, standing up and following John out of the restaurant. We didn't see Isabella or the hostess anywhere. I wondered where they disappeared. Maybe they were avoiding me now that they saw my necklace.

John didn't head in the direction of our bungalow, he turned back toward the small lobby building. He marched up to the small podium of a front desk and confronted a different man. "I need a lock for our door," he demanded without any explanation.

"Excuse me, Sir?" he asked John, not understanding him.

"Our bungalow," he said, raising his hands up in the air to form the shape of a house. "We don't have a lock on our door. Anyone can get in there. It's not safe or secure for your guests, is it?"

"Ah, none of our accommodations have locks on them," the employee stated.

"That's crazy!" John bellowed, loudly. "I've never heard of a place that doesn't have locks on their doors. I want a lock, now!"

The middle aged, well-dressed man in khakis and a purple polo shirt, said, "You're perfectly safe here, Sir. We've never had any problems at the resort since it opened."

"How long have you been in business?" John asked.

"We're fairly new here, sir. I'm the owner, Carlos,."

"How new?" John demanded.

"We took over this place about six months ago. We're in the process of rehabbing the guest's units. I believe you and your friend here," he stopped and motioned to me. "You both are in one of our newly renovated bungalows. Don't you like your accommodations?"

"The bungalow is lovely," I answered, interrupting John.

"It hasn't anything to do with the bungalow itself," John said, frustrated. "We were specifically told that we had to stay on this resort or the resorts on the beach to the north. It wasn't safe to head south. Now you're telling me that *none* of the accommodations have locks."

"Nobody would dare rob a guest here. Resorts are safe here on our island. Locals would be severely punished if they dared commit a crime on a resort's property." Carlos started getting nervous. He could see the anger building in John. I almost felt sorry for this handsome man, but John had a valid point. Nowhere is 100% safe from crime. We should know! Deer Creek never had any violent crimes, and now…well, you know the story!

John took a deep breath, "Okay, I'm the Chief of Police back in our home town." He pulled his wallet out of his shorts back pocket, flashing a gun in his waistband. Poor Carlos' reaction was priceless.

"No, no, we can't have guests running around with guns! That's very dangerous.

"Carlos, I'm the Chief of Police, remember? We always have to carry a weapon. I don't think you need to worry about me. In fact, you should be thanking me!"

"How's that?" I asked, confused at his comment.

He turned toward me and said, through gritted teeth, "Because we're safer now that I'm here. Nobody would mess with a cop!"

"Sure, okay, John," I said, laughing on the inside. A lot of good it does to have a cop from Deer Creek, Colorado waving a gun around in a foreign country.

He ignored me and turned his attention back to Carlos. "I want a lock, and I want it now!"

Carlos held his hand up and said he'd be right back. The man ran toward a door that more than likely led into an office. "There," John said. "Now we're getting somewhere."

"What's with everyone freaking out around this place? First, my necklace, and now, your gun."

"I guess we both have to remember it's a different culture down here."

"You're the one threatening Carlos!" I cried. "He seems like a perfectly nice man. Totally different than the last employee we encountered. That man was disgusting!"

"It's obvious, isn't it? The employees don't make a lot of money, because the owner's keeping it all. Didn't you see how nicely Carlos was dressed, and groomed, compared to the first guy?"

"Maybe," I said, vowing to keep an eye out on all the resort's employees. Something weird was happening around here, and I wanted to know what!

Chapter 14

It only took Carlos about five minutes when he reappeared suddenly. "Whoa," John jumped. "Where'd you come from?"

He didn't know how to respond to John's question. He shrugged his shoulders and held out a padlock and key. "This is all we have here. Will it do?"

John grabbed the lock and key and examined it thoroughly. "Well, it's not the best lock, but it should do as long as it fits the door handle."

I thanked Carlos, and then took hold of John's arm and led him away from the lobby. "See, it's all working out now."

"Let's see," he said, fiddling with the lock and key. "It' works at least."

We made our way past the green colored pool and concluded that it hadn't been renovated yet. Five minutes later, we arrived back at our bungalow. John quickly entered and searched the place to make sure nobody had been in there. When he felt it was safe and untouched, he left me on my own and headed to the front door to see if the lock would work. It didn't take longer than a minute when he returned and said it worked. "Not the best, but nobody can get in here without this key." John held up the one and only key.

"Uh, John," I said, hoping not to deflate his current mood. "What if there's more than one key out there? Maybe Carlos only gave you one of them on purpose."

"Ruth Ann!" John yelled, but quickly amended his outburst. "I'm sorry. I'm not yelling at you. I'm mad at myself for not thinking of that, too. Maybe I'll run back to the lobby and have another chat with Carlos."

"As long as you don't confront him, angrily. He might be more forthcoming if you're nice, and then he might tell you the truth."

"Fine, I'll try it your way, but I'll be able to tell if he's lying."

"You're the cop!" I said, smiling at John knowing he didn't always have that cop intuition!

John asked me to stay here and unpack while he ran back to the lobby. He didn't think it would take more than a few minutes. I told him to take his time because I had a lot of organizing to do. I also wanted to prepare *our* bed, and take a shower to get the stick off from traveling and walking around in the extreme humidity.

I looked at the time on my cell phone and it was already ten at night. I didn't like John walking around alone out there. Something about this place gave me the creeps. I'm hoping once we get accustomed, it'll stop and we can just enjoy the beach and the sea. I shook off my apprehensions and got down to unpacking. John wouldn't be long and I wanted to have my luggage unpacked. He could do his own.

I went inside the bathroom and into the closet. My suitcase was waiting for me there so I got down to work. There were plenty of hangars and a dresser where I could put everything that didn't get hung up. Within a short amount of time I had finished unpacking and headed out into the living area. I walked over to the couch and pulled off the cushions. I wasn't sure if I could or *should* pull out the bed. Maybe John would feel more comfortable doing that, but he wasn't here, and I wanted to get everything ready for our first official night alone. I piled the cushions on a chair and grabbed the handle of the folded bed. I pulled and the bed easily unfolded into a queen sized bed. "Now, where are the linens?" I asked out loud. I walked back into the closet and found them high up on a shelf. I grabbed the stepstool that was against the wall and was just tall enough to take hold of some sheets, pillows, and a blanket.

I thought John would've been back by now, but since he wasn't, I was going to get our bed ready. I hurried out to the living room and made up the bed and tried it out. "Comfy, for a pullout!" I hopped up, looked at the time on my cell phone. "10:45! Where is he?" Should I go and look for him, but there was no way I wanted to do that. I'd give him until 11:00, and then I'd head out and make my way up to the lobby. Maybe he got lost in the dark!

I decided the best thing I could do was to take a quick shower. I was sticky, sweaty, and probably not smelling my best. I grabbed a t-shirt and some shorts to put on afterwards in case I had to go outside. I turned on the shower, which was surprisingly large and modern. The hot water spilled out, and I hopped in and washed the day's filth away.

"11:10," I said, drying my medium length hair with a towel. "It shouldn't have taken John this long to check on another key for a silly old lock!"

I was beginning to get worried, when I decided it was best to head out and look for him. I kept reminding myself what the owner and the other employees have said. "It's safe as long as you stay on the property." Well, I'm not leaving the path or the property, so I should be okay.

I grabbed a flashlight I found in one of the drawers in the tiny kitchen and walked out the front door. It was pitch black out here! I bet John couldn't find the place and he didn't think to turn on the flashlight on his cell phone. I walked about ten feet when I heard a crunching sound. "John," I quietly called out, hoping it was him walking toward me.

No response. "John, is that you?" I said, a bit louder this time. Nothing. I contemplated turning around and going back inside the bungalow, but then I realized it was unlocked anyway right now. John had the one and only key! I didn't have a choice but to move forward. I took a deep breath and kept walking. I didn't hear any more crunching, and within a few minutes I could see the lights peeking through the jungle of the pool, restaurant, and lobby. "Phew," I said, quietly.

"Ruth Ann? Is that you?" a voice appeared out of thin air.

"John? It's me, Ruth Ann," I called out, louder.

John suddenly appeared right in front of me. "What are you doing out here?" he snapped. "It's not safe for you to be wandering around out here in the dark."

"But you didn't come back and it's been an hour. Where have you been?" I asked.

"Let's get back to the bungalow and I'll fill you in on everything. This place is starting to creep me out, too!"

We hurried down the sandy path, and if it wasn't for my flashlight, John would have walked right by the bungalow. "John, we're here," I said, grabbing his arm to stop him.

"Oh, yeah, right," he said, embarrassed.

He let me go inside first and as he closed the door he took the lock and hooked it on the inside latch. "This is ridiculous," he murmured. "We have to keep switching the lock from inside to out."

"It's not that big of a deal, John. It'll keep our stuff safe."

"Not very," he replied. "I don't like the security around this place."

"What security?" I questioned. "Nobody seems to care around here, but then they tell us it's not safe near here, too."

"I think we'll check it out in the morning when we can see better."

"Let's put this behind us for now. We're on vacation, finally. I plan on enjoying myself starting right now!"

John smiled, relaxed and said, "You're right, Ruth Ann. I'm going to hop in the shower. Why don't you pop that bottle of champagne I had delivered here earlier while we were eating?"

"You had a bottle of champagne delivered here?" I asked, stunned and pleasantly surprised. It wasn't like John to be prepared with a romantic gesture.

"I surprised you, didn't I?" he asked, smiling brightly. "I thought it would be nice to toast our trip and help us calm down from this long day."

"It really has been a long, exhausting day. I'm bushed."

John eyed me peculiarly and said, "If you want, we can hold off on the champagne until tomorrow. We'll be rested and excited about being here."

I wondered if he was thinking what I was? Do we want to have our first night flop because we were both too tired and irritat-

ed from the day's events or should we try and have a romantic in-
terlude because it was our first true night away together? But what
if we did go ahead and, you know…finally consummate our relationship and it was terrible?

"Ruth Ann?" John called out to me. "What are you thinking
so hard about?"

"Oh, sorry," I was just considering your suggestion about
saving the champagne until tomorrow."

"Well," he said, slamming the mini refrigerator. "We don't
have a choice."

"Huh?"

"They never delivered the champagne!" John exclaimed,
clearly agitated.

"Oh, that's okay. The thought was there and I really appreci-
ate it," I said, trying to calm him down.

He stomped over to me as I stood by the door to the bathroom
and said, "Tomorrow morning I plan on marching down and
speaking with Carlos. If he can't get things straightened out, we're
out of here!"

"Move again?" I asked, becoming irritated myself and it
wasn't because of the resort! John wasn't willing to go with the
flow. It wasn't that bad here, in fact, the bungalow was modern
and tastefully decorated. I'm sure when we wake up the view will
take our breath away and he'll forget about everything else.

"I'm sorry, Ruth Ann," he said. "This isn't what I expected
for our first night away together."

"John, stop worrying about everything! We're together and
I'm just happy about that."

"You're right," he replied, finally releasing the tension in his
face. "I'm taking a shower. Be out in ten minutes."

I let him go and headed over to the pull-out bed and plopped
down. It was actually quite comfortable. I think the mattress was
one of those memory foam ones that conformed to your body
shape once you lie down on it. "Ooh, this is comfy." That was all I
remembered!

Chapter 15

"Ruth Ann!" John called out loudly. "C'mon, wake up."

I opened my eyes and said, "Oh, I must've slipped off to sleep, sorry about that. How long have you been waiting for me since you got out of the shower?"

"Uh, about seven hours," he said, grinning at me from the other side of the bed.

"What!" I cried out. "Are you telling me it's morning?"

"Yep. I didn't have the heart to wake you after my shower. I admit, I took a really long one after the day we had, but not that long!"

I sat up and immediately wondered how horrible I looked. "Don't look at me!" I exclaimed. "I must look like a monster."

John laughed so loud that any cobwebs that were floating around in my head dissipated. "You don't look like a monster, Ruth Ann. You're just as pretty as always. That's one of the reasons I was attracted to you. You don't require all that makeup and stuff; you've got that natural look. So when you wake up, you look the same as you did when you went to sleep."

Okay, I knew he meant that as a compliment, but somehow it didn't make me feel any more confident about how I looked. "I'm going to run to the bathroom. I'll be out in a bit." I hopped off the bed before he could try and lean in for a kiss. It was bad enough how I most likely looked, but without brushing my teeth…yuck!

I hurried as fast as I could and threw my medium length brown hair into a pony tail since we'd be spending the day at the beach. Why wash it when it'll get all sandy and oily from the sunscreen? I threw on my new periwinkle blue tankini bathing suit and grabbed the matching skirt for additional coverage of my not so toned thighs. Once I cleaned myself up, I was ready to take in the view of the beach and head outside.

"You look ready to go," John said, checking out my bathing suit. I noticed he was already wearing his swim shorts and flip flops.

"Hey, you made the bed. I could've helped," I said, noticing the cushions on the couch and how he accidentally mixed up the bottom and back cushions. I didn't dare fix it until he disappeared into the bathroom so he didn't think I was correcting his thoughtful work.

"No problem, we're on this trip together. You don't have to do all the work."

"Did you sleep in your swim shorts?" I asked, wondering how he changed when he didn't come into the bathroom while I was in there.

"I was up for a little while before you. I already cleaned up and changed, and then I woke you up."

"Oh," I said, knowing I wasn't going to be able to fix the cushions for a while. I don't know why, but things like that, and crooked pictures, crumbs on the floor or counter, bother me until I can clean it up. "So, are we going to grab some breakfast first, and then head out to the beach?"

"I'm starving so I'd like to if that's okay with you," John replied.

"I'm hungry too. I wonder what they'll have for breakfast. Last night's dinner was American themed food. I wonder if they do that every night or was last night special?"

"I was so hungry by then, that it didn't matter to me. We can always go somewhere else, too."

"It's included in the price so we should try here unless it's really bad."

"Sounds good. Let's get going, huh?" he said, walking over to the door and unlocking the lock. "Hey, what are you going to do with that necklace you were tricked into bringing?"

"Oh, I almost forgot about that," I said, running back into the bathroom and then into the closet. I opened one of the dresser drawers and pulled out a pair of white socks I brought just in case I worked out (doubtful). I unrolled them and grabbed the aqua blue gem and hurried out of the closet. "What should I do with it? I don't want to wear it down to the beach, but I really don't want to leave it here."

"Wear it," John answered matter of fact. "Better safe on you than here. I don't trust this place. Anyone can get in from the sliders or the windows, too."

"But those have locks on them," I said.

"Anyone can break into those," he replied.

"Fine," I said, putting my necklace on. "Hey, it actually goes well with my suit!"

John shook his head in amazement. "That's just not something most guys notice, Ruth Ann."

"I do," I said, then walked out into the warm, morning air. "Oh, it's beautiful out here!"

"I have to admit this place is nice." We walked hand in hand up the now easily seen, sandy path past the pool and older bungalows. "Wow, I'm sure glad we got one of the new ones."

"I agree. I don't know how happy I'd be living in one of those," I said, noticing the small, rotting wood structures. "I bet they're full of bugs and other creatures, too!"

"Probably," John answered. "I want to stop in and see if Carlos is around. I have a few words for him. Why don't you get us a table and then I'll be right over?" John more or less demanded as he released my hand and headed down the path to the lobby.

I walked up to the opening of the restaurant and realized I might've made a crucial mistake. The last time I was in here I freaked out the waitress and hostess with my necklace. I quickly unhooked it and put it in my skirt pocket.

"Ah, Ms. Ruth Ann, you're back for breakfast, alone?" the same hostess from last night asked me, looking around for John.

"He'll be here in a minute. If you could give us our table, that would be great," I said a tad coolly. I didn't like the way she looked for John. Was she interested in him? I wouldn't doubt it. He was an extremely handsome, strong figured man that most woman would gravitate to. As she led me to the table we had the night before I asked her, "What is your name if I might ask?"

"Martika," she replied, enthusiastically.

"What a beautiful name!"

"Thank you. Here's your table and Isabella will be right with you. I see you're not wearing that necklace so she should be okay with you today."

"I still don't see the problem with it. It's a family heirloom, not this cursed piece from down here like you suggested."

"Ah, but you really don't *know* that for sure, do you Ms. Ruth Ann?" she asked.

"But I do," I announced. "I love that necklace and will probably wear it again. I hope that won't upset you and Isabella too much."

"Me?" she asked, innocently. "I don't have any of those superstitions like she does. She's a silly, local girl that doesn't know any better. I just wanted her to calm down last night so she could finish her work."

"Really?" I asked. "I thought you had a problem with it, too."

"Nope," she declared hastily, and abruptly turned to leave.

I wasn't alone for much longer when Isabella walked up to me with a pot of coffee. She was brimming from ear to ear and wished me a good morning as if she didn't remember who I was.

"Good morning, Isabella," I said, cheerily. "I don't drink coffee, but you can pour a cup for John. He'll be here in a moment."

"Oh, okay. Can I bring you anything else to drink?"

"I'll just grab one of those glasses of orange juice I see on the buffet table."

She shrugged her shoulders and sauntered off to a nearby table of four people. They were stuffing food in their faces from several plates on their table. "Wow, they must be hungry," a voice said from behind my chair.

"John! You startled me," I said, breathing to bring my heart rate back to normal. "Everything okay?" I asked.

"Yep, Carlos and I had a nice little chat. He apologized profusely about the mistake with the champagne and the lock. He promised nothing else would be missed."

"Great," I said, standing up and heading toward the food tables. "It looks like lots to choose from this morning."

"I'll grab my food and meet you back at the table," John said, heading to the omelet station. I went to the waffle station.

I filled my plate pretty full since I figured we'd spend most of the day on the beach. I grabbed a bowl of fruit, a large waffle full of maple syrup, some buttered rye toast and a large glass of orange juice. I sat down before John and started eating my waffle when Isabella reappeared.

"Ma'am," she said tentatively. "Can I ask you a question?"

I swallowed my bite of waffle and replied, "Of course, Isabella. What can I do for you?"

"It's not anything you can do, but…but I was just wondering where your necklace was? You know, the one you had on last night when…"

"When you flipped out and ran away in utter horror!" I finished for her.

She lowered her head in embarrassment and answered, "Yes, ma'am. I'm very sorry about that. It just it shocked me so."

"Why would it shock you?" I asked, wondering if Martika didn't talk to her about it last night like she said she did.

Isabella suddenly got fidgety and was about to bolt, when I grabbed her arm. "Please, please let me just get on with my work. I didn't mean to ask you anything!"

"Yes, you did, Isabella," I said, calmly. "If you wouldn't get into trouble I would ask you to sit down."

Isabella looked around the room and spotted her boss, Martika. "I'm going to get into trouble. I have to go!"

"Isabella, would it be easier for you to talk to me somewhere else? Please, I really want to hear what you know about my necklace!"

Isabella, surprising me, said, "You would do that for me?"

"Of course. I know you're working and don't want to get into trouble. You tell me when you can meet and I'll be there," I said, smiling at her so she knew I really meant it.

"Okay, I get off at 2:00 this afternoon. Can you meet me on the south side of the resort by the abandoned rowboat?"

"*Abandoned rowboat*?" I questioned her, confused. "Will I be able to find it?"

"Oh, yes, it's the only one right after you leave our resort."

"Give me exact directions quickly, Isabella," I requested.

"Follow the path to the beach. Turn left and walk about two maybe three minutes. You'll see a rotted, seaweed covered rowboat deserted on the beach. I'll meet you there at about 2:15, okay?"

"Perfect, got it!" I said and before I knew it, Isabella disappeared into the kitchen at the back of the restaurant.

John sat down just as Isabella flew by him. "Don't tell me she freaked out again!"

"No, no she was fine. I wasn't wearing the necklace. I don't think she even remembered me."

"Really?" John asked, surprised. "Oh, well, how's the waffle? They look good."

I cut a hunk with my fork and stuffed it in my mouth before I said too much. I didn't want to alarm John about my meeting with Isabella. He wasn't too happy I had the necklace in the first place. I figured if I learned anything, I would fess up. The only problem was…how would I get away without him? No sooner did the answer fall into my lap!

"Hey, how about we rent some of those paddle boards today?"

A lightbulb went off in my head! "What a great idea for you!"

"Me?" he asked, dumbfounded. "You don't want to do it?"

"I do, but I think the first time I would rather watch you."

"Are you sure? I don't want to do anything without you."

"I'll be right there on the beach watching you," I said, getting my free pass to meet with Isabella.

"Well, okay," he said, unsure of my motive. "I was told we could rent them down by the beach. We can go check it out after we're done eating."

"Sounds like a plan," I said, smiling inside.

We finished eating and left the resort's restaurant with no further contact with Isabella or Martika. As we walked by the pool we noticed it was being emptied. Carlos was standing over two men who were obviously working on the pool. He was frantically yelling at them, waving his arms high in the air in frustration. John, being the consummate cop, rushed over there. I stayed away, but could clearly hear the confrontation.

"What's going on here, Carlos?" John asked, out of breath.

Carlos abruptly lowered his arms, and turned toward John with a large grin. "Ah, Mr. Wilkinson, everything's fine here."

"It's John, and it sure doesn't look that way. You were really chewing those two out. Did they do something wrong?"

"Chewing?" Carlos asked, confused. "Is that a slang word from America?"

Frustrated, John said, "Yelling, cursing, screaming…"

"Oh, no, I was just trying to get these two to get moving with the pool. As you see, it's disgusting and nobody would dare go in it."

John eyed the remaining murky green water and said, "Agreed. It's gross. How did it ever get so bad?"

"As I told you last night, we're new owners here and the pool workers kept delaying coming here to fix it. I finally got them here and they're barely doing anything."

"I'm sure they need all the dirty water emptied. Then they'll clean it all up. I bet it'll done by tomorrow, right guys?" John asked the two nervous men.

They both nodded fervently and smiled at John. "Yes, yes, that's what we've tried to tell him."

"Well, Carlos? What's the problem?" John asked.

"No problem, I just want them to hurry it up. We have several guests who are complaining about the pool."

"They can go and enjoy the beach today and tomorrow the pool will be filled and ready to go," John said.

Carlos mumbled, "As long as the chemicals are in and it's up to standards."

"It will be, Sir," one of the pool workers said.

John stomped away and came back to me. "Wow, that was an unnecessary argument," John stated.

"Sounds like it," I said. "I need to stop back at our bungalow and grab the beach towels they left in the bathroom, and the sunscreen."

We walked hand in hand down the path to our bungalow. When we arrived the lock was off our door. "What the hell!" John screamed, running inside the bungalow. I followed immediately behind him.

"Who are you?" John demanded of the poor woman standing in the kitchen.

She obviously was terrified by John and went screaming out of our place. "John," I cried out. "She was a cleaning person. Couldn't you tell that?"

"How'd she get *in* here?" he asked, fuming.

"Oh, that's a good point. You had both keys, right?"

"Yes."

"Maybe the housekeeping staff has keys," I suggested.

"It's not even supposed to be locked, Ruth Ann! Carlos had to search for a lock and after our meeting last night he claimed he gave me the only other key."

"I don't know what to say, John. I just want to get out to that beach," I stopped and looked at the turquoise blue Caribbean waters. "Can we stop playing cop for a few days and just go enjoy ourselves?"

John calmed himself and grabbed me by the shoulders. "I agree, Ruth Ann. I'm sorry, it's just in my blood and hard to turn off when we're dealing with such incompetence."

"So, what are you going to do?" I asked, knowing the answer before he tried to explain why he had to search for Carlos again.

"I'm going to get you settled down by the beach. We'll get some lounge chairs, order a Pina colada for you, and then I'll run up to the lobby and find out why a housekeeper had a third key to this old lock."

I knew arguing would get me nowhere so I agreed. We walked a very short distance to the beach. We immediately spotted the numerous lounge chairs with attached umbrellas. John grabbed the closest one to the water and laid out our towels. We snapped them in place with the cute palm tree clips provided to us in our bungalows so the towels wouldn't blow away. "There, I see the Tiki hut where you can order a drink. Do you want me to do it or do you want to?"

"I'll do it. By the time I get us *both* a couple drinks you should be coming back."

John gave me a quick kiss and ran off. I sat down to take in my surroundings. I looked to the right where the Tiki bar was located, and then to the left (or south) where I would be looking for an abandoned rowboat. I couldn't spot it from where I was sitting, but according to Isabella, it wasn't too far down. However, it was the direction we were warned not to wander. I didn't have a choice, I had to find out what made Isabella so terrified when she looked at my necklace. Maybe Axel, Prunella, and I were mistaken about the origins of the Blue Ice.

Chapter 16

I stood up and hurried through the hot, fluffy sand toward the Tiki hut. It was only a short distance away, but I hurried because the bottoms of my feet were burning. "I'll get used to it," I muttered. Once I reached the Tiki hut, I noticed a sign listing the equipment the resort rented out. "Great," I said.

A man hopped off a metal stool from inside the hut and came over to me. "What's great, ma'am?" he asked.

"You rent the paddle boards here, too!"

"Yes, that and kayaks, rowboats, and paddle wheel boats."

"Do you need to reserve them or just come up and get them when you're ready?" I asked, curiously.

"It's best to sign up for one," he suggested, sliding over a clipboard with a sheet of paper attached.

I glanced at the empty sheet and made the second biggest mistake I've made so far. The first being my secret meeting with Isabella later in the day. I filled out John's name and our bungalow number on the paper for a time slot of 1:45 to 2:45. I figured it would give him enough time to get far enough out in the water so I could sneak off. He would see me watching him in the beginning, but then he would get a little further away and figure I was lying on my lounge chair out of his sight. But, I would actually be meeting Isabella down the beach.

I ordered my drink and a local beer for John. I had them stick the beer can in a large cup of ice because, knowing John, it would be flat and warm by the time he came back to our lounge chairs. I rushed through the hot sand on my tippy toes this time to avoid burning the bottoms of my feet. It wasn't as bad this time around, maybe I was getting used to it already.

Just after I lay back down, John came running down the beach. "Hey, that was fast for you!"

"Very funny, Ruth Ann. I know I was gone a long time last night, but this was an easy question for Carlos."

"Did you get the answer you wanted?" I asked.

"He quickly tried to manipulate the conversation and said housekeeping always had keys to any of the locks they've handed out to guests."

"I thought nobody ever locked their doors around here?" I questioned him.

"That's what I asked him," John replied. "He avoided my questions and concerns like a typical salesperson. I made it perfectly clear that there better not be any other keys out there or new issues during our stay. He promised again and again that everything was good."

"So, my thought is to let it go, John. Drink your beer and enjoy the beach and water."

"Oh, I need to find out about those paddle boards," he said, beginning to walk toward the Tiki hut.

"No," I called out to stop him. John stopped, turned and looked at me oddly. "I already handled it, John."

"How?"

"I reserved one for this afternoon," I said, hoping he would be okay with my choice of timing.

"Why so late? I was hoping to get a try at it, and then we can do it together this afternoon."

Quickly, I answered, "It was all booked up." I glanced at him innocently and added, "I hope that's okay with you."

"Oh, okay, it's no big deal. We have plenty of time to try it out if you change your mind." Phew, John accepted my little white lie and laid down on the lounge chair.

"Now, this is what I was looking forward to," he said, taking a large swig of his ice cold beer. "Nice touch, Ruth Ann," he said, sticking his beer back into the cup of ice. "Keeps it nice and cold."

"That was the plan. It's hot out here and I figured it would keep it just the way you liked it."

"You know me so well."

"Yes, John, I do."

We enjoyed the rest of the morning laying out in the hot, Jamaican sun. The breeze kept us cool, but I did have to get my feet wet a few times. John, on the other hand, marched into the water until it was over his head and dunked all the way down. As he walked out he shook his head and the water sprayed out from his thick, graying dark hair. It would've made a wonderful commercial for television! A handsome, graying, but extremely fit man strutting out of the water all wet!

"That felt great," John said, sitting back on the chair. "I'm going to grab another beer. Do you want another drink?"

"Nope, not yet. It's not even noon, I'd better pace myself."

John took off toward the Tiki hut and I hoped he only ordered a beer and didn't look at the empty clipboard. If he did, I would have some explaining to do.

Thankfully, John came back with a smile and another beer inside a new cup of ice. "That's almost too easy," he said, standing over me blocking the sun.

"What's too easy?" I asked. "Can you move a little to the side, please? Your kind of blocking the sun from my bottom half."

John jumped to the side and sat on the end of the lounge chair. "Sorry about that."

I closed my eyes and dozed off a little. The warm sun felt so good it relaxed me completely. The last few days had been so busy, I was finally settling down and it made me a bit sleepy. I could hear John talking away in the distance, but my mind wandered off...

I was alone on the beach searching for John. He was nowhere in sight. Where did he go? I put my hands over my eyes to block the blaring sun, but not a soul was in sight on the beach. What time was it? I tried to reach for my cell phone, but realized I left it back in the bungalow. Now what? I wasn't exactly sure where I was when the older woman I just left in the grass shack surprised me from behind...

"Ruth Ann!" I heard a strong voice calling my name. "Ruth Ann, wake up!"

I slowly opened my eyes and John's face was about two inches from my own. "What are you doing?" I snapped. "I just took a little nap."

"You were out cold! I didn't know you were so tired. You could've slept in a little later this morning," John said, concerned about my sudden drowsiness.

"I'm fine, John," I said, sitting up on the lounge chair. "I finally relaxed, isn't that what you've been saying I needed to do for weeks?"

"Um, yes, I guess I have," he said.

"It was such a busy week and traveling yesterday was tiring. The warm sun on my body totally relaxed me, but I'm feeling terrific now!"

"Great," John said. "Why don't we get some lunch and then we'll come back here before my paddle board time."

We left our towels on our chairs and headed up to the restaurant. I still had my swim skirt on and I checked to make sure the necklace was still inside. I put it in there so I didn't get a big emerald shaped suntan on my neck or scare off another employee. Once I felt the piece inside, I relaxed a little more and dove into a hearty lunch of salad, chips and guacamole, and a huge chocolate frosted cupcake. At least it wasn't too jiggly this time so I was able to eat the entire cupcake. Still not as good as my daughters, but doable.

"I'm stuffed," I said. "There's something about guacamole that fills me up."

"You ate enough of it, that may be why, too," John said, laughing.

"Very funny, John. I do seem to overdo it when it comes to chips and guacamole. That's why I balanced it out with a salad."

"Whatever makes you feel better," John said, finishing the last of his cheeseburger. "Let's stop off at the bungalow so I can use the bathroom before we head back to the beach."

"Sounds good," I said.

We walked past the pool and noticed fresh water was already filling up the cleaned pool. "That'll be nice to have a pool to float around in, too," I said, pointing toward the pool.

"Carlos sure got those two workers moving. It looks pretty good so far."

We unlocked the bungalow and noticed it was untouched. John's threats must've finally worked. If anyone was going to enter our bungalow, John would have to open it up for them. I wondered how they were going to clean the place, but for the time we're here, it didn't really matter too much.

"It's a little after one, what time am I booked for with the paddle board, Ruth Ann?"

"1:45-2:45," I replied, suddenly feeling a surge of anxiety. I realized the time was coming closer for when I had to meet up with Isabella. I didn't spot her in the restaurant at lunch, but maybe she was working at another part in the resort.

"Okay, I'm going to take a little swim in the water to loosen up. Want to join me?"

"Nope, I'm good right here," I said, lying back down on the lounge chair. "I'm going to get a drink soon, and then I'll watch you paddle board for a while."

John ran over the hot sand with his bare feet and splashed his way into deeper water. I watched as he swam back and forth a little and I had a moment where I thought I'd go out and join him. I wasn't fond of going in water higher than my waist. I loved to look at, float in, wade around in, but not swim in water. The feeling of a fish or whatever touching my legs or feet petrifies me. What if I stepped on one of those jellyfish?

As I lay there watching John play around in the water, I remembered the dream I was having before he woke me up. It was that same eerie dream I had before where I felt very uneasy, like something evil was about to happen. I must be subconsciously worrying about what Martika had said about my necklace being cursed. That was nonsense! Sure, we've had a lot of issues regarding it, but if I really thought about it, I can't say it was cursed. It may be a nuisance for anyone who had possession of it. Even now, it's a bit of a nuisance having it here with me. I really wished I didn't let Axel and Prunella convince me to bring it. It's nonsense that John thinks there may have been an ulterior motive. That's just the cop in him talking.

I brushed off the dream and told myself to enjoy the moment. These next few days were going to fly by, and who knows when we'll get to do this again. Little did I know that I should have definitely listened to my subconscious!

Chapter 17

John grabbed his towel and wiped himself dry. "Well, wish me luck," he said as he headed toward the Tiki hut to begin his time on the paddle board. I was going to make sure he could see me watching him for a while before I headed down the beach to meet Isabella.

I waited for him to get into the water with the board before I stood up and made my way to the water's edge. Once he was on the board, I noticed it wasn't as easy as it looked. John must've fallen off five times before he regained his balance and started moving along the water with the paddles. He tried to wave at me once, but landed smack dab in the water again. I laughed as I waded through the warm water following him for a little while. I was happy he was going the opposite direction I was about to go. I was worried a little that he would be going south instead of north. John definitely remembered not to go that direction since we were warned to stay away from going south. I obviously am not as good as a listener!

Once he was off and paddling, I headed back to my lounge chair. I looked at the time on John's watch under the chair. It was a little after 2:00, time to go. I needed to hurry so I would be back before John finished at 2:45.

I grabbed my cover up skirt and slipped it on over my suit. I grabbed a little purse I stuffed inside my beach bag and put the necklace in it and headed to the left down the beach. There weren't many people around us, but as I walked down the fluffy, dry sand I noticed fewer and fewer people. It took me about five minutes to realize I was definitely off the resort's property. The atmosphere changed from the clean, fluffy sand and beach umbrellas with lounge chairs to darker sand with crushed seashells and lots of rocks.

I was getting more and more anxious until I spotted the deserted rowboat. I didn't see anyone around, except for a couple of grass shacks here and there. I wasn't sure if people lived in those shacks or if they were used to store beach items or equipment. A chill ran up my spine when I remembered my first dream of being on a beach with a grass shack and an older lady appeared. Nonsense! It was just a dream.

I made it up to the rowboat and hoped Isabella would be here shortly. I didn't want this to take too long. John would have a complete meltdown if he knew what I was up to.

As I waited for Isabella, I looked at the upside down rowboat and wondered why it was here. There was a massive hole in the side, seaweed covered most of the bottom and a few creatures looked to be hiding inside it. I jumped about two feet off the ground when a little crab scurried over my foot and made its way underneath the boat.

I was about to sit down when I heard a crunch or two coming from the jungle near where I was standing. Isabella appeared from the deep jungle's edge. Before she came into the open beach, she looked around frantically. What was she so nervous about? I waved to her with a smile on my face hoping she wouldn't be so afraid.

"Ruth Ann," she said, huffing and puffing from running through the sand toward me.

"Hi, Isabella!" I called out loud and happy.

"Shhh," she said, still looking around to see if anyone was watching.

"Why?" I asked, curiously. "There's nobody around, and I was told I shouldn't be down this way."

Her eyes opened alarmingly wide and said, "Who did you tell you were meeting me here?"

"Nobody," I said, quickly. "We were told when we checked in to stay on the resort's property and not to wander south. He said it was dangerous down this way."

"It is, it is," she said, quietly. "We need to find a secluded spot. Follow me," she said, waving her hand for me to follow. I wasn't sure it was the wisest thing to do, but I needed to get to the bottom of this.

She turned toward one of the sporadically placed grass huts and went inside. There was no door on it, but strings of beads that dropped down and jangled when she went inside. I froze on the outside of the shack. Should I go in there? There was a familiar feeling about this shack, like the one in my dream. However, Isabella was a young woman and the woman in my dream was much, much older.

I pushed the beads aside and entered. The air was warm and extremely stuffy. Not good for a woman of my age. I had to make this meeting end quickly. It took a minute to adjust my eyes from the bright sun into the darkened shack. Once I got my sight back, I spotted Isabella sitting on a little wooden chair next to an old square shaped table. She motioned for me to sit in the chair opposite her.

"Why did we have to come in here?" I asked, curiously. "Are you afraid of being spotted by anyone in particular?"

Isabella bent over the table as if she didn't want to be overheard by anyone, even though we were alone. "I don't have much time, Ms. Ruth Ann, but what I have to tell you could change your life forever!"

"First," I said, wondering if this was some kind of trick John was playing on me. "Call me Ruth Ann, skip the Ms., okay?"

"Yes, yes," she said, rushed. "Did you bring the…the piece?"

"Why do you need to know that?" I asked, suddenly worried that I was going to be robbed and not given important information. Did I just fall into their trap?

"I ask because I don't want to see it. I've already risked enough seeing it the first time."

"Risked what? I'm confused, Isabella. What is so terrifying about it?"

"It's cursed, it's evil, it needs to be destroyed!" she cried out loudly, then throwing her hands over her mouth to stop her from spewing out more words.

"Nonsense," I said, trying to remain calm as she was becoming agitated. "Tell me why you believe it's cursed!"

"I don't have enough time to tell you the whole story, but I will tell you what I can."

"Please, and hurry. You're not the only one who's not supposed to be here. If John caught me going off on my own and walking into a strange grass shack, he'd ship me back to Colorado!"

"Colorado?" she asked, confused. "Is that in America?"

I looked at her, stunned. "Don't you know that?"

"No, no, I don't know much about other countries. I was taught by my grandmother, and she's the one who..." Isabella stopped talking and threw her hands over her mouth again.

"Who what?" I asked. "Is this all about your grandmother and what she's taught you?"

"Yes, I've heard many stories about local traditions and curses from my grandmother. She was my teacher, but not in the traditional sense. That's why I don't know a lot about schooling. I never went to an actual school. My grandmother taught me things she felt I needed to learn to survive here, in my country."

"But isn't it required by law that you go to school up to a certain age?" I asked, surprised at her ignorance.

"No, not here," she replied. "I, I was taught to work hard, stay loyal to my family, and marry the man I was told to."

"By whom?" I asked.

"My grandmother picked out my future husband."

"What! Why? And did you marry this man?" I asked, horrified at this poor girl's upbringing.

"No, no, I ran away and came to this resort where I met Martika. She took me in and gave me a job and a place to stay until I make some money. Then I plan on leaving this place, it's evil!"

"Evil?"

"Yes, there's many bad people around here. That's why I needed to speak with you. If anyone else from around here finds out about that necklace of yours, they will seek you out and kill you for it!"

"That's ridiculous!" I exclaimed. "You need to explain more, Isabella because this makes no sense."

"Please, listen to me and go home. I think it's already too late. If I spotted you in the necklace, and Martika did, then others may have, too."

"But you haven't told me why the gem is cursed and so evil?"

She stood up, peeked through the string of beads and came back and sat down. "Okay, we're still alone."

"Who else would come in here?" I asked, worried. "Does this shack belong to someone else?"

"Yes. Locals come here and meet privately at night. Nobody dares come here when certain people are staying here. They are bad people, Ruth Ann."

"Then why did we meet here?" I asked, irritated at this naïve girl.

"Because it's still daylight. The only one that ever comes here is this old lady."

"Wait, what did you just say?" I said, panicked. That old woman couldn't possibly be the woman from my dreams!

"There's an older lady, known to locals as a witch doctor."

I interrupted her and shouted, "a witch doctor!"

"Shhh, please, we don't want to be found. Especially if you're carrying that necklace in that purse of yours!"

"How'd you know I would be carrying it with me?" I asked, nervously.

"Because I feel it's presence," she said, holding her hands crossed over her heart. "My grandmother taught me that your body can sense when there's evil or goodness surrounding you."

"Maybe what you're feeling is goodness, and not evil."

"No, no, you need to listen and trust me," she said, panicking. "You and your boyfriend need to pack up and leave, today! Otherwise, you won't be safe here."

"But we won't leave the resort property, and then we'll be safe, right?"

"No!" she shrieked.

"Look, Isabella, I don't know what's going on around here, but where I'm from this would be considered ridiculous. If you don't tell me exactly why you think we're in trouble, then I'm done here." I stood up to leave, but she grabbed my arm.

I looked down at her trembling hand and halted. "Please, Ruth Ann. I will tell you a little." I sat back down and waited for her to explain. "My grandmother taught me things that have been outlawed for many, many years. There used to be people here, called…" she hesitated, scared to say the next word. "Obeahs."

"Obeahs?" I asked, never hearing the word before. "What, like a witch doctor or voodoo person?"

"Yes, but much, much worse. The government banned the practices of Obeah's long time ago, but that doesn't mean they don't exist."

"Tell me about these people, Isabella," I asked, now very curious where she was going with this.

"They practiced evil magic, sorcery, and potion making. The Obeahs used their supernatural powers to inflict torture, pain, and even death upon their enemies."

"That sounds like something that would've occurred centuries ago!" I said.

"Yes, but they're still around. My grandmother knows them. She is well known in my area for curing for those who have been sickened by an Obeah."

"This is unbelievable. You believe all this stuff?"

"Of course, it's true, Ruth Ann. You may need to be cured by one, too."

"Me?" I asked, shocked. "Why would I need a witch doctor to cure me? I didn't do anything wrong!"

"No, but this is when you need to listen closely to what I have to say." I nodded, enthusiastically. "My grandmother helps people get rid of their curses in many ways. She can help cursed people with her potions or even something as simple as a strand of hair or article of clothing to ward off the Obeah man."

"Okay, I understand what you're saying. One Obeah can ward off another Obeah's curses using potions or hair or clothing, but what does this have to do with my gem?"

"Ah, so you understand what my grandmother really is," she said smiling, but not a sweet smile. A more fiendish grin crossed her face.

"Your grandmother's an Obeah, but you didn't want to say it because what she does is illegal, right?"

"Yes, you do understand. That's why I know what I'm talking about."

"Wait a minute!" I cried out. "If you were taught by your grandmother, then that makes you an Obeah, too!"

"NO!" she shouted, but snapped her mouth shut.

"I don't understand," I said. "You seem to know everything about it, and you were taught by your grandmother. So, you tell me what I'm supposed to think?"

She lowered her head and spoke softly. "I disgraced my family so I had to leave."

"You didn't leave just because you didn't want to marry the man you were arranged to wed, right?" I asked, suddenly understanding this woman.

"No. I disgraced her by not wanting to follow her practice."

"You mean her practicing witchcraft or voodoo? Whatever it's called," I said, frustrated.

"Yes. You can call it what you want, it's wrong and against our laws, but for people who have lived here their whole lives, it's a part of their heritage."

"Just because your grandmother practiced it, doesn't mean you have to."

"It doesn't work that way down here, Ruth Ann," Isabella said. "I was born into it. I have the powers."

"Powers! What does that mean?" I asked, a little nervous for myself at the moment.

"Did you hear me when I told you I felt the necklace was with you?"

"Yes."

"It's because my grandmother passed down her powers to me."

"That's ridiculous!" I snapped. "You can't do that, can you?"

"If I showed any signs of having supernatural powers, I could take over my grandmother's practice once she passes on. But I don't want to, I hate having this power!"

"Then walk away from it and never look back," I said, realizing I might be venturing in an area I wasn't qualified for.

"I can't. It will haunt me for the rest of my life. My grandmother isn't well, she's sent my brothers to look for me, but I've been hiding out here. That's why I didn't want to be seen on the beach. I feel their presence getting closer and closer to me."

"Wow, this is unbelievable!" I said, but added, "But I don't see how that fits into the curse on my necklace."

"There's a lot more to this than we have time. But briefly, your gem, that beautiful blue emerald gem, was once used by an Obeah man to release a curse made from another Obeah man. That is one of the only ways to break an Obeah's curse."

"With another Obeah man's curse?" I asked, confused.

"Yes, yes, I know it's confusing, but your gem is very old. It may go back to the 1700's if I'm correct. I think the curse was never broken and until it is, it's a very dangerous piece to be wearing around here."

"Really?" I questioned her. "If you're right, what am I supposed to do?"

"I want to help you, but I can't. I'm not qualified to do it, yet. But if you want my advice," she waited for my response so I nodded frantically. "Then leave here and never come back here!"

"But how can I just up and leave? John will wonder what's wrong?"

"You need to go. I have a really bad feeling right now. Something bad is about to happen. GO!"

I didn't wait for her to tell me again. I jumped out of my chair and started to run out of the shack when I stopped, turned and asked, "Will I see you again? Will you be able to help me?"

"I don't know," the panicked girl replied. "Just go!" I ran out of the grass shack and headed toward the water's edge so I could make my way back to John, but I suddenly stopped, frozen in my stance.

I slowly turned around and noticed one of the other grass shacks. I had the strangest feeling I had been there before. I knew I should've run and kept running until I made it back to my comfy lounge chair. I couldn't help myself, I walked up to the entrance to this shack and was about to pull aside the string of beads when a voice called out from inside. "Come in, Madame, come in!"

The raspy voice came from an older woman. It must be the witch doctor, her grandmother. I panicked and took off toward the resort's beach without looking back.

I wanted to forget everything Isabella told me. I didn't know if I'd ever see her again. Maybe she was so scared now that Martika wouldn't allow her to work at the resort anymore. And what about Martika? How much does this 'hostess' really know about Isabella and her grandmother!

It didn't take long before I reached the resort's beach. I frantically looked out at the water and spotted John paddling his way back toward me from the opposite direction. "Whew, that was close," I said out loud.

He didn't even know I was gone. I wondered if it was difficult to paddle his way back with the current. That had to be the only reason he was gone for so long.

I walked along the water's edge trying to calm myself down. I noticed the waves had picked up since I'd been gone and it looked like John was struggling a bit to get back to where I stood. He was pretty far out when I noticed a large wave approaching him. I tried to scream out to him to watch out, but he couldn't hear me. In fact, he didn't see it hit him until it was too late!

Chapter 18

"John," I screamed as loud as I could. "Watch out!"

Too late, the wave hit John hard and he went flying off the paddle board and disappeared into the deep, rough water. I ran out a few feet trying to figure out what to do. I was hoping he was just underwater for a second or two and was not knocked unconscious by the board.

I desperately searched around for someone to help me when I noticed there wasn't anyone around. All I could do was watch as I ran over to the Tiki hut to get some help, but before I could a young man came running up to me asking what my problem was.

"My friend got knocked off his paddle board from a monstrous wave and he hasn't reappeared yet!"

The twenty-something man put his hand up to shield his eyes and peered out into the water. "I'm sure he's fine, ma'am, it's hard to see way out there. He's probably trying to get back to his board. Give him a minute."

"He might not have a minute!" I yelled, trying to get him to swim out there to save John.

"I'll go out there if I don't see him in a second. Don't panic, it makes things worse," he snapped.

"Panic! He may drown!" I wish I had learned to swim better because I wouldn't have hesitated rushing out there to find him.

Once the young man paced back and forth along the edge of the water and realized John was nowhere in sight, he called for one of his friends who was hanging out closer to the Tiki hut. The kid hurried over to him and they told me to stay back, they'll find him.

I watched as the two young, physically fit men swam out and searched around the empty paddle board. The second young man hopped up on the paddle board searching around him, while the other man dove down, and then reappeared, dove back down, and then reappeared. The once calm young men appeared to be panicking themselves now. What was happening! An hour ago we were enjoying our vacation sipping a few cocktails on the beach, and now…

"I'm sorry, ma'am," the out of breath young man said to me as he exited the water. "We searched all over the place. Are you sure he didn't swim to safety and you haven't spotted him?"

"NO!" I shouted. "He has to be out there! We need to call for help!" I screamed looking around me as a few stragglers came around us. "Does anyone know what I should do?"

"Ruth Ann!" A voice from a distance called out my name. I whipped my head around in hopes in would be John, but it wasn't.

"Carlos," I said exasperated. "I need your help!"

"I heard what happened. I've already contacted the local police, and they're on their way."

"Police?" I questioned him. "What good will they do?"

"They'll do a complete search of the water and grounds near here. We will find him," Carlos said calmly, but with a tone that hinted more at recovery than rescue.

"He's not dead!" I screamed, beginning to cry. "He knows how to swim and all he did was fall off a paddle board!"

"I heard he got knocked down by a wave, Ruth Ann. Maybe he hit his head on the board and couldn't get himself above water."

"Don't say that!"

"I'm sorry. You're right, we don't know if anything bad has happened to him. Why don't you go sit down on your chair for a moment? You look like you could pass out yourself."

"I will not sit until I see John standing next to me!" I declared. "I'm going to get one of those kayaks and take it out there. Maybe we just can't see him and he needs our help!"

Carlos grabbed my arm gently and pulled me away from the water's edge. "No, I need to stay here so he can see me when he gets out of the water."

"Ruth Ann, let us search. We'll come get you the minute we hear anything or find John. He's a tough, strong man. I'm sure he's fine," Carlos said, eyeing the other workers that arrived on the seen with much less confidence than he was expressing to me. I suddenly felt the weight of the world on my shoulders. I couldn't walk, talk or function anymore. I let Carlos lead me to my lounge chair and I sat in the middle of it staring out at the water. "Please, John," I begged over and over again. "Come back to me!"

I sat and watched as if it was a horrible nightmare. The local police and rescue squad arrived quickly. There were boats and men yelling around me and the water, but I couldn't react. I wanted to rewind the last two days and put me back in Deer Creek with my daughters and Prunella. I promised myself I would butt out of their lives unless they specifically asked me for help. I prayed and prayed with my eyes tightly shut until I heard a voice, Carlos', calling my name. "Ruth Ann, are you alright?"

I lifted my head and opened my eyes. "Please tell me you found him, alive?"

Carlos shook his head and that's when I spotted another man behind him. He was holding one of those old fashioned doctor's bags. "Who are you?" I asked him.

"I'm Joseph," he said kindly. "Carlos contacted me right away when he found out about your friend."

"Are you some kind of doctor?"

"Yes, I help out at the resort if they need me. I'm here to help you now, Ruth Ann," he said, kneeling down to eye level with me.

"Help me?" I asked, realizing what was happening now. "I don't need any help! John might need your help, but not me!"

"We haven't been able to locate John, yet. I thought I might be able to help you if you'd like something to help calm your nerves."

"You want to *drug* me?" I asked, stupefied.

"Just a mild sedative, that's all."

"That's the last thing I need right now! I want to stay alert and awake until I find John!"

"That may take some time," Dr. Joseph said. "Let me take you to your bungalow. If you don't want anything to help you, I can stay with you until we get word."

"Word?" I asked, angrily. "So, you think he's dead, don't you?"

Carlos and Joseph eyed each other suspiciously, and then Carlos jumped in before Joseph and said, "We don't know that, Ruth Ann. Let us conduct a full search of the area and the water. Maybe he floated down the water in the current and he got out of the water. If the board hit his head, maybe he doesn't have the capability of getting back here."

I thought about what Carlos said, and then I remembered what Isabella just told me not too long ago. She *felt* something bad was going to happen. She knew it! I had to go find her.

I stood up and told Carlos I needed to do my own search. He protested and wanted to send some men with me, but I flatly refused. I needed to do this on my own, but I told them to not give up looking and I'd be back soon.

I didn't leave Carlos or Joseph enough time to argue with me. I hurried through the sand and headed back to the grass shacks I recently ran away from in fear. Fear. Fear was now the thought of losing John, not some stupid curse about a gem that may or may not have originated from here. In fact, I forgot to grab my little purse out of the beach bag. I don't know what came over me, but I turned around and marched through the sand back to them and didn't say a word, but reached inside my beach bag and grabbed the small purse. I turned and hurried back down toward the water not only because it was easier to walk in, but maybe John would see me.

A few minutes into my walk down the beach, I felt a surge of anxiety run through my body. I was alone, all alone. I'm in a strange country with voodoo and witch doctors, and a rundown resort in the midst of a renovation with an owner that I didn't quite trust. I was confused, terrified, and on my way to find a young woman whose grandmother practiced a long forgotten profession of witchcraft and voodoo. What did Isabella call the person who practiced this? Ah, it was an Obeah man (or woman?).

I looked behind me but couldn't see the commotion that was happening at our resort's beach. I could hear activity out in the water. The motor boats were numerous and even a distant yell here or there, but nothing I heard signaled they found John.

I went around the small bend just before coming upon the broken down row boat. I looked over at a few of the grass shacks that were spread out and ran up to the one I was in with Isabella. I threw the beads aside and stumbled inside the darkened room. I was momentarily blinded from the change of brightness. I blinked several times to adjust, and when I did, I didn't expect to see who was already inside, and apparently waiting for me.

"Ah, so you've returned," the old woman said with a slow, soft tone.

"Oh," I blurted out ready to turn and run to another shack. Maybe I went to the wrong shack and mistakenly entered the old woman's place of business.

"Don't leave, Ruth Ann," she begged.

"Wait," I said, suddenly not afraid of her anymore. "How did you know my name? I've never met you before!"

"Ah, but you have," she said with a sly look in her face. "Think about it, Ruth Ann."

I stood frozen just inside the square room with its rock hard sand floor. Why was she saying I've met her before? I've only been in this country since yesterday and the only people I've met have been workers at the resort. The resort! If we only had our original reservations at the first, luxurious place none of this would've have happened. I wouldn't have met Isabella, and I would never have wandered off on my own to investigate a silly claim about curses and evil Obeah people!

"I don't know you!" I protested. "Why would you say we've met?"

"You're not opening your mind, Ruth Ann. Think back, we've come face to face before today." She watched me intently until the most bizarre thought entered my brain. It couldn't be! She reminded me of the woman I dreamed about before John and I came here, but that's impossible. It was just a dream I had a couple nights ago back in my bed in Deer Creek.

"Ah, I see you're finally thinking about it and if I can read you correctly, you've remembered where we've met."

"We never met. I had a dream a few nights ago far away from here."

"And…" the old woman said, nudging me to go on.

"And what?" I stammered. "We never spoke, I just had a few strange dreams about being alone on a beach and seeing an older woman in a grass shack. It's just coincidence, pure and simple."

"Nothing pure or simple about it, Ruth Ann," she said, changing her kind tone to a crosser one.

"Please, I really don't have time for this! I…" the old woman stopped me and motioned me to sit down with a wave of her arm. I followed her motion to a rickety old wooden table and chairs. I was in here before! Isabella told me earlier that other business took place in here, but I swore she told me that happened late at night. She also told me it was the kind of business I should stay away from.

"Please, who are you and why are you stopping me? I need to find the younger woman I spoke with here a short time ago."

"Isabella."

I was stunned. The older woman smiled and showed her unkempt teeth, or lack thereof, and the strangest sound came from her mouth. A laugh? Words couldn't describe the sound that sent chills up and down my spine. I actually pinched my arm to see if I could feel it because I had to be dreaming again. This could not be real. "Ouch!" I bellowed.

"Why did you do that to yourself?" the woman asked me curiously. "Oh, wait, you believe you're dreaming again, don't you?"

"Why, yes," I replied. "But I don't think you can feel pain in your own dreams, can you?"

"You're not dreaming, Ruth Ann. You were destined to come back here."

"Destined how?" I asked, wondering why I was still in here speaking with this woman. She wasn't going to help me find John.

"Isabella warned you that something bad was about to happen, didn't she?"

I looked at her oddly and replied, "Maybe."

The old lady leaned her hands on the table and hoisted herself up from the chair. I watched as she reached around her back with her wrinkled, withered hands and tried to straighten her back. She moaned, shook her head in disgust, and walked with an obvious limp toward me. She took a hold of my left forearm and, with more force than I thought possible, led me back to the table and pretty much pushed me into one of the empty chairs. The force was strong enough for the chair to waver backward and tipped the two front legs. I grabbed hold of the table to steady back to level ground.

When I looked up, she already had sat in the chair to my right. "Now, Ruth Ann. We're not going to get anywhere if you don't open up with me."

"I don't even know you!" I argued. "I don't have time to discuss my necklace! My boyfriend is missing!"

"Ah, the *Blue Ice*," she said, giving me a peculiar grin. "However did you name that? I see the color part of it, but where did the ice part come from?"

What did this woman just say? How did she know Prunella and I named the necklace, *Blue Ice*? I stared over at her and she sensed the wheels in my brain working. "Yes, I know the name of the necklace."

"But, how?" I asked, stupefied. "I've never even mentioned the necklace to you so how would you know the name we gave it?"

"Isabella informed me of its presence last night."

"Last night?" I questioned her, and then it hit me. It was only last night when John and I were having dinner and Isabella spotted me wearing the necklace. She freaked out and ran off leaving us with Martika. Martika explained how Isabella believed in curses and she felt evil when she saw my necklace. "So, Isabella ran to *you* after she saw me wearing the necklace, didn't she?"

"Yes, she did."

"But why? And who are you exactly?" I asked, trying to figure if any of this had something to do with what happened to John.

"Isabella is young, but very powerful. She hasn't realized the enormous power she has. It scares her, so she came to me for help."

"You didn't answer my other questions. Who are you?" I demanded.

"I'm Isabella's grandmother. You can call me Meme."

"Meme?" I asked, dumbfounded. I lowered my head and put it in my hands and shook it back and forth. This can't be happening…wake up! I have to be living in some bizarre dream. I thought this old woman told me to call her Meme. My great aunt's nickname was Meme, short for Irene, and my assistant at my antique store is Meme. If this woman says her name is Irene I'm going to drive myself to the nearest hospital and check myself in for observation.

"It's a family name, Ruth Ann. I'm sure you've known other strong, women named Meme!"

"No, well yes, but it wasn't her real name. It was what we called her."

"I know. It was her nickname," the old woman, Meme declared. "Are you starting to believe that I have a power your rational mind can't explain?"

I nodded my head in silence. I couldn't talk anymore. This woman had said things only my family should know. Plus, she knew that something bad was going to happen today. I gathered my wits together and blurted out, surprising myself, "I believe you! Please, tell me what I need to do now."

"Finally, can we both agree your doubts have been squashed?" Meme asked me.

"Yes, yes, please...what happened to John? I don't care about the necklace now. Just help me find John!" I begged of the old woman. "You're a witch doctor, right?"

"Oh, no, no. Don't call me that," she said, offended at the title I gave her.

"I'm sorry, but Isabella told me about you. She said you raised her and tried to force her to marry a man she didn't want to. She also said you wanted her to take over your practice since you were getting older."

"I did want her to marry. She has a good chance of passing her powers to her offspring. If she doesn't marry and have children, then our family heritage dies along with it! You need to understand how important that is."

"I do, I do, Meme, but right now isn't the time to worry about that," I said, pleading with her to stop worrying about Isabella and who she will or won't marry.

"Isabella's destiny is already put in place. She's just frightened right now. She'll come around, and you can help her."

"Please, Meme! I promise I will do whatever I can to help you and your granddaughter, but after we locate John."

"The two intertwine, Ruth Ann. Don't you get it?

"No," I screamed in frustration. I tried to calm myself by taking a few deep breaths. Then it dawned on me! "Wait a minute! Isabella told me she ran away from you, and her brothers are trying to find her right now. Now you're telling me she ran to you last night for help?"

"She lied to you."

"But why? I didn't do anything to her that would cause her to lie to me."

"She panicked."

"No, no," I bellowed. "She was scared last night when she first saw me wearing the necklace, but today, she seemed concerned about me."

"How was she concerned about *you*?" Meme inquired.

"She knew I only met her to find out why she was so terrified of the gem. When I told her I didn't really believe in all this...curse stuff, she became agitated and told me about her past and how she knew the gem was still cursed. She told me if I wouldn't do anything about it, that I should leave here right away and never come back."

"And you didn't believe her after she told you all that?"

"No, well, she did scare me, but I was confused about what she told me about my necklace. Or I should say the gem inside the setting, that is supposedly from Jamaica. I told her it was from...," the woman held her hand up to silence me.

"Sweden," she stated, finishing my sentence.

"Yes," I said, wondering if I needed to say anything at all. This woman was basically reading my mind and I didn't like it.

"You may have retrieved the gem from Sweden, but it is originally from down here."

"But how do you know that for sure?" I asked, tired of this conversation. "I mean; I haven't showed *you* the gem yet. Maybe you'll have a totally different reading from it."

"Why don't you pull it out of that purse of yours and show me?" she asked eagerly.

"Not until you tell me if John's still alive!" I demanded first.

The old woman stared me down, but I wasn't going to budge. "I can tell you this," she started to say slowly. "John did not drown. He's a strong man, and a little wave could not kill him."

"But then where is he?" I exclaimed in frustration. "He would've appeared by now, and he would never leave me hanging like this!"

"He didn't have a choice, Ruth Ann."

"What do you mean by that?" I ordered.

"Show me the gem."

I unzipped my small travel purse and noticed the old woman watching me with unhinged anticipation. I thought I saw a bit of drool fall down her chin. I pulled out the piece of tissue that I had wrapped it in to keep it concealed and laid it on the table. A set of crooked fingers reached across the table to take hold of it, but I slapped my hand over it. "Not so fast, Meme," I said, sliding the piece closer to me.

"But you made a deal with me."

"I will show it to you, in a moment. I need you to answer one more thing first." The old woman nodded. "If John didn't drown, and he's still alive, is he with Isabella or her brothers?"

"Ah, why would you ask that question?" she asked, impressed at my deduction.

"Because you just told me that Isabella and what happened to John were 'intertwined'."

"You listened closely, Ruth Ann. I know when a person's in severe distress, sometimes your focus becomes tunnel visioned. I will tell you that you are correct."

"Correct, meaning that John's with Isabella or John's with her brothers?" I asked, trying to figure out if my boyfriend had been kidnapped.

Meme held out her wrinkled old hand and said, "Hand me the necklace, Ruth Ann."

There was a finality in her tone. I wasn't going to get any more information until I let this Obeah woman hold my Blue Ice. I nodded and slid the piece of tissue over to her. She eagerly grabbed it from me and held the unseen piece in her hand. "I've waited a long time to see this again."

Again! What did she mean when she said *again*! I thought this piece had been in Prunella, Axel's, and my family for over a hundred years. How could she have seen this before? Only two answers popped into my head. The first, she'd been to Sweden at some point and somehow made her way into Axel and Prunella's life or she was over a hundred years old and the gem was actually here in Jamaica before it made its way to Sweden. I contemplated asking her, but she probably already knew what I was thinking.

I noticed she wasn't looking at me anyway. Maybe she wasn't reading my mind at the moment because she was completely obsessed with the tissue that laid in her hand. I watched as she took her other hand and slowly unwrapped the tissue and reached inside and grabbed a hold of the white gold chain the gem was attached to. Her eyes glistened when she took sight of the crystal clear blue gem. I watched her intently as her lips formed a smile I didn't think she could form. "Finally," she whispered as if speaking directly to the stone. "You've come home."

"Oh, no it hasn't!" I exclaimed. "It's my necklace, and the only home it has is with me in Deer Creek!"

The old woman didn't take her eyes off the stone. "You don't understand, Ruth Ann. There's a lot more to this than a piece of jewelry."

"What are you talking about?" I demanded.

"Ruth Ann, did you understand what Isabella told you about curses and the outlawed Obeah's?"

"Kind of, I guess. I figured most people would refer to you as a witch doctor since the Obeah practice has been illegal for hundreds of years."

"Yes, yes, you did hear that part. What about the reason for a person to contract an Obeah man? Do you know why?"

"No, and to be perfectly honest, I don't really care." I became agitated and ordered, "Now, tell me who has John? I showed you my necklace, now you tell me where he is!" I reached over the table to take back my necklace, but she snapped her hand shut.

"Not so fast, Ruth Ann. I understand you believe this is your family's piece, but it's not. I need to finish something that was started long ago, before you were born."

"Hand it over, Meme or I'll drag you down the beach to the police that are swarming all over the place searching for John!"

"No, you won't," she said, reopening her hand and glaring at the necklace. "If you do, you'll never see John again."

"So, you're threatening me?"

"No. I just think you value John's life more than this necklace," she said, holding it up in the air giving me a chance to rip it out of her hands, but for some unknown reason I didn't. I started thinking this woman was trying to control my mind!

Just as I snapped out of it, I lunged at Meme and grabbed the white gold chain hanging from her weak hand. "Got it!" I yelled, but was immediately interrupted by several men who stormed their way into the shack. I froze with the necklace firmly in the middle of my palm. I closed my fingers and made a tight fist. "What's going on?" I yelled as the men parted for a familiar face who just entered inside.

"Carlos!" I exclaimed. "How'd you find me?"

"Ruth Ann," he said with authority. "We need to leave, right now!"

"But, how did you find me?" I asked, fearing he might've searched the area to tell me they found John's body.

Carlos walked over to the old woman and sputtered out some words I couldn't hear or understand. She argued back with such ferociousness I thought the two of them were going to battle each other. She tried to stand, but he shoved her back in her chair. He ordered her to stay, that much I understood, and grabbed my arm and led me out into the blinding sun.

"What did you say to her?" I demanded. "She's a harmless old woman, Carlos."

"Harmless?" he questioned my inquiry. "She's a snake, and you have to promise me you'll never come back or try to find her again!"

I shoved my necklace into my swim skirt's pocket. I didn't want Carlos to see it. I wasn't sure if he was trustworthy anymore.

"Ruth Ann, you don't understand the local's ways around here. Some are very modernized, but some..." he hesitated and crossed himself. "Some, still believe in evil ways. You need to trust me about her. Stay away from her."

"Do you know who she is?" I asked, wondering if he knew one of his waitresses was her granddaughter.

"I know more than you need to," he said. "Let's get back on our property. It's not safe over here. Weren't you warned about going off on your own?"

"Yes, but after John and my..." I stopped, pretended to cough to cover what I almost confessed about my necklace.

"We never found a body," he said, coldly. "He may have swum for safety and we haven't located him yet."

"He's alive!" I insisted. "Meme told me he didn't drown!"

"Meme?" he asked suspiciously. "The old woman?"

'Yes, her name's Meme."

"Hmm," he said quietly.

I turned around and spotted the old woman standing in the entrance to her shack. She nodded her head and mouthed very clearly, "You'll be back." I watched as she turned around and went back inside the little grass shack.

I wasn't in the mood to argue with Carlos about her name or what she told me. I was curious, however, about Carlos' knowledge of Isabella. I waited until we were back to the resort's beach when I asked if him if the police escort from Meme's was necessary.

"We didn't know where you went, Ruth Ann. There's a lot of crime and strange things that happen down the beach to the south. We've warned all our guests to stay on the property or only head north. That's where all the other resorts are located, and they're usually very safe."

"*Usually?*" I questioned him. "We weren't told that!"

"There's always the occasional theft here or there. It happens everywhere!"

"Forget about all this for now. Tell me what you're doing to find John?" I demanded.

"We have the local police looking for him up and down the beach. I think we should take you up to your bungalow and have Dr. Joseph check you out."

"I'm fine!" I declared. "I don't need a doctor. Why would you think I needed a doctor? John's the one who's hurt!"

"Sit down then," he said, pointing to my lounge chair. I did as he asked and waited for him to continue. He looked around to see who could be listening. When we were alone, he said, "Ruth Ann, we don't have a lot of police here. It's not like back in the states where you can call in help from surrounding towns. I'm afraid that if we don't find any indication that your friend made it to the beach, they will assume he was…" he stopped, swallowed hard and said, "eaten or down at the bottom of the sea."

I jumped up and yelled, "Absolutely not! John's not dead, I told you that already. John didn't take that big of a spill, he's probably in some local's home recovering. He might not know who he is if the board hit his head hard enough."

"The police are going around to any residents that live near the beach or the resorts to the north. So far there's been nothing."

"It hasn't been that long," I stammered. "They're not going to give up already, are they?"

"No, but they will soon. The current could've taken him out further or…"

"Or eaten. Is that what you're eluding to?" I snapped, furious.

"It happens, Ruth Ann. That's why I think you should go lie down and let Dr. Joseph give you something to help you rest. Then we'll know more."

I pondered what he said. Maybe I should go along with him, and when they think I'm resting, I'll head back down to Meme. She was the only one who could give me answers. I knew it sounded naïve, but it's all I had.

"Fine, let's go," I said, standing up, grabbing my beach bag and heading toward the path that led to the first bungalow. I reached inside and pulled out the key John gave me. I unlocked the door and stepped inside the air conditioned room. Carlos pulled out his phone and quietly called the doctor. It didn't take long for Dr. Joseph to knock on the door.

"I'm going to leave you with Joseph. You're in good hands with him, Ruth Ann. I will be back shortly to fill you in on what we've found." With that, Carlos took off as fast as he could and headed back to the beach.

"So, Ruth Ann," Joseph said, calmly. "Carlos told me you would like something to help you rest. I think that's best. When you've woken up, hopefully you'll have the answers I know you're waiting to here."

"He's not dead," I stated, clearly. "But, I'll wait here for a little while and rest. What are you going to give me?"

He pulled out a few items from his bag. Uh-oh, I noticed he pulled out a needle and syringe. "No!" I cried out. "No needles!"

He eyed me strangely and put down the syringe. "Are you afraid of needles?" he asked.

Think fast, Ruth Ann! I quickly replied, "No, but I only trust injections from a doctor in an office or hospital. I don't know how clean these are. Nothing against you, of course." I watched to see if he bought my lame excuse.

"Oh, well, I guess I can see your point. It's no big deal," he said, rummaging around in his bag. He pulled out a small pill bottle and held it up close to his face. "I have these," he said, showing me the bottle.

"What are they?" I asked.

"Valium."

"That sounds harmless enough. I don't want to be completely drugged, just calmed down a bit."

"It'll help you rest for a few hours. By then, we should know more."

I agreed and Joseph walked over to the kitchen and opened the mini refrigerator and grabbed a cold bottle of water. He opened the palm of his hand exposing two little white pills. I knew I had to pretend to take them, but would he catch me? I took the two little pills in my hand and noticed he was watching me closely. "You don't have to stare!" I said curtly. "I'm not a five-year-old!"

"Oh, I'm sorry," he sputtered nervously, and turned his head toward the door hoping someone would come and save him. It gave me just enough time to drop the pills into my swim skirt cover up. By the time I raised my hand back up and took a big swig of water, he turned around and smiled at me. "There, that should help you right away. You should go lie down on the couch now."

I wasn't going to argue. I wanted him to *believe* I was going to sleep for a few hours without interruption. Then they would leave me alone and I could sneak out of here. I walked over to the couch, but didn't pull open the bed. "You can leave now. I'll be okay," I said, watching as the doctor nervously rocked back and forth. I was going to ask him why he was so anxious, but that would delay his leaving. I started to have a strong feeling that this doctor wasn't totally on the up and up.

"I'll give it a few minutes, just to make sure you're all right."

"I'm fine. Please, Joseph, I want to be alone now," I said, filling my eyes with tears so he got even more uncomfortable.

"Oh, I'm sure you do. I'll be back a little later," he said, backing up toward the front door. "If you need anything, come up to the lobby. I'll be waiting up there with Carlos."

"Sounds good," I said, pretending to close my eyes out of exhaustion. I peeked carefully as he left the bungalow. Once he shut the door, I sprang off the couch and ran to the front door. There was a window just to the left of the door and I very cautiously looked out from the side. I spotted Joseph standing just on the other side of the window. I was thankful the blinds were partially closed.

But why was he just standing there? He better not be standing guard outside my door! I watched for a second longer when I saw him pull out his cell phone. Who was he calling? I put my ear as close to the glass as I could without being spotted. I was about to give up when I heard Joseph talking.

"I gave her a double dose!" he argued from his end of the conversation.

"No! I won't do it," he bellowed. "She doesn't need the injection, too."

What! Whoever he was speaking with wanted me to get a shot, but a shot of what? If Joseph injected me with another sedative, I could die! I had to figure out who he was speaking with when Joseph yelled "Martika! She's knocked out completely with two pills I gave her. It should give you enough time to search the place and find Isabella."

"What!" I had to think quickly. Martika was going to come here and search my bungalow, but for what and how could I wait that long? She was also looking for Isabella so that meant she didn't return to her job as waitress.

"The necklace!" I murmured. Martika wanted my necklace for herself. What I wouldn't give to have John here with me right now!

Chapter 19

What was I going to do now? I had to get out of here, but if Marti-ka breaks in and I'm not here, then what? I had to think quickly, but carefully. I paced back and forth, but ended up back at the window to see if Joseph had left. I peeked through the window and saw Joseph, but he wasn't on the phone anymore. Carlos was now standing next to him. Either one of them could come inside here at any moment. I considered rushing back to the couch, but curiosity won out.

I hoped they would speak loudly enough for me to hear. Luckily, the glass was thin because I could hear them as clearly as if I was standing right next to them.

"Joseph, don't worry," Carlos said, becoming irritated. "She'll sleep for at least three or four hours, and when she wakes up she'll be so groggy she won't be coherent. It'll give us enough time to figure out what we need to do."

"But you didn't hear the tone in Martika's voice!" Joseph snapped. "She's changed. She's become cold and ruthless, Carlos. I don't want to be a part of this anymore. It's just a bloody neck-lace!"

"Shhh," Carlos snapped. "We don't want anyone to overhear us. Maybe we should go inside and finish our conversation."

I panicked, but before I ran back to the couch, I heard Joseph tell Carlos, "No, leave her alone. The poor woman's been through enough. She thinks her boyfriend is dead, and you and I know that's not the truth."

"What!" I cried out way too loudly. I slapped my hands over my mouth fearing they heard me, glanced outside and found them still arguing. Phew, they didn't hear me, but I had to be careful. Things were getting very complicated and my head was starting to pound.

They knew John was not dead. Why aren't they telling me this vital information? It couldn't possibly be over my necklace. I put that thought on hold and returned to the window to listen in some more. "Carlos, Martika's on the hunt. She wants to get ahold of that necklace before Isabella and her crazy family get to it first."

"I can't believe we caught Ruth Ann with Isabella's grandmother. How did she find out about her?" Carlos asked, confused.

"Only one person could tell her about Meme, Isabella," Joseph said.

"Meme, she's crazy!" Carlos declared. "They think the necklace is part of some old curse from years ago. You don't think Ruth Ann believes in all that voodoo stuff, do you?"

Joseph shrugged his shoulders. "Who knows. We don't know how much Ruth Ann really knows about it. Maybe we should just ask her."

"Ask who?" Carlos asked, stunned at Joseph's suggestion.

"Ruth Ann."

"Here's the problem with that. If we start asking all sorts of questions about Isabella and her grandmother, she'll get suspicious. Maybe she doesn't know why they want the gem, yet. That's why you drugged the poor woman, to buy us some time."

"I don't like this," Joseph said. "I'm a good doctor."

"Yes, but we didn't have a choice. We've got Martika on our backs and until she's satisfied, this will never be over."

"How did you ever get involved with her?" Joseph asked. "You knew she was a gold digger when you married her!"

Married Martika! No, I don't believe it. Carlos seemed more interested in men than women.

"You know why I married her, Joseph. She has a lot of incriminating information on me. She made me buy this run down resort because it's close to Meme's practice. I would never have bought this place, it's disgusting!"

"But you've been making great changes to it. These newer bungalows are really nice. Maybe when this is all over we can run this place and make some money with it!"

"I hope so, Joseph," Carlos said, gently rubbing his shoulder.

I get it now. Carlos married Martika because she was black-mailing him, but he wants to be with Joseph. At least that much made sense to me! But what did Martika have on Carlos that was bad enough to make him marry her and try and steal my necklace? That was the million-dollar question.

So, as I stood listening to them banter back and forth about how they were going to keep Martika at bay, I thought about my own conundrum. Who can I believe and trust? I have to think carefully because once I chose a side, I have to be right or John's life could end.

At least John was alive! I knew it all along. Meme wouldn't divulge where he was, but I didn't get a lot of time to pry it out of her when Carlos came barging in. At least that answered how Carlos knew where I was. They all do, but Martika, Carlos, and Joseph don't know what I know. It may sound confusing, but it's not to me anymore. I knew what I had to do…call Prunella!

I needed help, and Prunella would be the one who would come to my rescue. I would even agree with her bringing Axel along because when he's in full form, he intimidates everyone! I wanted to do one thing first, and that was to finish my talk with Meme. It was time to slip out the back slider and sneak down the beach.

Before I left the bungalow, I glanced outside to see if Carlos and Joseph were still there. They were gone and I needed to hurry. I hoped Carlos could talk Martika out of searching my bungalow while I was supposedly drugged. If she came here and I was missing, all hell would break loose!

I grabbed my skirt pocket and felt inside for the necklace. Still there. I quickly opened the front door, made sure the coast was clear, and put the lock back on, but didn't close the door just yet. I slipped the key in my other skirt pocket and felt the two little white pills. "Never know when these could come in handy," I thought. If the doctor said I'd be knocked out for hours on these, then so would another person!

I took the security pole for the slider and put it in so Martika couldn't break in. I grabbed a broom handle, broke it into three pieces and lodged each piece into the windows so they couldn't be opened. Once I felt the place was as secure as possible, I peeked out the front window to make sure the coast was clear and then headed out the front door, locking it and putting the key back into my skirt pocket.

I rushed down the sandy path as close to the edge of the jungle as possible. I didn't want anyone to spot me. Once on the open beach I moved quickly in and out of the palm trees lining the sand. I didn't notice any commotion on the beach. Obviously, the search for John was over, if there truly was an actual search. How could anyone fake an investigation of a man's drowning! When this was over, heads were going to roll!

Once I felt safely out of sight, I headed back onto the sand near the water. I had to think quickly. I made up my mind to find Meme and finish our conversation. I was hoping she'd be willing to negotiate a deal so I could see John. All she wanted was my necklace, and if I promised I'd give it to her, then perhaps she would grant my wish. It didn't mean I'd *actually* hand it over, but I could *tell* her I would. I wondered if she would believe me, I wouldn't!

I contemplated the situation between Carlos and Joseph against Martika. Carlos didn't like Martika very much. She obviously threatened to expose something big enough to get Carlos to go along with not only marrying her, but buying this resort near Meme's shack.

If Meme wouldn't cooperate, maybe I could go to Carlos and Joseph and convince them to join forces with me to take down Martika and Meme, and get John back unharmed. I thought they were less concerned about the necklace. Would Carlos be satisfied if I told him John and I would work together to get him out of Martika's control? Or would he panic because John's a Police Chief? Too many if's with my plan. I think the best place to start would be with Meme, and if that failed, then try Carlos and Joseph.

Just as I finished making my mind up, I looked up and realized I was standing in front of the grass shack. I knew it was dinner time and wondered if Meme would still be inside. I didn't notice any sleeping arrangement inside the shack, just a table and chairs. If she wasn't there, then what would I do? I needed to know where Isabella was too. I doubted she went back to the resort since Martika was on the hunt for her, too. Please let Meme be inside!

I walked up to the string of beads and pushed a few aside. I looked inside but didn't see anyone in there. "No!" I cried out when a hand touched my right shoulder, shocking me, I jumped around to see who it was. "Isabella!" I shouted.

"Shhh," Ruth Ann. "You can't go around yelling. It makes people very nervous."

"I'm so happy to find you, Isabella!" I said in a much lower voice. "Where have you been?"

"I told you, I've been trying to stay away from my brothers."

"And what about your grandmother. You told me you ran away from her."

Isabella nervously looked around before replying. "Yes, yes, her too."

"You're lying! You probably don't even have any brothers!" I exclaimed. "I met with her just a little while ago. She was inside this very shack!"

"She was?" Isabella asked, stunned. For a second I almost believed her!

"You know she was. Please stop lying. I know all about John being alive and from what Meme told me, she knows who has him. Why don't you tell me since you obviously know more than you've said before?"

"Come inside, Ruth Ann," Isabella insisted. "We don't want to be seen out here. "Whatever you believe, I'm still being hunted down by…" she stopped and snapped her lips shut.

"Martika," I said, finishing her sentence.

"You know about *her*?" she asked with a dumbfounded look on her face.

"Yes, I know a lot, now get inside and answer a few questions for me this time."

We went in and the minute I sat down at the table, out of sheer exhaustion and heat, another hand went across my face. "What the…" I whipped my head around and there stood Meme, Isabella's grandmother. I grabbed her hand and tore it off my mouth. Her hands smelled disgusting. I don't think Meme knew what a bar of soap was and I sure didn't want any of her germs entering my mouth.

"I'm sorry, Ruth Ann," the old woman said hoarsely. "I couldn't risk you screaming. The both of you were already too loud outside."

"I didn't see you in here when I looked in a couple minutes ago. Where'd you come from?"

"I was here. I heard you coming and hid against the wall."

"Why would you need to hide from me? And wait a minute, how could you *hear* me coming? I was walking in sand!"

Isabella interrupted my interrogation of her grandmother and said, "Who cares how she knew. You're here, and I bet we don't have a lot of time before the group from the resort realizes you're missing and come searching for you here."

I had to ask her who she meant by 'group'. I wasn't sure if Isabella was aware of Martika's blackmailing of Carlos. "You know who, Ruth Ann!"

"Humor me, Isabella," I said, sarcastically.

"Martika, that's who. She's after me because I tipped you off about your necklace. She was so mad at me that she threatened my life!"

"She threatened to kill you?" I asked, surprised at this turn of events. I knew they were trying to steal my necklace, but kill for it. Here we go again!

"Yes, many times. Martika's ruthless and so is her husband, Carlos. Watch out for him. She's the controlling one in their relationship, but he sure does whatever she tells him to do."

I accidentally blurted out, "That's because she's blackmailing him!"

Meme's unsurprised eyes informed me she was aware of this situation, however, Isabella looked astonished. "Martika is blackmailing Carlos?" she asked. "What's she got on him?"

"I have no idea. I just happened to overhear a conversation between Carlos and Joseph."

"Ah, I always thought those two were too close. Now it makes sense," Isabella said, slowly. "I knew there was more to Carlos and Joseph than a work relationship." She added, "But why'd he marry her?"

"Once again, I don't know. I just know whatever Martika has on Carlos, it was big enough to make him marry her and buy the resort."

I glanced at Meme who seemed uninterested. She sat down at the table with a few groans. I couldn't help but ask her what she knew about it. "Me?" she answered my question with another one.

"Yes, I saw the look in your eyes. You didn't look surprised at all!" I snapped my fingers and said, "Oh, wait a minute. You knew because you *felt it or dreamed it*, right?"

Meme's expression changed from pleasant to menacing. "After everything I've told you, you doubt me?"

"I don't know who to believe or what to think! The only thing I feel fairly certain about is that John's still alive."

"And I'm the one who told you, didn't I?" she asked.

"Yes, and I overheard Joseph on the phone with Martika. They think they drugged me and I'm fast asleep in my bungalow right now."

"I know, I know," Meme repeated. "I have a few spies of my own over there, and that's how I knew about Martika blackmailing Carlos."

Isabella bellowed angrily, "Why didn't you tell me? I thought you wanted me to take over for you, but you've never trusted me! How am I to help people if you won't confide in me completely?"

Meme looked from Isabella over to me and back to Isabella. "We should discuss this privately, Isabella. We don't need to bother Ruth Ann with our family disagreements, do we?" she asked with conviction.

Isabella straightened and smiled back at her grandmother. "Of course not, grandmamma. I'm sorry to have disappointed you."

The tension in the air was so thick I could've cut it with a knife, a very large bladed knife. "Enough of this. I need to know where John is before Martika does something desperate. What if she's already found out I'm not slumbering back in my bungalow? She could be raging down upon us at any moment."

"She would never come here, Ruth Ann," Meme said calmly.

"Why not? Oh, you mean she would send Carlos, right?"

"Well, yes, she would send Carlos, but there's another reason she won't come near me."

Curiosity kept winning out over solving John's mysterious disappearance. "And why not?"

Isabella shook her head vigorously at her grandmother. "No, no, please leave it alone, grandmother."

"It'll come out anyway, Isabella. We can trust Ruth Ann."

"You can?" I inquired, surprised myself.

"Of course. I know that you would no doubt hand over your necklace in exchange for John."

"Yes, I would," I said truthfully, but I hoped it didn't come to that.

"Martika is my grand-stepdaughter, Isabella's half-sister."

Chapter 20

"Your granddaughter!" I screamed.

"Keep your voice down, Ruth Ann!" Isabella snapped. "I thought you were smarter than this. You know if we get caught, you'll never see John again."

"What? Why?" I asked, exasperated.

"If Martika comes here she will put grandmother into a hospital for insane people, she's threatened it many times. She thinks she's crazy with all the premonitions she has, and the curses, don't get me started on that topic."

"What about you, Isabella? What would Martika do to you?"

"She'll kill me."

"But you're her sister!" I asked, shocked.

"Half-sister, Ruth Ann. We share the same father, not mother. My father cheated on my mother when I wasn't even alive. He got the other woman pregnant, but my mother didn't know it at the time."

"I did," Meme mumbled.

I glanced over at Meme and noticed the evil grin on her face. I could tell Meme and her daughter weren't close like I was with Lynne and Nancy.

"My father and mother started having a lot of problems when he found out about our family's practice. He thought my grand-mother and mother were phonies, and he couldn't stand it so he cheated. However, it wasn't until years later that my mother found out."

"How did she find out?" I asked, curiously.

"Martika showed up," Meme announced. "She marched up to my daughter's door and stated she was her husband's illegitimate child."

"How old was she when she did this?" I asked.

"About twelve. Isabella was only two at the time."

"So Martika is ten years older than you, Isabella?" I asked, even though it was rhetorical. Isabella nodded. "So, let me guess. Your mother kicked your father out and Martika stayed with you, your mother, and grandmother until she was old enough to be on her own?"

"Yes!" Meme said, hopping out of her chair faster than I thought possible. "I thought my daughter was crazy to do that. I told her to let Martika go with her rotten, cheating husband."

"Why didn't she?" I asked, wondering the same thing myself.

"Because Isabella's mother, my daughter, planned to place a horrible curse upon him and she didn't want an innocent twelve-year-old to pay the price for his infidelity."

"Wow," I said, shocked. "What happened?" I asked, dying to hear the story even though it was taking up valuable time.

"She placed a curse all right." Meme looked at Isabella who was standing in the middle of the shack, silent. "She set upon him a life of poverty, loneliness, and finally, he would succumb to a horrible, painful death from the bite of a snake."

"Did he?" I asked, amazed of what I was beginning to believe.

"Yes," Isabella said, somberly. "He lost both his wife and mistress. Then he wasted away any money he had on liquor. I tried to intervene, but he didn't want anybody's help. He knew by this time what was next so instead of waiting for a snake to attack him, he went and bought a lethal snake and let it bite him. It was quick, but very painful."

"So, you both think this happened because your mother placed an evil curse upon him?"

"Yes, do you doubt this?" Meme inquired.

"No, no," I said quickly. "I feel like I'm in a horrible nightmare and I'm waiting to wake up back home in Deer Creek."

"Well, you're not," Isabella said, tersely. "You need to follow my grandmother's instructions and then you can get John back. Once you and John have been reunited, you both need to leave here and never come back."

"If the curse with my necklace is broken, why can't we come back or stay here a few more days? Not that I would want to, but I don't understand."

"You will, Ruth Ann," Meme said, interrupting me. "But first, you need to listen very carefully to what I'm going to tell you."

"Fine," I said. "What do I need to do?"

"First, we're running out of time. I feel that someone's going to be checking on you soon. You can either run back to your bungalow and pretend to still be asleep or keep on the run like Isabella is doing at the moment."

"I don't know what to do, what do you think?" I asked Meme.

"I think you should stay away from the resort for now. I think Carlos and Doctor Joseph can be trusted, but they will need convincing. I can help Carlos with what Martika is holding over him."

"What is it?" I asked, feeling nosy.

"You'll find out soon enough. We need to have a plan first." Meme held off talking for a moment. She rested her head in her hands and started making strange, raspy noises. I frantically looked to Isabella for help. "Is she alright?"

"She's going into her trance, let her be, Ruth Ann."

I stood back with Isabella as Meme raised her head, and her arms thrashed over the table and started banging on it. "She's going to break her hands," I whispered to Isabella, but she shook her head for me to be quiet.

Meme started chanting words I've never heard of or could ever explain. It wasn't English or Spanish. It sounded like a bunch of mumble jumble, but after about five minutes she halted and opened her eyes. "Okay, I know what is needed."

"What are you talking about?" I asked, perplexed.

"I know who has John, and why they have him." Meme slowly stood up and walked over to me. She took my hand and closed her eyes. For a second, I thought she was going back into her trance, but she snapped out of it and said. "It's connected to you, Ruth Ann. Everything that's happening has to do with you!"

"Me!" I cried out.

"Let her explain, Ruth Ann. If you interrupt, she may not remember everything," Isabella murmured. I nodded instead of speaking since I wanted to hear Meme's version of what was happening.

"There's much to tell, Ruth Ann," Meme said, appearing older than a few minutes ago. "I'm going to start with why Martika is blackmailing Carlos." She looked at me and motioned for the both of us to sit down. This could take a while, even though Meme just warned me someone was going to notice I wasn't in my bungalow.

"Martika knows much more about our family then any of us imagined. Unfortunately, she wants to use our powers for evil. Isabella and I want to break curses, and help people rid themselves of evil. This is where you come in, Ruth Ann."

"But I've only been here a day. How could Martika plan all this when we've never met?"

"That's confusing, because I knew someone was arriving here that had an object from an old curse. I could *feel* it. I know you're still skeptical, but it's true. I didn't know it was you in particular until I found out from reliable sources that you and your friend checked in at the resort. Martika was the one who dumped your original reservation down the beach."

"Seriously?" I mumbled.

"Yes," Meme said. "Martika found out about your gem from your recent exploits in Sweden and Deer Creek." She turned her gaze to me from staring at the table. "You do realize you made the news in Sweden?"

"We did?" I asked, surprised. "I never heard that."

"Axel Eklund's an important man in those parts. He made the news, therefore you did, too."

"Oh, I get it. Axel made the news about his crimes when he was supposed to be shipped off to prison for a long time."

"Yes, but he escaped and went back to Deer Creek where he lives with his wife, Prunella, correct?" Meme asked me even though I was fairly certain she already knew the answer.

"Yes, but he didn't escape, exactly," I said, not wanting to get into the whole faked his death scenario.

"No, he pretended to be knifed and then it was discovered he wasn't dead." She held her hand up to stop my interrupting. "I know, it's a long story, but feel assured I know it all."

"Fine, so what does this have to do with now?" I demanded.

"Martika saw a picture of your necklace in the news."

"My necklace made news?"

"Not exactly. Axel made the news and there was a photo of you and Prunella. One of you were wearing the piece."

"Makes sense," I said, agreeing it could've happened.

"Martika immediately jumped on it and found out everything she could about all of you and where you lived."

"In Deer Creek!" I exclaimed.

"Yes, she even flew there a couple weeks ago to check it out for certain."

"Martika was in Deer Creek?"

"Yes, not for long. I don't know exactly what she did there, but I would have to say it plays a part in what's happening now. She came back and didn't say a word to Isabella, that's why she was so shocked when you showed up down here wearing the bloody piece!"

"Who was shocked, Martika or Isabella?" I asked.

"Isabella. Martika already knew you were coming here. In fact, it can't be a coincidence that you and John ended up here, don't you agree?" she asked strangely. "Somehow, Martika planted the seed when John called up to make reservations for the trip you two were going to take."

"That's impossible!" I bellowed. "I didn't even know about the trip until a few days before we left."

"I don't have those answers for you, but somehow Martika must've overheard or talked with someone who knew John was planning a trip for you."

"I still find that hard to believe. Nobody knew," I said, and then something hit me. What if John had confided in someone in town about surprising me with a trip and Martika just happened to be there when he did. Sounds nearly impossible, but it could've happened.

"I see your mind's trying to figure out how it could've happened, right?" Meme asked me.

"Highly unlikely, but there seems to be a slight chance that could have happened," I admitted. "But, how did Martika know about the gem in the first place? And there's no way Martika could've had Carlos buy this resort in the last couple days!"

"No, no, Martika had Carlos buy this resort some months back to keep an eye on me," the old woman stated. "She knew something was up."

"But that's way before I owned the necklace."

"I moved here from our little village before Martika bought the resort, and before you ask why I moved here I will tell you." She took a moment to get her breathing back under control and then continued. "I had a calling to come here, to this beach, this very spot. Don't ask me specifics, I don't usually work that way. It's always a feeling I get, and then it explodes inside my head. I knew something was going to happen that I *needed* to be involved in. I asked Isabella to come with me, and persuaded her to get a job at the restaurant in the resort. Of course she willingly came, because the young honor and revere their elders here, unlike many in modern times."

"So that's how Isabella came to work as a waitress," I said, and Isabella nodded.

"Yes, back to Martika and blackmailing Carlos. She didn't have the money to buy the resort."

"She found a person with money that had something in their past she could manipulate," I said.

"Yes. She knew Carlos from our village. He only left because he disrespected his family and had to flee."

"So, Martika took full advantage of that, didn't she?" I asked.

"Yes," Meme replied. "Carlos didn't really do anything horrible. He just neglected to inform his parents that he was gay."

"So what?" I asked, angrily.

"Ha! His parents are very wealthy. Not everyone approves, Ruth Ann. They are not like you or me. I would love my children and grandchildren no matter who they are or what they did. Carlos' parents aren't like that. If they ever found out about his choice to be with Joseph over Martika, they would disinherit him completely."

"So, that's why he married Martika. She knew he was gay, and she knew his family wouldn't approve. She blackmailed him into marrying her and he willingly agreed."

"But he'd rather be with Dr. Joseph, correct?" I asked.

"Of course. They are in love, but he despises Martika. Martika and Carlos had to appear to be a happily married couple who bought a resort on a lovely beach."

"That's what his parents believe," Isabella chimed in. "He would love to throw her out of his life, but he's used to nicer things and doesn't want to give it up or disrespect his parents. He agreed to go along until he found out the real reason she made him buy the resort."

"Carlos found out about Isabella and me moving here and our relationship to Martika. He threatened to blackmail her, but Martika could care less if people found out who we are. She would tell people Isabella and I are crazy and need to be locked up."

"And many people would believe that, wouldn't they?" I inquired.

"Unfortunately, yes," Meme answered. "It's an old practice, breaking curses, but if you have the power, it would be a sin not to use it for good."

"It is just for good, right?" I asked, wondering about the difference between good and evil curses.

'Yes," Isabella replied, eyeing her grandmother suspiciously. "We always try to resolve disputes or break curses, not cast them."

"But," Meme started to say and Isabella cut her off. "Grandmother, Ruth Ann needs to believe what we truly try to practice."

"So, you admit you've used your power for some evil, haven't you?"

"Not willingly. Only if we're backed into a corner, Ruth Ann," Isabella answered for her grandmother.

"We're wasting too much time!" The old woman spat out. "Let me finish, I'm feeling weaker by the minute."

I glanced over at Isabella to understand what her grandmother meant by her statement. "Grandmother's power drains her terribly. When she knows something's about to occur, she uses all her energy to keep the evil away, but that leaves her exhausted."

"She feels there's evil coming?" I asked, worried.

"Oh, yes," Meme replied. "It's already here, but I'm trying to fight it for you and your friend."

"John and me?" I questioned her. "But, this started way before we got here. I don't want to be blamed for everything!" Isabella put her young, unwrinkled hand on my arm and gently said, "We know it's not your fault. It's a fate you didn't ask for."

"Yes, you're right!" I stammered. "Why don't we just take my necklace and break whatever curse is attached to it? Then we can go on with our lives."

"It's not that easy, Ruth Ann," Isabella answered for her grandmother. Meme's eyes were closed and she was swaying in her chair. I noticed her almost fall off to one side or the other, but Isabella ignored it.

"Is she alright?" I whispered to Isabella.

"She's trying to rest and regain her strength. That's why I'm doing the talking right now."

I nodded and then said, "Meme said she knew who had John. Can we get that information out of her?"

"She will in a minute. Let her rest a moment."

"But we don't have time. Even Meme said they're going to figure out I'm not in the bungalow sleeping the drugs off."

"I don't think it matters anymore, Ruth Ann. I strongly feel my half-sister already discovered you are missing. She's very angry!"

"Are you sure? It's just a feeling, how can you know positively?"

Isabella looked at me strangely. "Please, we can't keep rehashing this. You either believe me and grandmother or not!"

"I don't have a choice."

"Yes. I also believe that Carlos can be trusted, but only him. I'm not sure about the doctor."

"Joseph?" I questioned her. "But I thought the two of them were a couple, behind the scenes, but still a couple."

"Something's not right about that, Ruth Ann. I don't know what exactly, but hopefully Grandmother can fill us in."

"You think Joseph is working with Martika and he's faking it with Carlos?"

"Possibly. I don't think they're too many people we can trust. You need to promise to stay loyal to us or the curse can't be broken."

I waited too long to respond when Isabella cried, "You have to promise, Ruth Ann!" I saw the intensity in her deep, golden brown eyes and felt like I could see inside her soul. I knew that instant I could trust her and nodded eagerly.

"I do believe you, Isabella. I feel that I can trust you deep in my gut." I realized what I just said and so did Isabella.

"Ah, maybe you have the power, too!" she said, smiling.

"No, I just have a stomach that tells me who I can trust or not. It's just a gut feeling as we call it."

"Oh, well maybe that gut feeling could be used to guide you further as we come across our next incident."

"What next incident?" I asked, curiously. "I thought you needed your grandmother to tell us what to do next."

"I do, but I also have an idea of where she wants to lead us." Isabella walked silently over to her grandmother and gently jostled her. Meme took a few shakes, but suddenly her eyes popped open.

"I'm okay," she said, rubbing her temples with her crooked fingers.

"Even though I couldn't speak, I heard everything Isabella told you. She was right…," Meme stopped to smile as broadly as an old woman with missing teeth could smile. Isabella stood a little taller in that moment, and I hoped this dispelled any doubt about her loyalty to her grandmother.

"Right about what, exactly?" I asked.

"Trusting Carlos. I've known that man his entire life and he's only going along with Martika because he's terrified of his parents finding out about his chosen lifestyle."

"I don't know if it's chosen or," I stopped speaking because it wasn't worth going into that topic. The two of them looked at me like I was an alien. I doubted they would understand anyway. "Okay, so we can trust Carlos. Should I find him and speak to him? Maybe I can bring him here and you can help him solve the Martika issue." I hesitated just a second then added, "Is that who has John?"

"I think you'd better sit down again, Ruth Ann," Meme said, pointing to the empty chair next to hers. "I think what I'm about to tell you might shock you."

"It's not John, is it? He isn't dead!"

"No, no, he's fine," Isabella said, rubbing my shoulder while she stood behind me. I turned up to her and asked her to stand or sit so I could see her. I didn't want any signals she might send to her grandmother that I couldn't see. I wasn't that loyal to them, just yet.

Isabella stood behind her grandmother and rested her hands on Meme's shoulders. She gave them a little squeeze and told her grandmother to continue.

"We will get Carlos in due time, Ruth Ann. I need to get something else off my mind so it opens up room for more information." I thought that was a peculiar statement. It's like throwing up food so you can eat more, kind of a disgusting analogy, but that's what entered my head.

"Go ahead, please, Meme," I begged. "It's getting dark outside and I'm worried about John!"

"Don't you find it funny that Martika was able to locate the gem in Deer Creek?"

"I guess so, but she heard about us on the news I thought?"

"Yes, but you weren't mentioned in the news, just Axel," Meme said.

"But Axel also has a large mansion in Deer Creek. He bought it when…" I stopped because I didn't want to go so far back in time when I thought Axel was a criminal.

"I know all about that, Ruth Ann," Meme stated. "But Martika went to great lengths to get to Deer Creek and snoop around town. How did she find out that John booked a trip to this very spot?"

"That's too much of a coincidence for me!" I bellowed.

"Exactly," Isabella intervened. "My grandmother thinks Martika may have an ally working with her."

"Do you know who? And do I know them?"

Meme and Isabella exchanged a quick glance with one another. "Hey," I exclaimed, "I saw that! What was that look for?"

"This is why I asked you to sit down, Ruth Ann," Meme said, motioning once again for me to sit down. I can't count how many times I sat and then stood up out of shock, and then sat back down again. "What are you getting at?"

Meme waited for me to sit down. I slowly sat back in my chair not taking my eyes off of her. I wanted to see if she was exchanging looks with Isabella. "Okay, I'm sitting so tell me who you think is helping Martika?"

"Prunella and Axel," Meme announced out of the blue.

Wait, what did she just say? I couldn't respond to such nonsense. I shook my head out of frustration and finally, when I thought I could speak, Isabella said, "I agree."

"You agree?" I asked Isabella. "You both don't know what you're saying. Maybe your *powers* are off kilter."

"No, Ruth Ann," Isabella said. "Look at my grandmother." I followed Isabella's hand motion toward her grandmother. Meme was back in her trance, rocking back and forth violently. Isabella was about to intervene when Meme popped her head back up and shouted, "NO!"

It shocked the two of us so that I fell off the chair and landed on the hard, dirty sand floor. Isabella rushed over to stand next to her grandmother and grabbed her shoulders to wake her out of her state.

I pulled myself back up to my chair and watched as Isabella gently shook her grandmother and spoke to her with a firm voice. "You need to rest. You don't have to do this. Ruth Ann and I are both fine, but you need to wake up now and rest!"

Meme's wild eyes opened wide and she glanced up at her granddaughter, and then over to me. Sweat was dripping down the old woman's face, and Isabella kept wiping it off with her bare hands. "It's okay, you don't have to use so much energy. It's not good for you anymore."

"What's not good?" I asked, anxiously. "What's going on!"

"Give her a minute, Ruth Ann," Isabella said. "I'm sure she'll explain why she had the outburst."

"She screamed no, Isabella. That sure doesn't sound good to me. I want to make sure something didn't just happen to John!"

"No, no, John's still okay, Ruth Ann," Meme said, wearily. "He's with...he's with...Joseph!"

"No way!" I replied, exasperated. "Joseph's with Carlos and you just told me that Carlos was trustworthy."

"But Joseph isn't. He's bad, very, very bad," Meme said, gaining some strength in her voice.

"Is Carlos aware of Joseph's betrayal?" I asked, knowing the answer right after it left my lips.

"Of course not!" Isabella bellowed. "Carlos would never drug or kidnap another human being.

"Because you know him so well?" I asked.

"Yes, and don't bother trying to dissuade me. I know he's one of the good guys. He's just gotten himself wrapped up in a messy situation."

"Messy situation!" I exclaimed. "I'd say it's a little more dangerous than a messy situation!"

I rubbed my aching head. First, Meme and Isabella informed me of an alliance Martika formed was with Prunella and Axel. Next, she told me that John was being held by Carlos' significant other, Dr. Joseph. I was beginning to wonder if I could trust Meme and Isabella! My mind raced, and I had to shut it down. I took a deep breath in and said, "How do I know who to trust? What if I'm being naïve in trusting you two!"

Meme hissed a few incoherent words, and Isabella just threw her hands up in the air. "Why would we go through all of this, and confide in you if we were lying to you? What benefit would there be with us?"

"I'll tell you how you benefit!" I snapped. "You both want my necklace!"

"Everyone wants the bloody necklace, Ruth Ann!" Isabella retorted. "At least we told you upfront, and didn't kidnap your boyfriend and drug you!"

She had a point. I have to work with someone, but if they try and tell me Prunella and/or Axel are involved in all this, I'll find a way to end this myself!

"So, can we move forward, Ruth Ann?" Isabella asked, closely watching Meme straighten up in her chair and regain full consciousness. "Look, my grandmother has restored her strength. Let's see what we should do next."

Of course she regained her strength, I thought to myself. I agreed to believe them, and not Martika and Dr. Joseph. Miraculously, Meme came to just after my choice was made. "Meme, if

Martika knows I'm not in the bungalow anymore, where does she think I went?"

"Here, of course," Meme stated. "She now knows you've met me and more than likely, Isabella. I'm sure she's waiting for Joseph to march down the beach and grab you."

"What do you mean grab me?" I asked, curiously. "As in take me back to the resort or throw me wherever John is."

"That's the question I'd like answered myself," Meme replied. "I think she's fuming mad at this moment, and raising quite the ruckus back at the resort. Carlos won't know what it's about. She'll probably tell him you've woken out of your drug induced slumber and walked off. He won't think to come here because Martika doesn't want Carlos knowing too much. She will think of some excuse and Joseph and Martika will come here alone."

"Why don't I leave and hide-out near here? That could confuse them, and hopefully they would rush over to wherever they're holding John, and I'll be right behind them." I suddenly liked my plan. It could possibly lead me right to John.

"That's too risky," Meme said. "If they find you, they'll force you to give them your necklace, and I hope you know what they might do to you!"

"Nothing!" I answered. "If they got my necklace, then I'm no use for them anymore."

"Exactly," Isabella chimed in. "Think about it, Ruth Ann. You're a U.S. citizen. If you were released where would you go?"

"To the police, of course," I replied. "Ah, I see where you're going with this. Martika won't let me leave of my own free will. She'll need to kill John and me!"

"Yes, Ruth Ann," Meme said, quietly. "Like I said, your plan is too risky."

I panicked. "How are we going to find John if we don't force them or follow them?"

"I have a few ideas," Meme said.

Chapter 21

I looked around the shack as darkness filled the room. Isabella lit a candle on the rickety wood table, but it didn't help the eerie surroundings. I shivered a little, not out of cold, but of fear. I didn't think going back to the bungalow was going to happen anymore. I wanted Meme to hurry up and give us her plans so we could end this nightmare of a vacation. I just wished I could contact Prunella for help.

"By now, Joseph and Martika know you're gone. They're probably thinking of how to dispose of you at this very moment. I want to help you, Ruth Ann. Do you believe me? I need to know you completely trust me." Meme stared into my eyes as if she was looking deep inside my brain. I knew I had to trust her or whatever she had planned wouldn't work.

"Yes."

Meme hesitated a second while she stared me down in deep concentration. "If you don't give me your full trust, nothing will work. My powers to help work by trust. Therefore, I need it to be a mutual trust. Do you understand me, Ruth Ann?"

"Yes." I had to open my mind and let her in. It was a terrifying thought, but what other choice did I have!

"Okay, I feel you letting me in," she said, still staring me down. "I think we're on the same page so let's begin."

"Begin what?" I asked, confused.

"I need to use you to put a curse on Martika and Joseph."

"What!" I exclaimed.

"We've been fooled by Martika."

The look on Isabella's face said it all. She barked, "You think *Martika* has her own powers?"

Meme's gaze left mine and landed on Isabella. "Yes, I do. It may not be as strong or controlled as ours, but I think she's tried to learn how to plant curses herself."

"You can learn to put curses on another person?" I asked, stunned.

"I think she's so obsessed with Ruth Ann's necklace that she's realized Isabella and I aren't insane. She did her own research on the practice and possibly found out she or perhaps Joseph have their own power!"

"Oh," I bellowed. "That's why she could be using him! He could place a curse on me or either of you."

"It does make sense," Isabella stated. "More sense than Martika having powers."

"Yes, the more I open my mind for the possibility, the more my feelings are waking up."

"So, what are we going to do about them?" I asked. "Time is running out for us."

"No, Ruth Ann," Meme said, smiling wryly. "You hold all the cards, so to speak."

"I don't understand," I said.

"They can't do anything to John or you until that necklace is in her hands. Until then, you hold all the power. Do you understand?"

"I understand that when they get the necklace, and then they'll kill John and me. But how does that give me any power?"

"That gem you made into a necklace has strong currents running through it. I believe once I break the old curse, the stone will be ignited and instilled with new powers."

"New powers instilled?" I questioned Meme. "You mean, the old curse has nothing to do with why Martika really wants it, right?"

"Yes."

"She needs you too?" I asked and Meme nodded eagerly. "Martika will force you to break that old curse so she can hold the newly empowered piece and do…what with it?" I asked, thinking I understood, but I really didn't.

"Once the gem is clean, it wipes out the evil that's associated with it. The person who has possession of it once the curse is lifted has a very important choice."

"What are you talking about, Meme?"

"The person can either use the piece for evil or for good." Meme waited a minute to see if I would interrupt, but I wanted to hear more first. "Good, you're listening, Ruth Ann. If Martika is the person who's holding the gem when the curse is lifted, we know what side she'll take, correct?"

"Evil," I mumbled, but Isabella and Meme heard.

"Exactly. We can't let that happen, can we?" I shook my head and Meme continued. "We have to keep Martika away from your necklace until the curse is lifted and *you* alone decide it's future. I'm assuming you would choose the right direction."

"Of course I would!" I announced. "So, that's why all sorts of bad things have happened since I've had this necklace?" I asked.

"Yes. We need to break the curse correctly and with the right person. That person is you, Ruth Ann," Isabella stated. "My grandmother will be the best person to take care of this."

"That's why you want my necklace. You didn't want to keep it from me, just to break the old evil curse."

"Yes, Ruth Ann. You finally understand and believe me," Meme said, smiling. "Now, we have a few problems associated with this though."

"What? Just do whatever you need while I hold the necklace. Then we can find John and get out of here!" I said, impatiently. "I'm sorry to say this to either of you, but I don't ever want to come back here again!"

"I don't blame you, Ruth Ann," Meme said. "But it doesn't work that simply."

"Please explain, Meme. We don't have a lot of time!" I demanded.

"We have several problems. The first one is the curse on your gem was placed over a hundred years ago. Second, Martika and

Joseph are after the gem, and thirdly, we need to rescue John before Joseph injects him with a drug that will kill him."

"Is that what you see?" I asked, scared to death.

"Yes. I can feel their anger growing and Martika has ordered Joseph to kill John if they don't get their gem back soon."

"How soon?" I demanded.

Meme put her head into her hands and squeezed so tightly I thought she'd break her skull. "I can't see that yet, but I feel it could happen soon unless…"

"Unless what?" I yelled.

"Unless we give them what they want," Meme answered.

"But you said if we give them the necklace they'll still kill us."

"Yes. You didn't let me finish, Ruth Ann. We let them believe we'll go along with them to buy us some more time."

"Buy us time to break the curse and find John, right?" I asked.

"Yes, and to find out if your cousin, Prunella, and her husband, Axel are somehow involved."

"I don't believe that part. There's no way Prunella or Axel would betray me."

"I feel they are involved, though. I just don't know for sure if it's against you or to protect you."

Isabella added, "Or somehow protecting themselves."

I turned and looked over at Isabella. "Why would they need to protect themselves?"

"I'm not sure, I just feel strongly about that scenario, too."

"Ah, my granddaughter caught something her grandmother didn't. That's because I'm growing weaker and weaker." Meme's eyes rested upon Isabella's with such love and trust I couldn't help but believe I made the right choice.

"Okay," I said loudly, snapping them out of their daydream with each other. "What do we need to do to make Martika believe we're willing to work with them?"

Meme kept her gaze on Isabella. "You know what needs to be done, right?" Isabella nodded and started to back away toward the door.

I cried out, "Wait! Where are you going?"

Meme nodded at Isabella, and she turned and scurried out of the shack into the darkness.

"Why did you let her leave?" I pleaded. "You didn't explain where she was going or why she couldn't tell me!"

"It's okay, Ruth Ann. I will explain what she's going to do. I didn't want her to wait any longer so I let her leave."

"Where's she going?" I asked, staring back at the jiggling beads.

"She's sneaking back into the resort."

"To my bungalow?"

"She'll stop there and see if anything is happening, but I sent her to find Carlos. Isabella completely trusts him so that means I do too. She will tell Carlos what's happening between Martika and Dr. Joseph. Once he calms down from the initial blow, he'll understand what needs to be done."

"What?" I cried out.

"The first step of our plan is the see if Carlos truly doesn't know where your boyfriend, John is. If Isabella believes he's telling her the truth, then she'll get him to feed false information to Joseph. Joseph does have strong feelings for Carlos, but his greed has won out. He may take this information and give it to Martika or he'll back off and leave willingly."

"You think Joseph will just leave without the gem? I thought Martika needed him because he's the one who has power?"

"He might have some power, but not enough to break the curse himself. That's what I'm going to have Isabella tell Carlos who in turn will tell Joseph. He'll also tell Joseph that Martika will kill him if he doesn't break the curse while Martika's holding the gem."

"I get it!" I stammered. "It could work."

"I hope so, Ruth Ann," Meme said, looking exhausted. I felt sorry for the old woman. She's led a rough life full of poverty and a bizarre power that most people would call insane.

"What do you and I do now?" I asked, curiously.

"We could wait for Isabella to return or you could go get us some water and food from a local vendor I know of not far from here."

"You want me to walk around in the dark?" I asked, hoping she was joking.

"Yes, you can do it. I'm thirsty, and I bet you are too. It's only about a five-minute walk from here in the opposite direction from the resort. It'll get you out of here to clear your head and if by chance Martika or Joseph do show up, you won't be here."

That's true, I thought. I could use some night air to clear my head and I was thirsty, and hungry. Meme said it was close and assured me I would be safe. After all, she was the one who would know if I'd be in any danger. "Okay, I'll go," I said, standing up from the table and stretching my stiff, tired body. "I don't have much money, but I do have a few dollars. Do they take dollars where you're sending me?"

"No, just tell them Meme sent you and they will supply you with a few items."

Meme gave me some simple directions and told me not to stray from the route. I assured her I had no intention of going off on my own. I made sure she was settled and then took off through the beaded entry and headed south, away from my cozy bed back in the bungalow.

I stepped out into the night air and expected to feel a cool breeze. How wrong was I! The air was still and stifling, not a palm frond blowing. I walked close to the edge of the jungle until I came upon an entrance with two totem poles. "This has to be the place." I walked passed the totem poles into the jungle on a moist sandy path. Meme told me to go a minute and then turn right on a grassy path that led deeper into the jungle. I had the flashlight Meme handed me aiming down and found the path with no problem. I didn't like it, but I had to stay strong and hope Meme didn't lead me into a trap.

After another minute, Meme said I'd come to a large opening in the jungle where a small local store would be located. Most people don't even know about this place, and I could see why. It was in the middle of nowhere, and looked like a rundown small house. I noticed a small light was next to a door and headed directly for it. Meme told me not to knock too loudly because I didn't want to startle the owner inside. "Why would you have to knock to enter a store?" I whispered.

I made my way up the three rickety stone steps and opened the screened door. I gently knocked on the wooden door and waited. When no one answered, I knocked a little louder, still nothing. I banged harder, and was rewarded with the door flying open and there stood a little old man. He had to be about a hundred by the way he stood hunched over and bald. He didn't recognize me and was about to slam the door shut when I put my hand on the door and cried, "Wait!"

He hesitated a moment before trying to shut the door again. I called out, "Meme sent me," and he halted.

"Meme?" he questioned me. "You know her?"

"Yes, yes. She sent me here and told me to tell you she needed some supplies. That's all she said you would need to know."

The old man quickly pulled me aside and looked around to see if I was alone. "Nobody is with me," I stated.

"I needed to make sure. Come in, hurry up, come in."

I walked inside the tiny, dimly lit room. It must be the foyer, but super small. The both of us barely could stand side by side inside the room. He motioned for me to follow him and took off through another door. I hurried through the door and stepped inside another larger room. The shelved walls were full of jars, bottles, root vegetables, fruits, nuts and seeds. He grabbed a large burlap bag from a center island and starting filling it with a few jars and bottles. Then he stuffed in some straw and added more items. I couldn't see exactly what he was loading into the bag except when he grabbed a large handful of beets. "Beets?" I questioned him. "What do we need those for?"

He ignored my questions and kept to himself. Once he was finished he walked over to me as I stood by the doorway. "Take this back to Meme. It should be everything she needs."

"What's in there?" I tried asking the older man.

"Too many things to explain. I know what she needs to perform," the man shut his mouth so tightly that I thought he'd break the few teeth he had.

"Perform what?" I demanded. "Curses!"

He nervously spat out a few incoherent words and opened the door for me to leave. "Go, be careful on your way back."

I turned to ask him why I should be careful when he gave me a shove out the front door and slammed the door. I walked down the steps with the large, heavy bag and realized I needed the flashlight to lead the way. I set the bag on the sandy ground and reached inside my skirt to pull it out. I felt the necklace in the other pocket and gave a sigh of relief. I wasn't sure if Meme or the man in the store played a trick on me to get the necklace out of my pocket. I turned on the flashlight, picked up the bag and hurried back to the shack where Meme was waiting.

"You made it!" she exclaimed.

I nodded, out of breath, and looked around the shack for Isabella. "She's not back yet?"

"No."

"Do you think she's in any trouble?" I asked. "Maybe I should go look for her."

"I don't think that's safe, Ruth Ann."

"I'll be really careful and not let anyone see me."

"Give her a little while longer. I have a feeling she'll bring back lots of information and maybe even Carlos."

"I hope Isabella can convince Carlos to help us. I know his feelings will be hurt once he finds out about Joseph, but it's better he finds out now before things get worse."

"Very wise, Ruth Ann," Meme stated. "Carlos will believe Isabella. They go too far back for him not to believe her. He hasn't known Joseph too long."

"I wonder if Martika pretended not to know about Carlos and Joseph's relationship. Maybe she's the one who knew Joseph first and the two of them came up with this plan of him falling for Carlos."

"I have to agree with you."

"Thanks," I said, slightly relaxing for the first time in a long while. I didn't have a reason to relax, but I felt safe with Meme for some unknown reason. I knew she would lead me to John, save Carlos, and even prove Prunella and Axel weren't involved with Martika.

Meme watched me and said, "I will do my best."

A chill ran down my spine even though the heat inside the shack was overwhelming. That woman read my mind, and even though it was a compliment to Meme, it gave me the creeps knowing she could understand how my mind worked. I decided to ask her bluntly, "Are you constantly reading my mind, Meme?"

"No, I had a strong feeling a minute ago, and your thoughts popped inside my head. You have to be thinking passionately about something, whether it's good or bad, and then it passes over to me."

"I don't claim to understand your power, and never thought I'd meet someone like you, but I'm sure glad you're on my side."

"I can assure you I am on your side, Ruth Ann."

We spent the next several minutes unloading the items from the burlap bag. Meme let me help her, and I asked many questions regarding the contents of some of the bottles and jars. "They're mostly herbs, spices, and liquids that I need." She pulled out a few water bottles and we both opened one up. "Drink up, we need to stay hydrated."

I swigged the bottle down and felt hundred times better. I grabbed a handful of grapes that she placed on the table and started munching on them. Meme cut a few slices of a sweet smelling bread directly on the old wooden table. I didn't care if the table was clean or not. I was hungry and took a slice of the bread and devoured it. "You are hungry," Meme said, smiling. "I'll cut you another slice." I thanked her and ate another slice, a few more grapes, and a handful of nuts.

"I feel a lot better," I announced.

"You need your strength," Meme said. "I do too," she said, grabbing a slice of the bread and eating it.

"Shouldn't she be back by now?" I asked. "I feel pretty revived. Maybe I'll take a peek down the beach and see if I can hear anything."

"No, stay here. It's not safe down there."

"Are you just saying that or do you know something's happening?" I asked inquiringly. "You don't think Isabella's in any danger, do you?"

"No, but I think she's struggling with something or someone."

"Maybe I could help her!"

"No, just wait here, please," Meme begged, and then we heard a loud thumping noise just outside the shack.

"What was that?" I asked quietly, but scared.

"Shhh," Meme whispered, and then stood up and creeped toward the opening of the shack. I followed so closely behind her that I stepped on her linen skirt and she almost tumbled forward. Surprisingly, Meme caught herself and stayed upright, but the glare she threw back at me was disturbing. She put her crooked finger to her mouth to keep me quiet.

We could hear movement right outside the shack, but it was completely black outside. The only light came from the single candle burning on the wooden table. I was frightened, but Meme appeared calm and steady. Knowing her, she already knew the cause of the commotion outside.

Then suddenly, the beads parted and in walked Isabella. I was so excited to see her that I didn't notice the look on her face. She shook her head violently to stop me from moving any closer. What was her problem? She was back and now we could find out if Carlos was willing to go along with our plan. Whatever that plan actually was!

As she made it all the way in, I noticed an arm sticking through the beaded entry. On the end of the arm was a hand...holding a gun in Isabella's back! "What's going on here!" I screamed, and then the gun changed direction and was aiming directly at my heart. "Hey," I snapped.

"Don't move an inch," the voice called out as the person stepped all the way inside.

"Martika!" I bellowed. "What are you doing?"

She ignored my question, but gave Isabella a little shove over to her grandmother. They were forced into the corner and the two of them sat on the hard sandy ground. Neither of them spoke a word, but I could see no fear in their eyes. I whipped my head back around to see Joseph standing inside the shack also. "Dr. Joseph!" I announced. "What a surprise seeing you here."

"Ah, Ruth Ann, you think you have it all figured out don't you?" he glared over at the two women huddled in the corner and then returned his gaze to me. "You trust these two! One is too old to do any harm, and another too young and stupid to be able to cause any harm." He laughed a sickly, loud, laugh and added, "And you're a fool for trusting them."

By now, everyone who knew me well enough, would tell you I didn't take kindly to insults. I stomped over to him and stood within an inch or two of his face (or chin in my case), and said, "You're a low life, loser doctor who drugs innocent, weaker woman! You're not a man, you're a coward. A coward who doesn't have the balls to stand on his own two feet and tell Martika to get lost. Let her get the blessed necklace herself! You had a good thing with Carlos, and now you blew it!"

Well, if looks could kill, I'd be dead, buried and forgotten after that declaration. Joseph raised his arm to take a swing at me, but Martika screamed, "Stop, Joseph!" he followed her orders and lowered his arm, but used his shoulder to knock me to the ground. I wasn't about to let this loser get the best of me so I pulled myself up, brushed the sand off my swim skirt and top, and smiled right back at his face. "I got to you, didn't I?" I commented, sarcastically. I backed away just as he spat out some disgusting liquid from his smelly mouth.

"Enough!" Martika yelled. "Ruth Ann, you go over by my two relatives while I think of what I'm going to do to you all." She turned her attention back to Joseph and told him to keep watch outside the shack. He moaned and groaned, but followed her orders. I slowly sauntered over to where Isabella and Meme were still huddled, shocked at my behavior.

"You're making it worse," Isabella whispered to me as I stood at her feet.

I didn't respond, but I knew she could be right. I couldn't help myself. It's been a long twenty-four hours and I was agitated, tired, and ready to find John.

Martika paced in front of us waving her handgun. "Well, well, what am I going to do with you three?"

"You can't do anything until you get what you want, can you Martika?" I asked, taunting her.

"Stop, Ruth Ann," Isabella ordered, quietly.

"Yes, Ruth Ann, you may want to hold back on the comments. I do believe I am the one who has all the *power* now!"

"You only have a gun for your power, Martika," Meme chimed in. "You and I know that unless you get a hold of the piece you've been searching for, you can't or won't do anything to the three of us."

Martika's expression changed to anger. "You, old woman, don't know everything! I only really need to keep Ruth Ann alive. The two of you can be disposed of easily."

"No, Martika," Meme started to say, disagreeing with her. "You think Joseph has the capabilities to rid the gem of its curse, but he's a low life hack who doesn't have any power. He's been fooling you and you can't even see that!"

"You're lying!" she yelled. "I've seen what he can do, and I feel confident he can handle some silly old curse."

"What's he shown you, Martika?" Isabella asked. "Silly tricks that anyone can learn from a magic book!"

"Shut up!" she snapped. "You both are trying to save your lives and will say anything."

"You know I'm right," Meme said, grinning. I could tell from the expression on Meme's face that she knew she was getting to Martika. Maybe Martika would think twice about ending their lives. At least I hoped so, because I sure didn't want to do this alone.

Martika stared at Meme, deep in thought. Meme's eyes didn't leave Martika's either. I knew that look! Meme was reading Martika's mind and by the grin on Meme's face, she was winning.

"So," I said, interrupting the mind game between Meme and Martika, startling the both of them. "Why don't we get down to business. I need to know where you've stashed my friend."

"Ah, John," Martika replied. "He's quite handsome."

I ignored her comment and demanded to know where he was. Martika laughed in my face and said, "Maybe I'll keep him for myself. He'd make quite the lover, and," she paused and checked me out from head to toe, "you can't be satisfying a man like that!"

"Shut up!" I yelled. "You don't have a chance in hell with him. He's not into sleazy, lying, murderous women!"

Martika stepped up to me and slapped me hard in the face. I fell back a step or two, but didn't fall. I wasn't going to let her know just how much her slap hurt. I didn't even grab my face with my hands and I can assure everyone, I wanted to. "So, let me add to my previous statement. He also doesn't care for women who assault other women."

Martika was about to come at me again, but thought twice about it. She turned around and checked on Joseph who was standing just outside the entrance. Some words were said between the two of them, but I couldn't hear any of them. She came back in and said, "No sign of your little friend, Carlos, yet."

"What did you do to him?" I asked. "He is your husband!"

"Ha! He's no more my husband than John would ever be yours. Carlos was a means to an end, that's all."

"So, you admit you used him to marry you, buy the resort, and then have him fall for Joseph."

"Yes to all of the above, Ruth Ann. He was so scared of his family finding out that he was gay, that he jumped on my proposition."

"That's horrible, Martika," I said. "He didn't do anything wrong, but you found the one weakness he had, his parents."

"And I'd do it again, Ruth Ann. Carlos will be fine if he cooperates and does as he's told."

"So, he knows about Joseph now?" I asked curiously, feeling sorry for him if he found out Joseph used him.

"I didn't have to tell him. Joseph was the one who tied him up right before we headed down the beach to find you. He'll be detained for quite some time. At least enough time for us to end all this."

"Just curious, Martika, what do you mean by end all this?" I asked.

"Let's see, first I want you to tell me where that little necklace is. I searched the entire bungalow and couldn't find it and John was searched thoroughly," Martika hesitated a moment, and then added, "he enjoyed every minute of my hands running up and down his body, and in his pockets checking for the gem."

"Knock it off, Martika," I snapped. "John would pummel you if you actually did that!"

"Believe what you want, Ruth Ann. John was clearly into me."

"Oh, just so you know, I'll never tell you where my necklace is. It's safely stowed away in a place you'll never find." I was hoping she wouldn't have Joseph pat me down to see if the necklace was somewhere on me. I was beginning to think she wouldn't because who would be so stupid to have a priceless, cursed gem right in their pocket!

"Oh, I'm fairly certain you will, Ruth Ann," Martika said. "I'm holding valuable merchandise."

"John," I murmured.

"Yes, and don't forget about your new friends here," Martika said, eying Isabella and Meme.

"They're your family!" I proclaimed. "Isabella's your sister and Meme's, well she's not your blood relative, but you've known her for years."

"Half-sister," Martika corrected me. "And Meme's just a silly old woman who's wasted her entire life practicing some pointless rituals. She's used more people than I ever did."

"I have not used anyone, ever!" Meme demanded forcefully. "I've helped hundreds of people whose lives have been ruined by those 'silly' curses. You're just jealous of Isabella because she got my powers and you were just an abandoned child from a worthless man!"

"He was my father!" Martika yelled at the old woman. "It was *your* fault he died so young and left me at your doorstep."

"Correction," Meme said. "My daughter placed the curse upon him, not me. And we took you in and raised you to be a hard-working, respectable woman, but you were a rotten little girl."

"I wasn't rotten! I was neglected and once I was old enough to run away from all of you I did!"

Isabella's face softened. "Martika, you and I were once very close. I never treated you badly, in fact, I would give you my food when you were hungry, and I told you I loved you and never wanted you to leave!"

"You were a foolish little girl," Martika hissed. "I was much older than you, and you idolized me. You wanted to come with me when I was getting ready to leave that rundown, filthy household."

"Not because I wanted to get away from my mother or grandmother. I didn't want you to be alone!"

Martika didn't respond. I was hoping Isabella's pleading would soften her hatred a little, but I was clearly mistaken. "I'm done with the three of you for now."

"Wait, where are you going and what are you going to do with us?" I asked, anxiously.

"Oh, you're not going anywhere just yet. I've got a few loose ends to work out. Joseph will stay here to keep watch. Unless, Ruth Ann…you're ready to divulge where the gem is?"

"No," I stated.

"Then I'll leave you with Joseph," she replied and turned to leave.

"What if Joseph tries to hit me again?" I asked, stopping her just before she reached the doorway.

"That's your problem now, Ruth Ann. I suggest you keep your mouth shut so he doesn't have a reason to slug you!" With that, she exited through the beads and into the still night.

Chapter 22

"Now what, Meme?" I asked her. "You have a plan to get us out of this, don't you?"

Meme stayed silent, curled up in the corner. Isabella stood up and started walking around the shack. "Let us think, Ruth Ann. My grandmother needs to run things through her mind. I believe we had a plan, but now that we've been captured by Joseph and Martika, we need to revise it. At least we know John's alive and somewhere near here."

"How do we know that?" I asked.

"She was teasing you with him, Ruth Ann. I'm sure he's fine, and he has to be close because Joseph's here, and I would bet my life on it that she went to John now."

"She better keep her hands off him!" I hollered.

"Keep it down in there!" Joseph yelled, sticking his head through the beads. "Or do I need to make you keep your mouth shut?"

I stayed silent and didn't react to him. I knew what he was capable of and wanted to keep my face free from his hands. Isabella plopped down on one of the wooden chairs at the table. "You might as well sit down too, Ruth Ann. We've got a long night ahead of us. I feel pretty certain of that."

I agreed and sat down. I grabbed a handful of the sunflower seeds from the bag on the table. I needed to keep up my strength and keep my mind sharp. I had to think of a plan that could get us away from Joseph.

"Aha!" I said, hopping out of my chair. "We're going to be okay."

"And how do you know that?" Isabella asked without much confidence in her voice.

"Carlos will rescue us," I announced. "Martika said he was tied up and indisposed temporarily. I'll bet he's freed himself by now and is coming up with a plan to get us out of here."

"You think?" she asked.

"He's got to be. Martika said he knew what they were after, and he knows Joseph's betrayed him."

"Maybe he'll try to get through to Carlos," Meme said from the floor. "He could try and fool him thinking he'd help Joseph."

"Maybe Joseph's not too smart and Carlos will say he'll handle us so Joseph can go and help Martika," I suggested. "If he falls for it, we're free to find John."

"That's if Carlos is able to or wants to help us," Isabella said. "And, if Carlos knows where they're holding John."

"We have to keep positive thoughts, Isabella," I said.

"Yes, yes, Ruth Ann's right!" Meme said, trying to stand. I hurried over and gave her some help. "Positive thoughts yield positive outcomes. You know that, Isabella."

Isabella nodded her head, but her facial expression didn't give me much confidence. "I know grandmother. I'll try and keep positive thoughts."

"That's better. You, of all people, know how important it is to keep our mind open and positive. Otherwise, evil can seep in and change us."

"Change you?" I asked. "You mean if you let evil inside your mind you can turn into an evil person?"

"It tempts us, Ruth Ann. That's all I meant by that. We don't want to be tempted to do work for immoral, ruthless people. I want Isabella to remember that I've always tried to use my powers for good."

"I do know that," Isabella said, smiling at her grandmother. "I will never forget it."

"Good. Now, let's hope Carlos gets here soon," Meme said.

"You think that'll happen too?" I asked.

"How do you think you thought it? I had just put it into my own mind and you picked up on it," Meme said.

"Are you saying *I* read *your* mind?" I inquired, stunned by her statement.

"You're picking up on it quickly, Ruth Ann," Meme said, grinning. "I'm not passing my power to you, I'm passing thoughts to you. It's different."

"Oh, so I don't have any power?" I asked, a little disappointed.

"No, you have an open mind which can be beneficial for people like me who want to help you along. However, if you let evil people into your mind it will only hurt you. Remember that always, Ruth Ann."

"I will!" I said. "I'll close off my thoughts if I can."

Meme got back to Carlos. "When Carlos gets here, he's going to try and convince Joseph to find Martika. He's going to tell him Martika's going to stab him in the back and take the gem for herself. Carlos will need to persuade Joseph that he still wants a relationship with him, even though he betrayed him."

"Do you believe Joseph will fall for it?" I asked.

"I'm not sure yet. If not, Carlos will have to overpower Joseph and take him down. Once he's out of the way, we can get out of here and hope that Carlos knows where we need to go." Meme paused, took a step toward the table and held on to it. "I'm afraid I might not be able to go."

"What, why?" Isabella asked, horrified. "I won't leave you behind!"

"I'm too old to run. I'll just slow you down."

"We won't leave you behind, Meme," I said. "They'll kill you!"

"Maybe it's time, Ruth Ann. I'm okay, really."

"It's not going to happen," Isabella declared. "Carlos will convince Joseph so we won't have to worry about leaving you or anybody behind."

Time passed slowly. Joseph didn't come inside except to stick his head through the noisy beads to make sure we were behaving. The three of us sat at the table silently waiting for Carlos to appear. Finally, after what seemed like hours, Meme raised a finger to her mouth and gestured for us to stay quiet. "Someone's out there with Joseph."

I could hear low voices bantering back and forth, but I couldn't make out any words. After several minutes, the beads spread and in walked Carlos with Joseph right behind. I didn't know what direction this would lead, but Carlos quickly answered my prayers.

"Joseph has agreed to help us."

The three of us didn't speak a word. We waited for confirmation from Joseph before asking any questions. "Carlos is correct. If I keep my alliance with Martika, I will be betrayed. She will not share any of her wealth with me so I might as well be happy with the man I've fallen in love with."

Carlos smiled and grabbed Joseph's hand and gave it a tight squeeze. He released his hold and walked over to me. "Ruth Ann. I'm so unbelievably sorry that you've been involved in this whole nightmare. I need you to know I was kept in the dark until recently. However, I did know about Martika blackmailing me, obviously, and I had a feeling she was doing the same thing to Joseph."

I couldn't help but ask, "Did you know about John not drowning?" I wanted to see if he would tell me the truth. I'm fairly certain Meme or Isabella would call him out if he was lying.

"No. I swear I wasn't privy to that information." He turned to Joseph and his happy expression faded. "Joseph explained what happened and even how he drugged you." Joseph's head fell toward his chest in embarrassment, and Carlos continued, "I don't condone or forget what he did, under Martika's orders of course, but he knows he's fully responsible for his own actions. I am extremely thankful he didn't give the additional shots Martika tried to get him to give you. If he did, you'd probably," Carlos stopped speaking, swallowed hard trying not to get choked up.

I finished his sentence, "I'd probably be dead."

"Yes," Joseph replied for Carlos. "It would've been considered an overdose because you were so distraught from John's drowning."

"Martika thought of everything, didn't she?" Isabella asked, angrily. "My sister is a cold blooded murderer!"

"Yes, she's nasty," Carlos answered. "I, I never wanted to team up with her. It's just that…she had me over a barrel so to speak."

"We know, Carlos," I said, sympathetically. "Don't worry, we'll handle Martika."

"That would be nice, Ruth Ann. I don't want anything material, like the necklace I've heard about. I just want my life to go on in peace, and that means not disappointing my parents."

"We'll figure it out, but first, we need to have a plan for finding John and stopping Martika," I said.

Meme turned her attentions to Joseph. "Will you tell us where John is being held?"

"I, I want to, but if Martika found out I told you, she'll kill me, too."

"Joseph, you don't have to say a word. Just tell me you want to help us and let me see you mean it."

I knew what Meme was doing! She was using her power to get inside his mind. If he truly wanted to help us, Meme would be able to see it. However, if Joseph was just going along with Carlos, then Meme would be able to see that, too.

Joseph appeared nervous. His eyes were twitching rapidly and I noticed little beads of sweat beginning to drip down the side of his face. It was humid and steamy, but he wasn't sweating until Meme requested his help. I watched him carefully as he wiped the sweat off his face with his perfectly manicured fingers. I never looked closely at this man until now. He wasn't unattractive, but not as good looking as John. I could see why Carlos was attracted to this man who was probably in his forties. The graying hair at the temples and around his sideburns made him look distinguished. He was also in pretty good shape, tall, slim, and dressed like he had money to burn in his khaki shorts and teal green short sleeved shirt.

"I told you all that I want to help. I don't know what else to say!"

Carlos watched him closely, too. His eyes surveyed the rest of us as we stared at Joseph almost yielding him to break down. "What?" Joseph demanded. "You're all staring at me like I'm lying. I promise, I'm not. Martika's evil, and she made me work with her."

"We know, Joseph," Meme replied. "But we need to know we can trust you."

"What can I do or say to convince you?" he asked, calming down.

"Just agree to work with us," I insisted. "Martika's feeling backed into a corner, and she could do something horrible to John!"

"Or us," Carlos reminded me. "If she comes back here and sees that I escaped and went running to save all of you, then I'm a goner, too."

"We're all goners, Carlos," I reminded him.

"Fine," Joseph bellowed. "I'll help you, but I think we need to do this my way."

We stared at him in shock. I was the one who spoke up. "What do you mean we do things your way?"

"I think I should keep working with Martika. Let her believe I'm still on her side."

"Go on," Meme said.

"She's either with John right now or checking on her husband. You all agree with me?" We nodded. "If she finds Carlos missing, she'll be back here pretty quickly, but if she's with John we might have a little more time."

"Maybe you should be standing outside the shack pretending to be guarding us," Carlos said. "That way you'll see her coming and can warn us."

"But Carlos, there's nowhere to hide in here. If she shows up and you're here, she'll blow a gasket!" Joseph's concern seemed genuine, and I bet those words convinced Meme to trust him and now she might be able read his mind.

Isabella spoke up and said, "If my step sister finds Carlos in here we can tell her that he's a prisoner like the rest of us."

"Great idea," I said. "That would definitely show Martika that Joseph was still loyal to her."

"Okay, that has to be our last resort," Joseph said, heading through the beads into the warm night air. "I'll peek my head in from time to time to see if you all come up with our next move."

"Wait a minute!" I cried out. "Joseph never told us where Martika's holding John."

"It's okay, Ruth Ann," Meme said. "I think he was more concerned about Martika showing up and discovering he's betrayed her. Let me see what I can come up with, and then we'll bring Joseph in to help us."

I went and sat back down at the table. Isabella and Meme were huddled together across the table deep in discussion. I was hoping Meme or Isabella was getting a reading on where John was. I didn't want to talk much because I wanted to be able to hear anyone coming from the outside. Joseph popped in and said the coast was clear, and then went right back to his post.

Carlos was near the doorway pacing back and forth. I left him alone because he had a lot to lose if things didn't work out. He would lose not only Joseph, but his family. Family. I couldn't help but think about my daughters, Prunella, Axel, Inga, Sherman, and Alex. What were they doing now? I wondered if they had tried calling me? I doubted it because they were giving John and me our space to enjoy our first vacation. Ha! If they only knew...

"That's it!" I announced loudly. I hopped out of the chair and ran over to Carlos. They all stopped what they were doing and stared at me when Joseph stuck his head in and snapped, "Shhh, do you want to be heard all the way down the beach!"

"Sorry," I replied softly. "I had an idea."

"What?" Isabella asked me first.

"I need to get my cell phone."

"Why?" asked Carlos.

"I know who can help us. It might take a little while for them to get here, but I know they'd risk their lives to help me."

"Ah, you're talking about Prunella and Axel," Isabella said before Meme could get the words out.

"Yes! They'll take Axel's private plane and be here in a few hours. I know they'll rush down here and help us find John and take down Martika."

"But Ruth Ann, don't you remember my feelings about them?" Meme reminded me.

"I think you're wrong about them," I said. "They're my family. They would never do anything to hurt me."

"No, I just know they're involved somehow," she said, closing her eyes tight and scrunching her face up.

"There she goes again," I said to Isabella. "She's trying to go back into her trance, isn't she?"

Isabella nodded, Carlos looked confused so I explained how Meme's powers worked. He laughed at first, but I told him she wasn't a fraud. It took some convincing, but I think Carlos was beginning to believe Meme and Isabella had an unnatural power that could help us.

"If you say so, Ruth Ann," Carlos said, still unsure. "What's her problem with your cousin and her husband, Axel?"

I pulled Carlos aside and explained that Martika went to Deer Creek to find the necklace. She found out all sorts of information, including the itinerary of my trip to Jamaica. Meme also believed she was in contact with Prunella and Axel at some point regarding the gem. He was mesmerized at what I told him, and it finally convinced him to believe what Meme and Isabella were saying about the curse on the gem and how we needed to break it.

"Martika really believes Joseph has some sort of power and he could break the curse on the gem, too?" he asked, dumbfounded. "But, he's just a regular doctor, isn't he?"

Joseph stuck his head in and said, "Yes, Carlos. I'm just a *regular* doctor. I hope that doesn't disappoint you!"

"I didn't mean it like that. I'm just shocked Martika believed you could break some goofy curse, that's all."

"Actually, Carlos, I was the one who convinced her that I could break the curse. I know I was out of my mind when I agreed to work with her, but that gem is worth so much money, I guess greed got the best of me."

"Have you even seen the necklace, Joseph?" I asked, curiously. "How could you be attracted to a gem that you've never even seen?"

"I saw it on television. Martika came to my office one day for infection she caught and it was on my television. We both saw it together, and it was like the gem was calling for us to get it! I can't explain it; it was very bizarre."

"That's because the power this particular gem possesses is very strong," Meme said from across the room. "Most people just glanced at it on the television, but you and Martika sensed the importance of the gem."

I asked Joseph, "So you two didn't really know each other, but happened to see the gem on television and agreed to work together?"

"Kind of. Martika noticed the look in my eyes after seeing it and she said she just had to find that necklace. I told her I wanted in, and that's where it all began."

"Did you go to Deer Creek, too?" I asked, curiously.

Meme answered for him, "No, he did not."

Joseph eyed the old woman in fear, "How did you know?"

"I just know," she replied.

"Well, no, I stayed back and…," he hesitated and glanced at Carlos. "That's when I met up with Carlos."

"Oh, I get it," Carlos said. "Martika goes off the Deer Creek while you stayed here to lure me in. Martika had already set her plan in motion by blackmailing me and forcing me into buying the resort. Am I right so far?" Joseph nodded, ashamed.

"But Martika couldn't have known John and I were coming down here and staying at the very resort she forced Carlos into buying?" I asked, quite perplexed.

"Martika didn't make me buy the resort until *after* she came back. She had already forced me to marry her, as you all know, and threw Joseph at me." Carlos paused and added, "Sorry, but it is what it is!"

"Yes, and when she found out you two were coming here to Jamaica, she was ecstatic!"

"Because she didn't have to chase me in my own home town, right Joseph?" I asked, figuring it out piece by piece.

"Exactly!" Joseph cried out. "If her plan didn't work here, she was going to get me and Carlos to go to Deer Creek!"

"What!" Carlos yelled and threw his hands over his mouth to silence himself.

"Yes, Carlos," Joseph said. "Martika's original plan was for the three of us to go to Deer Creek. I am a doctor and I would somehow worm my way into your household as a doctor and search for your necklace."

"I don't know how that would've worked out. Axel would never allow a strange doctor to just roam around his house."

"I'm sure we could've come up with something, Ruth Ann," Joseph said. "But it wasn't necessary. You came here, and with the necklace!"

"I didn't want to bring the necklace!" I announced.

"Prunella and Axel convinced you, didn't they?" asked Meme.

"Yes, but, wait a minute! That's what you already knew, isn't it, Meme?"

Meme nodded slowly. "I think that's why I'm reading they're involved, but why would they want you to bring the necklace down here?"

Isabella declared, "Maybe they knew about the curse and wanted Ruth Ann to break it for them!"

"Nonsense," I said, but doubted the words right after they fell out of my mouth.

"Think about it, Ruth Ann," Isabella said. "That could've happened."

"So, you *all* think Martika befriended Prunella and Axel and convinced them that the gem had a horrible curse placed upon it a hundred years ago?" I waited for a response, but nobody spoke up. "And, Martika told them the best way to break this curse was to make me bring the necklace down here. Once I was here, somehow the necklace was going to be stolen and…" I stopped speaking when a nasty thought entered my head.

"Prunella and Axel have some money troubles. If the necklace was somehow stolen, they could collect the money from insurance and all would be fine," Meme said, finishing my thought exactly.

"Yes, Meme, that was the thought I just had."

"I know."

"I don't believe they would put me in that kind of danger," I stated, doubting my words and beginning to think the theory of getting money from insurance was stronger.

"Martika probably promised you wouldn't get hurt," Carlos said. "She can charm anyone when she puts her mind to it. Look at me, I married her and trust me, I can't stand her!"

"Maybe," I said. "But there's only one way of finding out, isn't there?"

"It's too risky, Ruth Ann," Carlos told me. "You can't leave here by yourself."

"Why don't you come with me?" I asked Carlos. "My phone is at your resort."

Joseph popped his head inside once again, "Hey, you never told us where you've hidden that precious necklace of yours?"

I wanted to reach down and touch the necklace through my swim skirt, but didn't dare. Nobody would think I was foolish enough to have a priceless piece of jewelry on me.

Carlos gasped loudly, "Please tell me you didn't hide it in your bungalow? I'm sure Martika ransacked that place." Carlos turned to Joseph who was still partway in the shack. "Did you search Ruth Ann's bungalow or did Martika?"

"I did after I supposedly drugged her, but Ruth Ann was smart enough not to ingest those pills."

"Did Martika search the place also?" I asked.

"I'm sure she did," Joseph replied. "If she found that neck-lace, we would know about it. That much I'm sure of."

"I agree," I said. "But did you remove any other items from the bungalow…like my cell phone?"

"Nope. I saw it lying on the side table next to the couch," Jo-seph told me. "I doubt Martika would do anything with it, she was so focused on the necklace."

"That's great!" I exclaimed. "I need to go get it!"

"Wait, Ruth Ann," Carlos call out. "I'll go with you. It's safer with the two of us."

"Hold on," Isabella said. "What if Martika shows up and Ruth Ann's missing, again?"

"Yeah, she'll kill me for sure if I let Ruth Ann escape," Jo-seph said, worried. "I don't know when she'll be back."

"We have to risk it, Joseph," I said. "We can hurry and be back in fifteen minutes. She's gone about an hour or so."

"Fine, but if I get killed over this, I'll come back and haunt the two of you for the rest of your lives!"

"Gee, thanks, Joseph," Carlos said, sarcastically. "We'll be back before she gets here."

Carlos grabbed my arm and we hurried out of the shack. The beach was pitch black. I couldn't see a thing. I didn't have the flashlight anymore and we had to go by the moonlight that faintly lit the beach. Carlos led the way as I held his arm. "We're almost there," Carlos stated, pointing the lights we could see in the distance.

"Finally, I can see where I'm going," I said, releasing his arm. "We haven't seen a soul out here. Nobody walks the beach at night around here!"

"They do, just not on this side of the beach. Remember when you arrived and we warned you to stay on the resort's property or to the north?" I nodded, remembering exactly when we were told. "We're on the south side of the beach. It's not the safest place to be walking around."

"Then let's get out of here!" I demanded, picking up my pace.

Just before we stepped onto resort property, Carlos halted and held his arms out to the side. "Hey," I said, running into his backside. "What did you stop for?"

"We need to stay out of sight of my employees."

"Why?"

"We don't want them to alert Martika that they saw us and we definitely don't want to run into Martika!"

"Good point."

"No more talking, Ruth Ann. We need to stay as quiet as we can. Follow me," he said, heading off toward the jungle. "We need to be careful in here, too. I don't want us to get bit by a snake or nasty spider!"

That didn't even enter my mind until he put it there! "Can't we just stay on the outskirts of the trees?" I asked, hoping he would oblige.

"My white shirt, and your bright skirt can be seen from far away. I think if we just go a little bit into the jungle we should be safe."

I followed closely behind Carlos as he weaved in and out a few palm trees and small shrubs. It wasn't as bad as I thought since it appeared there was a narrow path that Carlos was taking. "We're not the first ones to go this way," I said.

"No, people explore the resort's grounds all the time. Most people don't listen to our advice about reptiles and insects that could potentially harm them."

"That's reassuring," I said, mockingly. "Let's get out of here, it's dark and I'm getting itchy all over!"

"Almost there," Carlos said, just as he exited through a thick clump of bushes and stepped directly onto a small sandy patch that led right onto our back patio of the bungalow.

"We're here!" I announced, loudly. Carlos gave a nasty glare and whipped his finger over his mouth motioning me to shut mine.

"Okay," he whispered. "I'm going to walk around the bungalow, you wait here."

"No way!" I said. "We're sticking together."

"Fine," he said, and took off to the back sliders. The bungalow appeared pitch black inside, but it was difficult to tell since the heavy blinds were shut. I know I didn't shut them earlier in the day, but Martika and who knows who had been in there, too.

We walked around the side and Carlos peeked inside the windows. "I don't see any reason why we couldn't go it. Nobody seems to be in there or guarding the place," he said, peering around the corner looking for the front door.

"Good, let's go in," I said, pushing Carlos a little to the side and walking right up to the front door. "The lock's gone," I noticed. "A lot of good that did in the first place."

"I told you that it wasn't needed," Carlos stated. "If somebody wanted in, they would be able to with or without a lock."

"That's not very reassuring."

"Let me go in first, just in case," Carlos said, standing in front of me at the door.

"Okay," I replied, stepping to the side. "I doubt someone would be in there in the dark."

"You never know with her," Carlos said, reaching for the door handle and giving it a slight push. "Here we go." Carlos opened the door enough to stick his head in. "Dark."

"I'm assuming we can't turn on any lights," I said.

"No."

"I won't be able to find anything," I stated. "The last time I saw my cell phone it was on the table next to the couch. I know basically where that was." I carefully started walking into the main room of the bungalow. I recall there being a lot of open space in the middle so I headed straight in and walked with my hands out in front of me feeling my way over to the couch. It didn't take but a minute before my knees ran into the pulled out couch. "The bed was never made," I said.

"From when Joseph drugged you?" he questioned me.

"Yeah, but I thought I just laid down on the couch. I pulled the bed back into the couch earlier today."

"I'm sure Joseph or Martika pulled the bed back out of the couch to search it."

"Makes sense," I said, and then felt for the end table. "Here it is!" I exclaimed, holding my cell phone in my hand.

"Great, turn the flashlight on your phone," Carlos said.

Within a few seconds we had a small beam of light that showed the mess around us. "They ripped this place apart!" I said, angrily.

"I sure hope you didn't leave that precious necklace of yours in here."

"No," was all I replied. I wasn't ready to tell anyone that the item everyone desired was right in my pocket.

Carlos eyed me peculiarly and asked me, "Please tell me you don't have the necklace with you right now?"

"I'm not ready to tell anyone where it is. Just know this, it's quite safe." I ignored his looks and took a quick look around the bungalow. "They didn't take anything from what I can tell, but they clearly went through *everything*!"

I picked up a few loose items and placed them on a chair here and there and headed into the bathroom. Even that was destroyed. Every drawer and cabinet had been opened and emptied. I went inside the closet and so much for unpacking! All our clothes were thrown on the floor and our suitcases were on top of the strewn clothes wide open. "Unbelievable," I said, disgusted. "I feel so violated."

"She's desperate, Ruth Ann. Don't worry about this mess. We can get this cleaned up in no time."

"I know it's just stuff, but it makes me so mad!"

"We need to get back to business, Ruth Ann. Call your cousin and see if she's willing to help us."

"Yes, you're right," I said, dropping a pair of sandals I picked up from the floor.

I asked Carlos to give me a moment alone so I could make the call in private. He smiled and left the closet where I was standing. I knew it would be late back in Colorado, but not as late as it was here. I decided I was going to make a quick change of clothes so I wasn't stuck in my bathing suit any longer. I grabbed a pair of khaki shorts because it had many pockets and a couple of them were zippered. I threw on a tank top and grabbed a light jacket. I wanted to be prepared for an extended amount of time away from here so I grabbed whatever I felt I needed and filled my pockets. My necklace was more secure in one of the side zippered pockets, too.

"What are you doing in there, Ruth Ann?" Carlos called out to me.

"I changed my clothes, and now I'm going to make that call. I'll be out in a couple minutes. Just keep watch, please."

I listened for Carlos' footsteps to fade away on the tile floor, and then I turned to my cell and made the dreaded call. I didn't know if I was hesitating because I was worried Prunella and Axel were somehow involved or was I thinking they wouldn't help me? I was about to find out.

Chapter 23

I opened up my contacts on the phone and pressed Prunella's name. "Here goes," I said, fearing either the phone wouldn't have service or she wouldn't answer.

"Hello," a muffled, tired voice answered. "Ruth Ann, is that you?"

"Yes, yes, it's me, Prunella."

"Is everything alright? Why are you calling so late?" she asked, her voice quickly gaining strength.

"No!" I cried, literally. "Everything's horrible!"

Prunella gasped and I could hear her trying to wake Axel. "Tell me everything!" she asked calmly, knowing I was far from calm.

"I need your help!"

"Ruth Ann," a male voice answered. "It's me, Axel. Prunella put you on speaker phone so we can both help." He hesitated a second and said, "Please tell us what's going on, and talk slowly if you can."

"I'll try," I said, taking a deep breath in to calm myself down. "It's John, he's been kidnapped and, and," I stopped talking to figure out where to begin this unbelievable story.

"Voodoo and witchcraft!" Prunella bellowed. "This is crazy, Ruth Ann!"

"Start from the beginning, Ruth Ann," Axel requested. "I'm pretty sure you've left a lot out and we need to hear *every* detail so we can fix this."

Fix this! I wanted them to say they'd hop on Axel's private plane and hurry down to me. Instead they want every detail so I might as well start from where we were rejected at the first resort two days ago.

"So, let me get this straight, Ruth Ann," Axel said, interrupting me before I finished my story. "John went paddle boarding because you wanted to meet up with this Isabella woman and find out why she freaked out when she spotted the necklace you were wearing, right?"

"Yes!"

"Why didn't you just talk to John and explain to him you wanted to find out what was wrong with Isabella?" Prunella asked.

"He wasn't thrilled that I brought the necklace along on our trip. He went into full cop mode after we found our current bungalow didn't have any locks."

"So, you tricked him into paddle boarding at a certain time so you could go down to the unsafe part of the beach to meet Isabella?"

"Yes, I know now that it was stupid of me, but I can't go back and redo anything. I just want your help!"

"Of course," Axel replied. "I'll call the pilot and get my plane fueled and ready to go. We'll be there by lunchtime."

"Thank you," I said, relieved. "I don't have much time so I'm going to give you directions on how to find me. Hang on a second," I said, opening the closet door and looking for Carlos. I found him pacing nervously around the main room and he wasn't expecting my sudden appearance.

"Don't do that, Ruth Ann!" Carlos barked, holding his hand up to his chest. "You almost gave me a heart attack!"

"I need you to tell me where you think we'll be around lunchtime." I said.

"Why?" he asked, puzzled.

"Prunella and Axel are coming down here to help us find John and get rid of Martika."

"Tell them to meet us at the grass shack. We might not be there, but we'll make sure someone is there to lead them to us. I'm not even sure where we're going anymore!"

"Okay, I'll give them the best directions I can." I was about to put the phone back to my ear when Carlos suggested that he give the directions. He quickly instructed Axel and hung up.

"Let's get out of here now, Ruth Ann," Carlos said, anxiously. "I don't like it here. I feel like at any moment Martika could come in and blast us!"

"You mean *shoot* us?" I questioned, and Carlos shook his head vehemently. "No, she wouldn't do that. I think she'd just threaten violence and take us prisoner like John."

"You don't know how vicious that woman can be, Ruth Ann," Carlos said, suddenly shivering. "She's a solid block of ice when it comes to emotions."

I didn't want to waste any more time either, so I grabbed whatever I thought was necessary and we headed out into the dark night and made our way back to the shack. We were steps from the bungalow when Carlos grabbed my arm and forced me to stop.

"Hey," I said. "What are we stopping for?"

"I have one question for you, Ruth Ann. You can choose to tell me the truth or not." I nodded and told him to ask me whatever he wanted. "Did you grab your necklace while we were in your bungalow?"

"No," I replied, truthfully.

He appeared stunned, but took it in stride. "Okay, thanks for being honest."

I felt horrible lying to Carlos, but I still wasn't sure who I could trust. Of course I didn't take the necklace out of the bungalow because it was still in my shorts pocket. We didn't run into a soul as we hurried down the beach. Carlos and I pulled the hanging beads aside and entered the shack.

"Where are they?" I shouted. "Nobody's in here!"

Carlos didn't respond, but walked the entire perimeter of the tiny shack. "There's nowhere for them to hide, Carlos!" I snapped. "I doubt they'd all fit under the table."

"What happened?" he asked desperately, even though he knew I couldn't answer him.

"Okay, let's try and stay calm. I think one of two things could've happened. Either they took off because they knew Marti-ka was near or…" I stopped and Carlos finished my sentence, "she caught them and forced them to go with her."

"I find it hard to believe one woman could force Meme, Isa-bella, and Joseph to leave."

"Not if she had a gun pointing at them," Carlos replied.

"Then let's go look around," I suggested, walking back out of the shack. Carlos was right behind me and we stood on the sand staring out toward the beach.

"I doubt they would go near the water," Carlos said. "If they left on their own I'm sure they would head toward the jungle."

"I agree," I said. "Hey, do you think they would go to the house where Meme sent me to earlier?"

"What house?" Carlos asked, confused.

"An old man runs some sort of shop not far from here. I think I can get us there again if I use the flashlight on my cell phone."

"We might as well check it out. I don't see why they'd go there, though."

"Maybe Meme and the old man are friends and he's helping them hide."

Carlos shrugged his shoulders and we took the path I took what seemed like days ago. It wasn't easy, but we wound our way through the path and came to the clearing where the little house sat. "There it is!" I cried out.

"Shhh," Carlos insisted. "We don't know how safe it is here."

"There's nobody around!" I snapped back at him. "There's a light on the front door, let's go knock on it and see if he's there," I said, beginning to walk over to the stairs that led to the front door.

"No, Ruth Ann!" Carlos loudly whispered, grabbing my arm to stop me from going forward. "It's the middle of the night. We can't just go knock on some old man's door."

"But I got the impression that Meme and the old man are much closer than we know. He knew exactly the items she needed earlier without me telling him. He trusted me because I was sent to him from Meme."

"Yeah, but," he hesitated, and then said, "I guess we don't have anything to lose. Let's see if the old guy's awake or not."

"Good," I said, releasing his grip and marching over to the front steps. I raised my hand to knock on the outer door when the door flew open. I almost fell back down the steps, but thankfully Carlos was there to catch me. "Wow," I said, stunned. "You startled me!"

The old man quickly recognized me, but glared at Carlos. "Who is he?" he barked.

"He's my friend, and we're looking for Meme and her granddaughter. Have you seen them?"

"No."

"Please, you can trust me. Meme sent me to you earlier. If she didn't trust me, why would she do that?" I begged of the man.

He didn't answer, but thought deeply about my comment. I watched him closely as his closed mouth parted open and the few, stained teeth he had left appeared. "Yes, yes, you have a point, but, I haven't seen her."

"Are you protecting her?" Carlos asked from behind me. "We're in a lot of trouble, and we're worried that Meme and her granddaughter, and a man named Joseph were kidnapped."

"Kidnapped!" the old man hissed. "Meme would never get herself kidnapped. No matter what condition she might be in."

"What do you mean by that?" I questioned. "Is something wrong with Meme?"

"Um, no, she's just getting older, and, and she wants Isabella to take over her practice. Meme's just fine," he insisted, but I felt differently. I think he was covering up something about Meme's health.

"Fine, but if they're not here, do you know where they might've gone?" begged Carlos. "It's very important that we find them before they get hurt!"

"Hurt!" yelled the man. "You didn't say anything about one of them getting hurt." He waved us inside the tiny foyer and immediately headed through the only door that led to his store. It wasn't much better than the foyer with the walls of shelves and merchandise strewn over the floor, but at least it gave us a moment to breathe and figure out our next move.

"So, Ruth Ann," Carlos said. "What are we going to do now?"

"I don't know Carlos," I answered. "You're from this area. Where could they have gone?"

"We're forgetting the other option, Ruth Ann," Carlos said. "Martika could've captured them."

"Martika!" the old man bellowed. "No, no, she can't take them, she's a very dangerous woman!"

"We know," I said to the troubled old man.

"No, you don't get it. She's dangerous in many ways."

"Tell us what you mean?" I asked.

"She's been here before, a lot."

"Really?" I asked. "I thought this shop was for locals and for special customers like Meme."

"It is," he replied. "When she first started coming here I thought she was from one of the local villages, but when she started asking all sorts of questions I got suspicious."

"What kind of questions?" asked Carlos, curiously.

"I, don't remember," he said, rubbing his forehead with his weathered hand. "I told Meme about her and she told me never talk to her again!"

"Did you talk to her again?" I asked tentatively.

"Yes, I did," he answered, lowering his head in shame. "I betrayed Meme because she offered me lots of money."

Carlos gently touched my shoulder with his hand so he could take the lead and said, "It's okay, we understand you don't have a lot of money and if she offered you a large amount, it's understandable that you would take it."

He perked up a little with Carlos' statement and said, "Yes, yes, that is what happened!"

"Tell us what she wanted from you," Carlos asked.

"She asked many questions about my relationship with Meme."

"She knew you and Meme were friends?" I asked, surprised.

"Yes. She said Meme and she went way back, and then I got confused," he said, visibly getting concerned.

"Why would that confuse you?" I asked, even though I knew the answer.

"I didn't get why Meme told me to stay away from her when Martika told me they had been really close."

"Yes, I can see how that's confusing for you, but you ended up talking to her anyway," Carlos said, taking over the conversation again.

"Yes, I did. Martika wanted to know about the items I've supplied Meme. She was curious about what I knew about Meme's power to rid people of curses."

"Can you even answer those questions?" I asked, curiously. "I mean, isn't Meme the one with the power?"

"Meme definitely has powers, but she needs specific ingredients from time to time, and that's why she comes to me. I can get everything she needs. I don't have any power, but I can supply her what is necessary for her to help people. I'm kind of like the pharmacist and Meme's the doctor!" The old man grinned proudly.

"That's a good analogy," Carlos said before I could dispute his rather extreme analogy. "Can Ruth Ann and I call you by your name if you don't mind?"

The old man looked nervously from Carlos to me, but nodded and replied, "My name's Felix."

"Great, thanks Felix," Carlos said. "Let's get back to Martika. Did you tell her what Meme used to break her curses?"

"No, I couldn't," he answered eagerly. "Every situation is different and I can't remember everything Meme needs."

"But you knew what Meme needed when I saw you yesterday," I said, wondering if he wasn't telling us the entire truth.

"Yes, that was just a basic necessity kit, Ruth Ann. When Meme has a client that needs her help, she comes in here with a list. Every person requires different ingredients depending on the level of the curse."

"The level?" inquired Carlos.

"Some curses are petty, no big deal, but some are much more difficult and require many challenging ingredients that only I know how to get."

"Did you tell Martika that?" I asked.

"Yes," he answered, worried. "Did I do something wrong? I didn't tell her too much more, except…"

"Except…" Carlos repeated, waving his hands to get him to continue.

"Except, I accidentally blurted out that Meme warned me not to talk to her."

"You did?" I asked Felix.

"She was pushing me, and I got frustrated. The woman started out kind, but when I wouldn't tell her about some root she asked about, she went off on me! She started yelling at me and told me if I didn't tell her everything I knew about Meme and what she needed to rid curses, she would come back and hurt me."

"So, you blurted out that Meme said she was evil, right?" Carlos asked.

"Yes!" Felix bellowed. "Martika is evil. You should've seen the fire in her eyes."

"Oh, I've seen it before, Felix," Carlos admitted. "Martika is not my friend, just so you know."

"Mine either," I added. "She may have kidnapped Meme and her granddaughter. That's why we need your help."

"Don't forget Joseph," Carlos mentioned.

"Unless Joseph is still pretending to be on Martika's side," I said.

"I doubt that anymore, Ruth Ann," Carlos said.

"I know, I was just hoping," I replied, sullen and discouraged.

"We need to rescue Meme and Isabella!" Felix blurted out. "What can I do to help?"

"Can you tell us where Martika was going?" I asked, doubting he would know anyway.

"She must be close by, because she's been around here several times."

"How many?" Carlos asked. "I thought after you told her she was evil, she left."

"She left after she threatened to hurt me," Felix reminded us. "She didn't get any other information from me, but I've seen someone stalking out my house lately."

"You never told us that!" Carlos exclaimed. "That's important, Felix. Who have you seen?"

"A big man has walked around my house several times the last couple days."

I looked at Carlos and whispered, "Ever since John went missing I bet."

"Yes, and when Martika spotted your necklace back in the restaurant."

"That wasn't very smart of me," I said, touching my side pocket and feeling the bulge of the gem hidden inside.

"Why would you think you'd be in danger down here? You didn't even want to bring the necklace down here, but your cousin and her husband convinced you. You didn't know that was the plan all along."

"Wait, what?" I asked, puzzled. "What do you mean it was the plan all along?"

"If Martika went to Deer Creek and met with Prunella and Axel, they may have formed some kind of alliance. I'm sure Martika lied to them or even subtly suggested something about how lovely the necklace was she saw on television and how valuable it was."

"So, you're saying that Martika knew Axel was in financial trouble and could've suggested the necklace get stolen and then they would acquire the insurance money?" Carlos nodded slowly. "That seems far-fetched and how would Martika know about Axel's money problems anyway?"

"Because it was all over the news in Stockholm," Carlos said. "Even I heard about the infamous Eklund's and how their pier was blown up."

"You did?" I asked, wondering if Carlos knew about Martika's plans, too.

"I see the look in your eyes, Ruth Ann," Carlos said immediately. "And just so you know, I had no idea what Martika's plans were when she blackmailed me into marrying her and buying the run down resort. I hope you can trust me."

I wanted to, but there were too many twists and turns in his story about how Martika found out about my necklace and came to Deer Creek. Until I come face to face with Prunella and Axel, I wasn't going to completely trust anyone!

"Carlos, I want to trust you. If I trust anyone right now, it's you. You've given me no reason not to."

"I'll take that," he replied, and then turned back to Felix. "This man, can you describe him?"

"Yes, yes, he's about twice as tall as me," Felix said, raising his arm up in the air to support his statement. "He wasn't dark, like most of the locals down here."

"You mean he was white or Caucasian?" I asked, a little surprised.

"Yes, yes, very white."

"Was he American?" Carlos asked.

"I don't know. He's very tall, big and muscular with yellow hair and blue eyes. I don't know if that's what American's look like, but that's him."

"Did he see you?" asked Carlos.

"No, I'm sure Martika told him I was an old man who couldn't see very well."

"But you can, right?" Carlos inquired.

"Yes, my eyesight is perfect still, surprisingly enough. I know I'm in my late eighties, but I'm strong and still have a working mind."

"Good, good," Carlos said, thinking hard. "So this man, did he ever speak any words to anyone, like Martika?"

"Nope. He just walked around and around my house, and then he'd disappear into the woods. Then he would reappear and do the same thing."

"Carlos," I started to say. "You know what that means, don't you?"

"Yes, Martika has hired help. That's not good for us."

"He may have hurt John, too," I said, worried. "And now if Meme, Isabella, and Joseph have been captured, we're in bigger trouble."

"I know, Ruth Ann," Carlos said, discouraged. "But we still don't know that for sure."

"Hey!" I cried out. "Felix, you said the man would walk around the place, and then disappear, right?" Felix nodded. "But he would come back. How long was he gone before he reappeared and started pacing around your house again?"

"Not long. Maybe every thirty minutes or so, why?" he asked.

"That's great!" I blurted out. "That means wherever they're holding John, and maybe the others, it has to be close by. What do you think, Carlos?"

"I think you're probably right!" he agreed, smiling. "We should search the surrounding area and see if we find another house or," he slammed his fist on the counter in the middle of Felix's room. "What if they're all back at the resort in one of the older bungalows?"

"No, Martika wouldn't be that stupid, would she?" I asked.

"It's brilliant, actually. That lets her keep up her appearances at the restaurant and lobby, but still close enough to get here or the shack."

"You could be right, Carlos. I think we should check it out. How many bungalows are there?" I inquired.

"Let's see, there's yours, and another newly renovated one down by the water, but I think it's already occupied with another guest. Then there's at least ten more along the path from the pool area down to the beach."

"Then we'll check each one out!" I demanded.

"Some of them are occupied, but I'll go and check the register and see which ones are open."

"You mean the yellow pad of paper?" I said, teasing Carlos about the way they checked guests in.

"Yes, Ruth Ann. We haven't updated the resort with computers yet. That was next on my list, actually."

"I'm sorry, I was trying to lighten up the mood. It's bad enough what we're going through. I feel strongly that John and the others are still all right, but for how long?"

Felix wanted to accompany us back to the resort, but Carlos was able to dissuade him. "We need you here in case Meme and the others show up. You can fill them in on where we've gone."

"What about the big guy outside?" he asked.

"Stay inside and don't confront him," Carlos ordered. "He hasn't tried to come inside your place yet, so I think you're safe."

"Okay, I'll do what you ask because I don't want anything bad to happen to Meme and Isabella. They mean a lot to me."

We walked into the tiny foyer and Carlos carefully peeked outside to see if the tall, big, blonde man was wandering around outside. "Coast's clear right now so let's go, Ruth Ann."

I turned to say goodbye to Felix, but he had already disappeared into the larger room and shut the door. I heard a click or two and figured he had locked himself inside. "Let's go!" I said, hurrying down the steps onto the sand.

Carlos grabbed my hand and rushed me into the dense jungle. "I wonder if we should wait here a little while and see if he shows up?"

"But it'll waste valuable time, Carlos," I whispered.

"Think about it, Ruth Ann. We won't have to guess where he's going then. He'll come here and check out Felix's place to see if anyone has shown up, and then he'll lead us right to where John's being held."

"You're right!" I replied, thrilled at his quick thinking. "But what if he catches us?"

"We'll stay hidden. I've been around this place long enough to stay hidden in the jungle. Follow me," he said, gripping my hand in his sweaty hand and dragging me a little deeper into the jungle. It clearly wasn't on a path, and Carlos wouldn't let me turn on my flashlight. I hoped he knew where he was going, because the last thing we needed was to get bitten, stung, eaten or strangled by whatever is lurking in this jungle!

He came to an abrupt stop and I bumped right into him. "Hey," I said. "Some warning would've been nice."

"Sorry, I think we've gone far enough. I doubt the fool would go here," he said, wiping the dripping sweat off his forehead. "It's steamy in here, isn't it?"

"Yes, but I'd rather stay way out of sight from this man. There's something odd about this man who's been scouting out Felix's house."

"What?"

"Why would Martika hire a blonde, blue-eyed man? I get that she wanted someone big and muscular, but why not a local?"

"Good point. Got any theories," Carlos asked, smiling in the dark at me, but I could still make out his grin.

"Yes, I do, Carlos," I replied snottily. "If you knew about my past few months, you would know the answer already."

"Please, do tell," he said.

"I think Martika went to Sweden to seek the necklace, but it wasn't there anymore. She met up with some unsavory people over there and brought one (or maybe more than one) man back with her to help. She knew she couldn't do the physical part of the kid-napping without some help."

"She thought she had Joseph."

"Joseph! He's a doctor, not a criminal," I retorted. "He may have been convincing enough to Martika about being able to break curses and all, but he surely wasn't big or strong enough to handle John!"

"You have a point, Ruth Ann."

"Wow," I said too loud, and Carlos reacted by slapping a hand over my mouth. "Ouch," I cried.

"You have to be careful, Ruth Ann," he snapped. "I'm starting to understand the kind of person you really are."

"What's that supposed to mean?" I barked.

"No, no, I don't mean that in a bad way, Ruth Ann. I just meant I see you as a strong, energetic, stubborn woman who speaks her own mind and doesn't let anyone take advantage of her."

"Oh, I guess that's not so bad," I said, not agreeing with the stubborn part. "I do drive John mad when I don't listen to him and end up in trouble. Kind of like now!"

"I don't want you on my bad side, but if you would've just let John know about Isabella's initial reaction to the necklace, none of this might've happened."

"You don't know that, Carlos," I snapped, knowing deep down he could be correct. I eased up a bit and added, "I know, Carlos, I already feel horrible enough without you pointing it out to me."

"Sorry."

"Let's change the subject. How long are we going to wait here?"

Carlos lifted his wrist up so he could see the watch he was wearing. "It's five in the morning now. Prunella and Axel won't be here for several hours. We've only been here about ten minutes, and Felix said he thought the big guy came around every thirty minutes or so."

"So wait another twenty minutes?" I asked.

"Yes."

We stood in silence for a while trying to hear any footsteps or wild animal sounds. I was thankful we didn't come into contact with anything more than a few mosquitos when Carlos grabbed my forearm. "What?" I asked, but this time I was quiet and whispered.

"I hear something," he replied. "Listen."

We froze in our spots and leaned our heads forward. I couldn't hear a thing, but Carlos squeezed my arm tighter. "I think someone's out there."

"I don't hear anything."

"Shhh," he said. "There's definitely something or someone out there."

I finally heard a muffling or crunching sound. "If it's him, he's not walking on the sand," I said, quietly.

Carlos nodded, with wide-opened fearful eyes. What if the man Martika had watching the place didn't just walk around Felix's house? What if he also walked around the surrounding jungle, too and we didn't think of that!

I wanted to move because the crunching sound was getting closer. I tried to get Carlos' attention, but he looked terrified. It was time that this strong, smart, and stubborn woman took the lead and got us away from here. I took a hold of his arm this time and pushed him deeper into the jungle.

Once I woke Carlos from his petrified trance, he was able to take the lead and move us far away from the approaching noise. "I think we're safe enough now," he whispered. "I don't hear the crunching sound anymore."

I nodded, but didn't speak. In the distance I spotted a dim light. It had to be the man searching Felix's grounds. "Look," I quietly said. "He's halfway between us and Felix's house."

"Yes, don't move an inch," Carlos replied. "Let's see if he keeps going."

We stood motionless and waited for the light to move on. I think if we would've stayed where we were, we would've been spotted. I was thankful that I was able to get us deeper into the jungle so Martika's hired man didn't find us. However, it was time for us to follow him.

I nudged Carlos and we carefully stepped closer to where the man had just been. We could vaguely see the light ahead. "Don't make too much noise, Ruth Ann."

We stayed close enough to follow him until the light suddenly went out. "Oh, no," I exclaimed. "Where'd he go?"

"I don't know," Carlos said, frustrated.

Even though the air was stifling inside the jungle, I had a sudden chill run through my entire body. Something wasn't right, but what? I knew we had to find this man so he could lead us to John. Carlos took off running without me, and I couldn't see a thing. I wasn't about to be left alone in this thick, scary rainforest so I headed in the direction Carlos ran. I didn't make it too far when I tripped over a rock on the ground. I went flying down, and thankfully wasn't hurt.

"Ruth Ann!" Carlos called out to me. "Are you alright?"

"No thanks to you," I snapped, looking up at him. "Why did you run off without me?"

"I thought I heard a noise so I ran after it. It wasn't him, though, it was a small animal."

"You can't just take off and leave me alone in the dark, and in the jungle!"

"I'm sorry, Ruth Ann. I didn't have time to explain," Carlos said, frustrated. "Let's get out of here. I think we've lost him so we might as well head back to the resort and check out the bunga-lows."

Discouraged, and a little sore, I followed Carlos back to the path that took us onto the beach. The mysterious man had vanished into thin air. It was our best lead, and we blew it. Now we had to sneak around the resort. I was terrified to go back.

Chapter 24

Carlos wanted me to wait on the beach until he was able to get up to the lobby and grab the guest list, but I flatly refused. He didn't want to waste any more time than was necessary so he allowed me to follow him, but on his terms.

"We're not going on the main walkway that takes us past the pool and restaurant."

"Fine, I get it."

"Stay right behind me. If I jump off to the side, you jump, got it?"

"Yes."

"Okay, once we get close to the lobby, I'll hide you in a storage shed that's next to the pool. Once I get the sheet, I'll come get you."

"I don't like that idea, but I guess we don't have any choice."

Carlos hurried to my bungalow and we glanced inside the windows, but it was dark. I suggested we do the same with the five bungalows we passed along the way to the lobby, but he refused. "What if a guest saw us looking inside their window? That would infuriate them and they would report it. We don't need to tip off Martika."

"I get it. But what if you're spotted by someone Martika has paid to keep watch for you?"

"It's almost sunrise. There's really nobody around until after six in the morning. I'll be careful."

We made it to the pool successfully. The lights inside and around the pool were off. There were a few lampposts scattered around the pool and restaurant, but we didn't spot a soul. Carlos headed toward a small shed that was off to the side of the lobby and motioned for me to go inside. He told me to not say a word, but wait for him to return. I didn't like it, but he promised he'd be back in less than five minutes.

"Hurry up!" I said.

"Don't worry, I doubt Martika's around here now. I think she's with the others, wherever they are."

"Probably getting sleep, unlike us!" I complained, remembering it wasn't too long ago that I pulled several all-nighters trying to find murderers.

At least I was able to turn on the light inside the shed. I looked around and spotted shelves full of pool towels, chemicals, and a large pole with a blue net to skim debris out of the pool. I was thirsty and should've asked Carlos to grab something for me while he was in the lobby. I grabbed a towel and folded it in half, and then in half again. I dropped it on the floor and sat on top of it. I was tired, and wondered if I just closed my eyes for a minute I would get rejuvenated.

"Ruth Ann, Ruth Ann," a voice called out to me. "Wake up!"

I couldn't understand why John was waking me up. I just went to sleep and was having the worst nightmare. John was kidnapped, and I was running around chasing witch doctors trying to break curses. I was so tired, please let me get some more sleep.

"Ruth Ann!" Carlos yelled louder, and grabbed my shoulders and shook them forcefully.

"I'm up, I'm up," I growled, but then looked up and saw Carlos. "Oh, it's not a nightmare, it's real, isn't it?"

"I'm afraid so, Ruth Ann," he answered, helping me to stand up.

"Did you get the list?" I asked.

"Yes."

"See anyone?"

"Nope."

We stopped our banter and walked out to the pool area. "Maybe you should remain back in the shed. It's safe in there."

"No way!" I cried out. "I'm going where you're going."

Carlos shrugged his shoulders and walked around the pool and onto a side path that I had not been on before. "Where are we going?"

"There are three bungalows down this way, and none of them are occupied."

"Why not?" I asked, wondering if anyone really stayed at this place.

"Because these bungalows haven't been renovated."

We walked a minute or so when Carlos pointed to a small bungalow. "Wow, this place looks like it could tumble down," I said, looking at the worn building. "It looks about as good as those shacks down the beach."

"I think they're a little better than those," Carlos snapped. "At least these have running water, a bathroom, and a bedroom."

"No electricity?"

"Nope, not yet. That's part of the renovation I planned on doing soon." Carlos frowned, and I picked up on his use of the word 'planned'.

"You think after this is over you'll get rid of the resort?" I asked, interestedly. I thought what he had done to my bungalow was wonderful. It was roomy, and had nice amenities.

"I think so, Ruth Ann," Carlos replied. "I think this place will be too hard to be around."

"Don't let Martika bring you down, Carlos. I think this place has a ton of potential."

Carlos perked up and nodded, but a second later he appeared deflated. "I see your point, but don't forget about Joseph. He betrayed me, too."

"But he redeemed himself," I declared, reminding Carlos that Joseph was willing to help us.

"Unless he was lying, and stayed on Martika's side. We really don't know yet since we haven't found the others."

"We will. I think they may be in one of these run down bungalows," I said, not as confidently as I should have. Carlos walked up to the dark building and looked inside a window. "It's pitch black in here. I don't think anyone's in there."

"Could they be sleeping and Martika wanted to keep it dark inside?"

"I doubt it. Unless she drugged everyone," Carlos stopped speaking and I knew what he was imagining.

"No, Carlos. Joseph didn't drug them like he supposedly did to me."

"You don't know that for sure, Ruth Ann."

"I feel quite sure," I answered, actually unsure.

"Let's go on to the next one. It's only a short distance from here."

I followed Carlos down the sandy path, but I noticed it was becoming slightly light outside. I was happy for the light, but worried we'd be spotted. "Here it is," Carlos said, walking right up to the window on this bungalow. "Nope. All dark again."

"So there's another one around here, right?" I asked him, looking around but not spotting any new building.

"Yes, but it's a little way down the path toward the jungle. It might be a better location for Martika since it's away from the action of the resort."

"Action?" I questioned Carlos. "What action?"

"I meant the employees of the resort who clean the pool and lobby area, and the restaurant workers, and don't forget house-keeping."

"Oh, I get it."

We trudged down the path and I noticed it wasn't as sandy. We were actually walking on matted down grass. Carlos stopped before I could see any bungalow. "What'd you stop for?"

"I have an uneasy feeling about this, Ruth Ann."

"You really think they're in this one, don't you?"

"I do."

"Then let's go see!" I said, invigorated and awake at the prospect of finally setting my eyes on John.

"It could be very dangerous. I think you should hang out back here while I sneak up on the building and take a quick peek. I don't want to risk either of us making too much noise."

"We're walking on grass, Carlos. What noise can we possibly make?"

"I just don't want to risk anything happening to you. There could be a guard walking around the building keeping an eye out for us."

"Oh, like the one who was checking on Felix's place?"

"Yes. You heard Felix. He was a big, blonde man and I can guarantee you he's packing a gun."

"I'm sure he is," I said. "I'm not afraid of that, Carlos. If you only knew what I've been through the last few months, you wouldn't worry so much about me."

"You can tell me all about it when we're safe and far away from here."

"Deal, but I'm still following you."

"Fine," he retorted, giving in to my demand. "But if I tell you to run, you run!"

"I know, I know. Just like before," I said, starting to walk around him to take the lead, but he held me back.

"No, no. I go first."

I quietly asked him how far away the bungalow was, but he only shook his head and stomped forward. I guessed from his lack of communication that we weren't far away. The further we walked, the darker it got. I knew the sun was starting to rise, but we were going deeper into the thick jungle. What kind of guest would want to rent this bungalow? I know, a very, very private guest or one who didn't want to be seen. This was a perfect hideout!

"Okay, it's right around the bend up ahead. I think we should move forward, but keep a sharp lookout for any noise or feeling we're being watched."

"*Feeling?*" I asked strangely. "Don't tell me you're like Meme and Isabella!"

"No, no, that's not what I meant. Don't you get uneasy feelings when you're about to dive into danger? I know I do."

"I guess so. It's happened so often lately; you'd think I would."

Carlos slowed his steps and walked with a light foot. There were twigs, leaves, and miscellaneous items that could make sounds when stepped on. My eyes were whipping around from the ground to the front of us to each side. I didn't spot anyone or anything until Carlos pulled me abruptly to the ground. I didn't see it coming and landed hard on a rock with my hand. My immediate reaction was to yelp out loud, but I knew I had to restrain myself.

After rubbing my sore hand, hoping it wasn't broken or sprained, I looked up at what Carlos was staring at. He shook his head at me so I wouldn't speak, but he didn't have to. I saw what had startled him and forced him to throw us to the ground. It was the same man we almost ran into in the jungle near Felix's house.

We ducked behind a grouping of palm bushes and watched as the man tramped through the foliage and headed on to the grassy path. I whispered just as he was out of earshot, "I think he just did a search of the area and now he's going back to the bungalow. I think you were right! They're in there for sure."

"I agree, Ruth Ann. Give him a minute to get further ahead and then we'll get closer."

We waited about two minutes, and then Carlos stood up, brushed himself off and reached his hand out to help me up. I know I didn't require his assistance, but it was a kind gesture so I took him up on it. I stiffly rose and stretched out my arms over my head and twisted my body back and forth to loosen up my back. "Are you alright?" Carlos asked, watching my motions.

"Yes, just a little stiff. I'll be fine."

"Let's go, but watch where you're walking. I don't want you to step on anything that'll alert him to turn around."

"I won't," I said, watching the ground already. It was bright outside and Carlos told me it was near seven in the morning. I was counting each hour until Prunella and Axel arrived. I couldn't wait to see them, and to clear their names with our new group here in Jamaica. I didn't believe Prunella or Axel would do anything to risk my life, but there was a small churning in my stomach at the thought that Axel needed money and was using me to get it. I shook off the thought, for now. I stayed close on Carlos' heels as we made our way back to the grassy path.

"Do you think it's wise to walk on the path?"

"Probably not, but it's the quickest way to the bungalow."

I understood his thinking, but if we got captured then it wasn't very wise of either of us. I didn't argue with Carlos, but followed him until he made a quick stop. "We're as close as we can go on the path. Follow me."

Carlos pushed aside a large bush on the left side of the path and went past it. He left the bush open so I could fit through and then went into the deeper foliage. I wasn't a fan of going back in there, but we couldn't risk being seen by the guard and I doubted he would go in this thick group of bushes. "Okay," Carlos murmured. "Hold my hand. I'm going to make our way right up to the bungalow from the side." He reached out and held his hand out for me to grab. I took hold and silently prayed that he knew what he was doing.

He used his free hand to push aside any loose branches as he carefully strode closer and closer to the bungalow. I had no idea how far it was since I couldn't see more than the bush or tree that was in front of us. It was dark, damp, and extremely hot in the jungle. There was nowhere for the air to move and I was suddenly feeling claustrophobic. "How much further?" I asked quietly. "It's really hot in here!"

"We're here," Carlos replied, stopping in his tracks.

"I don't see anything," I said, adjusting my eyes to the brightness that appeared out of nowhere.

"The sun's coming up so it's hard to see, Ruth Ann. The bungalow is just to our right. It's in a small opening in the jungle so that's why the sun's so bright. It's hitting the metal trim around the roof and windows and blinding us."

"Do you see the bungalow?" I asked him since he was in front of me blocking most of my view.

"Yes."

"Can you see anyone?" I asked, anxiously.

"No."

"Can you stop the one word answers! It's really annoying."

"Sorry," he choked on the last comment and replied, "Oh, sorry about that. I'm not trying to be sarcastic. I'm looking to see if there's anyone around. We don't want to be surprised, do we?"

"No, but I'm getting impatient. I want to see if this is the place John's being held and if Meme, Isabella, and Joseph are here, too."

"I think we already know the answer to that, Ruth Ann. Why else would a guard be walking around the jungle?"

"Good point, but we don't know for sure that Meme and the rest of them are here, too."

"No, and I hope they're not. It'll be easier to free one person than four."

"Trust me, if John's conscious, he'll help us once he sees us."

"As long as they don't have a gun on him. We don't want them to shoot first, and then grab us!"

"No. We can't let that happen." I didn't want to think about that so I quickly changed the subject. "What are we going to do now?"

"Well, I'm going to have a look inside the side window. I'm just hoping we can see inside."

"You think it'll be closed up, don't you?" I asked, worried.

"Not exactly. The reason why I had us come to this side is because the bungalow is open on the other three sides. This particular side has trees right up to the structure. There's no reason to shut the blinds since nobody would think a person would come to that side."

"Oh, that's good. Are you waiting to make sure the guard doesn't plow through the jungle anyway?"

"Yes, and I'm trying to stop my hands from shaking."

For the first time it hit me that I wasn't the only one terrified. Poor Carlos was scared, and I bet he wasn't used to running around after criminals. "I'm scared too," I told him. "But we're close, I can feel it."

"Me, too," he said, smiling back at me. "I'm going in. Stay here."

"I'll be right behind you so don't try and stop me."

"I didn't think I could. I spoke too soon. Now I know you pretty well, and I won't fight you about anything again."

"Thanks," I said, taking Carlos's comments as a compliment.

He stepped over a few loose branches and pushed aside a couple bushes when he came up to the side of the bungalow. He put his fingers to his mouth to make sure I understood there was no more talking. I nodded, and watched what he was doing, excited at the prospect of John being so close inside this bungalow.

Carlos felt along the wood siding of the bungalow and knelt down low. I followed suit, and when I looked up I noticed why he leaned over. It was a window or kind of a window. The large opening was enclosed, but with a piece of plastic that fit nicely in the opening. I wondered how air got in and out, but then I noticed it flipped open and was held in place with a long rod. It was definitely not a secure bungalow, but who would come all the way in the jungle to find this place!

Carlos slowly rose and with the help of his hands on his quadriceps, pulled himself halfway up. He stuck his head just to the bottom of the window and tried to look inside. I really wanted to look, too, but waited for Carlos to report what he saw. It didn't take long when he knelt back down to the ground next to me. He motioned for me to follow him around the back side of the bungalow. I was worried where we were going, because he told me this was the only safely enclosed side.

I wanted to ask him why we were going to unsafe territory, but couldn't so I crawled next to him as he went toward the back. Carlos stood up and reached his hand down to help me. I didn't take it this time, and glared at him, waiting for an answer to why we were putting ourselves out in the open.

"They're gone," Carlos said in his regular voice.

"What!" I bellowed, and then threw my hand over my mouth.

"It's okay. I think we just missed them."

"How on earth do you know that?" I asked, very confused. "We just saw that guard!"

"I think he was here looking for us, Ruth Ann."

"But why…how?" I asked, frustrated. "We just got here!"

"I just know, let's go inside. Maybe there's a clue or two in there."

Carlos walked around to the front of the rundown bungalow not worrying about the guard anymore. I didn't understand what was happening. Why would Carlos not be worried about the guard when we just saw him?

"It's okay, Ruth Ann," Carlos said, almost as if he read my mind. "I think the guard was checking here one last time to see if we had shown up. He probably is on his way back to report to Martika that we were nowhere in sight."

"You think so?" I asked, deflated.

"Let's go check it out before we make assumptions." Carlos entered the unlocked bungalow and disappeared inside. I hurried after him and walked into a dark, smelly, hot open room.

"This place is disgusting," I said, looking around at the dirty cement floor and sparse furniture. "Did anyone *ever* stay in here?"

"Not since I've owned the place. I only knew it was here from the blueprint of the resort we were given when we purchased the place."

"Hasn't anyone ever cleaned the place?"

"Probably not. It was going to be torn down anyway so why bother?"

I shrugged my shoulders and started looking for signs that John or the others had been here. Carlos did the same. It didn't take long before Carlos called me over to a couple of cots at the back of the room. "He was here, Ruth Ann."

"What'd you find?" I asked, eagerly.

Carlos held up a small piece of wood. "Look at this."

I grabbed the flat, hand-sized piece of wood. "I don't see anything."

"Turn it over, Ruth Ann."

I turned over the flimsy piece and gasped. "John! He scratched his name in the wood."

"Yes. Now we know he was here, but keep looking for clues."

I went over to the small kitchenette and opened a mini refrigerator. There were a few water bottles, an apple and an orange. I grabbed a bottle of water and opened it up. I drank eagerly and took another one for Carlos. He took it right away and drank the bottle in one long swig. "Think the apple and orange are safe?" I asked him.

"Rinse it off in the sink," he answered, pointing to a small, dirty, rusted sink in the corner of the kitchenette. "I know it's gross, just let the water run a minute and then rinse the fruit off. I think it'll do us a lot of good."

I walked over to the sink that was located in the front of the bungalow. There was a small cut-out for a window and another piece of thin plastic inside the opening. I tried to look outside, but it had a thick film and I wasn't about to touch it. Carlos took the orange. I knew he did it to make it easier for me. Eating an apple was much easier than an orange.

I continued looking around the small room as I munched on the surprisingly crisp, red apple. "I don't see anything but garbage," I said with a mouthful of the sweet, juicy fruit.

"Don't just surface check. Dig deep into the piles on the floor, the counters, and the furniture. You never know what you might find, like..." Carlos stopped speaking and grabbed another item from the floor at the back of the room. "Hey, look at this!"

I rushed over to him and tried to get a peek at what he was looking at. "What is it?" I asked, not able to see anything at all.

"It's a ring," Carlos answered, holding a shiny little object out so I could see.

"Is it important? I don't recognize it, do you?"

"Yes, I do, Ruth Ann." He held the ring close to his face and gazed at it admiringly. "It's Martika's."

"Really?" I asked, wondering why I should care about a ring that belonged to Martika. We already knew John had been held prisoner in here by her.

"It's a ring given to her by her father."

"Isabella's father, too, right?" I asked, questioning Carlos' assumption that it was Martika's. Maybe Isabella had a ring like that, too.

"Oh, it's hers all right," he replied, smiling. "She told me all about this ring when we were actually getting along."

"You two got along? I thought you were blackmailed into marrying her and buying the resort."

"I was, but before that time. Martika had known me from our village and she was a pretty, outgoing girl that I once had a huge crush on, until..."

"Until you realized you weren't attracted to women, right?"

"Yes. Martika and I were close years ago. She's had that ring ever since her father was cursed out of their lives."

"Meme told me about Isabella and Martika's father. He cheated on Isabella's mother for years and Martika was a girl when she showed up on their doorstep. I was told Isabella's mother took her in, so why would Martika want to betray them?"

"Martika thought she was better than them. She told me her life was horrible, full of witches and crazy stuff."

"But you were close to Isabella, too?"

"Yes, I was. I tried to get through to Martika, but I think she was jealous, really, that she didn't have the powers Isabella, Meme, and her mother possessed."

"You think so?"

"Oh, yes. Martika would get angry and complain all the time about those woman, but I knew deep down she envied them. I think that's why she's trying to destroy them."

"What about that ring your holding? What did Martika tell you about it?"

"Her father gave it to her before he sent her to live with the others. He told her that it would always protect her from the evilness in the house where Meme lived. He told her to be a good child and young woman so she wouldn't..."

"Be cursed?" I asked.

"Yes. He believed he would die in excruciating pain so he chose to speed up the process and went and got himself killed out in the jungle."

"So, it was true what I was told about how he was cursed and ended his life by being bitten, stung, and whatever else to death!"

"Oh, yes. I was around when it happened. That's why I tried to get Martika to either lose the anger she held inside or leave and never come back."

"She left, didn't she?"

"Yes, but she still obviously held onto her rage."

"I'll say," I mumbled. "Is the ring valuable?"

"I think it's just a cheap, local stone," he replied, handing the ring over to me.

I took the ring and placed it in the palm of my hand. It was a pretty little thing with an oval shaped green-blue stone, and a couple of diamonds (or fake ones) on each side. The setting was in silver, which isn't overly expensive, but I'm surprised she would leave such a sentimental piece behind. I put the ring in the same pocket as my necklace. I wondered if the good and evil with the two pieces would neutralize and end this nightmare, but no such luck. Carlos decided we better get back to the grass shack and wait until Prunella and Axel arrived. I agreed because we had no idea where to look anymore.

"What about the other bungalows?" I asked. "We only checked a few."

"We'll go by the others on our way back to the beach. They aren't as secluded as this one was, but who knows...Martika may be thinking we'd never suspect her to hide hostages in plain sight."

"We still don't know if it's just John or if Isabella, Meme, and Joseph were captured, too."

"It sure would appear so," Carlos said, deflated. "This place was a mess and if they did leave another sign, we'd never find it with all the garbage everywhere."

"I know, it's depressing."

"Yes, it is," he replied. "Let's head out."

We took off down the grassy path instead of lurking around in the jungle. Carlos felt we were fairly safe since the guard just checked this place and found nobody around. We finally ended up back on the sandy path that would eventually lead to my bungalow, but Carlos headed toward the beach in another direction.

"There are three other bungalows down this way," he said, pointing to the right. "It's light outside so we need to be extremely careful."

I nodded and followed him as he made his way a short distance and then pointed to the first bungalow. It wasn't as bad as the last few, but still needed major repairs. The building was solid, but vines had overtaken the entire bungalow. It was set in a sunnier environment except for the overgrown foliage that surrounded the bungalow. Carlos walked up to the front door and pushed it in without any hesitation.

"Hey, what if they're in there!" I cried out, taking a step back just in case.

"Then they'd catch me, and you would need to run for your life."

"That's not very nice of you, Carlos," I snapped, knowing he was being sarcastic. "Be careful!"

Carlos disappeared into the bungalow. He didn't come out for a couple minutes and I got extremely anxious waiting for him. Did I go in after him or run for the grass shack and wait for Prunella and Axel? My question was answered immediately when Carlos reappeared in the doorway. "Nobody's been here, Ruth Ann."

"Don't do that to me again!" I yelled. "You went inside and didn't tell me if it was safe or not. I didn't know what I was going to do!"

"I told you, run!"

I ignored him and waited for him to lead the way to the next bungalow. It didn't take long since it was only about fifty steps from the last one. It was a replica of the last one. I didn't worry this time as he entered the place and came right back out. "Nope."

We walked back on the path and headed a little closer to the beach. The bungalow in my view was parallel to the one John and I were staying in. Carlos marched up to the broken down door and pushed it in. I was about to yell, "watch out," because the door was coming off its hinges. Carlos had a good hold on the loosely hinged door and carefully closed it leaving me standing just outside the front entrance. I leaned against the front of the bungalow wishing I could close my eyes for a few minutes. I really was getting too old for this, I thought to myself. I barely have caught up with sleep from the last escapade!

I closed my eyes and waited, and waited. Carlos didn't come back out as quickly as the other two bungalows. I forced my eyes open and creeped around to the side of the bungalow and looked for a window. "There's no window on this side," I said quietly to myself. I didn't have a choice but to go around to the back. I knew there had to be a sliding glass door or at least a large window back here. It was facing the sea, and the whole point of these bungalows near the water is to *see* the water.

I reminded myself that this wasn't a renovated bungalow like mine, but there still should be an opening of some kind. Well, there was, but it was more like a large whole hole with a piece of plastic duct taped over it. I wasn't worried about being seen since the plastic was so blurry and filthy nobody would spot me. I kneeled over and crept over to the side of the opening and stuck my head inside. I tried to see if Carlos was still inside, but I couldn't make out much of anything. I had to go back around and push open the front door and peek inside. The one thing I was sure of was that there was no noise coming from within. Maybe Carlos had found a clue.

I made my way carefully back to the front door and gently grabbed the door handle and gave it a slight push. I was thankful the door didn't make an ounce of noise as it opened a couple of inches. I stuck my head in the opening and looked inside. It was dark, and I could only make out some basic furniture. I decided it was safe to enter since I couldn't hear or see any movement so I pushed the door open widely enough for me to enter.

I stepped inside and immediately took a quick tour of the place. I didn't want anyone to sneak up on my side or behind the door that I had just opened. "Nobody," I whispered. "Carlos…are you in here?" No response. I looked at the sparsely furnished room and noticed it was much cleaner than the other ones. There wasn't any garbage or mess on the floors and counters. The little kitchenette was in pretty good shape with a full-size refrigerator, microwave, and a nice faucet and sink. I was just thinking the place wasn't too bad when I heard a low moan coming from somewhere inside the bungalow. My heart started racing as I slowly turned away from the kitchen and gazed out at the large open living area. I knew I had to find out what or who made that noise.

I walked around the room and couldn't find the source of the noise so I went over to the one and only door in the room. It had to be for the bathroom and closet just like my bungalow. I reached to open the door fighting the powerful urge to back away. I couldn't, and I knew it. Carlos could be hurt in there so I turned the knob and pushed open the door.

I entered inside the small bathroom. I didn't see Carlos, but I knew I had to check the closet. I walked through the bathroom to the other end and pulled open the sheet that was used as a door from to the closet. I stepped inside and that's when I saw Carlos! He was on the floor, his wrists and ankles tied with rope.

"Carlos!" I yelled, startling him out of his slumber. "Wake up, wake up! Did they drug you?"

Carlos' eyes opened and he whipped his head back and forth to get me to take out the gag I hadn't noticed was shoved into his mouth. I fell to the floor and pulled out a dirty rag that was stuffed inside his mouth. "Chloroform," he spat out, gasping for air. "It was a light dose, so I wasn't totally out."

"Who did this to you?" I demanded, trying to untie his wrists, but failing since they were tied so tightly. I told him to hold off speaking until I ran out and found something to free him with. I didn't want to stand there and listen to his account just in case whoever came back and found us. I wanted Carlos free to get up and run alongside me!

Carlos nodded and closed his eyes again. I didn't think his body was as quite clear of the chloroform as he did. I used the time to run to the kitchen and open a couple of drawers. "Bingo!" I cried in triumph. I picked up a pair of rusty old scissors and ran back to the closet. Carlos was out again, and I needed to wake him out of his drug induced sleep. I first cut off the ropes from his wrists and ankles, and it didn't stir him. I stood up and went back into the bathroom and filled a small plastic cup that was sitting on the sink counter and filled it with some cool water. I hurried back and took the cup of water and threw it on his face.

Carlos gagged on the water and screamed, "Why'd you do that!"

"To wake you up!" I barked back at him. "You were out again."

"I was?" he asked, wiping the rusty water from his face with his hand.

"Look, you're free and don't even know it."

Carlos' gaze left mine and slowly moved down toward his hands and feet. "Oh, thanks," he said, trying to sit up. "Whoa, I'm a little dizzy."

"Take it slow, but we need to get out of here. Whoever did this to you may be coming back." I realized he hadn't told me who it was that did this to him, but I think I had a hunch.

"I don't think he'll come back. It's that big, blonde, monster of a guard Martika has working for her."

"Tell me what happened, but quick."

Carlos started talking as he sat up, and then began to stand with my assistance. "I stepped inside and immediately a hand wrapped around my mouth and pulled me all the way in. It was her guard, and he was smiling disgustingly as he dragged me into this closet and threw me to the ground. He pulled out a rope he had wound around his shoulder and tied me up.

"Did he say anything to you? Did you try and fight him?" I asked.

"You think I could fight him! He's a beast!"

"Fine, but did he speak?"

"Yes, a little. He was mocking us and saying we're stupid trying to think we could out maneuver them."

"Did he mention John?" I asked, hoping to get some news about his condition.

"Yes. He said he's tired of lugging that big cop around."

"What do you mean *lugging*?" I asked, terrified at the potential meaning of the word.

"He means John's been a bit difficult to handle, so they've had him drugged most of the time so he won't keep fighting them."

"That's horrible!" I yelled. "Who's doing the drugging? I have to ask you, I'm worried Joseph never turned to be on our side."

"I know," he said, dispirited. "I think Joseph played us unless he's just acting and trying to keep John and the others safe. We just don't know anything yet."

"Did he mention Meme or Isabella?"

"No."

"I wonder if they're not with John. Maybe they didn't get caught and are hiding out somewhere until they know it's safe."

"They're part of the reason this is happening, Ruth Ann!" Carlos spat. "If they didn't fill your head with all these curses and voodoo stuff, you might not be in the place you are right now!"

"But," I couldn't think of how to reply to Carlos. He was partially correct in his outburst.

"Think about it. If you didn't care about Isabella freaking out at the sight of your necklace, then you wouldn't have gone in search of her and met Meme."

"You do make a good case."

"I'm sorry. I'm not trying to blame you. Let's get out of here and go and wait near the grass shack."

"But won't they know that's where we're heading?" I asked.

"No. I told the big thug we'd find them, and we'll eventually beat them at their game. I accidentally blurted out that you will never hand over your necklace."

"You did what!" I shouted. "You didn't!"

"I'm sorry, but he was goading me and I lost my temper. That's when he stuffed the chloroform rag in my mouth."

"I can't be mad at you, Carlos. You're deep in this too, and you're helping me. They know about the necklace, so it's not such a big slip up after all."

"Thanks," he said. "What time is it anyway?" Carlos inquired, looking for his cell phone. "It's gone!" he yelled. "He must've taken it from me. Great, just great!"

"I still have mine, but there's no service around here. It's been a pain from the moment we checked into this resort."

"Sorry, I haven't cleared that little problem up yet. It's a remote area, and I was hoping to work on that in the near future."

"Hopefully it won't matter for long. I plan on going back home and staying put."

"Under normal circumstances, you would love it down here. The warm air and sea, the locals are usually very friendly, and no snow."

"I would normally agree with you, but…"

"Say no more, Ruth Ann. I get it." Carlos made it out into the main room of the bungalow and took a quick survey of the place. "Looks clear," he said. "I may think of relocating myself once we get out of this mess. I've about had it, too!"

"You could come back to Deer Creek with John and me. You would love it there!" I said, excited at the prospect of Carlos joining our little gang back in Deer Creek. I was growing closer to Carlos and the thought of leaving here and never seeing him again didn't sit well with me.

Carlos held me back until he knew the coast was clear. He stood just outside the front door and waited a minute before waving me to follow him. We hurried down the short path since this last bungalow was so close to the open beach and water. "Don't we need to hide?" I asked, wondering why Carlos was heading to the middle of the beach.

"Why?" It's early morning, and most people get moving a little later around here. We take it slowly, unlike most Americans who rush, rush, and rush some more."

"Life gets busy," I replied, thinking he had another good point.

"It shouldn't be long before your cousin shows up. I think we'll be able to come up with a solid plan then."

"Let's hope so!" I said, hoping that was true. I had a little bit of an upset stomach thinking Prunella and Axel might be involved already, and not on my side!

Chapter 25

As we walked down the sunny beach, I noticed only a few walkers around. The resort employed a few locals to rake and pick up the beach so it was free of debris and looked soft and fluffy. "At least I got the beach part of our resort looking good," Carlos added as he noticed my smile staring at the workers.

"It is a beautiful beach, Carlos. You've got that part of the resort looking spectacular." I quickly amended my comment and said, "Oh, and the updated bungalow is really nice, too."

"Thanks, but there's so much to do around here. I wonder if it'll ever get done. And now with my situation with Martika…"

"You don't need her to fix this place up! You're smart enough on your own or remember…you could always come back with me!"

Carlos didn't reply, but trudged through the damp morning sand and stopped every now and again waiting for me to catch up. He was much faster at walking through the sand than I was, but I had to admit, if I lived around here I would never need to use my elliptical again!

About ten minutes later, Carlos put up his hand to stop me. "We're almost here," he said, quieting down. "I doubt anyone would be here, but let me check it out first."

"I think we're better off together, don't you think?" I said, hinting at the last time he went off by himself and got chloroformed.

"Yeah, I guess you're right."

"It's okay, Carlos. Why would you think they'd grab and drug you, too?"

"To keep us from finding out where they're keeping the others."

"John, you mean. I'm starting to have my doubts about Meme, Isabella, and Joseph."

"Me, too," he said solemnly. "I really thought Joseph was a good guy."

"He may be. Give it time before you totally condemn him."

"I guess so."

Carlos and I saw the few grass shacks nearby. He led me toward the jungle entrance and we walked up to the shacks from the backside. Even though we could still be spotted, we weren't walking directly up to the front entrance from the beach.

"Okay, we're here," he whispered. "I think we should both jump inside and if it's empty, great, but if they're in there, we catch them off guard with the element of surprise."

"I'm assuming you're talking about Martika and the guard, right?"

"Yes, oh, I wasn't trying to frighten your cousin and husband. I figure we still have some time before they show up."

I pulled my cell phone out of one of my short's pockets and hit the button to turn it on. "No service, but it's already after ten in the morning. They could be here as early as now if they took off right after we hung up with them."

"True. It sounds like that Axel person has a lot of contacts. He's a big shot, isn't he?"

"Yes, and no. He was a successful business man back in Sweden, but when his business blew up, I think it humbled him a little. And let me stress the words 'a little'," I said. "He's a very confident man, but even with everything he's done to me, he's always been kind to me. I know that sounds conflicting, but I can't explain it myself. That's why I'm having a difficult time believing he would put me in any danger down here."

"I guess you'll find out soon." Carlos added, "Are you going to ask them about it right away or wait to see if the fess up to anything?"

"I really don't know yet. I need to see how they act and what they ask me, first."

Carlos nodded and motioned for me to walk with him up to the hanging beaded doorway. The sun was bright, but inside the shack had been pretty dark. We stood, side by side, waiting to jump inside and see who was in there. Hopefully, it was empty.

"One, two, three," Carlos murmured, and then we grabbed some of the beaded strings and pulled them aside. "Now!" he hollered as we jumped inside the shack. I noticed my eyes were closed and I was holding my breath.

"It's okay, Ruth Ann," Carlos said calmly. "It's empty."

"Phew," I answered, opening my eyes and taking a deep breath. "I really didn't know what to expect."

"I didn't either," Carlos admitted. "I didn't want to scare you, but I thought it was about a fifty-fifty chance the big guy was waiting in here for us. They must think we wouldn't return here, but they don't know about your cousin coming here."

"Joseph could've warned them," I said. "He knew I was going to contact them."

"Maybe he did, and maybe he forgot or chose not to mention it to Martika."

"If he is with Martika," I repeated to Carlos. "Maybe he ran away and is waiting for this to blow over."

"You think he's a coward?" Carlos asked, stunned at my suggestion.

"No, I mean I don't know!" I quickly replied. "It was just a thought that entered my head."

"Oh, sorry for jumping down your throat. Why don't we see if there's any food left in here? I'm starving."

I walked over to the rickety wooden table and found the bag I brought back from Felix's under the table. I picked it up and plopped it on top of the table. I reached inside and found some nuts, an apple, and a couple bottles of water. "Jack pot!" I exclaimed. Carlos hurried over and eagerly downed one of the waters and munched on a large handful of nuts.

"This is perfect," he said, satisfied. "Protein and water!"

"It would be perfect if there was some chocolate in there, too!"

Carlos chuckled and said, "I can see you have a sweet tooth, Ruth Ann. I do, too!"

We finished one bag of nuts and I stuffed another one inside my side shorts pocket. The ring and necklace were in the other pocket, but I thought we might need some food if we were chased out of here. Carlos suggested I sit down and lay my head on the table. "I'll be the lookout for the first hour unless your family shows up. You need some sleep."

I didn't argue, but went over and sat down on the hard, wooden chair and laid my head in my hands. It didn't take long until I felt slumber take me away. I wasn't totally asleep, just enough where I could hear what was going on. Carlos was mumbling to himself as he paced the shack. I was too exhausted to yell at him to stop, but it was annoying.

I didn't think I was resting for more than ten minutes when Carlos started shaking my shoulders. "Get up, Ruth ann. Get up!"

"What!" I demanded. "It's only been a few minutes. I need more time!"

"It's been two hours!" he replied tersely. "I hear voices nearby. We need to be alert and ready to act."

Carlos didn't have to tell me more than once. I hopped out of my chair and straightened my hair and clothes. I had to look horrible! Prunella will march in here all pristine and beautiful, but this time it didn't matter. I couldn't wait to see them. It felt like it'd been weeks, not just days.

"I hear the voices, Carlos. I think I hear a woman's voice. Wait, I hear more than one woman!"

"It could be Martika with Isabella and Meme!" Carlos replied, nervously. "We should hide somewhere!"

I looked around the square one room shack and snapped, "Where? The only thing in here is the table and chairs!"

"Forget it. It's too late. I think we're about to find out who's here," he said, pulling me to the side next to the front entrance.

The beaded strings slowly parted and I saw a large, black shoed foot step inside. "Stop it!" a voice barked back at the others. "I don't want to be the first one to enter!"

Wait, I know that voice, I muttered quietly. Carlos turned and gave me his, "What do you mean?" look on his face and whipped his head back to the large body juggling to get inside.

I shoved Carlos away and rushed over to the halfway in guest. "Sherman!" I cried out loudly.

"Sherman?" Carlos questioned me as if I was a crazy person. "Who is Sherman?"

I ignored Carlos and concentrated on the man trying to avoid coming inside the shack. It was his unlucky day because I reached out and grabbed his arm and pulled him all the way in. "What the…" Sherman yelled.

"Sherman, it's me, Ruth Ann!" I cried out, grasping him in a tight bear hug. "You're here, too!"

"Ruth Ann?" he questioned, wondering if I looked so terrible he didn't recognize me.

"Yes. Are the others coming?" I asked, wondering what was taking so long for Prunella to get in here.

"I was their guinea pig, Ruth Ann," Sherman spat out, and then he yelled, "It's okay, Ruth Ann's in here."

Immediately the strings parted and in came Prunella, Axel, Inga, and last, but not least, Alex. I was so flabbergasted. They all came to rescue John and me!

Prunella rushed to me and took me in her arms. "You look okay. A little worn and frazzled, but you look good."

Axel nodded and stood next to Prunella. "Can you talk, Ruth Ann?"

"Yes, yes," I said over and over again. "I'm sorry, I'm so shocked you all came."

Axel spoke up and said, "We brought the troops, Ruth Ann. We're here to rescue John and you!"

"I don't need rescuing, but John's in serious trouble."

Carlos stepped up and cleared his throat. Alex was about to apprehend him when I yelled to stop. I explained who Carlos was and that we've been searching and chasing after John and his captors. "He's totally trustworthy," I reassured them. "We need to explain everything that's been going on the last twenty-four hours."

"I can't believe that's all it's been," Carlos mumbled.

"I know," I said, patting his hand. "Let's fill them in."

Prunella, Inga, Sherman, and I sat down at the table. Alex, Axel, and Carlos stood around us. I could've cried at the support that surrounded me. It was impossible that Axel and Prunella would've participated in any wrongdoing with Martika!

I finished telling them everything that happened once John and I stepped off the airplane. Well, almost everything. Carlos glared at me, but I ignored him. I didn't want to divulge the potentially negative part until I felt it was necessary so I left out about Martika supposedly hooking up with Axel and Prunella back in Deer Creek.

"That woman came to Deer Creek and spied on all of us?" Inga asked, angrily. "And how could she have found out about your trip?"

"I know, it's sounds crazy, but she did and now she's got John."

Carlos added, "Don't forget about her guard and the others."

"Others, what others?" Axel asked, perplexed.

"Joseph, Isabella and Meme," I answered, filling them in on the theory they may have been taken prisoner by Martika also.

"Or they're hiding out like you guys," Sherman added.

"We are not hiding out, Sherman!" I snapped across the table at him. "We've been running all over the place after these criminals. They're actually laughing at Carlos and me!"

"It's okay, Ruth Ann," Axel said, glaring at Sherman for being so insensitive. "We can figure it out now."

I looked up and noticed how quiet Alex had been. "I know you're new to the family drama, but how are you doing, Alex?"

He stirred back and forth a little, nervously, and then said, "I'm fine. I just don't understand what the fuss is about."

I reminded him not long ago he came barreling in the library waving a gun and demanding the necklace. He lowered his head in embarrassment and said, "You're right, but I only did that because I was told how valuable the gem was. Not that it was cursed."

"We didn't know about the curse until a day and a half ago!" I expressed, looking over at Carlos who was staring at Axel and Prunella to see their reaction. I quickly glanced and did the same, but their faces showed no apparent guilt.

"Ruth Ann," Carlos interrupted. "Can I have a private moment with you, please?"

The others looked at him like he was crazy, but Inga was the first to speak up. "Hey, what do you want with Ruth Ann that you can't say to us? We've known her a lot longer than you have!"

"It's okay, Inga," I said. "Give me a minute with Carlos and I promise we'll fill you in on the conversation anyway."

Carlos grabbed my hand and forced me to stand rather abruptly. He pulled me outside the shack. "What's wrong with you!" he snapped in a quiet, but abusive tone.

"Look," I said like a mother about to scold her child for disrespecting her. "It's up to me to tell them, not you."

"But it's really important to find out if they were in on it with Martika. Why can't you see that?"

"I do, Carlos, but I have a plan." Carlos didn't argue back, but waited for me to continue. "I want them to confess, not the other way around. If I confront them, they'll get defensive and potentially lie. If they see what's going on here, I feel certain they will confess any possible wrongdoing."

"You know they did!" he snapped. I couldn't disagree with him at the moment. It didn't look good for Prunella and Axel in regards to their association with Martika.

"I'll go along with you, but only for a short time. If they don't tell you they've been in contact with my wife very soon, I'll bust them!"

"Agreed."

We walked back inside the shack and I nearly fell into Inga. "Oh, sorry, Ruth Ann," she said, obviously trying to eavesdrop on my conversation.

I glared at her irritably, "Did you get any good information out of spying on us, Inga?"

"Me, spying?" she asked, innocently. "Why would I need to spy on you two?"

"Why don't you just tell me what exactly you think you overheard?"

"Nothing. I heard nothing."

"Enough of this," Axel jumped in. "We need to come up with ideas of where this Martika woman has John."

"That's just it. We're at a dead end. We thought they may be in one of the resort's bungalows, but that failed," I said.

"Well, the guard was all around the place, Ruth Ann," Carlos reminded me.

"You mentioned some other place," Inga said. "Fred or Frank's…"

"Felix!" I shouted out. "We should go find Felix and see if he's heard from Meme. They're really close."

"Then let's go," Axel said, eager and ready to move on from the stuffy little shack.

Carlos agreed it was a place to try, but he didn't seem confident we'd find anybody there except the old man. I kind of felt the same, but it would buy us time to think of a better plan or persuade my cousin and her husband to tell me what they really knew.

I warned them that we'd be stomping through the jungle and it was wet, steamy, and itchy with the leaves brushing up against our bodies. I mainly told them because I didn't want Sherman complaining the entire trip. We were quite the group. Axel and Prunella dressed in their expensive clothing, Sherman and Inga in their household uniforms and big clunky shoes. Quiet Alex was dressed most appropriately. He wore a pair of water resistant, khaki shorts, a t-shirt that would air dry instantly, and a pair of lightweight hiking shoes. Hmm, I thought quickly to myself. Why was Alex the only one dressed for this climate? I wondered if maybe he knew more than he was admitting to.

Carlos and I led the pack out of the shack and down to the sandy path that took us deeper into the jungle. I knew Sherman would start complaining once we were in the thick, dark rainforest.

"How far is this place?" Sherman inquired, batting at the several flying insects that were invading his personal space. "Should I have received shots for doing this?"

We ignored Sherman's endless questions when Carlos came to a halt. "Nobody speak!" he ordered in a low voice.

"Why, what's happening?" Inga asked, ignoring his request to be quiet.

"Shhh," he barked. "I hear something up ahead."

"You think it's that guard again?" I asked, faintly.

"Maybe. Let me go ahead and take a quick look. It's too hard with all these people to be invisible. I'll go and see what's going on. We're getting closer to Felix's place anyway."

I turned back to the others and explained what Carlos was doing. I noticed Axel and Prunella exchange a peculiar glance. What was that about? I really wanted to catch them, but this wasn't the right time. I didn't want any argument to get loud, and if they did betray me, I would get very, very loud!

We huddled on the narrow path and waited until Carlos returned. He ran up out of breath and said it was a false alarm. "Probably a wild animal."

"Wild animal!" Sherman bellowed. "I didn't sign up for being killed by a wild animal!"

"Stop complaining," Axel ordered. "You didn't have to come on this trip. We warned you it might get rough."

"I had to come. It's an honor thing," he said, standing straight and trying to wipe away the creases in his dirty white shirt. "Really, this is so uncivilized!"

"Go back to the shack," Alex suddenly chimed in and snapped. "In fact, I'll take you back and return here before anyone even moves."

I thought it was necessary to break this disagreement up so I stepped toward the back of the line where Alex and Sherman were face to face glaring at each other. "Knock it off. We're sticking together for now." I turned to Sherman and said, "You knew what you were getting into so please stop complaining."

"Fine," he replied, bitterly.

"We need your help too, Sherman," I added quickly, knowing it would boost his confidence.

"Yes, you usually do."

Carlos started walking again, pushing aside the loose branches and leaves that were invading the grassy path. "Here," he said.

"Here, what?" Axel asked.

"We're here," he said, pointing toward an opening that appeared out of thin air. "It's afternoon now, and the sun's streaming through. We'll be spotted if we all go marching up to the door. I think we should break into two groups. If one group gets caught, then it leaves the other group to save us."

"Good idea, Carlos," Axel said. "Let's see...Ruth Ann and Carlos should stick together since they know this Felix guy. Why don't Inga and Alex go with your group. That leaves Prunella, Sherman, and me in the other group. What do you think?"

"Sounds good," Carlos said. I'm sure he was relieved he didn't have to be stuck with Axel and Prunella. Actually, I'm relieved because now I didn't have to worry that he would accuse Axel or Prunella of being in on this whole affair.

"Ruth Ann and I should go up to Felix's door. Alex and Inga should stay slightly behind us."

"Why!" Inga demanded, irritated.

"Because Felix is an old man who doesn't trust many people. I've only met him twice, and the first time he was very curt with me," I explained. "He was much nicer when Carlos and I were there together."

"Yeah, hopefully the old man can tell us if he's seen Meme, Isabella or Joseph."

"He has," a voice spoke out of nowhere.

We all jumped and whipped our heads toward the direction of the sound of the strange voice. "Joseph!" I screamed too loudly.

"Shhh, Ruth Ann," he said, covering my mouth with his sticky hand.

"But where'd you come from?" I asked, pulling his hand away.

"I made that noise Carlos heard a few minutes ago. I didn't know it was you so I jumped inside a bush over there and wiggled the branches. Carlos assumed it was a small animal causing the movement."

"You're correct," Carlos said, coolly. I had two immediate thoughts come to mind. Was Joseph guarding the prisoners inside Felix's house or was he inside with Meme and Isabella hiding out and waiting for us to show up. There was only one way to find out, be direct.

"So, Joseph, are you here with Meme and Isabella or are you back in Martika's good graces and guarding Felix's house because John is in there as a prisoner?"

Joseph looked terribly offended. He opened his mouth to speak, but slammed it shut. He looked to Carlos for his help, but Carlos stood his ground next to me. "Well," Carlos said. "We're waiting for you to answer Ruth Ann's question."

"I can't believe you'd think I'd betray you! I told you I was forced into helping that woman. I thought we cleared that up earlier."

"I thought so, too," Carlos said. "Where are Meme and Isabella?"

"Inside with Felix. We fled the shack when we saw Martika and her guard coming down the beach."

"Didn't they see you leave the shack?" I asked, curiously.

"No, there's a back exit. Didn't you know that?" he asked, surprised that we had no idea about any other exit out of Meme's shack.

"No. There's no door at the back of the shack," I stated.

"It's not a door. It's just an exit through the wall. If you didn't know it was there, then you would never suspect a way out."

"Oh, I wonder why Meme never mentioned it to me."

"She's an old lady, Ruth Ann," Carlos said. "Maybe she forgot."

"I doubt it, but what excuse do you have for Isabella? She's young and bright, and I bet she knew about the exit."

"Who cares about the secret door out of the bloody shack!"

Axel bellowed. "Can't we just go inside this house now?"

"Not all at once," Joseph said. "Felix will panic and so will Meme."

"Meme's the witch doctor, right?" Sherman asked, sounding a bit cynical.

"I don't know what her title is, but she has some kind of power that enables her to help people break curses that have been bound against them." I added quickly before the criticisms started pouring out. "She's not crazy. Isabella has the same power, but she's young and her grandmother, Meme, wants her to take over her business. Don't judge them. Wait and see for yourselves."

Joseph and Carlos appeared on better terms. They suggested I come inside Felix's house with them before we come and get everyone else.

"No way!" Prunella cried out. "We're not letting you out of our sight anymore. We travelled all the way down here to help you, you can't shut us out!"

I had to kick Carlos in his shin to keep him from commenting back to Prunella. I had the same urge to blow her out of the water, but it still wasn't the right time. I needed to speak with Meme and Isabella first. They will advise me on how to handle my cousin.

"Fine," Carlos interjected. "Prunella can come with us, too. That's enough people for now. We must go now. We're wasting valuable time."

Joseph, Carlos, Prunella, and I headed through the last part of the jungle and out into the open grass space. Felix's house was smack dab in the middle like it dropped from space and landed there. Joseph led our group, but stopped on the steps to the front door. "I need to warn you about something first, Ruth Ann."

"What?" I asked, wondering why I was the only one included with his warning.

"It's about Meme," he said, watching me intently. "She's grown weaker since you've seen her last."

"But it hasn't been that long! What's wrong with her?"

"Old age, Ruth Ann. That's why she's been so insistent about Isabella learning everything from her."

"She's dying?" Prunella asked, sad.

"I think so," Joseph replied, bluntly.

"And you've examined her, too? I mean, you really are a doctor, right?" I asked, stumbling through my words.

"Yes, I've watched her closely. I think she knows it too, but what I can tell from my quick examination is that she's failing."

"That's horrible!" I exclaimed.

"It's part of life, Ruth Ann," Carlos added. "She's got to be about ninety or more, don't you think?"

"Yes, she won't tell me exactly how old she is, but my guess is about ninety-four," Joseph answered.

"Wow, that's up there," Prunella said. "We should get in there while she's still coherent and can help us."

"I agree, let's go inside," I said.

Joseph opened the door and we followed, well tried to follow, into the tiny foyer. It wasn't large enough for the four of us so Carlos waited on the front step until a couple of us entered inside the store I had been in before.

Once we were all inside, I couldn't help but notice nobody was around. "Where are they?"

"Probably hiding out somewhere," Carlos replied. "Felix should be here any second. I'm sure he heard the bell ring when we entered."

We waited only a minute or so when Felix entered into the small room that was used as his store. "Hello, Ruth Ann," he said, eyeing Prunella with raised eyebrows. "And who is this lovely young woman?"

"It's my cousin, Prunella," I answered, giving her a gentle shove toward his direction.

"Oh, hi, Felix," Prunella said, cheerily. "It's nice to meet you."

"Yes, yes, I see Carlos is here, too," he said in a less than cordial tone.

"Why wouldn't I be here? I've been running around with Ruth Ann from the beginning. You know that. Have I done something to offend you, Felix?"

"No, I didn't mean it that way. I'm just worried that all these people are involved."

"There are more outside, Felix," I admitted, hoping he wouldn't freak out.

"How many more?" he inquired, rocking back and forth nervously. "I don't want anything bad to happen here. It's all I've got!"

"Nothing will happen to your store, Felix," Prunella replied. "I won't let you lose your store, I promise."

Felix eyed her suspiciously. "I don't know you, why would you say that to me?"

"Because you've helped my cousin, and anyone who helps her when she's in trouble is okay in my book. If anything happens to your stuff, I promise to replace every single item!"

"You would?"

"Of course!"

I watched their exchange and hoped Felix would trust Prunella and open up to us. I knew he had a bigger part in this, I just didn't know what yet.

"Can the others come inside, too?" I asked, anxiously. "I don't want Martika or that guard of hers to catch them outside."

Felix cautiously nodded. I opened the door and stepped through the foyer onto the front landing. I waved to Axel who was pacing frantically back and forth just outside of the sunny grassy opening. He called to the others and they rushed to the stairs that led to Felix's house. "Hurry up, we're so many now it'll be easy to be spotted," I pleaded.

Inga and Sherman went first into the foyer, and then Axel and Alex brought up the rear. I was the last one to enter back inside the store. "We're all here. Now, where are Isabella and Meme?" I asked Felix.

"They're well-hidden here," Felix answered. "But I know they'll want to speak with Ruth Ann."

"Not us?" Prunella asked, perplexed. "Why can't we all talk to them? I think you should have them come out here so we can talk as a group and come up with a solid plan."

"Meme wants only Ruth Ann right now," Felix insisted.

"Let me go, Prunella. I'll talk with Meme and see how she's doing, and then come back here."

I didn't leave any of them a choice and took off through a well-hidden door with Felix. There was a staircase that led downstairs. "Where are we going?" I asked him.

"I know back in the states you would expect the bedrooms to be upstairs, but in the heat of the jungle, we go downstairs."

"Oh, Meme's down in a bedroom of yours?" I inquired, worrying she was worse off than I expected.

"Yes. She's grown weak and I thought it best that she rests comfortably."

"I agree," a male voice spoke up out of nowhere.

"Joseph!" I cried out. "You startled me."

"I think I need to check on Meme's condition. I knew Felix wouldn't mind me interrupting your talk, right?"

"If you think it's necessary," Felix replied. "I agree that helping her is out of my powers now."

"You were treating Meme?" I asked, confused.

"Yes. For a long time, I've been Meme's healer. I only give her vitamins and herbs, but it's above my expertise now."

"So, you're not just a store owner for locals, are you?" I asked.

"No."

Felix didn't care to explain further so I dropped it, for now. I knew there was more to this old man than just a local grocer. Once I find out how Meme's doing, and speak with Isabella, I plan on questioning Felix more.

"I assume Isabella's with Meme?" I asked.

"Yes," Felix answered. "She's been in silent meditation with her grandmother. She's trying to gather as much knowledge from her before it's too late."

"It's getting that close?" I asked sorrowfully.

Before Felix or Joseph could answer me, a door opened up at the bottom of the stairs. "Come in, Ruth Ann," Isabella called out to me. "We have a lot to discuss, and not a lot of time."

I hurried down the narrow, hardened mud packed steps into a small corridor. There were three doors and one was opened by Isabella. My assumption would be two bedrooms down here and one bathroom, but I wasn't so sure about the bathroom. Maybe it was outside or upstairs.

"How's Meme?" I asked before entering inside the bedroom.

Isabella's head was sticking out of the room, but she stepped fully out into the small corridor. "She's so weak, Ruth Ann. I'm scared that she doesn't have much time left."

"I'm so sorry, Isabella. What can I do to help the both of you?"

"I need you to listen, and learn."

"Learn what?" I asked, confused. "I know Meme sees and feels things that are happening, but has something else happened with John?"

"Too much for me to talk about out here." Isabella eyed Felix and Joseph and asked if they could wait out here.

"Let me check her vitals quickly, and then I'll leave you three alone," Joseph requested. Isabella nodded, and let Joseph inside the room. Felix, Isabella, and I stood in the damp, dark and empty corridor. I decided I'd ask Felix a couple questions while we waited.

"So, Felix, are there two other bedrooms down here or a bathroom, too?"

"What does it matter!" he snapped, surprising Carlos and me.

"I was just curious, that's all. I've never been in a local Jamaican home."

"Oh, it's just extra rooms. One's a storage room for my store, and the other one's another bedroom."

"Where do you have a bathroom?" I asked, wishing for one so I could throw some water on my face.

"Upstairs, off the kitchen."

"Oh, that's right. I haven't seen any room beside the store."

"Yes, I live here so there has to be a bathroom and a kitchen. They're very small and bare, but they suit me just fine."

I decided to halt my questions. Felix appeared irritated and I didn't want him to close up. I watched Carlos as he stared up at the ceiling, ignoring our conversation. I was so thirsty and hungry and wished Felix would run upstairs and grab food for us. I wanted to ask, but decided to wait until after my conversation with Isabella and Meme. I didn't have to wait long. Joseph slowly opened the door and stepped out.

"You can go in, Ruth Ann. Keep her calm, though."

"Why would I get her upset? She wanted to see me, remember?"

"Yes, but I know how desperate you're getting in the search for your boyfriend."

"I am, but I promise not to upset her. I'm hoping she can do all the talking and tell us what we need to do to end this. I'm tired, hungry, thirsty, and I want to go home!"

Nobody responded to my little outburst except for Joseph opening the door and waving me in. I didn't want to leave Carlos out there, but Joseph was there for him and hopefully the two of them will have a private conversation about their own relationship.

I walked inside the dark, cool but humid room. There was barely any furniture except for a small cot against the wall, where Meme was lying, and a metal chair with Isabella sitting on it. I noticed a small side table with an old, chipped porcelain pot filled with water, and a rag hanging over the side of it.

"Sit down, Ruth Ann," Isabella said, standing up and motioning for me to take her seat. "My grandmother's voice is growing weaker, and you need to be close to hear her."

I gently squeezed Isabella's arm as I took her seat. I looked over at the small, frail woman who clearly had gone downhill in just a day. Her eyes were closed, but I did notice her chest moving slowly up and down. She was still alive.

Chapter 26

"Come closer, Ruth Ann," a strong voice called my name, even though the body looked close to death. "We have much to speak about."

"Can't Isabella tell me everything?"

"No. She knows a lot, but not all. I'm trying to teach her, even now, when I'm so close to my end."

"Don't say that!" Isabella cried. "You can't leave me. I'll be all alone!"

"No, you won't," I interrupted. "You have us now."

"Yes, Isabella. Listen to Ruth Ann. She will not abandon you."

"Never," I stated clearly.

"We need to talk quickly. I think we're about to be interrupted soon with news."

"News about what?" I asked, worried.

"I think we're about to hear from Martika about her demands."

"What demands? She has John and I need to find him!"

'You know what I'm talking about Ruth Ann. The necklace or should I say the gem inside your necklace."

"They want it."

"Yes. Martika wants it badly. She's greedy and wants to be rich and powerful. She thinks the gem will bring her all of that, but she's sadly mistake."

"Why did you want it?" I asked Meme, even though it came across disrespectfully, which I didn't mean. "I'm sorry."

"No, don't be sorry. You didn't know us, but now you know that I only wanted to rid the stone of the dreaded curse put upon it a hundred years ago. If it's the last thing I do, then I can pass at peace."

"What needs to be done to rid the gem of the curse?" I asked.

"We need certain items. I, I tried to tell Isabella. She can fill you in on that when we're done here. When you get the necessary items, bring them back to me and I'll break the curse. Until then, your boyfriend's life will be at risk."

"They'll kill him, won't they?" I asked, worried.

"Yes, and then they'll come after each one of you. I will tell you this much, it won't end without fatalities, Ruth Ann."

"Even if we break the curse in time?" I asked, terrified of what she implied.

"Yes."

"But why? If we reach John in time why would anyone have to die?" I asked terrified.

"I just see what's about to happen, I don't have control over it."

"But if you know what's about to happen, then tell me and we can protect that person."

"It doesn't' work that way, Ruth Ann," a weakened Meme stated.

"Tell me who you think is going to die?"

"I don't have a clear view of that yet. I just know at least one person will die before the curse is broken."

"Tell me what I can do to prevent this from happening? Can I just hand over my necklace to Martika and let her deal with the curse?"

"No, the curse won't leave you and your family until it's broken," Isabella chimed in. "That much I know."

"She's right, Ruth Ann."

"Tell me where they are, Meme. I want to go and get John."

"Not until you get me my items. I don't have much time, and I need you and the others to hurry. The faster I break the curse the fewer lives will be at stake."

"Fine," I said deflated. I turned to Isabella and asked, "Can we hurry and get what your grandmother needs?"

Isabella grabbed my arm and pulled me away from Meme. "She needs to rest now. Let's leave her with Felix and Joseph and go."

I walked back over to Meme and gently patted her withered hand. "I promise I'll be back!"

Meme's eyes remained closed, but she spoke softly, "I know you will."

Isabella and I left Meme with Felix and Joseph and headed back upstairs. Carlos kept asking what was going on the whole way back to the others who were waiting in the store.

Isabella snapped at Carlos for the last time and said, "Just wait, Carlos. I only want to say this once."

We met up with Inga, Sherman, Axel, Prunella, and quiet Alex. Inga and Sherman were arguing about a few items they were examining on a shelf, and Prunella and Axel had their heads together whispering. They looked a bit too suspicious to me! And that left Alex. He stood in the middle of the room, leaning on the counter, alone.

"Ruth Ann!" Prunella cried out as we entered Felix's store. "Finally."

"Yes, we've got to talk, all of us," I said, letting Isabella come forward. "This is Isabella, she's Meme's granddaughter. Isabella will explain what we need to do next."

All eyes upon Isabella made her nervous. She wasn't used to being the center of attention. Not because she wasn't young and beautiful with her dark long silken hair and flawless tanned skin. In fact, I saw the glimmer in Alex's eyes when he first laid eyes on her. He stood up straight and flashed a smile that showed off the one dimple he had on his cheek. He was a handsome young man, and Isabella definitely took notice.

"Ruth Ann and I have been told by my grandmother that we need to break the curse of your family's gem."

"Can't we do that after we rescue John?" Axel asked, impatiently.

"No. Please don't ask any questions until Isabella's done explaining," I said, sternly.

"The curse will cause at least one death among us if we don't break it."

"What!" Inga bellowed. "Did you just tell us that one of us is going to die?"

"Yes. That is why you must listen to me and do as I say. We don't have much time. My grandmother's getting weaker by the hour and she needs to be the one to break the curse. She's known about this for most of her life."

"Can't you do it?" Prunella asked.

"No."

Nobody asked why, but waited for Isabella to explain what we needed to do. "First," Isabella continued. "We need a personal item from all the members of your family who have come into contact with the necklace."

"So," Sherman began to say. "Inga, Carlos, and I don't need to contribute a personal item?"

"Yes, you're correct."

"But not all of our family is here!" I cried. "My two daughters, Lynne and Nancy, are back in the states and they've touched the necklace before."

"I need something from them. Did you bring anything with that they've used themselves?" Isabella inquired.

I thought of my belongings back in my suitcase. I know I must have something from Lynne and Nancy. Think, Ruth Ann, think! I closed my eyes tightly and pictured packing my suitcase..." Wait!" I yelled. "I borrowed a pair of silver dangly earrings from Nancy."

"That's great, Ruth Ann. What about your other daughter?" Isabella asked urgently. "We only need one thing from her."

"I, I don't know," I said worriedly. "I'm trying to picture all the stuff I brought."

"Ruth Ann," Prunella interrupted. "Didn't Lynne give you her velvet pouch to keep our necklace in?"

"Yes!" I exclaimed. "She knew I didn't want to take a box along because it took up too much room, and my suitcase was popping at the seams. She lent me her favorite red velvet pouch with a cupcake imprinted on it."

"That's even better!" Isabella said, excited. "The more personally attached the item the more power it holds."

"What about everybody else here?" Carlos asked, impatiently. "We need to get a move on!"

Axel pulled out his pocket watch. "It belonged to my grandfather and means a lot to me." He looked over at Isabella and asked, "We will get these items back, won't we?"

"Yes."

Prunella pulled out a hairpin from her neatly coiffed bun. "It's antique, too. I don't have a lot of possessions from my mom, but she gave me this when I turned twenty-one. She said it belonged to her grandmother." Prunella added it to the pocket watch Axel laid on the counter.

All eyes turned to Alex. He looked nervous and said, "What? I don't have anything valuable with me. All I've got is…" he pulled out a few items from his shorts pocket and studied them in his hand. He hesitated a tad too long as if he was going back and forth in his mind whether he wanted to give something up. "Why do I have to do this? I just met these people."

"Yes, Alex, just cooperate. Whatever you have will be better than nothing," I said, pleading him to open his closed up hand.

"Okay," he said, slowly opening his tightly bound fist. "This has to be returned to me."

"What is it?" Inga asked, eagerly trying to take a peek. "Whatever it is has to be really tiny!"

"It's a coin."

"A coin?" Sherman questioned, mockingly. "That's all!"

"It's very important to me. It was my mom's." He held out a silver oval shaped coin. I walked next to him and picked it out of his hand. It was trembling slightly as I took it from him.

"Poopsie's?" I questioned him, puzzled. "What's this?"

"It was a coin my mom had for years. She got it at a store a few hours from where we lived."

"What's so special about it other than it was your mom's?" I asked.

"Her dad used to call her Poopsie Pie when she was young and she spotted this coin in a store and bought it. She felt her dad, my grandfather, was always with her when she carried it."

"Then it is *very* important," I said, smiling at Alex. "I promise you that it will be returned to you."

"Thank you," he said, kindly. I watched as he put the other loose items back in his side pocket. I knew it was difficult for him since he didn't say much about his parents, except the story his mother told him about our necklace.

"So, we have Prunella, Axel, and Alex's items," Carlos said. "We need Ruth Ann's."

"But mine are back in my suitcase in our bungalow," I reminded them. "How are we going to get them?"

"Simple," Sherman interrupted. "We walk back down the beach and get your suitcase."

"It's not exactly that simple, Sherman," Carlos retorted. "We have kidnappers and murderers after us!"

"Oh, yeah, that's right."

"We've got to have those items, Ruth Ann," Isabella said. "It's a risk we need to take."

"We don't all have to go," I said. "I'll go with…?"

"Me," Carlos said, volunteering. "I'm the obvious one."

"And why are *you* the obvious one?" Axel inquired, rudely.

"Because it's my resort and I know the way."

"He's got that one on you," Inga said, chuckling slightly, but stopped as soon as Prunella glared daggers at her.

Just as we were about to decide who would stay and who would go, a knock occurred outside the front door. We jumped instantaneously, and rushed over to the door that led into the tiny foyer. "Who could that be?" Inga asked.

"It can't exactly be Martika or her guard!" Sherman exclaimed.

"Felix should answer the door," Isabella said. "But he's down with my grandmother."

"I'll open it," Alex suggested. "Nobody knows."

"Look out the side window first," Carlos recommended, and Alex nodded. He opened the door and shut it behind him. We didn't want any of us to be spotted just in case it was someone associated with Martika.

It didn't take long before Alex returned. We barely let him shut the door behind him when I blurted out, "Who was it?"

"Let him come in first, Ruth Ann," Axel said.

"He's in, he's in. I need to know who was at the door!"

"It was a young boy."

"Was he here for Felix?" Carlos inquired.

"No."

"Come on, Alex, spill it!" Inga hollered.

"I'm trying. It was a young local boy who said he had a message for, and I quote, *the two bumbling idiots and the two crazy witches*."

Carlos took a deep breath and said, "He means, Ruth Ann and I, and Meme and Isabella."

"I think we understood what the boy meant," Axel said. "What's the message, Alex?"

"Here it is:" Alex read it out loud.

Stop running all over the island looking for John. You won't find him until I have the necklace in my hands where it belongs. Forget about Isabella and her crazy grandmother. There's no such thing as a curse. She's trying to fool you into giving it up to her. At least I'm being honest and telling you what I want.

If I don't get what I want by the end of the day...you see that red spot on the back of this paper? It's his blood, and there'll be plenty more to spread. In fact, there'll be buckets and buckets of it! Do what I say and I'll give him back to you. Don't follow my instructions and I've warned you what the consequence will be.

Alex paused and looked up at us. "Here's the red spot she's referring to." He held the paper up for us to inspect. I didn't need to see it. I knew she wasn't kidding. "Shall I continue?"

"Yes," Axel answered for the group.

"Here are her instructions:"

Ruth Ann, only. I don't want anyone following her or with her. If I find out I was betrayed, John dies. Bring the necklace back to the grass shack on the beach. You know the one. I'm aware Meme has taken a turn for the worse so she won't be there or Isabella, my beloved half-sister. Bring only the necklace and yourself at midnight tonight. I want it to be dark and empty. Remember, if you don't do as I ask, John dies, and there could be others that won't come out of this alive.

Martika

"Well, that's NEVER going to happen!" Carlos screamed, grabbing the note from Alex's hands and inspecting it. He looked at Axel, frustrated, and demanded, "You won't let her do that, will you?"

"Carlos, we don't have a choice," Axel admitted, to my surprise. "If any of us goes with her, John will be killed. We can't risk that happening."

"But if we let Ruth Ann go alone, she will die!" he yelled. "Don't you get it? She's a ruthless murderer and even if Ruth Ann did give her the necklace, Martika can't risk being caught by the authorities. She'll murder Ruth Ann, John, and come for each one of us until there's no more witnesses!"

I watched the argument go back and forth until I couldn't take it any longer. "Carlos!" I shouted over their bickering. "Maybe it'll happen just as she wrote in the note."

"None of you know that woman like I do. I've been on the butt end of her blackmailing and I can tell you first-hand that she has zero morals or feelings for others."

"All she wants is the necklace," Prunella said entering the conversation. "We just have to hand it over, and it'll be over."

That was it. Carlos let out all the words I didn't want him to say. "You both knew about this, didn't you?" Carlos screamed, totally losing his cool. "You and that husband of yours already met with my supposed wife and planned this whole thing, didn't you?" Carlos accused, standing with his feet apart and hands on his hips. "Don't stand there speechless like you don't know what I'm talking about. You know *exactly* what I said is true! Both of you met with Martika back in that town of yours, what's it called again?" Carlos became flustered looking for help.

"Deer Creek," Sherman quietly responded.

"That's it! Deer Creek. Martika flew all the way to Sweden and found out you were in Colorado, not Sweden. She met with you and your wife and found out all about the mysterious gem she's after."

"Nonsense!" Axel snapped, in a cool and calm manner. If I was being accused of a horrendous wrongdoing I didn't do, I'd be kicking and screaming until everyone believed me.

"It's not nonsense, is it?" I asked, eager to get to the truth. "You and Prunella knew about Martika, didn't you?" I directed my question right at Prunella. If she had any part in this, I would see it in her eyes.

"Ruth Ann," Prunella cried. "It isn't what you think."

"Prunella," Axel barked. "Don't."

"I have to. Ruth Ann's my family and she's in a horrible position because of us."

"We didn't know what Martika had planned, Prunella."

"But look what's happened, Axel," she pleaded.

The rest of us watched their exchange, feeling like we were invading a private conversation. I felt like I was in a tunnel and I couldn't see the light at the other end. My head started spinning and I almost fell to the ground. Carlos, my hero, grabbed my arm and held me upright. "Are you alright?" he asked, gently.

"I'm fine. I just got a little woozy. I think I need some water," I said, pointing at one of the shelves with bottles of water. Alex hurried over and grabbed one and opened it up.

"Here you go, Ruth Ann," he said. "I think we should all drink water, too." It was a good moment to pause and calm down.

"Okay," Inga said, startling us. "I, for one, need to understand what's happening. First, this little boy hands us a note and asks Ruth Ann to deliver the necklace to that shack we were in a little while ago, right?" I nodded. "If you don't go alone, John could get killed, right?" I nodded. "Now, Carlos disagrees with you going alone thinking that woman will kill all of us anyway, right?" I nodded. "Then, out of nowhere, Carlos freaks out and starts accusing Prunella and Axel, oops, I mean Mr. Eklund of being involved with Martika in stealing the necklace." Inga paused without looking at anyone. "But what I don't understand is why would Prunella and Mr. Eklund need the necklace? They are already part owners of it!"

"For the insurance money," Carlos blurted out much to my dismay.

I whipped my head to see Axel and Prunella's response. Neither of them denied or admitted what Carlos said was true or not. "Well?" I demanded.

"It's too long to explain now," Axel replied, curtly. "I think our best option is to get back near the shack and check it out. If it appears safe, Ruth Ann should go in and hand over the necklace to Martika."

My anger took over any rational thinking I was trying to display. "IT'S TRUE! Isn't it?" I yelled at Axel and Prunella. "You forced me into bringing the necklace down here so it would be stolen, and then you could collect an obscene amount of money from insurance. Am I right?" I asked, my face hotter and redder than I think it's ever been. "Don't lie to me or tell me to wait for a better time for your stupid explanations. I want the truth NOW!"

Prunella grabbed her husband's arm and shook it. "Axel, please. We need to come clean."

"I knew it!" Carlos bellowed. "It's true that you met with my wife and planned this whole thing, didn't you?"

"NO!" Prunella cried back. "We didn't know any of this was going to happen."

"Enough!" Sherman shouted, surprising us all with his unusual outburst. "Someone has to take control of this situation and it might as well be me. Prunella," Sherman turned his attention to his great niece. "You tell us what actually happened because I feel strongly that we'll hear the truth versus bits and pieces of it from Mr. Eklund." Sherman avoided eye contact with Axel since he had just totally disrespected his employer.

"Sherman!" Prunella bellowed. "I can't believe you just said that about Axel."

"I didn't mean to sound disrespectful, but you have a bigger heart, and I know you would never do anything that would hurt Ruth Ann."

"I would never," she answered slowly and tenderly. Prunella turned to me, her eyes implored for my understanding and attention.

"Go on, Prunella. We're burning daylight here," I said impatiently, not sure I would forgive her or not.

"Okay. You know that Axel's money has been tied up with legal troubles. We both felt it would've settled eventually on our side, but we needed money to get his shipping company back up and running. We got desperate, Ruth Ann," Prunella stopped and waited for some kind of reaction from me, but I didn't give her one. I stared directly at her, but didn't say a word. "We received a mysterious visit from this woman we'd never met before. Her name was,"

Carlos interrupted and muttered, "Martika."

"Yes," she answered, humbly. "Martika forced her way into the library and demanded to speak with Axel and I followed her in." She took a moment and glanced up at her husband who motioned with his head to continue. "This woman, Martika, knew way more about us than she should have. She had been to Stockholm and had spoken with previous employees of Axel's and found out about the dock's explosion and Axel going to jail and of course, the famous necklace."

"So what!" Carlos yelled. "Why would you make a deal with the devil? You must've known she was evil when she revealed your personal affairs!"

"Yes, but she pointed out, however wrong it was, that she would pay an exorbitant amount of money for the necklace."

"But how does insurance fit in then?" Alex inquired, curiously.

"We would get almost double the amount of money. Martika would pay us, and if we truly lost the necklace, then we'd get the insurance money, too."

My voice took over, even though it was without emotion. "So, you made a deal with Martika to get the necklace for her. She would pay Axel this unknown amount of money and turn around and steal it from me. You talked me into bringing the necklace on my vacation with John because it would be so nice to wear it and show it off a little. I refused profusely in the beginning, but you and Axel convinced me it was all right. You both mentioned the insurance would kick in if anything bad happened to it. Unbelievable! I should've read through your trick before I took one step onto that airplane. How could you do that to me?" I didn't wait for a response since I was on a roll. "And now, your plan completely backfired and John's been kidnapped and his life is being threatened. I've been through hell and back, and could be killed myself! How dare you both!"

Carlos was the first to my side. "Take a deep breath, Ruth Ann. You need your strength." He rubbed my back and I stopped my rant to take in some very needed deep breaths. Carlos' glare at Axel and Prunella was terrifying. I looked at the shocked and dumbfounded expressions on Inga and Sherman's faces knowing they were totally in the dark about what their boss, friend, and family member had done.

Inga snapped her mouth shut after hanging wide open. She shook her head furiously and cried out, "No! Please tell us that this isn't true, Prunella?"

"I'm sorry, Inga. I know I've disappointed all of you. I, I never meant any of this to happen."

"What exactly was supposed to happen?" Carlos inquired, fuming.

"We were to convince Ruth Ann to bring the necklace down here. She was to leave it in the bungalow and it was to be stolen," Axel said, simply. "That's it. There was never supposed to be any danger or kidnapping. I don't know why Martika took it this far. She even gave me a portion of the money for the necklace before she got the piece in her hands."

"Where'd she come up with that kind of money?" Carlos asked rhetorically, since none of us knew the financial status of Martika, Carlos, Joseph, Meme or Isabella for that fact.

"She's your wife," Inga spat. "Don't you know where she got that kind of money?"

"No. We're not hurting, but I had no idea she had enough money to pay off the Eklund's."

"She did," Axel said. "She gave us enough money for me to restart my shipping company back in Stockholm. It was in the millions."

"Really?" he asked, bewildered and furious all in one.

"I don't care about the bloody money!" I hollered, vehemently. "How could you risk John's life and my own?"

"We didn't think…" Prunella stopped talking and threw her hands up to her face to cover the tears streaming down her cheeks.

"That's right, you didn't think!" Carlos shouted. "You could be an accessory to murder now!"

"Nobody's been murdered, Carlos," Axel corrected him. "We won't let that happen."

"But my grandmother told Ruth Ann and me that even if Martika gets the necklace, someone would be killed."

"I thought you said all we needed to do was give the necklace to her and nobody would be murdered," Inga said, terrified.

"Inga, Meme told me that there would be a fatality no matter what."

"Did she tell you who?" Inga asked, anxiously.

"No. She claimed she couldn't see that yet. She wanted us to get our items to her so she could break the curse, and then she'd tell us where to find Martika."

"But now we got the demand letter and that changes everything," Alex said. "Now what do we do first? Do we let Ruth Ann go to the shack or give this Meme woman our items to break the curse first?"

Isabella cleared her throat to get our attention. "That wasn't everything we needed to supply for my grandmother."

Confused, I asked, "There was more? I didn't hear more, Isabella."

"She told me before you arrived. I knew there'd be more, and she made me wait for you, but I have other items I need."

"Like what?" Inga asked.

Isabella hesitated, moved nervously back and forth in her spot and finally said, "Your family isn't the only items we needed."

"*Who else's family is there?*" I demanded. "Please don't tell me it's the cursed family that we know nothing about!"

"Well you kind of do know about the other family that was originally cursed."

"Meme said it was cursed over a hundred years ago! How would I know someone from this island?" I asked, confused.

"Well…the gem was here a hundred years ago and then stolen and taken to Sweden where Axel and Prunella's families fought over it."

"I know that part of the story, but what about before?" I asked, never imagining there was a past beyond what I learned from Axel and Prunella.

"The origin of the stone has connections from Jamaica to Sweden, Ruth Ann," Isabella explained. "The stone was cursed because a descendent from your family stole it from Martika's great-great-great, I'm not really sure how many 'greats', but quite a long time ago, grandmother."

"You've got to be kidding," Axel chortled, but not jokingly. "You're telling me that a past family member of Martika's actually owned the gem here in Jamaica and one of Prunella's or my ancestors stole it and took it back to Sweden where we fought over it for the next hundred years?" He laughed again and said, "That's ridiculous!"

"Yes." Isabella waited for any our responses, but we were quite speechless. So that's why Martika was so set on getting the precious necklace from me. She wanted it back to where she believes it truly belongs. A pang of guilt surfaced and I suddenly felt sorry for her, but not for long. Martika could've just confronted us and discussed the matter without going to such an elaborate scheme.

"Who cares about the past of the gem!" Alex snapped, impatiently. "What do we need to do *now* to end this?"

Even I knew the past played a huge part in our current situation, but it was Isabella who kindly said, "Alex, you've recently lost your mother and discovered a whole new part of your family you didn't know existed. If your mother didn't tell you about the necklace, you wouldn't be standing here surrounded by family." Alex lowered his head, but not before a quick glance in Axel's direction. It was one of those uncomfortable moments. I can't explain why Alex looked at Axel, but when their eyes met, I knew there had to be a deeper involvement between the two. I added a mental note to pursue this when we get home.

"Well said," Sherman announced. "I recently divulged I was Prunella's great uncle and now I have a whole new family, too!"

"Okay, I get it," he said, admitting defeat. "I'm thrilled I found Prunella, Ruth Ann, and the others, but we need to get a move on. What are we going to do first? Go after a personal possession from Martika or have Ruth Ann show up at the shack with the necklace?"

"We locate Martika before she kills John," Inga declared. "But where is she? Didn't your grandmother say she knows where they are, but won't tell us until she breaks the curse?" Inga waited for Isabella to respond, but first added, "It's impossible! If we don't give Martika what she wants she'll kill John, and if we hunt her down she'll find out what we're up to and kill John!"

"We won't let her kill John!" Axel barked. "Enough of killing John! We'll get Ruth Ann over to the shack and she can get something from Martika *without* handing over the necklace."

I whirled around to face him and snapped, "And how do you propose I do that when a gun will be aiming at my head!" I hadn't forgiven either one of them for putting us into this horrible situation. If they would've told me they were in financial troubles maybe I could've helped, but they chose to lie and force me into bringing the necklace down here in hopes it would be stolen.

"I'm thinking, Ruth Ann," he admitted. "I'm hoping they won't feel threatened by you and Martika there alone."

"And why couldn't they feel threatened by me? I've proven I can stand up to just about anyone lately, haven't I?"

Prunella nudged her husband and she quickly replied, "Of course you're strong and smart enough to handle her. I believe my husband meant that it isn't like you were going in there with back-ups. Martika will be on high alert having the shack watched from all directions."

"I think so, too," Carlos said. "My wife isn't stupid, that's for sure, but she can be outplayed." We turned to face Carlos who had been standing by the front door, pacing.

"Go on," Axel said, interested in what he meant by his comment.

"Martika had a few weaknesses. That's the only positive thing I've learned from her since she blackmailed me into marrying her."

Axel interrupted him and asked, "Yeah, you never did explain what she's blackmailing you with?"

"Never mind that, Axel," I chimed in. "It's personal and has nothing to do with our current predicament."

"But," he said, and I held up my hand and repeated, "Please, it has nothing to do with this. Let him be."

"Fine, but hurry and tell us what her weaknesses are. We're supposed to get Ruth Ann moving in a few hours."

"Martika has been a jealous, greedy woman her whole life. She was jealous of Isabella," Carlos smiled at Isabella who appeared stunned by his statement. "Yes, jealous that you had a doting mother and grandmother. She played off the crazy part of your family, but deep down she was jealous, plain and simple."

"Wow," Isabella mumbled. "I never knew. Maybe if she talked to me we would've been on the same side and not going through this."

"Too late now," Axel remarked. "Go on, Carlos."

"I am!" he barked. "Besides the jealousy, which ate away at her soul, she always wanted better. She always complained about this crummy, poor town and how she was going to bust out of here someday. She was always working on a plot to make it big. She once tried out for a beauty pageant, but she got cut in the first round."

"I remember that!" Isabella shouted.

"You remember why she was so upset, Isabella?" Carlos asked.

Isabella lowered her head to the dirty, cement floor and replied, "Yes."

"What?" Alex asked anxiously, wanting to know what she meant.

"It's nothing, really," she said, modestly.

"Tell them," Carlos insisted. "It makes my point clear about her."

"She was upset that I tried out along with her, but in a different age level, and got further along in the process. I looked up to her when I was young and impressionable. I didn't know she was jealous of me. I was much younger, and I didn't have anything to be jealous of."

"You were gifted, Isabella," Carlos said, smiling brightly at her. "You had powers like your mother and grandmother, and that made Martika green with envy."

"But she thought we were freaks!"

"Out of jealousy only."

"It's making sense now," I said. "Martika wanted powers like you, but she didn't have them so she left and plotted against your family. She wanted to destroy you all!"

"I guess so," she answered. "That's so sad."

"Sad?" Axel asked her. "She's sick, twisted, and disturbed! The woman kidnapped a man and is threatening to kill him. You can't possibly feel any empathy toward her!"

Isabella didn't respond. Carlos sensed her embarrassment and went on. "So, I've told you about her past with greed and jealousy. There might be a way to get an item from her without risking Ruth Ann seeing her at all!"

"How?" I asked, excitedly. I wasn't thrilled about confronting a wild woman like Martika, alone.

"Isabella needs to pour on the charm and reach out to her half-sister. She can tell her she's sorry about everything that's happened to her and offer her assistance. She can tell her that her grandmother's dead and now she's her only family left."

"You're kidding, right?" Alex asked, sarcastically. "The woman's deranged. She won't fall for this!"

"It might happen," Carlos replied. "What could we lose? If Martika refused to let Isabella into her life, then we'll figure out another way. I don't think Ruth Ann going into the shack alone is a smart plan. Once Martika gets a hold of the necklace, she'll have no use for Ruth Ann or John!"

"I agree," Prunella said. "But your grandmother won't tell us where they are!"

"I can convince her otherwise. Maybe she'll agree to go along with us if I promise I'll bring back *all* the personal items we need to break the curse."

"Is that all we need, Isabella?" I asked, curiously.

"Well," she answered, and then hesitated.

"Well what?" Axel asked, worried.

"We also need items from my mother and myself."

"Why? You're not part of this family, are you?" Alex inquired.

"No, no, not like that. It's just Martika who is related to me and it will help with breaking of the curse."

"Why don't you go talk with your grandmother, Isabella?" Carlos asked, giving her a gentle nudge toward the basement door. "We'll come up with other options while you're gone."

Isabella disappeared into the basement. I had an idea. "I know it's a risk my going to the shack alone, but what if Isabella and I go together? She can appeal to Martika and I can try to get an item from her."

"But you'll have to turn over the necklace!" Inga exclaimed.

"Not if I don't have it with me," I said. "I could tell her I didn't trust her and I'll tell her I'll hand it over once I've seen John. That may buy us some time."

"I don't know," Axel said, clearly thinking about my suggestion.

"What will it hurt?" I asked.

"She told you in the note to come alone or John dies," Alex reminded us. "Bringing Isabella is a risky move; don't you think?"

"But it's her sister," Inga stated. "I don't think she'll hurt her. I think Martika's worried about being attacked by us if Ruth Ann's not alone."

"True," Alex said. "It could work, I guess."

"Good. When Isabella comes back, I'll tell her the two of us are going to the shack. Our main objective is to grab something of hers and make sure John's still alive and well."

"It's sounds awfully dangerous to me," Sherman contributed. "I think we should all go in there and surprise her. We'll grab her and force her to hand John over or we'll kill her!"

"That's a good plan, Sherman," I said, not wanting to discredit his efforts. "But if she has a gun or her guard has one, somebody could get killed."

"She's dangerous. I think we need to go in with females because she thinks we're weak anyway," I said. "Unless she's afraid of Isabella and her 'powers'."

"They're not that kind of power, Ruth Ann," Carlos said. "They see and feel things that are going to happen, not exactly a threatening control."

"But I thought they could place curses on people?" I asked.

"Yes, they do actually," Carlos said slowly, and then a huge grin crossed his face. "Hey, that's a good point, Ruth Ann!"

"What?" I asked, wondering what idea I had.

"About curses."

"Oh," Axel said, quickly understanding Carlos' intentions. "We have Ruth Ann and Isabella go in there and if Martika doesn't cooperate, Isabella will threaten her with a curse!"

"Exactly," Carlos said. "That'll scare her to death!"

"Why didn't we think of that before?" Inga asked, exasperated.

"I don't know," Carlos said, stunned himself. "We did now, so I think that's our best plan."

"As soon as Isabella comes back, we'll go find Martika and end this," I said.

We stood around a few more minutes when Isabella appeared out of thin air. "Hey, where did you come from?" I asked, seeing her standing next to me at the counter in the middle of Felix's store.

"I came through the stairs," she replied, innocently. "What's going on up here?" She eyed each one of us as we stood frozen, staring at her.

"Oh, how's Meme?" I asked, worried that she had passed away while we were up here scheming.

"Weak, but alive. She told me where I could find my sister. It's not far from here, Ruth Ann."

"Why are you addressing only Ruth Ann?" Prunella inquired.

"My grandmother doesn't want anyone else to get involved except for Ruth Ann and me."

"That's funny," Sherman said. "That's exactly what we planned while you were in the basement checking on your grandmother. How did your grandmother know that?"

"Seriously, Sherman," I snapped. "Meme can see what's going on even if she's not there. If it's a strong feeling, she becomes weaker and weaker because she uses all her energy to identify her visions."

"It sounds a little hokey," Sherman muttered, but one glare from Isabella shut him up. He wasn't totally convinced Isabella couldn't throw a curse on him!

"Ruth Ann and I will head out now. All of you stay here, and we'll return as soon as we can."

Not one, but several in our group protested. "No!" Axel declared. "I know we said you and Ruth Ann should go to the shack alone, but that was with us at a close distance. There's no way I'll allow you to take Ruth Ann to some unidentified location. Tell us where you're going first!"

"No, sorry. That's all I can say. If I don't follow specific instructions from my grandmother, people will get killed."

"Killed!" Sherman bellowed. "Let them go!"

"You coward!" Inga yelled at Sherman. "We'll follow you, but at a safe distance so we won't be seen."

"I don't want you following, please," I begged. "I'm safe with Isabella. Her grandmother would've told her if we would be in danger going alone. The quicker we go, the quicker we get back."

I grabbed Isabella's arm and headed out the front door. We didn't wait for any further protests. We were wasting time. It was evening now as we headed into the dark, wet jungle. I grabbed a flashlight before we left the store and turned it on. "There, now we can see."

"I don't need a flashlight, Ruth Ann," Isabella announced. "I know this area quite well."

"It makes me feel better."

"Fine. Stay right behind me and don't speak until I give you a sign it's okay."

"Sounds good," I said, slapping my hand across my mouth. I had a way of talking without thinking. It usually got me into trouble and that shouldn't surprise anyone who knows me!

Chapter 27

I didn't keep my silence too long. "Where are we going, Isabella? I whispered. "I thought we were going to the shack?"

"No, not yet. First, we're going to your bungalow and picking up the earrings and that red velvet pouch, and then I want to check out another place. It's not far from here. That's why Martika and her guard were able to show up near us so many times."

"Please don't tell me she's back at the resort!"

"Yep, that's exactly where she is."

"Carlos and I checked all the bungalows and they were empty."

"Well, he missed one," she stammered, pushing her way through a thick area where the path was non-existent. "It's where housekeeping stayed when there was a full staff. They would come from their villages and stay at the resort for two weeks, and then go home for a weekend, and then return to the resort to work. Many resorts do that down here, Ruth Ann."

"It's probably better accommodations than what they're used to at their homes."

"Oh, yes. Getting a job at one of the resorts on the beach was like winning the lottery down here. The pay isn't great, but staffers get to eat, sleep, and drink for free."

"Sounds like a job I'd like!" I said, trying to lighten our mood as we hiked through the dark, damp jungle.

I tripped over a large branch and nearly fell into Isabella. "Be careful, Ruth Ann!"

"I can't see very well. You need to slow down a little. I'm not as young or familiar with the terrain as you are!"

Isabella slowed her pace, and I was able to keep up with her without tripping, running into low hanging branches or other unknown elements, which I didn't want to know about anyway. We walked about ten minutes when she halted. "We're on the outskirts of the resort."

"I don't remember coming this way ever, even with Carlos," I stated, wiping the sweat that was dripping down my neck.

"There's many ways to get around here. I've been sneaking from the resort to the shack and Felix's for a long time now. I don't think Carlos left the resort as much as I did. He's not used to 'roughing' it like I am."

I didn't comment, but she was correct. I could tell from Carlos' manicured hands that he hadn't trudged around the jungle and chased after kidnappers in quite a long time.

Isabella slowed her pace even more. I could see the lights from the lampposts around the resort up ahead through the trees. "We're almost at the bungalow, and the compound."

"Compound?" I asked, confused.

"It's just what the staffers called their building."

"How big is the place?" I asked, thinking it was just a small building.

"It's not much bigger than your bungalow, but it has five tiny bedrooms with just a bed, wash basin, and a small dresser to hold personal items."

"So five bedrooms. I assume there's a bathroom or two and a kitchen?"

"One bathroom, and not exactly a kitchen, but a sink and small refrigerator are in there. Oh, and a microwave."

"Doesn't sound too bad," I said, tentatively. "It's small and only one bathroom doesn't sound convenient, but as you said it's better than where they came from."

Isabella didn't respond, but walked up to the edge of a grouping of trees and told me not to talk anymore. She pointed to the side of my bungalow and whispered that it appeared dark and most likely safe inside. She stood guard at the front door as I rushed in and headed through the mess and found the earrings and red velvet pouch on the bathroom counter. I felt quite sure Martika or her guard opened it up thinking the necklace was inside. Ha! Hope they were totally disappointed when they found it empty! I shoved it in my pocket and headed back to Martika. "All clear out here," she told me. Let's get over to the compound."

Soon, we were there. I noticed the back of a cement dwelling with a broken light on the side of the back wall. It was very dark out since the small building blocked the surrounding hotel lights. Isabella grabbed my arm and pulled me down. "Hey, give me a warning, would you!"

"Shhh," she snapped.

I noticed five small, square windows on the back end of the building. They were all dark, but open aired. There were no blinds, drapes or other window coverings. My heart was beating faster, thinking we could peek in and spot John.

"Are you going to look inside?" I whispered.

"Yes." Isabella motioned for me to stay put. She crawled over to an abandoned wood crate near one of the windows and stepped on top of it to look inside the windows.

I gave her a second before I couldn't take it any longer. I stood halfway up and stepped over to her as she was peering over the edge of the window. "Anyone in there?"

Isabella hopped down and glared deep into my eyes. I didn't have to hear her response because I felt it burn inside my brain. Nobody was in there, but don't do that again!

She grabbed the crate and dragged it to the next window. She stepped on it and shook her head at me. I got it, don't ask any questions. She'd tell me if she found John or anyone for that matter. I leaned against the building and closed my eyes. I started to pray that John was safe inside one of these rooms when Isabella took my arm and pulled me over to the last window on the far right back side of the building. She pointed up at the window and pushed me to get on the crate to take a look.

My heart leapt when I thought of what I might find inside the room. Isabella's expression was neither terror or happiness. I took one step up and grabbed the outside edge of the rough cement window opening and slowly brought my face close enough to look in. What I saw startled me so I fell back and landed on my backside on the ground. Thankfully, I landed in a pile of foliage that softened the blow, a little. Isabella hurried over to me and helped me to stand.

"You saw?" she whispered in my ear.

"Yes," I said, horrified at what I saw and sore from what I landed on. I rubbed my butt as I contemplated what I just saw. "Who was that?"

"It was the groundskeeper at the resort, Ruth Ann."

"But why would she have done that to him?" I asked, shocked at the sight just inside the window.

"I think he was in the wrong place at the wrong time. Martika has nothing against him."

I know it was horrible seeing a dead man lying on the cold cement floor, but I was also grateful it wasn't John. The groundskeeper's throat had obviously been slit and there was a pool of blood surrounding the poor man's body on the floor.

"Now what?" I asked, concerned about where Martika was now.

"She may be in the living room of this building. It's small, but I think she would keep John in her sight at all time. We better get out of here before the guard comes out and checks the area."

"Did you see the guard or her inside?"

"I spotted the guard walking in the hall just outside the bedrooms. I think he was going to the one bathroom at the end of the hall."

"So, they really are in there! I want to get in there so badly, but we have no weapons."

"No, I think our best bet is to go the shack and wait for midnight. It's getting close anyway. Martika may have already left and the guard is standing watch over John."

"I can't leave without seeing him, Isabella. We're so close, but we can't do anything about it! I can't take much more of this."

"Just know it'll be over soon, Ruth Ann. I think we'll be able to sneak something from Martika without her even knowing."

"But she's expecting me to hand over the necklace, Isabella. How are we going to handle her in the shack? Do I give her the necklace?"

"NO!" she cried, too loud. She grabbed my hand and dragged me into the jungle so quickly that I didn't have time to object. We went a short distance when she stopped and told me to listen. "The guard was outside the building. I heard him. I was stupid to shout so loudly."

We stood a few feet inside the jungle away from the building and watched as a flashlight moved across the back of the building. It was the guard. He was checking out the back of the building. Hopefully, he wouldn't come to where we were hiding, but then he would have to leave John alone longer than he was probably ordered to. Suddenly, we heard his voice, "Just somebody from the resort. Probably some fools in the disgusting pool!" He turned and headed back around the side of the building out of our sight.

"Phew, that was too close, Ruth Ann."

"And it wasn't even me who did that one!" I chuckled, even though it wasn't a time to crack a joke. I just do it sometimes when I'm under a lot of stress. It helps me relax so I can think more clearly.

"I'm sorry, Ruth Ann," Isabella said. "I didn't mean to yell like that. I just feel it would be a huge mistake to give her the necklace."

"I understand you want to let your grandmother break the dreaded curse, but I'm risking John's life. I wouldn't be able to live with myself if anything happened to him."

"I understand. Let's just try and see if I can swipe something from her first. We can tell her we didn't think she'd show up at the shack anyway and that's why you didn't bring the necklace." Isabella eyed me apprehensively and said, "You don't actually have the necklace with you, do you?"

"I haven't told anyone where it is, Isabella," I replied. I knew it was safe inside the side pocket of my shorts. I didn't even tell Carlos I had it with me, either.

"But you know that's it's safe, right?" she asked, worried.

"Definitely."

"Martika will be furious when she finds out we didn't bring the necklace, but I'm hoping it'll buy us some time."

"We can tell her we need to go to the place where it's hidden," I said. "Also, we can say that we've been too busy trying to rescue John, and haven't been able to retrieve the necklace."

"I don't know if she'll buy it, but we don't have any choice now."

Isabella took off and headed for the sandy path that led down to the beach. "It's pretty dark out here. I think it's safe we take the path now."

"Good. I'm getting sick of hiking through the jungle. I've been just waiting for a snake or spider to attack me!"

We made good time getting down the deserted, dark beach and over to the shack. "It's really dark," I said.

"You can't even make out the group of shacks right ahead. I don't see any lights from them which makes me think Martika isn't there yet," Isabella announced.

"If she'll even show up!"

"Why wouldn't she?" Isabella asked, confused. "She wrote you the note and told you to meet her here."

"I know, but they always seem to be one step ahead of us and I don't know how."

"We know she's got the one guard, but maybe she's got others following us."

"I didn't think of that. We could be followed right now!" I remarked, looking around me, but seeing nothing move.

"I don't think so, Ruth Ann. I'd have some sort of feeling that we were being followed."

"You would?"

"Yes, and I bet you would, too. I'm sure you've had that feeling that somebody's watching you before, right?"

"I guess so."

"Well, it's the same thing."

Isabella treaded through the sand and marched up to Meme's shack. I was a few steps behind her, but close enough to see the place was pitch black. "Are you going in?"

"Yes. We'll wait for midnight and see what happens."

Isabella disappeared inside the shack and I stood outside in the moonlit night waiting for her to call me in. I noticed a dim light beginning to glow and Isabella told me to come in. She had lit the tiny candle on the wooden table. "This will have to do, Ruth Ann. We have no other light except your flashlight and I'd like to save that for emergencies."

"Sounds good," I said, sitting down on one of the chairs. "It's weird that just hours ago I was sitting here with Meme hearing all about the curse and waiting for you to appear."

"It seems like days ago."

I looked at my dead cell phone and wondered what time it was. Isabella held out her arm and showed me her battery powered watch. "It's 11:45," she told me. "Not much longer."

We didn't have to wait too long before we both heard a rustling outside. It couldn't have been from the sand, but maybe the jungle behind the shack. "I think somebody's coming, Ruth Ann."

I nodded, anxiously, and noticed Isabella went and stood to the side of the beaded strings that was used as a door. "Shhh," she said, quietly. "When she sees me she'll be furious, but let me do the talking, okay?" I nodded, and we waited for the sound of the tinkling beads and then a hand appeared through them.

"Ruth Ann, are you in here?" a female voice asked.

"Yes," I replied with a shaky voice.

"Are you alone?" she asked, still only seeing the hand holding the beaded strings.

"No, she's not," Isabella responded instead of me.

Without hesitation, the strings whipped apart and Martika stormed in with raging eyes searching for her half-sister. "Isabella!" she hollered. "Where are you?"

"Right here," she replied, coming in to view from behind Martika.

"What are you doing here! I ordered, yes demanded, Ruth Ann to come alone or her boyfriend will be killed!"

"Knock it off, Martika," Isabella snarled. "You won't kill him before you get your hands on that precious gem."

"So, you're calling my bluff?" she asked with fiery, red rimmed eyes that one would expect to see on the devil, himself.

"No, you know it wasn't safe for Ruth Ann to come here alone. You wouldn't have done it either. It wasn't like I let one of her family members or Carlos bring her. I'm the least threatening person of all of us and you know it!"

"You were always a weak little girl, Isabella. You idolized me for years!"

"You're right! I was jealous of you and wanted to be just like you. Why did you leave me?" she asked, truly appearing heartbroken by Martika's betrayal, but I knew it was an act. At least I hoped it was an act!

"I didn't have a choice, Isabella. Your mother and grandmother hated me and never wanted me in the first place. The only connection you and I had was our father, and you know what happened to him."

"Yes."

"I did feel bad back then, but you didn't try and escape from them and try and find me, did you?"

"I was a child!" she stammered. "I did end up finding you recently, didn't I?"

"Yes, and I was truly happy to see you until I found out about your grandmother and your plot to get the necklace from Ruth Ann, too."

"I'm not plotting anything, Martika! All we want to do is break the evil curse. You want it for greed and money, and that's different!"

"Yes, poor me. I want a better life for me since I was raised in such squalor that I barely had clean clothes and a full tummy. You should understand that, too!"

"But I wouldn't lie, kidnap, and murder to get a better life!"

"I don't want to do that, but things got out of control so I had to protect myself."

"With the guard?" I asked, interrupting their exchange.

"Yes, that's right. I found him back in Sweden before I flew to that little dumpy town of yours back in the states."

"It's not dumpy!" I shouted.

"Ruth Ann, please," Isabella said, eyeing me anxiously. I shut my mouth and listened to the two reminisce about their unfortunate past and how they ended up in two totally different places in their lives. I was standing near the wooden table and then leaned against the back of one of the chairs. My hand carefully reached down to my pocket and felt the hard lump near the side of my thigh. Still there, I said to myself silently. I then felt another smaller lump. Oh no! I forgot all about the ring Carlos discovered back in one of the bungalows. Coming here was a wasted trip! I already had a personal possession of Martika's. The ring her father gave her.

I frantically tried to think of a way to get out of here without risking our freedom. I decided I had to risk pulling her ring out of my pocket and trying to wave it at Isabella behind Martika's back. I couldn't let Martika see me, but I had to try. I walked near the two women as they continued their argument and stood behind Martika. Neither one of them took notice of me until I started waving the tiny little ring up in the air and hoping Isabella would spot it. It worked! Isabella almost choked on her words when she caught site of the blue-green stone ring.

Martika noticed Isabella's abrupt change of demeanor. "What's wrong with you?" she barked.

"I'm, I'm too upset to continue. We don't have the necklace with us right now."

"WHAT!" she screamed with intense rage in her voice. "I demanded it to be brought to me at midnight. Why would you betray me? You know the consequence!"

I stepped a few feet away from Martika and exclaimed, "You don't understand! I have to go and get it. We've spent the last day or two chasing after you and that guard of yours. If you would've stopped changing locations continuously, I would've been able to get my necklace out of it's safekeeping."

Martika was speechless. I wasn't sure if what I said was working or not. She could either order the guard back at the staff's housing to kill John or allow me a little more time to get the necklace and come back.

"I don't believe you!" she said slowly and eyed me suspiciously. "You're trying to trick me, aren't you?"

"NO!" I bellowed.

"Are the others outside waiting to grab me?" she asked, appearing paranoid whipping her head around the room looking for someone to pop out and attack her.

"No, it's just Ruth Ann and me," Isabella protested. "Let us go and, and…I have an idea."

Both Martika and I said, "What?"

"If we promise to go and get the necklace and come back, will you go get John?"

I thought for a slight second Martika would go for it. "Are you crazy?" she laughed, devilishly. "You're just like your mother and grandmother! All I have to do is dial one number and your boyfriend's as good as dead!" Martika pulled her cell phone out of her skirt pocket and held it up for us to see.

"If you kill him you'll NEVER see that necklace!" I screamed having enough of this. "Listen here. It's our turn to tell you what to do! We *will* go and get my necklace and while we're gone, you *will* go and bring John back here. If you don't do as we ask this time, you *will* never get your hands on that gem. Got it?" I demanded with as much strength I could muster.

Isabella smiled briefly and watched as her half-sister's glare bore through my own eyes. "You can't tell me what to do! I want the necklace first, and then you'll see John. That's if he still wants to see you."

"Wait, what did you just say?" I asked, stunned at her statement.

"He and I have been having a nice little time, Ruth Ann. You know, he's quite the attractive guy, and so strong!"

"That's ridiculous," I replied, doubting the words she was beginning to imply. "He would never betray me with *you*!"

"Are you so sure about that? I'm a beautiful, young woman. I'm sure he's quite willing to satisfy my needs."

"Only to get away from you!" Isabella screamed.

"He wouldn't touch her!" I responded to Isabella. "He wouldn't want to get a disease!"

Well, that did it. Any hope of compromise was over. Isabella knew it so she quickly ran over to the table and blew out the candle putting us into complete darkness. I felt a hand grasp mine as I was pulled out into the warm night air.

We didn't speak. Isabella ran as fast as she could drag me until we were far away from the shack. Finally, when she thought we were safe, she stopped.

"I can't keep going, Isabella," I said, gasping for air. "You go; I'll find my way back to Felix's somehow."

"I'm not leaving you, Ruth Ann."

"Where are we?"

"We're taking a back way to Felix's. I don't think even Martika or her guard will know about it."

"Good. I'm too tired to be chased at the moment."

A few minutes later Isabella had us back on kind of a path. At least it wasn't tramping through fallen branches, leaves, and rocks. "It'll be easier now," she said, releasing my hand and walking in front of me. The path was very narrow, only about a foot or so wide, but at least I felt safer than before. "We're here."

"Here, where?" I asked, not recognizing anything about where she stopped. "Are we at Felix's place?"

"Yes, but from the other side of the house. I thought it'd be safe to go in through the basement entrance."

"There's a basement door?" I asked, wondering how I didn't notice it when I was down there earlier. "Why didn't you point that out earlier?"

"It wasn't necessary."

"C'mon, Isabella. What if someone used the door and went after your grandmother?"

"She's well protected with the others."

"Joseph was still down there with Felix when we left. Hopefully they'll still be there."

We hurried through the small, open grassy area and made our way down a narrow set of cement stairs. "Nobody even knows these stairs exist. They're well hidden," Isabella said.

"Until we took the first step I didn't see a thing!"

We hurried down the cracked cement steps and came up to a solid wooden door. Isabella reached up to open it, but it didn't budge. "Locked."

"How are you going to get in?"

"I'm going to knock!" she stated, wrapping hard on the door.

We waited, and when nobody answered, Isabella knocked as hard as she could. A few seconds later we heard a number of metal noises which sounded like locks being undone. "There," she said. "Somebody finally heard me."

"Carlos!" I cried out. "You're down here."

"I've been going back and forth checking on everybody." Carlos eyed Isabella with a worried look. "Your grandmother needs you."

"Is she…" I started to ask, but Carlos shook his head.

"Barely," Joseph muttered from behind Carlos. "Hurry up and get in here. We don't want to be heard."

Isabella rushed in and disappeared into the bedroom where her sickly grandmother lay. I stood in the small hallway outside the room and interrogated Carlos and Joseph. "What's going on here? Is Meme near her end? How's everyone upstairs?"

"Easy, Ruth Ann," Carlos said. "I'll get to your questions, but first, tell me what happened with you and Isabella? Was Martika there?"

"Oh, yes, she was there," I replied.

"Alone?"

"Yes."

"Wow, I thought she'd be smarter than that," Carlos said, laughing. "We should've come along and forced her to take us to John."

"She's a crazy woman!" Isabella called out from inside the room. "She thinks my grandmother and I are, but it's her who's not right in the head!"

I stuck my head inside the room and spotted Isabella sitting on the side of the bed near her grandmother. I noticed Meme's eyes were slits and she seemed at the end of her life. Isabella waved me inside, but I hesitated not wanting to interrupt their last moments together.

"No, no, it's okay, Ruth Ann," Isabella said. "My grandmother wants to talk with you."

I slowly walked to the bed and stood next to Isabella. She was holding Meme's hand and rubbing it with the other hand. "She's weak, but still sharp."

"That's good," I said, not knowing what to say or do.

"Ruth Ann," Meme spoke meekly. "I'm glad you're alright. I was worried Martika would hold you hostage until you gave up the necklace."

"Nope. I'm still here and I wouldn't let Martika capture me! She needs me to bring her the gem she wants so badly."

"She thinks the gem will bring her great fortune and happiness, but it'll only bring her despair and loneliness."

"Grandmother knows this for sure, Ruth Ann. Anyone who's had that gem understands things never seem quite right, and some people who've possessed it have not lived long enough to enjoy it."

I listened carefully to what Isabella and Meme said and thought about all the problems I've had since I've come into contact with the gem. Back in Deer Creek when it first arrived, Doug was brutally attacked and left for dead in his bank until I arrived. Then the security guard, Paul was thrown into a hole in the basement floor and I was shackled to a wall. I was able to escape, but was captured again and flown to Stockholm and held captive in Axel's estate until meeting Prunella, Inga, and Sherman. Once we all escaped from there we ran around, narrowly escaping an explosion at Eklund Industries' pier. Come to think of it, there's been too much heartache attached to the gem. Especially looking back at Bert, who was horribly burned to death and to poor Helena who also lost her life.

"I believe it," I said, resigned to the fact the curse had to be broken immediately. "Can you break the curse with what Isabella and I brought you?"

"Isabella was just going over the items with me."

"Yes, grandmother. We have Martika's ring, Prunella's hairpin, Axel's pocket watch, Alex's coin, Lynne's velvet pouch, and Nancy's silver earrings." Isabella hesitated and asked, "What would you like to use, grandmother?"

Meme released Isabella's hand and moved it back to her side and felt along her leg for the pocket in her skirt. She reached in and pulled a small item out of the pocket and held it up for Isabella to take.

"What is it?" I asked, eagerly.

"It's my wedding band," Meme replied. "The love of my life. I keep the ring with me at all times."

"That means it's an extra special personal item," I said, smiling.

"Isabella, you know what you have, too," Meme said, tapping the hand that held her wedding band with her shaky hand.

"Yes." Isabella stood up, reached inside the pocket of her own skirt and pulled out her own tiny item. "It was my moms," she said, holding a small gold cross in her hands. It surprised me. I guess seeing them as Christian didn't cross my mind with their practice of the supernatural.

"My daughter," Meme started to say. "She did not keep her wedding band since he betrayed her with Martika's mother. She spat on it and cursed it."

Isabella nodded, but I could see the pain in her eyes. She didn't want her father cursed and killed. "It's very nice," I said, talking about the gold cross. "Now can we break this blessed curse?"

"Not yet," Meme weakly said. "Where's your personal possession, Ruth Ann?" Then she added with more power in her voice, "And the necklace?"

"You need something from me, too?" I asked, surprised. "I thought you would just need the necklace."

"I need both."

I didn't have anything with me. What would I do now? Just as the panic was setting in, Carlos came barreling through the door. "We have a problem," he said, trying to get his breath back.

The three of us turned our attention to a frightened Carlos. "What happened?" I said first.

"Martika's guard is outside the house. Felix went out when he heard some racket outside thinking he had a customer. He didn't want anyone coming inside and finding the rest of us standing around his store."

"Did Felix confront the guard?" I asked, worried.

"Yes!" Carlos said, frantically. "He shot him!"

"WHAT!" I screamed.

Isabella asked the more important question now. "Is he dead?"

"I think so," Carlos said. "All the poor guy did was walk down his steps and the jerk pointed his gun at him and shot him! He didn't even get a chance to speak. It was horrible!"

"Where's Felix now?" I asked, appalled at what Carlos reported. "Please don't tell me he's still lying outside."

"It's too late, Ruth Ann," Carlos said. "Felix was killed instantaneously, and it was too risky for one of us to go out there and bring him somewhere until we can properly lay him to rest."

"That's horrible!" I cried. "Why'd that guard have to shoot him? I don't get it. Felix has nothing to do with this."

"I know, Ruth Ann," he replied, solemnly.

"I told you people were going to die," Meme suddenly spoke with a stronger voice. "I just wasn't sure who."

"I wish we could've had a warning. Then poor Felix wouldn't have gone outside to see who was out there," I said, wishing Meme and Isabella had a clearer vision of what was happening.

"Now what do we do?" Carlos asked, looking to Meme for the answer.

"We need to work on the curse."

"But I don't have anything personal with me!" I exclaimed. "I didn't think *I* needed something, too."

"Everyone, including you, Ruth Ann, who had direct and personal contact with it needs a personal item," Isabella answered for her grandmother.

"That means I have to go back to the bungalow, again. My belongings are still there."

"Is that where the necklace is hidden, too?" Carlos inquired.

"No," Meme answered instead of me. "Isn't that right, Ruth Ann?"

I decided it was the right time to divulge the exact whereabouts of my necklace. "You're right, Meme. I should've known you would know."

Meme's eyes twinkled as she stared at me. "It's okay now, Ruth Ann. We're all on your side and you now know that."

"You're right, Meme." I put my hand inside my pocket and pulled out the Blue Ice. I held it up for Isabella, Carlos, and Meme to see. "Here it is."

"Ah," Meme groaned. "It sure is."

"It's beautiful!" Carlos said, greedily. "Can I hold it?" he asked, his hands trembling with excitement.

I clutched it close to my heart and clamped my fist shut. "Not yet," I said, doubting any of their sincerities suddenly.

"Ruth Ann," Isabella said softly. "By now you should know the risks we would take for each other. It's not because of the necklace, but because of the relationships we've formed since meeting you. Please let my grandmother hold the necklace. It'll give her such pleasure."

I listened intently, but something in me was screaming to not let go of the necklace, not ever. "I'm not sure," I mumbled. "I have an awful feeling inside right now."

"It's fear of letting go, Ruth Ann," Meme declared, gently. "I can't do anything with your necklace in my condition. You can trust me, really, you can." Meme raised her arm off the bed and reached her hand in my direction. "Let me hold it for a minute. It'll give me strength to go on a little longer."

Well, how could I not oblige that plea? I unclenched my fist and walked over to the bed where Meme lay. I gently set the necklace in her wrinkled, open hand and watched as the gleam in her eyes brightened bringing new life that rushed through her body. "Magnificent."

"It is, isn't it!" I agreed. "But we still can't break the curse right now, can we?"

"No," Isabella said, leaning over the bed to get a better look at the necklace lying in Meme's hand. The strength of her previously shaking hand increased, and she brought the gem close to her face and stared at it hypnotically. "Finally, we meet again," she mumbled to herself. "It's been a very long time."

Wait a minute! The necklace was passed from Axel's family to my family to Prunella's family in Sweden for many, many years. How old was this woman anyway? I believed the necklace had been in our hands for about a hundred years, and I thought the curse was placed on it before that time. Meme couldn't be that old, could she? Even if she was around about a hundred years ago, she would've been a small child at most.

"I know what you're thinking, Ruth Ann," Isabella said. "My grandmother is very old, but I'll let her explain how she came into contact with the piece since the curse was placed on it."

I looked at Meme who was still staring at the gem and ignoring the rest of us. "I have seen the gem before. I was in Sweden years ago when I first fell in love."

"I don't understand," I said, completely baffled.

"When I was a young girl I was very adventurous. I wanted to see the world, but didn't have the means to do so. I was working on the beach making baskets and weaving blankets one hot, sunny day when a young man approached me. He was very tall and handsome. I was supposed to be married soon, and I wasn't in love with the man I was to marry. So, when this beautiful man started talking to me, lonely, poor me, I felt important, different. He came around daily for about a week when he asked me to join him for the day. He said he'd show me a different side of the island, not just the poor side."

"And of course you went, didn't you?" I asked.

"Yes, yes. I was young and stupid. Times were different back then. People didn't commit the horrendous crimes like they do these days, but there still were bad people out there."

"Was he one of them?" I asked, curiously.

"Not at first. He showered me with flowers, trinkets that were expensive. He told me not to marry the other man and asked me to come back to his home in Sweden."

"You just dropped your life here and followed this stranger?" I asked, wondering if I would've done the same given the circumstances.

"Yes. I desperately wanted a better life and I thought I loved this new man in my life. I didn't understand my powers at the time. I knew I was different, but wasn't sure how to handle it. Most of the people in my village thought I was just a quiet, strange little girl."

"You had those visions early on, didn't you?" I asked.

"Yes, but I didn't know how to control them. It was hard because my parents didn't tell me about our special abilities yet, and I thought I was too different for people in my village. So, I went with him back to Sweden."

"Stockholm," I said.

"Yes."

"What happened, grandmother?" Isabella asked, just as surprised by this story as I was. Obviously, her grandmother had never told her about her past indiscretion.

Isabella, Carlos, and I were so caught up in Meme's tale that we didn't notice the group gathered at the doorway. Meme did though and said, "Why don't you all just come in so Ruth Ann doesn't have to repeat it later."

I whirled around to find Axel, Prunella, Alex, Inga, Sherman, and Joseph piling into the tiny bedroom. There was barely enough room for all of us, but I didn't care. I desperately wanted to hear the rest of Meme's story. "Go on, please, Meme," I said.

"I went with him to Stockholm and he didn't take me to his home. He told me I had to understand his life over there first. He was a little older than me. Well, a lot older, but it didn't matter to me. He said he had a wife…" Meme was immediately interrupted by Isabella. "You went and had a relationship with a married man?"

"I didn't know in the beginning, and when I found out it was too late. I was in love and this man was very wealthy. He promised me he would leave his wife and move me into his home as his new wife. I believed him, but remember, I was young and stupid."

"Don't tell me," Isabella said, ignoring our blank, shocked stares. "He lied to you."

"Yes, he did. Instead of making me his wife, he left me as his mistress in his home disguised as a maid."

"A what!" Inga bellowed.

"Yes, Inga, I was this man's housekeeper."

I noticed Axel becoming nervous. A few drops of sweat slowly fell down his cheeks, and his face turned a deep shade of red. Prunella and I looked at each other in acknowledgement, but I let Prunella confront him. "Are you okay, Axel?" she asked, worried. "I know it's pretty hot, but down here it's much cooler."

"I'm fine," he stammered. "Let Meme go on with her story."

Meme turned her attention to Axel. "You figured it out, didn't you?" she asked him.

Axel pushed through Sherman, Carlos, and Joseph to get a little closer to Meme. "Yes. It was my grandfather wasn't it?"

"You've got to be kidding me!" I cried out loudly. "Is *everybody* connected to this necklace!"

"I'm so confused," Prunella said. "Am I to believe that Meme was involved with your grandfather, Axel? And she came all the way from Jamaica to Sweden to live as your grandfather's mistress and housekeeper!"

"Seems so," he answered, truthfully. "I had no idea. Do you believe me?" he asked directly to Prunella.

"Of course I do," she replied sweetly and innocently. I, on the other hand, wasn't totally convinced of his ignorance.

"I've about had it," I snapped. "Meme, are you telling me you stayed his mistress and that's how you saw the necklace?"

"Oh, yes. The minute I was privileged to see the necklace I knew my destiny why it led me to Sweden with this cheater." Meme hesitated, took in a deep, raspy breath and said to Axel, "I'm sorry. I didn't mean to disrespect you."

"No, no, what he did to you was terrible," Axel said out loud, but I bet it made him look back to poor, dead Helena. She was his not so long ago housekeeper mistress. He even got her pregnant and then she was murdered by Axel's lunatic nephew, Finn.

"Can we get back to the future," Sherman interrupted. "I get the past has merit, but right now there's a dead man outside and a lunatic guard with a gun. What are we going to do to get out of this?"

"Sherman's right," I said. "We still have a huge problem."

"What now?" Inga asked irritated.

"We have most of what we need to have Meme break the curse except for..." I was rudely interrupted by Sherman as he shrieked, "Except for what!"

"I was about to tell you, but you interrupted me!" I snapped at him. "I don't have my own personal item to give to Meme."

"You have your necklace!" Sherman stated. "If that's not personal to you I don't know what is."

"But it can't be the necklace," Isabella said. "Each of us have given up an item, and Ruth Ann is no exception. Ruth Ann needs to go and get something...and quickly!"

"Are you suggesting Ruth Ann go back to her bungalow and grab something from her suitcase?" Prunella inquired, horrified at the thought. "There's no way. That madman is outside waiting for one of us to take a step out of here!"

"I know," Carlos said. "We need a distraction."

"What kind of distraction?" Sherman asked, suddenly aware that someone would have to pose as the 'distraction'.

Nobody spoke up. Axel started pacing the outer walls since there was no room in the middle of the bedroom. I got dizzy watching him walk the three walls, stop and turn, and go back and forth. I felt a sudden sense of desperation filling every breath inside my heavy lungs. This was all my fault! If I didn't convince John into taking me away from Deer Creek none of this would've happened. I won't take the blame for bringing the necklace down here. Axel and Prunella were to blame for that one! If they would've just confided in me about their dire financial situation I would've helped them come up with a better, safer plan. Finally, an idea popped in my head...

"I've got an idea." Everyone stopped what they were doing and turned their attention to me. "I think we would agree that we need to flush out Martika's guard, right?" Nods around the room showed me they agreed. "Okay, so what we need to do is divert his attention to the back of the house with some sort of loud noise or explosion. The man will come running back here, but we'll be ready for him."

"But he's got a gun!" Sherman bawled. "He'll shoot first, ask later."

"Not if we catch him off guard. We'll surprise attack the man. I doubt he even knows about this back door. I never did."

"He probably has walked all the way around the house, unlike you did, Ruth Ann," Carlos said.

"But the staircase is so well hidden, it looks like a part of the house. Maybe he didn't notice it."

"Possibly," Carlos said.

"It's risky, Ruth Ann," Axel said. "But I think Alex and I can take the guy." Axel looked at Alex to see if he was a willing participant.

"And how do we do that?" Alex asked, not appearing surprised with Axel's request.

"I think Ruth Ann's idea about a loud explosion is a good starting point. If we startle him even for a minute, you and I could pounce on him without him seeing it coming."

"How are we going to create this explosion you're talking about?" Inga asked, suddenly intrigued and excited. "Maybe there's something upstairs in Felix's store that could cause the noise."

Inga was about to head out of the bedroom and upstairs when Joseph told her to wait. "I can help you with that. I'm the doctor, let me find something that could work. I don't want any of you concocting something that will backfire in your faces."

"Fine," Inga agreed. "Let's go."

Inga, Joseph, and Sherman headed up the stairs. "Let's give them a few minutes, and then we can determine who's going to go and get Ruth Ann's belongings," Axel said.

"I'm going," I declared. "I know where my stuff is."

"You can't go alone," Prunella expressed, terrified of the thought of letting me out of her sight again. "I'll go with you."

"I'll go, too," Carlos said. "The three of us should be safe if Axel and Alex keep the guard at the back of the house long enough."

"Well, it sounds like we have a plan, finally," I said, feeling a weird sense of relief even though nothing had been resolved.

Isabella spent the next few minutes at her grandmother's side while Prunella, Axel, Alex, Carlos an I discussed several scenarios in case we got separated for a longer period of time.

"So, you understand that you can't just walk back up to this house when you come back, right Ruth Ann?" Axel asked me, ignoring Prunella and Carlos.

"Of course, Axel. I'm not stupid. Unless we have reason to believe the guard's gone or taken care of, we won't walk up to the house until you've given us a sign."

"The sign will be when you're near one of you will throw a branch at the back door from the edge of the jungle, but out of sight of the guard." Axel continued, "We'll divert the guard to the front of the house and you three will run as fast as you can back inside. Got it?"

"Got it," Prunella and I said together. Carlos just nodded, probably wondering what he had gotten himself in to.

A few minutes later, Inga, Joseph, and Sherman came rushing down the stairs. Or I should say, Inga and Joseph did. Sherman clearly didn't rush. He sauntered down the cement stairs as slowly as he could. It was obvious he was out of his element.

"We got it! Inga shouted. "We've got something that will definitely distract the guard."

"What is it?" Alex asked eagerly.

"You won't believe what we found," Inga said excited. She had her arms behind her back and slowly brought them forward holding what looked like sticks of dynamite. Surely I had to be mistaken.

"Dynamite!" Joseph announced, hugely irritating Inga since she didn't get to tell us.

"Why would Felix have dynamite in his store?" Axel asked Meme and Isabella.

"Felix has, I mean had, many customers with...how do you say it, odd requests. Maybe someone needed it for some reason or another," Isabella answered. "It doesn't surprise me. Anything we've ever needed, he was able to get. And trust me, my grandmother sometimes asked for peculiar things herself!"

Sherman cleared his throat rather loudly. "You have forgotten one possible outcome. The guard may have left after he shot and killed Felix."

"Possibly," Axel said. "Hopefully you're correct and Ruth Ann, Carlos, and Prunella will not need our little diversion to get out of here."

Inga waved the dynamite in the air, yielding Carlos to yell at her. "Stop doing that! Do you want us to be blown up!"

"Easy, it's not ignited."

"It's a volatile explosive. Who knows what could happen," he stated.

Inga set the sticks gently on the table next to Meme's bed and backed off a little. "It's all yours," she said.

Alex walked over and inspected the sticks. "Looks good to me. Let's do this." He picked up only one of the three sticks and walked out of the room. "I don't have anything to light it with."

Inga whipped out a lighter from her pocket and threw it at him. "I found this upstairs, too."

Alex and Axel walked to the door that led to the back of the house. He waited for Prunella, Carlos and me to hurry upstairs and wait for the explosion before we made a run for it. If we saw the guard head to the back of the house, we were to fly out of the house and make our way into the jungle.

It didn't take long before we heard a thunderous bang that shook poor Felix's house. "Let's go!" Carlos yelled, opening the door to the front of the house.

What we forgot to expect was Felix's body. It lay near the bottom of the front stairs. Thankfully, he was face down so I didn't have to see the ghastly expression on his face. "Don't look Ruth Ann, Prunella," Carlos ordered, dragging us both by our arms away from Felix's lifeless body.

"It isn't right leaving his body there open and exposed. It's so disrespectful," Prunella stated.

"We'll take care of him soon," I said. "We didn't have a choice and even Felix wouldn't want us to risk our life trying to move him."

When we were far away from the house, I had to stop running. "I need a second to catch my breath."

"I think we're safe now so let's take a moment to go over our plan," Carlos said, barely out of breath.

Prunella bent over gasping for air, which made me feel a little better, actually. Carlos tried to make us feel better by mentioning he was used to the humid climate down here and we weren't.

"What time is it?" I asked, noticing the sun was making a slight appearance through the trees. "I think I've been up for two solid nights!"

"That's not good," Prunella said. "You haven't had any sleep?"

"I've had bits and pieces here and there, but we need to finish this today."

"We will. Let's get back to your bungalow and grab your item quickly. Then we'll hurry back to Meme and she can finally break the curse," Prunella said.

"But we still have to get John back," I reminded her.

"We will. Once the curse is broken, we'll start having good luck for a change."

"I hope so."

"Me, too," Carlos said. "Then we can all get back to our normal lives, whatever mine will be that is."

"We'll figure that out once we're safe," I said to him.

Carlos waited until we were ready to move on. "Follow me. It's getting lighter and I don't want us to be spotted. I'll follow this sandy path until we get closer and then I'll take us inside the jungle until we come up on the back of the bungalow. I think we should be okay."

"You *think* we should be okay?" Prunella asked him, worried.

"We've been one or two steps behind Martika the entire time. I'm not jinxing us."

Carlos didn't make us run any more. He walked at a brisk pace, but one that didn't get me out of breath. About five minutes later, he stopped and headed through a bunch of low bushes and told us to follow. Here we go again, back into the jungle. I've been lucky so far not being eaten, bitten, stung or whatever else could attack me.

"I can see the bungalow. I'll have you two stay near the edge of the jungle while I go in the back slider and check it out."

"No, we stay together!" I ordered, not leaving Carlos any choice. I pushed him aside and stepped into the little grassy area behind the bungalow on the beach. I walked up to the glass slider and grabbed the handle. It wasn't locked so I slid the door open just enough to stick my head in and see if it was clear.

"Wow," I gasped. "The place has been torn to shreds since the last time I was in here."

"I'm sure it's been checked and re-checked, Ruth Ann. Martika probably thinks your necklace is still in there somewhere," Carlos said. "Let's get in there and get what you need. I don't like being here. I feel like we're sitting ducks."

"I agree," Prunella said, whipping her head around making sure nobody was following us.

"Hey, Ruth Ann," Carlos started to say. "What did you do with the necklace after we saw it back in Meme's room?"

I patted my side pocket of my shorts and smiled at him. "It's not leaving my side."

"I understand, but I have to admit it makes me a little nervous with you walking around with that thing."

"Ruth Ann would never leave it back at Felix's house. It has to stay with one of us," Prunella said.

I eyed her suspiciously. Just a few days ago she was willing to have our necklace be stolen so Axel could receive the money from Martika and an enormous amount of insurance money.

"Coast is clear for now," Carlos said, checking out the entire bungalow. "Go and get something now. I want to get out of here."

I hurried into the bathroom and went straight for the closet. My suitcase was in there, but none of the contents were inside. They were thrown all over the floor and anything I had hung up was ripped off its hanger. "Unbelievable," I muttered.

I found my purse on the floor, and the contents strewn next to it. I reached down and picked up a pen. I knew most people wouldn't think a pen was important, but this one was. It was from my father's company. I've rarely used it so the ink was still fresh. I don't know why I never got rid of it, but I didn't. I stuffed it in one of the pockets of my cargo shorts and left the closet. Prunella and Carlos were sitting in a couple of chairs waiting for me.

"Got it?" Carlos inquired, hopping out of the bamboo chair.

"Yep, let's go," I said, heading toward the back slider.

Just as I was grabbing the handle, Carlos pushed my hand out of the way and knocked me to the floor. "What the…" I bellowed.

"Shut up!" he snapped in a quiet, but extremely forceful tone.

Prunella was behind the two of us and immediately dropped to the ground. She whispered, "What's going on?"

"It's Martika, her guard, and, and…" he stopped, turned to look over at me kneeling on the ground with a stunned expression on my face.

"Oh, my…God!" I stuttered. "It's John!"

Prunella crawled next to me and peeked out the back sliding glass door. "It is John! He's okay, Ruth Ann."

"Yes, but he's got a gun shoved in his back and they're walking right toward us!" Carlos said, pulling us away from the door. We crawled over to the front of the bungalow and he forced us out the front door.

"NO, I can't leave! John's right here. I can almost touch him he's so close."

"We can't risk getting caught, Ruth Ann. That guard will shoot John first, and then ask questions."

Prunella reached out and squeezed my hand gently. "He's right. We need to break the curse first, and then we'll come back and rescue him."

"But how could you both suggest we walk away when he's right here!"

"We'll look through the front side window and see what they're doing here. Maybe they've been hiding out here, too," Carlos said, bending over and walking over to the window on the side of the door. I wanted to look with him, but he put his hand out to stop me. "Too risky. Let me look alone."

I backed away and stood with Prunella a few feet away from Carlos and out of sight from the bungalow. I leaned against a tall palm tree and took a long, calm breath in. "He's alive."

"Yes, and we'll get him out of this alive."

"I can't just walk away knowing he's in there, Prunella."

"We might not have a choice, Ruth Ann. I think it's safer to go back to Meme and the others. We know where he is now, and they don't have a clue we're here."

"But the guard was with her so that means he wasn't at Felix's house anymore."

"We had no way of knowing that. He must've taken off after he shot Felix. I bet he came back and reported what he did to Martika."

"How could you and Axel get involved with that woman!" I asked, furious with my cousin.

Prunella remained silent, but hopefully contemplating her imprudent decision.

"I wish you could've trusted me enough to tell me about Axel's business troubles. Maybe there was another way that didn't involve risking people's lives!"

"I'm so sorry, Ruth Ann."

"Unfortunately, this time sorry doesn't cut it," I said, exasperated and obviously still full of rage. I knew my anger resurfaced because I felt so hopeless right now with John being held captive by a lunatic. He looked okay, tired and beaten, but he was still able to walk on his own.

"Okay, they're in there and John's tied up to a chair. They put duct tape over his mouth to keep him quiet."

"Did he fight them?" I asked, worried about John's temper getting him into more trouble with the guard.

"Actually, no." Carlos hesitated, and then said, "He was smiling at her."

"Smiling?" Prunella asked, perplexed. "Why would he be smiling at Martika?"

"It's obvious, isn't it?" I asked. "He's playing her, plain and simple. He's trying to stay on her good side hoping she'll tell him something of importance or maybe he just doesn't want to get beaten up by that guard!"

"Probably," Carlos answered. "Let's go." He bent over low and hurried around the side of the bungalow and into the jungle. Prunella and I were right behind him, even though it took every ounce of what sanity I had left to walk away from this bungalow. "I promise; we'll be back soon."

Chapter 28

It didn't take long to get back to Felix's house. We knew the guard and Martika were back in the bungalow so Carlos marched right up to the front door and entered. Upon entry, he was grabbed, thrown to the wall and a hand slapped against his face. Prunella and I hurried in to try and diffuse the volatile confrontation. "Stop!" I cried out loudly.

"It's just Carlos," Prunella said, grabbing her husband's hand and pulling it off Carlos' face.

Alex pulled Axel away from Carlos and let him go free. "You weren't supposed to come in the front door!" Axel bellowed. "What if the guard saw you and shot the three of you!"

"That wasn't going to happen. We just left them back at the bungalow, with John."

"What!" Axel exclaimed. "John was with them just sitting around your old bungalow?"

"No, no," I said. "We went in and found the place ransacked. It was a mess, but I was able to grab an item for Meme. When we were about to leave, Carlos spotted Martika, her guard, and John walking toward the back slider. We fell to the ground and crawled over to the front door. Once outside, Carlos peeked in the window and saw the three of them. We high-tailed it back here and figured it was safe to come in the front door."

Prunella quickly asked, "Hey, I didn't see Felix outside anymore. Where is he?"

"We went out and put him in a safe place until we can contact the authorities."

"Where?" I asked, suddenly picturing him in one of the bedrooms downstairs.

"There's a small shed out back. It's somewhat cool, but it's the best we could do at the moment."

Carlos shook them away and started walking toward the basement stairs. "C'mon, let's get this over with." He opened the door to the basement and disappeared down the stairs.

I followed, and then Prunella, Alex, and Axel went down into the basement. We found Meme, gasping for breath and Isabella patting a damp washcloth on her forehead.

"Is she okay?" I asked, walking over to the bed. I knew it wasn't an appropriate question, but the words came out of my mouth before I could think.

"No," Isabella replied, turning toward me with tear stained eyes.

I didn't know what to say or ask since we needed Meme conscious right now. After I gently rubbed Isabella's shoulder to let her know I understood what was happening. I looked over at Meme who had turned a sickly gray shade. Her mouth was trying to speak, but her gasping breath wouldn't allow it.

"She sees you, Ruth Ann," Joseph said, standing behind me. "I think she's trying to say something."

I bent over and put my face close to hers. "It's okay, Meme. I'm here now, and you can rest in peace knowing you're about to break the curse that you've waited most of your life for."

"I, I don't know if...I," Meme stopped her whispers at me and tried to lick her dry, chapped lips. "I don't have the strength anymore."

"Yes, grandmother, you can!" Isabella cried, squeezing her hand so tightly I thought it had to hurt poor Meme. "I can't do it, I'm not strong enough!"

"You must break the curse, Isabella," Meme declared. "I can only die in peace if I know you will do as I taught you. Can you do that for your grandmother?" Meme begged, her wild eyes racing from Isabella to me.

"I, I don't know," Isabella said, crying so hard she was having a difficult time thinking straight.

I thought it was time to interfere. "Isabella," I said with a confident strength in my voice. "Your grandmother needs you to complete her last dying wish. Of course you will do as she asks, right?"

I gave her a little nudge with my elbow. It woke her up from her hysteria and she wiped the tears running down her face with her young, delicate fingers. "Of course I will," she said, stronger than I thought she was capable of. "My grandmother has taught me well. I can help all of you so there will be no more curse resting on the Blue Ice."

"Here, here," Sherman bellowed from the back of the room. "I'd say that was exactly what your grandmother needed to hear."

"And the rest of us agree, too!" I declared, smiling at Meme to show her we would be just fine and she was free to be at peace.

"Let's do this," Carlos said, anxiously. "Once the curse has been broken, we can march over to the bungalow and overthrow Martika and her guard."

"I hate to be the bearer of bad news, but," Alex began. "She still wants the necklace whether there's a curse on it or not."

"He's right," Axel said. "We need to stock up on some weapons and bulldoze our way in and surprise them. We'll wait it out until we see the guard's distracted, and then we can plow in and take over."

"Sounds a bit risky," I said.

"Not if we get the guard while he's doing a check of the grounds," Alex said. "If he's outside, a few of us can overtake him while the rest of you go inside and surprise Martika."

"We need to put a rush on it, though," Carlos said. "She's got to be getting really impatient, and an impatient Martika is a dangerous Martika."

"I agree," Axel said. "Let's do this curse breaking thing, can we?"

I looked over at Isabella who turned three shades of white. "It's okay, Isabella. You can do this. Your grandmother's here by your side and I bet she'll guide you through the process. Right

Meme?" I asked, and she forced a crooked smile at me. "See, she smiled."

"Yes, I guess she did," Isabella replied. "Okay, first things first."

"What?" Prunella asked impatiently. "What's first?"

"I need you all to leave."

"What? Why?" Inga yelled. "I want to see this!"

"NO!" Isabella snapped back at her. "Only Ruth Ann and Prunella can stay in here."

Axel didn't like it. His immediate reaction was to blow up. I could see his point. Axel was a part of the history of the necklace, and felt he should stay. "Isabella," he said, trying to regain his composure. "Don't you think I should be here, too?"

"No."

I stepped in before Axel took his temper to another level. "Isabella, Axel's family has been just as involved with the necklace as Prunella's and mine. Maybe he should be here?" I asked, hoping she saw it my way, but she fervently shook her head.

"Axel, please. We don't have a lot of time. Isabella knows what's needed, so why don't we let her. I promise I'll tell you everything that happened," Prunella said, sweetly.

He wanted to protest some more, but Prunella's gaze begged him to concede. Finally, he said with resistance, "Fine, but I don't like it."

With that, Axel stormed out of the room followed by Alex, Carlos, Joseph, Inga, and Sherman. Isabella stood up from Meme's side and closed the door. "We need complete silence and privacy," she said, walking to the nightstand and pulling open a drawer.

"Do we have all the items?" Meme asked in a strong, healthy voice that stunned me.

"Wait, aren't you dying?" I asked, confused.

"Yes, but not just yet."

"Was that an act before?"

"Not all," she answered, sitting upright in her bed. "I'm weak, but not gasping for my last breaths."

"But why did you have to pretend you were in your last minutes of life?"

"You'll see soon," Meme replied, grabbing the bowl that held the valuable personal items.

Meme held each one up, studied it and placed it back in the bowl. "The priceless ring from Martika, the coin of Alex's, Prunella's hairpin, Axel's pocket watch, Nancy's silver earrings, Lynne's velvet pouch, and Ruth Ann's father's pen."

"Don't forget yours and Isabella's," I said, quickly reminding her.

"Yes, I have my wedding band, and Isabella's mother's gold cross."

"Sounds like we have it all," I said, excited.

"We have all the personal items we need to break the curse, except we need the actual gem, Ruth Ann," Meme said, holding out her now steady hand.

I reached inside my side pocket and pulled out the necklace. I held it up and looked deeply into it. Would I see a difference after the curse was broken or was this just a bunch of hype and nothing would happen? I handed Meme the necklace and watched as her eyes sparkled with new life and possibly a little greed.

"Now what?" I asked, trying to bring Meme out of her trance.

"Isabella has the other ingredients I need so I will begin my spell."

I was instructed to sit down on one of the chairs on the other side of the room. Isabella stood closely to her grandmother and pulled out tiny glass jars one at a time as her grandmother requested. I had no idea what was happening except that Meme mumbled out words I'd never heard before. I could make out the sounds, but not one recognizable word. Isabella had darkened the room by turning off the one light, and lighting a couple of candles on the table next to Meme's bed. The room glowed eerily, and the shadows that flitted across the wall began to freak me out a little. If I could explain, I would say the shadows resembled people running around the walls waving their hands and disappearing as fast as they appeared. Maybe they were all the people who had come into contact with the gem and had been cursed by it. They could be the people escaping from within the gem and being released. I wanted to remember to ask Isabella when this was over, even though it sounded farfetched.

I couldn't see Meme's face, but only heard her voice. It stopped as suddenly as it started, and then Isabella blew out the candles and the room was in complete darkness. I wanted to say something, but remained quiet. It wasn't long before Isabella switched on the light and the room lit up brightly.

"There," Isabella said. "It's over."

I stood up and walked over to the bed and looked down at Meme who had my necklace clasped in her hands with the gem dangling over her fist. "Is she sleeping?" I asked Isabella. Meme's eyes were closed and she appeared so calm and peaceful.

"She's gone."

"Gone?" I questioned her. "What do you mean by *gone*?"

"She passed away, Ruth Ann. My grandmother has died." I looked at Isabella and saw the tears streaming down her smooth, dark skin.

"How, why?" Was all I could mutter. "You mean breaking the curse killed her?"

"It is why she held on, Ruth Ann. Now that the curse has been broken, she was free to leave us."

"I'm so sorry, Isabella," I said, suddenly wiping away my own tears. "She had a good, long life, and now she's with your mother."

"Yes, I have to believe that too, Ruth Ann."

"What can we do now?" I asked, wondering if it was appropriate to reach down and take the necklace out of Meme's lifeless hands.

"I will go get Joseph so he can examine her one last time, and then we'll go up and talk with the others."

"Should I stay here?" I asked.

"If you would, please. I don't want to leave her alone just yet."

"Of course," I said, watching as Isabella slowly turned her attention away from her grandmother toward the door.

"I'll be right back."

I nodded and went and sat at the edge of the bed with Meme. I knew I should be the one to take the necklace out of her hands so I carefully unclenched her still warm fist and gently removed my necklace. I held it up high in the air and inspected it thoroughly. Nothing. There was nothing different about it, which kind of disappointed me. I think I was expecting something magical to occur.

Within a few minutes, Joseph and Isabella came back and I stood up, gave Meme one last gentle tap and backed off. "She's definitely gone," Joseph said, taking the sheet and covering her up. "Would you like some time with her alone, Isabella?" he asked.

"Yes, please."

Joseph grabbed my arm and led me out of the room. He closed the door behind her and I could now hear the sobs escaping from Isabella's mouth. I felt the urge to not go too far from her, but wanted to give her enough privacy to grieve.

"She'll be all right," Joseph said quietly. "I have a feeling your family won't leave her alone, right?"

"Of course not!" I said. "Isabella is a part of our family now."

"That's makes me feel better, Ruth Ann."

"We need to go upstairs and talk with the others," I said. "I'll stand here for a couple of minutes and then go up. Will you tell the others I'll be right up?"

That was my cue to Joseph to leave me alone. He nodded his head and went upstairs. I waited until I didn't hear any more sobs from Isabella and was about to go upstairs myself when I heard her speak. I walked closer to the door and put my ear up to hear a little clearer.

"I won't let you down, grandmother. I promise to always carry on our family ways and I won't ever let the gem get too far away from me."

What did that mean? Why would she care now about my necklace? I wasn't going to question Isabella too soon, but trust me, she will answer my questions when the time was right.

I turned and headed upstairs to the others who were eagerly waiting my return. Prunella was the first one to rush over to as I stepped out of the basement stairwell. "Ruth Ann! Are you okay?"

"I'm fine."

"Tell us what happened. Joseph wouldn't say a word except for you were coming up soon."

"Meme passed away right after she broke the curse."

"She did?" Axel asked, waving me over to the group in the middle of the store room.

"Yes."

"Start from the beginning, Ruth Ann," Inga asked. "What happened after we left?"

I explained what transpired while Meme and Isabella were breaking the curse. They were stunned that Meme was able to sit up and handle it herself. "She was faking with us?" Sherman asked, regretting his words immediately after they came spewing out of his mouth. "Sorry. You caught me off guard with her spurt of energy."

"That happens," Joseph said. "Many people have one last bout of energy and sometimes words from a comatose patient come screaming out."

"Wow," Sherman muttered. "Go on, Ruth Ann."

"It was scary going through it," I said, explaining the shadows flying across the walls.

"You think it was people leaving the gem?" Alex asked, skeptically.

"I don't know for sure. I'm sure my mind was imagining things, too," I said.

"I don't know," Carlos said, jumping in the conversation. "Strange things happen, you know."

"Yes, how exciting except for Meme passing away that is," Prunella stated, but felt bad saying it out loud. "Sorry, it's hard knowing what to say in this situation."

"I feel bad for the old lady, but we have more to deal with," Sherman reminded us. "What do we do now?"

"We overtake Martika and her guard," I responded. I turned to Axel and asked, "Right?"

"Yes. While you were gone we searched the store and found one gun, a machete, and a few small hunting knives. I think we can handle that guard with what we found."

"Hopefully without any more bloodshed!" Isabella said, appearing out of thin air.

Prunella was the first one to her. She threw her arms around Isabella and hugged her tightly. Isabella let her hug her, but only for a minute. She pushed Prunella away abruptly and said, "My grandmother died for that necklace. I want this over!"

"Here, here," Sherman bellowed. "Let's go!"

"Not so fast, Sherman," Axel said. "We have to agree on our plan."

"What plan?" Carlos asked. "We go over to the bungalow and wait for that guard to do his rounds around the perimeter. When he does we surprise attack him, and the others go inside and overtake Martika. That shouldn't be too difficult because I don't think she had a gun, just the guard."

"Yes, yes, that's perfect. Let's go!" Inga said, hungrily. She clearly was one who loved the danger and excitement. Maybe housekeeping wasn't the right occupation for her.

The group decided on how we were going to break up to pull off our coup. Axel, Alex, and Inga were going to wait for the guard and Carlos, Prunella, Sherman, and I would storm in the bungalow and surprise Martika. Joseph thought staying back with Meme was the right thing to do, even though I thought he just didn't want to fight with the rest of us. I wasn't totally sure he was on our side, and I believe Carlos felt the same way because he didn't argue about Joseph staying behind either.

Chapter 29

Everyone went downstairs and said their good-byes to Meme. Isabella chose not to since she had already said good-bye. It was obviously too difficult for her still and I promised myself to make sure she was included in our family and to hopefully convince her to return to Deer Creek with us when this was all over.

It was only about ten minutes down the beach to the resort. However, Carlos chose to take the long, complicated way back to his resort. Didn't that just figure! I had enough of the jungle and the bug bites running up and down my arms and legs. Nobody complained so I went along with the group. I was too exhausted to argue anyway.

About ten minutes of tramping through a narrow, grassy path through the jungle and I started to hear a few grumbles from the crowd. Sherman was the first one to protest, which didn't surprise me since he was swatting at everything in his path. "I better not catch some weird virus!" he muttered. "There's a lot of bugs attacking me in here!"

"You'll be fine, Sherman," Inga snapped. "Just keep your mouth shut or they'll fly inside your mouth and lay eggs in there!" Inga couldn't help but smirk as she turned away from Sherman. It did the trick, Sherman slammed his mouth shut and kept it tightly closed. Not a bug or word could enter or escape.

"It's not much further," Carlos announced. "It's the middle of the day. I didn't want any of us to be spotted down by the beach."

I couldn't tell if it was night or daytime inside the deep, dense jungle. I followed Carlos, and everyone else fell behind as he led the way in the dark. Every now and again a sliver of sun peeked through the trees, but not enough to light our way. "Okay, we're here."

"Here, where?" Axel asked from the back of the group.

"We're just on the outskirts of the jungle. Ruth Ann's bungalow is located there," he pointed ahead.

"So, where does this guard walk when he's doing his surveillance?" Axel asked, pushing his way to the front where Carlos and I stood.

"Well, I don't know exactly," he responded. "Ruth Ann and I have witnessed him check his surroundings every thirty to sixty minutes. I feel fairly confident he'll do that here, too."

"Let's split up here, then," Axel suggested. "I'll stay here with Alex and Inga, and you go to wherever you're planning on entering the bungalow."

"What if we get split up?" Prunella asked, worried. "We can't let that happen anymore."

"It won't," he assured her. "But we're too big of a group to stay together so splitting up now would be the safest idea."

"Don't worry, Prunella," Carlos interrupted. "It's not that far to the bungalow and I'll point out exactly where we'll be in relation to Axel, Alex, and Inga. We won't be that far apart."

"Okay, sounds like we don't have a choice."

"No, if we want to get John out of there," I said.

"And catch Martika," Carlos added.

"Don't forget about the guard!" Inga said. "We've got to at least subdue him."

"What do you mean, *at least* subdue him?" Sherman asked.

"Well, if he goes after us, we'll do what we have to be safe."

"You mean you might have to kill him!"

"It could happen, Sherman," I said. "This guy's already proven he doesn't mind murdering innocent people."

"Felix," Sherman mumbled.

"Yes, he killed him for no reason," I said. "He's sick, but we'll try and keep him alive so the police can deal with him."

"I don't care what you do to him!" Carlos declared. "Kill him just to be sure he doesn't come back after us!"

"Let's get going," I said, anxiously. "I'd like to get in position and be ready when the guard comes out of the bungalow. I don't want him to return before you guys overtake him and were inside trying to get John out of there."

"Okay, Ruth Ann, Prunella, Sherman, follow me," Carlos said. "Axel, Alex, and Inga, watch where we go. You'll get a pretty good view from the edge of the jungle."

Carlos led the way right up to the edge. He held his hand up to make sure we didn't speak. He motioned for Axel, Alex, and Inga to stay put and watch where we headed. Carlos took us around the edge, but still hidden from the side of the bungalow.

"We're going to go in the front door?" I whispered, getting a nasty glare from Carlos. He nodded, and went around the bungalow disappearing from the others sight.

He took us from the edge of the jungle to the front of the bungalow. There came a point we had to cross a small sandy area that would take us to the front door, but we weren't going to do that until we knew for sure the guard had left the bungalow. Carlos barely whispered, "We need to see if he goes out the front or the back slider."

"But how will we see if he goes out the back?" I questioned.

"Hopefully we'll hear him."

We positioned ourselves in a few waist high bushes to wait for the exact moment when we could explode into the front door and hopefully throw Martika off for just a split second. It should be enough time for Carlos to aim the gun at her and force her to do as we ask. That's if everything went according to plan.

Sherman started fidgeting while kneeling on the ground. "My knees are killing me!" he complained. "I won't be able to get myself up fast enough to follow you into that bloody bungalow!"

I knew exactly what ran through Carlos' mind. *We really don't want you following us inside that bungalow because you'll probably mess the whole thing up!* I smiled at him and nodded, acknowledging I knew what he must be thinking. Carlos held back a laugh and shook his head at Sherman. "It'll be fine, old man."

"Did you just call me an 'old man'!" Sherman tried to stand, but Prunella pushed him down with her hands on his shoulders. "Sherman, this isn't the time for arguing. Do as Carlos said."

Sherman huffed and sat on his butt on the sandy ground, surrounded by thick bushes. We waited and waited. I felt on edge, but I knew I didn't have any choice in the matter. There was no other solution but to wait it out. I spotted Sherman looking at his watch several times and even noticed Prunella asking him once or twice. Suddenly, everything changed.

Carlos quickly held his finger to his mouth. I twirled my body to face the bungalow. I couldn't see any movement, but I clearly heard what I thought was voices. We listened attentively.

"I'll be back in a few minutes. You stand guard and don't leave him alone for a second!"

"Uh-oh, that was Martika's voice," Carlos whispered. "We never considered her leaving instead of the guard."

Terrified, Prunella asked, "What do we do now?" "We stick to the plan," I stated. "Once Martika's out of sight, we force our way in and pray that we throw this guard off while he's not holding his gun. Carlos will aim his gun at him and hopefully force him to give up, don't you think?"

Carlos looked panicked. "This wasn't supposed to happen!" he said, nervously. "Now what, think, Carlos, think!"

I went over and tapped him gently on his back. "It's okay. We can do this, but we have to go now. Are you ready?"

"No, yes, I don't know," he said, anxiously trying to make up his mind. "I guess we don't have a choice. The others will have to take down Martika, but that shouldn't be a problem for the three of them."

"They have it easier than us!" Prunella declared. "But, we've got to go!"

Carlos pushed his way through the bushes and Prunella, Sherman, and I followed him onto the sand. "Once I open the door, I will rush the guard, holding my gun at him. You three run over to John and release whatever they've got holding him down. Got it?"

"Yes," I replied for the three of us.

Carlos bent over to pass close to the side window near the front door. He waved us over, but before he grabbed the front door handle, he snuck a peek through the little window. He shook his head, "I can't believe we're doing this," he murmured and then reached out, took a tight grasp on the handle with one hand, gun in the other, and threw open the door with so much force it slammed against the inside wall.

Carlos rushed inside screaming, "Put your hands up!"

Prunella and I ran in behind him and spotted John in a wooden chair in the middle of the room. He looked horrified, and confused. His mouth had a dirty rag stuffed in it, and his hands and feet were tied with ropes. I watched as the guard tried to go for his gun on the kitchen counter, but Carlos beat him to the punch. He aimed his gun at the center of his body and told him to freeze. "Sherman," Carlos yelled at the frigid butler in the doorway. "Take his gun from the counter and hold it on him."

Sherman didn't move. I turned away from John and ran over to help Carlos. I grabbed the gun and held it at the guard. The guard started choking on a bite of a sandwich he was eating, but raised his arms high in the air. I yelled over to Prunella to start untying John, but she was already in progress.

"Ruth Ann!" a familiar voice cried out my name. "What are you doing here!"

"Saving you, John," I said, still aiming the gun at the guard. "You'll be free in a minute, and then you can take this gun from me and handle the guard with Carlos."

It didn't take long for Prunella to free John since she found a large knife sitting on one of the end tables. She carefully cut the ropes, and John was up and hurrying to my side. There was no time for sentimentalities yet, but they would definitely come later!

"Give me the gun, Ruth Ann," John ordered, but with a kind tone. "I can take it from here."

Carlos never stopped holding the gun at the guard. John wanted to ask so many questions, but I explained it was too long and too complicated. "Where's Martika? She'll be coming back soon," he said.

"Axel, Alex, and Inga are handling her right about now," Prunella said, laughing. "I can't believe they would have a difficult time overthrowing her."

"They better not," John said.

John demanded Sherman hand him the rope from the ground. Sherman hopped to it, and within a few minutes, the guard was gagged and tied. He begged and pleaded with us to let him go, and promised he would tell us everything we needed to know about Martika's plans. "Too late now," I said, just before John shoved the gag into his mouth. "I think we just blew her plans out of the water!"

"She's got more up her sleeves," the guard divulged. "Don't think it's over just because you say so. I don't see her here, captured by your other friends."

"Shut up!" John demanded and shoved the gag into his mouth.

John took over the show. He told Carlos to stand guard with his gun aimed at the guard until he came back. "Where are you going?" I asked, not even thinking he'd leave me again.

"I've got to go and see what's going on with the others. Carlos has it handled here. That guard was her muscle, but I don't trust her. She's evil, and it wouldn't surprise me if she tried to pull a fast one on Axel, and the others."

"What on earth could she do, John? It's three against one, and she doesn't have a weapon!" I cried out.

"I just don't trust her. I'll go and help them, and bring them back here. That way both of them will be under one roof until we get the local police here."

"Fine," I said, resolved that I wasn't going to win this one. He was determined to take over now that he was free.

John took off through the front door and disappeared outside. Carlos stood frozen with the gun aimed at the tied up guard on the ground. Sherman announced he was going to use the facilities. "I feel atrocious. I'm all grimy and sticky. I'll be right back."

"I have to agree with him," I said to Carlos. "I can't wait to take a long hot shower and put on some clean clothes."

"And sleep, Ruth Ann. Don't forget about our lack of sleep the last couple days."

"I'm so overtired, I'm not tired anymore!"

Carlos laughed, and I noticed he was relaxing just a little, but I knew until he saw Martika in handcuffs, he wouldn't totally settle down. "I don't trust that woman. She's pulled off quite a lot lately."

"I'll say! She's been all over the place trying to get my necklace. From Sweden to Deer Creek and back down here. She's manipulated so many people, and almost got away with it."

"But she didn't."

"No, Carlos, she didn't." At least I hoped she didn't get away. I don't see how Axel, Alex, Inga, and now John would let that happen.

Once Sherman returned, I followed suit. I went into the bedroom and directly into my torn apart closet to grab some fresh clothes. Once I found another pair of shorts that would securely hold my necklace and a tank top, I went into the bathroom and contemplated taking a quick shower to wake me up. I figured I only had a few minutes, and I told myself to do it quickly, so I did. I hopped in the shower and blasted the hot water all over my sticky body. Once I lathered my body and my hair, I rinsed rapidly and threw on my clothes. "So much better," I mumbled, combing my hair and putting it up into a tiny ponytail. I marched back into the living area and found it empty!

Chapter 30

I yelled out loud for Carlos and Sherman, but nobody answered. "Where'd everybody go?" I asked, even though I knew I wouldn't get a response. I panicked, and ran to the back sliding glass door and opened the heavy glass door. I knew not to run out into the open until I carefully looked around. I couldn't hear or see any sign of movement or voices so I stepped out into the hot, sunny late afternoon air. Why would they abandon me? I knew something bad had to have happened for Carlos to leave me alone in the bungalow.

I decided to walk around the entire bungalow before deciding what to do. I could always make my way back to Felix's house where Isabella and Joseph were, but that's not what I wanted to do. I started to move to the side of the bungalow when I looked down at the sand. I noticed an object lying just outside of the back slider. I bent down and picked up the shiny gold object and held it close to my face. "It's Sherman's gold pinky ring. Why's it lying in the sand?"

My mind rushed with horrible thoughts of what could've happened inside the bungalow. How could that guard untie himself and attack Carlos and Sherman? Or maybe John came back and rushed them out to get more help and didn't have time to inform

me. That didn't seem logical, though. John would never leave me
alone. I shoved the ring in my pocket and trampled through the hot
fluffy sand toward the side of the bungalow. Nothing. I walked
around to the front and noticed the door was ajar. Did they leave in
such a rush they didn't shut the door or did Carlos or Sherman
leave the door slightly open telling me that's how they left the
bungalow? I really didn't know, and my mind went through that
horrible tunnel vision reeling me deeper into despair.

"Think, Ruth Ann, think," I muttered. I snapped out of the
horrific visions I was imagining, and started thinking rationally.
"Keep looking around. If I don't find anything to tell me where
they went then I'll go back and find Isabella and Joseph."

I felt a surge of strength come over my entire body and also a
great deal of anger. How dare they leave me alone! I opened the
bungalow door and before I left I made a thorough check of the
place. It really was empty. I didn't know the back way to Felix's,
but I knew how to get there from the beach and the grass shack
Meme used to inhabit. I hurried down the path, not running into
anyone, and made my way to the beach. The cloudless sky was
breathtaking, but the heat was nearly unbearable. I just took a
shower! Oh, well, onward.

I nearly made it to the grass shack Meme used to sit in, when
I noticed a flash coming from within the shack. Somebody was in
there! I didn't want to rush in, just in case it was Martika, but I had
to see who was in there. I walked toward the shack from the side
since there were no windows, just an opening for the door. Once I
arrived, I leaned as close as I could to the side of the shack to see if
I could hear any voices, but it was silent. I slowly walked around
to the front of the tiny shack and forced myself to take a look
through the string of beads used as a door.

The minute my head was close enough to take a peek, a hand
reached around from inside and pulled me forcefully in. "What
the…" I bellowed loudly.

"Come in, come in, Ruth Ann," a female voice called out, letting go of my arm.

I looked up at the woman who I never expected to see free
again. "Martika, it's you."

"Of course it's me, Ruth Ann. I'm not stupid enough to get
caught by your group of incompetents!"

"Where are they?" I demanded.

Martika howled a disgusting sound which I took for her laughing. "You think I'm going to tell you!"

"I'm alone, Martika. What could I possibly do to you?"

"You're not as innocent as you appear, Ruth Ann. You seem to worm your way out of everything I've thrown at you. Now it's just you and me."

"How did you fool Axel, Alex, and Inga?" I asked, more curious than worried at the moment. How on earth could those three let her go!

"Simple. I was ready for an attack at any moment. When I saw them running at me waving a gun, I pulled mine out first and shot before they could react. They were so worried about Axel, that they didn't see my guard come up and take them prisoner."

"Your guard was tied up back in the bungalow! How did he get to you so quickly?"

"My guard was tied up, but what you *all* missed is that there were *two* guards. Identical twins!" Martika laughed, loudly.

"You've got to be kidding!"

"Nope. I knew it would come in handy at one point. Now your friends are relatively safe and tucked away neatly until you cooperate with me."

"But you said Axel was shot! How is he? He isn't dead, is he?"

"No, no. I know how to aim. I just grazed his leg. He's only got a superficial wound that my guard already cleaned up. I just wanted them distracted for a second so I could capture them."

I silently thanked the heavens that Axel was all right. Then I went on, fuming, "What do you want!"

"Seriously? You know *exactly* what I want, Ruth Ann. Why would you ask such a dumb question?"

"I'm not giving it to you until you take me to the others."

"I don't think so. Once you give me the necklace, I will call and have your friends and family released."

"I don't trust you. Why would I believe you?"

"I don't see you having much of a choice, Ruth Ann."

"Well, I think I do. Take me to them." Martika didn't respond so I added, "Why would I give you the necklace without physical proof you haven't killed any of them? Plus, if I hand over the necklace you could kill all of us so you don't get pursued the police."

"The police?" she asked, humored. "The local police don't care about this. They're a bunch of fools."

"But the United States authorities will care. Wiping out several American citizens would cause quite the attention."

I could almost see the wheels turning in her head. That was the last thing Martika wanted. "Fine. I'll take you to them, and then you hand the necklace over. If you try anything, I'll not only kill you, but the others, too." She added quickly before I could repeat myself again, "Don't bother trying to scare me with the whole American citizen thing, I'll cover my tracks one way or another."

Martika turned and whipped apart the string of beads and headed out into the sunshine. She waited for me to follow as she headed directly into the jungle. "Where are we going?" I asked, knowing she wasn't going to tell me.

"Shut up! I don't want to hear another word from you, got it?"

I didn't answer her, and she whipped her head around and repeated, "Did you get that?"

"You told me not to say a word, so I'm not!" I spat out, smiling on the inside since it infuriated her.

"Stay close. I don't plan on losing you again."

I followed Martika into the jungle, yet again. When I get out of this mess, I'm going to make a solemn promise never to walk into a jungle again! She went deeper and deeper into the dark, humid rainforest. I had never been this direction before, not that I always knew where I was going, but it was never this far inside the jungle. Martika had a large machete, probably from Alex or Axel, and she kept swatting at one branch and another. I was concentrating on not falling, and making sure no insects landed on my body.

About fifteen minutes later, Martika halted. "We're here."

I looked around at my surroundings and said, "Here, where? I don't see anything but trees, vines, and bushes!"

"It's on the other side of that rock," she said, pointing to a massive piece of stone I didn't notice. The large rock was as big as a house, and she marched right over to it and waited for me. "You promised you wouldn't try any funny stuff. Stay next to me the entire time. I don't want you to see your friends and run over to them. The guard will shoot you, got it?"

"Shoot me, but why? If I'm with you, then he'll know you've caught me."

"Just listen, and stop asking such annoying questions."

Martika walked around the side of the rock and a beautiful, newly built villa appeared out of thin air. It was rather large and built out of local woods and stone. There wasn't a sidewalk, just a grass path that led to a large, double front door.

"Does someone live in there?" I asked.

Martika walked right up to a few wide stone steps that landed on a long front porch. She took in a deep breath and turned around to face me. "I had this built recently. It's my hide-away from the world. I love this villa so don't make me do anything to it you'll regret."

"What would I do to make you damage your precious little villa?" I asked, sarcastically.

"Little!" she huffed. "This place is quite large, Ruth Ann. It has four bedrooms, a large gourmet kitchen, and a massive great room."

"So," I stated, uninterested. I didn't want her to think I was impressed. "These kind of houses are a dime a dozen back in the states."

Martika's nasty glare sent chills up my spine. "It's got a gigantic master bedroom closet and every detail inside took taste and money. I spared no expense with any of it!"

"Great, Martika, just great. Now can we go in and see my friends or do you want to give me a tour first?" I couldn't resist goading her. I hoped I pushed her to a point that it alerted everyone inside to our presence.

"Ruth Ann!" she shouted angrily. "Shut your mouth. I know what you're trying to do!"

"And what is that, Martika?" emphasizing her name in a childish tone. "I'm not trying to do anything except get my friends and family out of your villa and go home!"

"You'll be lucky if anyone goes home alive!" she hollered, loudly.

"You promised nobody would be hurt, Martika! If you even try to go back on your word, I won't hand over my necklace!"

"All I've got to do is kill you and then search your lifeless body for the gem."

"Who said it was on *my* body?" I asked, trying to trick her, even though it actually was just sitting in my shorts pocket.

Martika thought long and hard about what I said. She started to speak, but snapped her lips shut tightly. Finally, after several attempts at trying to respond to my statement she said, "You're bluffing."

"Try me," I said, quickly calling her bluff even though I didn't want her to actually shoot me and then search my body.

"Just stop talking, could you? I know you can't help yourself, but it's giving me a migraine!" Martika pulled out her cell phone and a second later was ordering her guard to open the front door.

"Stay next to me," Martika ordered. "No walking anywhere near your friends."

"Fine."

We waited until a large, blonde haired man opened the locked front door. "About time," she snapped, pushing him aside and entering the massive great room.

"Ah," she said, smiling. "I do love this place."

"Yes, yes. Take me to my people," I demanded.

"In due time, Ruth Ann. First, this is *one* of my guards. So don't think if you get through him you're home free to release your friends."

I thought about her statement, and knew she had another one exactly like him. I nodded in acknowledgement and waited for her to move further inside the room. She took a few steps forward and said, "This was built to resemble a log cabin."

I looked around the room and she was correct. It wasn't at all tropical. There was no rattan furniture and palm tree plants or accessories. This place was more suitable for Deer Creek with the walls built of large logs, and a large stone fireplace along the one side wall. The couches and chairs were covered in a heavy, thick forest green fabric. I didn't spot any of my friends or family inside this room. "Where are they?" I asked, curiously.

"They're safely tucked away, Ruth Ann."

"You didn't drug them or anything, did you?"

"Nope."

"Can we go see them now? I don't understand what you're waiting for!"

"I will take you to them after I have a private chat with my guard."

I watched as Martika pulled the guard away from the front door where I was standing. She leaned close to him and listened as the large man whispered in her ear. Unfortunately, I didn't hear a word.

Within a few minutes, Martika marched back over to me and said, "Let's go."

I didn't ask where because I was fairly certain she wouldn't tell me anyway so I stuck close behind her as she walked through the great room and down a hall to the right. There were several closed doors in this hall which I gathered were bedrooms. "You put them into your bedrooms?" I asked, wondering if they were separated.

"Do you have a problem with that?" she barked. "I didn't want them all together."

"Because they would have a higher probability of overtaking you and your guards, right?"

"Possibly, not likely, but possibly."

"You know I won't tell you where the necklace is and I will not hand it over until *all* of us are released and free to leave this place."

Martika shot me an angry look and nodded. She reached out to open the first door on the left. "Stay out in the hall," she said, opening the door with one of the keys she took from the guard. She entered and quickly came back in the hall saying nothing. I tried to look inside the room, but she slammed the door before I could see anything. Martika walked to the door across the hall this time. She did the same thing and slammed the door. After a total of four rooms, she turned around and told me to follow her.

We walked back through the great room to the opposite side and walked down a much wider hallway. We passed a large room that was obviously a dining room, and then entered into the kitchen. She was correct in saying it was top of the line. There were two sets of double ovens, two refrigerators, a large six burner stove and a massive marble island in the middle of the room. "You're loving it, aren't you?" Martika asked, seeing I was impressed from the expression of awe written on my face.

"It's nice."

"Nice," she muttered. "Those appliances cost more than my husband paid for our wedding!"

"Wedding!" I laughed. "What wedding? You conned him into marrying you!"

"Be quiet!"

I watched as she opened the refrigerator and grabbed one bottle of water, and a small bottle of Prosecco. She grabbed a wine glass from a cabinet above a small wet bar on the far end of the long kitchen. I patiently waited as she opened her Prosecco and poured it into the glass. Martika slowly sauntered back to me as I leaned against the island and wondered if I was going to get the water bottle.

"Here you go, Ruth Ann," Martika said, handing me the cold bottle of water. "I don't want you passing out on me."

I eagerly drank the water and felt instantaneously refreshed. It was true that as long as the human body gets hydration it really doesn't need constant feeding.

"Now, this is how it's going to go down," she said, finishing her full glass of bubbly. "I'm going to bring one room of people into this kitchen and have them sit at the table. It would be nice if you just handed the necklace over at that time, but knowing you I'm sure that won't happen." She waited for my response, but I just leaned and stared at her.

"Okay, so once you see they're all right, I'll go and get the second room and so on. After all of them are in here, you will hand me my gem, understand me?"

I still didn't respond. "Ruth Ann! Are you listening to me?"

I was, but I couldn't help but stare at a plate of muffins on the counter near a large coffee machine. I knew she was speaking, but my mind wandered and I started counting the delicious looking pastries. Four blueberry, four apple cinnamon, four pumpkin, and four..."

"Ruth Ann!" she hollered. "Are you listening to me?"

I shook myself out of the trance and looked back to Martika who was staring at me waving an empty wine glass in the air. "Ruth Ann!"

"Yes, yes, I heard you. I'll do as you say."

"Wait here." Martika stormed out of the kitchen and disappeared into the hallway. She left me alone? I questioned her motives, but where would I go anyway? I could try and open one of the other doors, but I would surely run into Martika as she was bringing the first group into the kitchen.

So, I decided to wait here and hoped she brought John in. He would be the most determined to overtake the guard and Martika. Guards, I corrected myself. There were twin guards.

As I was waiting, my gaze went back to the muffins. I didn't think it would hurt to grab one, so I hurried over to the counter and picked one of the pumpkin muffins. I took a large bite and tasted the cinnamon first, and then the burst of pumpkin and vanilla hit my taste buds next. As I chewed the best muffin I ever ate, I wondered why Martika would have a plate of pumpkin muffins. It didn't seem like something that would be available down in the Caribbean, but here it was.

I finished the muffin in about four huge bites, and was about to grab one of the apple cinnamon ones when I heard voices coming near. "They're coming!" I said, excited about who would enter the kitchen first.

"Ruth Ann!" Inga cried as she stepped inside the kitchen, followed by Axel and Sherman. "You really are here!"

"Inga," I called out, excited to see the three of them. They looked good, even Axel, who walked with a slight limp after being grazed by one of Martika's bullets.

"Axel, are you okay?" I asked, looking at his leg to see if there was an obvious injury.

"Good as new," he said, snarling at Martika. "Don't think this will slow me down at all," he replied, giving his right leg a little pat.

"That's good to hear," Martika commented. "Not that you'll be running any time soon."

"Knock it off!" I said to her. "Go get the others," I demanded.

Martika ordered the three of them to sit at the large round table in a small nook off the main kitchen. "Don't move an inch," she said, turning and walking out of the kitchen.

"We should get out of here!" Inga exclaimed, ready to run.

"She knows we won't go anywhere without the others," Axel said. "Just sit and wait. We'll come up with something once we're all together again."

"I agree, Axel," I said, walking over to the platter of muffins and offering them to Axel, Inga, and Sherman. They each grabbed one and stuffed them into their mouths.

"I was starving," Sherman said, ignoring his proper upbringing and wiping his mouth with his forearm. "Can I have another?" he asked, eagerly eying the full plate.

"Of course," I said. "Just as long as you leave some for the others."

It didn't take long for Martika to return with Alex and Carlos. "Hey, where's Prunella?" Axel asked, worried about the whereabouts of his wife and my cousin.

"She's just fine, Axel," Martika snapped, shoving Carlos into the middle of the kitchen.

"Was that necessary?" Carlos barked. "Remember, I am still your husband!"

"That's a joke!" she howled with laughter. "It never was much of a marriage, was it Carlos dear?"

"That's because you blackmailed me into marrying you!"

"You forgot to mention that you're gay, too. It's not like we ever consummated our marriage."

"Even if I was the last straight man on earth I would NEVER have slept with you! You were a sweet child, but you grew up to be a disgusting, murderous, lying, miserable, bitter, revengeful human being." Carlos looked over at our group by the kitchen table and said, "Did I leave anything out?"

Inga chimed in to stick the knife a little deeper into Martika's back and added, "kidnapper, thief, and ugly, too!"

"How dare you!" Martika shrieked. "I'm the one with the gun and I can substantiate a few of those words!" She held the gun up and aimed it over at the kitchen table. She released the safety and I quickly decided to diffuse her temper.

"Stop it, Martika! Everyone's just sick and tired of what you've been doing. Can we get this over with? Go get Prunella."

"Not so fast, Ruth Ann," Martika replied, lowering her gun to her side. "I want to see the necklace before I go get your cousin. If you don't have it on you, then I bet Prunella does."

"No she doesn't!" I exclaimed. I was about to put my hand in my pocket when Axel shouted at me, "Don't show her anything, Ruth Ann. She needs to get Prunella and bring those two goons she has as guards in here. Once she's released us, then you can hand over the necklace."

Martika glared at Axel and shouted back, "You don't give the orders around here, got it?"

"Actually, you don't know *who* actually has possession of the necklace right now. Are you willing to risk not getting it all?" Axel knew he had her under his thumb so he continued. "I suggest we move this party into the great room so we have more room. Then you go get my wife and bring her to me. Once you've done that, then one of us will retrieve the necklace." He hesitated, took a breath and added, "After you've put down all your weapons, that is. And that includes the guards, too."

Martika was clearly incompetent at being the one in charge. She raised her arms in exasperation and waved the gun at the table. "Get up, all of you."

She was actually listening to Axel's demands. Not the smartest woman in the world either. We could've added that to the list, too! "Everyone get up and head to the living room. Don't try to come after me or I'll shoot the first person I see."

Axel caught my eye, and I could tell from his look that he had a plan. I wished I knew what it was, but hopefully when we're closer to each other he'll inform me. John was awfully quiet during the exchange of insults and demands, but I didn't doubt he was doing this on purpose until he was ready to pounce.

We piled out of the kitchen and walked through the hall past the dining room into the massive great room. Martika motioned for us to sit on the arrangement of couches that were smack dab in the middle of the room. I finally was able to get near John. It had been days since I've felt him next to me, but it seemed like years. He grabbed my hand and sat down on a couch with me. On my other side was Alex. The three of us sat on the smaller couch while Axel, Inga, Sherman, and Carlos were on the long couch next to ours. Martika stood in front of us and pulled out her cell phone. She didn't speak, but a few seconds after she put her phone in her pocket, the twin guards appeared.

"They do look alike," I said, staring at the identical twins. "They sure don't look very pleasant."

"No, they don't," John replied with a whisper. "I've got a plan, Ruth Ann. Axel and I came up with it back in the kitchen."

I didn't want Martika catching us conspiring so I didn't reply right away. When she left us alone with the guards, I asked John, "Are you going to tell me what it is?"

"No, too risky. Just go along with whatever Axel and I do, got it?"

"But what about the others?" I asked, worried that Inga would try something on her own.

"They won't. We passed the information onto them at the kitchen table."

"Where was I when you planned this?" I asked, a little irritated at being left out.

"You were over at the island, remember?"

He was right. I never did sit down at the kitchen table. Martika kept me separated from them probably for that very reason. It must be why she held onto Prunella, too. She was the other owner of the necklace.

I tried to imagine what John and Axel could do with two armed guards standing over us. Neither one of them had a weapon that I knew of, but they must have something in mind or they wouldn't be risking all our lives.

Martika took too long bringing Prunella back. I started noticing Axel becoming anxious. John could read my mind and whispered to be patient. The right time will come, and they'll make their move, but was he sure Axel could wait for the right time? We were about to find out.

Chapter 31

When Martika failed to show up, John and Axel started exchanging glances with each other. Carlos, Inga and Alex tried to hone in on the exchanges, and finally, John obliged. The guards were oblivious to us. I started thinking we could hold an all-out conference without the guards reacting.

Suddenly, John nodded over to Axel and the others. Within seconds, Axel fell to the floor holding his chest. John hopped off the couch rushing to Axel on the floor. The guards didn't know what to do. They yelled at John to return to this seat, but John screamed back, "This man's having a heart attack! He needs help, NOW!"

The guards looked dumbfounded. They mumbled back and forth to each other, but neither one forced John to get back to his seat. John motioned to Carlos to make his move. Carlos stood up, walked over to one of the guards and begged them for their cell phone. Neither one of them would hand it over or they didn't understand English. "Please, he's dying!" I hollered, standing and going to Carlos' assistance.

I spotted John's disapproving look, but felt Carlos needed help. Inga suddenly slipped around the back of the couch and I could see her barely crawling around to the side where the guards were standing facing Carlos and me.

It all happened so fast. Inga jumped one of the guards, and Carlos belted the other in the face. There was no reaction from the guard, except that it infuriated him. Carlos was obviously in severe pain from trying to knock out the guard with his fist. I felt it was time to help. I lifted my foot just before the guard was about to grab Carlos' throat with his hands. I kicked as hard as I could in an area the guard would surely feel. "I did it!" I yelled as the guard keeled over in distress. Carlos grabbed his gun and turned to find John next to him with his hand out ready to take it.

"Good job!" John said, slapping Carlos on the back and smiling over at Inga who had single handedly disarmed her guard.

"He had a little help," I reminded both of them. "I was the one who…" Carlos cut me off and snapped, "We know, we know. You kicked him in the balls!"

I laughed and waited until both guards were gagged and tied up so they could not escape. "We have a huge problem," Alex reminded us after stepping over one of the guards.

Axel looked grim. "I'm brutally aware of it. Prunella and Martika never returned. She's keeping her for assurance."

"Let's check out the villa and find them. They couldn't have gone far," I said.

"We stick together this time," John demanded. "Nobody goes anywhere alone."

Everyone agreed without argument. We hurried down the hall to the bedrooms and found them empty. "We figured that," Axel said. "I'm sure she took Prunella out of the villa."

"But now where?" I asked, exasperated. "Where could she possibly take her?"

Carlos immediately answered my question. "I think I know where she's gone. Follow me." With that, he took off out the front door.

"Stay together," John yelled up to Carlos. "Not everyone can run as fast as you!"

Carlos slowed his pace and waited for the group to come together. I had no idea what he was planning, but he seemed confident about where Martika went. "She's desperate now. I think she's going to try and flee the country with Prunella."

"But where?" I asked, trying to catch my breath.

"Think about it, Ruth Ann," John said. "Martika is leaving in a hurry without any money or luggage. She needs Prunella to supply her with all of that. I think she's going to try and get back to Deer Creek before any of us and empty out Prunella and Axel's money."

"What!" Axel yelled. "I didn't even think of that!"

"I think so, too," Carlos replied. "However, she'll make one more stop before leaving."

"Don't leave us in the dark, Carlos," Axel said.

"We're almost there," Carlos said.

I felt like I've been here before. We were on the path back to the resort that Carlos and Martika owned. Maybe she did need to grab something before leaving.

"Her passport," Carlos said. "She can't leave the country without it."

"Good job, Carlos!" I cried out. "If she tries to sneak on, it could be worse for her. But if she takes Prunella onto a plane as her companion it won't look suspicious at all."

"But why would Prunella go through with it?" Inga asked, confused.

"Prunella thinks our lives are in danger. She'll go along with Martika for that reason alone," Axel said.

"Yes, and I bet she left with Prunella way before we overtook those guards," John added. "Martika thinks we're still being held prisoner and doesn't know we're right behind her."

"Exactly," Carlos said. "We sneak up on her and surprise her."

"We have to be careful she doesn't get sight of us. She could shoot Prunella!" Sherman said.

"We will," Axel replied, looking a tad worried himself.

Carlos came up to the outskirts of the resort near my bungalow. John took my hand and held it tightly as we passed the bungalow. We went off the path and snuck around the back of the other bungalows and the restaurant. Carlos whispered that they had a two room bungalow just off the lobby. I don't recall seeing it before, but to be honest, John and I didn't exactly have a lot of time at the resort before he was kidnapped.

"John, Axel, and I should go in. The rest of you stay out here while we take care of her," Carlos said.

"But," I was immediately interrupted by John. "No, stay back with Inga and Alex for protection."

"Hey," Sherman protested.

"Sherman, you need more protecting than anyone!" John barked. "Just stay back," he said, becoming frustrated with the arguing. "Inga, take this gun and keep a sharp lookout."

Inga willingly grabbed the gun and we watched from the back of the small bungalow as Carlos led them around to the front. Before they could've made it to the front door, we heard two loud bangs coming from within. Inga, Sherman, and I didn't wait for permission, but ran as fast as we could to the front of the bungalow.

The front door was wide open, and without any hesitation, we rushed inside. "Oh, no!" I cried. Martika was standing with her arm tightly around Prunella's throat holding the gun at her head. My eyes left those two and spotted a man's body on the ground. I knew it wasn't John from the clothing, but couldn't place who it was.

"Joseph," Carlos screamed. "You shot him!" My mind reeled wondering how and why Joseph suddenly appeared.

Martika's eyes were wild with rage. "What are you all doing here! You should've been back at the villa. I left instructions with the guards to shoot each one of you until that damn necklace was handed over to me or one of the guards!"

"I knew you wouldn't have let us go!" I screamed, furious. "You were going to kill us all along!"

"Of course, you fool."

John took that moment to rush at her, but she spotted him and was about to shoot when another person ran from behind and knocked Martika and Prunella to the ground. "Isabella!" Carlos yelled, rushing to her aide.

Martika dropped her gun, but not far from her body. She rolled over trying to reach it while Prunella tried to get away from her. Isabella almost had the gun when Martika took hold of it and aimed it at Prunella. "Don't shoot!" Axel screamed, grabbed John's gun from his hand and shot Martika right in the middle of her chest. She dropped the gun from her hands and stared at the people around her. "How could you!" she said, blood gushing from her chest. Seconds later, she was dropped to the ground, dead.

"Joseph," Isabella said, rushing over to his body that lay on the ground not far from Martika's lifeless one.

"He's dead," Carlos said, standing up from his partner's side. "From what I could tell, he died immediately."

"Why did she have to kill Joseph?" I asked, confused, but relieved the woman was finally stopped.

"Joseph was a hero," Isabella said, with tears streaming down her anguished cheeks.

I went over to the couch and grabbed a green cotton blanket and covered him. I looked around for something to put over Martika, but I didn't see anything. Carlos suggested I go in the bedroom and pull off the comforter from the bed and throw it over her.

Once both bodies had been covered, John asked Carlos for her cell phone since it was the only one left that had any battery life or service. He called in the local police and suggested we step outside until our statements could be made. I had no problem with John's request, and it appeared nobody else did either.

Once out of the bungalow, I finally asked what time it was. "It's Tuesday evening, Ruth Ann," Prunella told me. "We've got to get home for Thanksgiving Dinner!"

"I forgot all about that. Hey," I blurted out after a thought entered my head. "Do my daughters know you came down here?"

"Yes," Prunella answered. "Well kind of. I told them we were flying down here because our necklace was stolen, and you were beside yourself."

Anger surged inside my body. I knew it was petty considering there were two dead bodies just feet away, but they lied, plain and simple. "I know you're disappointed in me, Ruth Ann," Prunella admitted, lowering her head. "But I didn't want to worry your daughters. I hope you understand why I lied and why Axel and I made the huge mistake of convincing you to wear the dumb thing down here anyway."

"I'm still pretty upset with you and Axel, but I'll let it go for now. When we get home we need to have a long, difficult talk about what led to this. Agreed?"

"Yes, Ruth Ann," Axel answered for Prunella. I knew she felt horrible, but that didn't excuse their behavior. I wanted to make sure I understood their financial situation that led them to con me. I didn't think I was the type of person who could be fooled so easily. So, I was just as mad at myself as I was at them.

It took a while for the police to get here and take our statements. It wasn't as if they had Martika alive to book for her many illegal actions, but the two guards were still alive and the police assured us they would be thrown in jail.

"Good," Carlos said. "Let's go back to the restaurant and eat and have a few drinks to celebrate."

I walked over to him and quietly said, "I know you're upset about Joseph, but he was a good guy and he died trying to save us all."

"I know, Ruth Ann. That's why I want to make this a celebration."

Inga jumped into the conversation and asked, "Can we at least take a shower first?"

Everyone laughed and Carlos suggested we take a few bungalows to refresh ourselves and meet back at the restaurant. He would be waiting for us, and Isabella said she would wait on us, even though we told her she was beyond serving us now. "It's okay. I'll do it one last time," she said, smiling. "I want to. My grandmother would be proud of me for not letting my half-sister win."

"She definitely would!" I agreed, wishing Meme could be with us to celebrate.

John and I didn't get to have our old bungalow alone. There were only two refurbished units available so we had to share. There were a few bungalows that none of us were willing to stay in so John and I readily agreed to share. He pulled me aside first and I knew before he asked me that I would tell him I agree to a re-do vacation in the near future.

"I promise," John said. "After the holidays…just you and me!"

"I'm going to hold you to that, John."

"I'm sure you will!"

After John, Prunella, Axel, and I finished cleaning ourselves up, we headed down the sandy path once again past the pool and up to the restaurant. Sherman, Inga, Alex, and Carlos were waiting for us outside the restaurant. "We're all here," Carlos said, leading the way to our large table. Isabella was there ready to serve us one last time, and we ate, drank, and laughed for the first time in what seemed a century.

"So, I guess you'll be leaving tomorrow?" Carlos asked, while Isabella stood behind him curiously wanting to know our response.

"Yes. We have a holiday in less than two days. We'll get home with enough time for Inga to prepare a full Thanksgiving meal," I said, smiling over at her waiting for her to complain, but she didn't.

"I look forward to it. Ms. Lynne said she'd help me, and I will definitely call her the minute we land!"

"Great," I said, turning my attentions to Carlos and Isabella. "I'd like it if the both of you joined us?"

Isabella's eyes lit up, but Carlos' didn't. "Carlos, you okay?" I asked, wondering if he was too sad to make the trip.

"I'm good, Ruth Ann."

"Well?" Prunella asked. "We'd love for you both to stay with us. We have a huge estate and plenty of room. Please say you will!"

Isabella's eyes welled up and she nodded her head not able to speak. "It's okay, Isabella. I'm sure your heart is broken over your grandmother, but I believe she would want you to go."

"Then I will!" Isabella announced, smiling broadly for the first time ever since I've met her.

"Carlos, we're waiting for your answer," I said, all eyes on him.

"Well, I don't know what my plans are for the future now, but I'm sure I can get away for a little while....so.... YES! I'll fly to your cold state and spend the holiday with all of you."

"Then it's settled. We leave tomorrow," I said, feeling happier than I had in a long time. I reached to my neck and clasped Blue Ice whispering, "Thank you Meme. You broke the curse!" But then an eerie thought crossed my mind. Meme told me that once the curse was broken a choice will have to be made.

"The gem can now be used for good or for evil!"

The End

About the Author

Karin Richardson graduated from The University of Iowa with a communications degree. She currently resides in a suburb of Chicago with her family.

Richardson's aspiration has always been to complete a series of mystery novels for readers of all ages. *CURSED ICE* is the third book in this Deer Creek Mystery Series. Look on Amazon for the first two books, *BLUE ICE* and *ICE QUEST*.

When she's not **in the Dominican Republic** admiring a pet monkey, Richardson is hard at work on book four!